# WORLD RUN

## THE SECOND WILD CHANCE HOGAN RIDE

### BY K. RANDALL BALL

### BOOK 2

5-BALL, INC.
– 2016 –

First published in the United States in by 5-Ball, Inc.

First published in paperback 2016

ISBN 9780965160551

The second Chance Hogan book is published by 5-Ball, Inc. We grant discounts on the purchase of 12 or more copies. For further details, please write to:

5-Ball, Inc.
200 Broad Avenue
Wilmington, California 90744
Or Bandit@bikernet.com
www.Bikernet.com

Printed and manufactured in the United States of America

First edition: March 2016

Cover art by Pamelina with spot art by Jon Towle.
Editing by Bruce Snyder and Faith.
Interior design by David G. Barnett/Fat Cat Graphic Design.
www.fatcatgraphicdesign.com

Library of Congress Catalog Card Number: 2016906199

For Alison Ball, the fourth Mrs. Ball who returned to find Nirvana and help me in my search.

# -1-

# CHANCE TEARS LOOSE

Chance Hogan woke with a start. He sat up in the messy bed, pushed his long hair into a ponytail and grabbed a rubber band off the nightstand. Walking to the kitchen, he reflected on the iron box of hell he just closed. He was just a loner biker trying to find work in a small seaside town when the girl he dated was killed. For a year, he was the single, most sought after suspect while one girl after another was brutally murdered.

No one else was accused until they discovered the murders were the crazed notions of a depressed police officer and his psycho mistress. He was relieved but humbled as he stumbled to his partially refurbished kitchen. His life was a shattered mess and he still dodged cops who thought he was as guilty as any grubby, no-account biker. He was a publicly proclaimed hero by a small influential group in San Pedro, California, while the rest of the gun-toting police force smacked a bounty on his ass. He fired up his rusty coffee pot and brewed a fresh pot.

His Spanish stucco 1937 seaside home was a mess, strewn with newspapers and takeout Chinese food cartons. He opened the front French doors, walked onto the deck overlooking the harbor and snatched up the morning *Seaside Post* newspaper. The publisher smeared the front page with photographs of the Hispanic officer and his sneering mistress, coupled to postage stamp sized images of each of the girls they'd killed. Chance scanned the article, tossed the paper in an over-flowing shit-can and turned back to the kitchen to make his coffee with a heavy dose of cream and sugar.

He returned to the wooden deck to sit, ponder and look at the harbor. Relieved but anxious, he sipped his hot coffee from a stained ceramic mug. An officer still sat in a black and white cruiser down the block from his small stucco pad. Chance's 6'2" frame was still bruised from the beatings, and he needed a workout. After the coffee, he dressed and meandered to the garage. For the first time in a long time, he could tinker with his bike in the drooping, termite-infested garage.

He rolled his chopper out into his small yard and as the sun blazed in from the east and lit the sprawling harbor, Chance hosed it down then shot it with a fine motorcycle cleaner and rinsed it off. On the run for a while, the bike took the brunt of the action and was filthy from stem to stern. He rolled the chopper back into the garage and up on the lift, where he carefully strapped it down. The Handy air ram lifted his bike to bench level. He disconnected the air compressor and hooked it to an air gun to blow the water off the bike. He couldn't believe he was free from the carnage. He changed the oil and adjusted his brakes on the Harley-Davidson Evolution-powered machine that was his ticket to freedom and his only real possession. The phone rang in the garage and Chance picked it up.

"Hey, Chance. Get your ass to the Dojo, it's about time." Dick Bondano, the acclaimed Filipino Sifu, harassed Chance for months during his harried times. Chance thought it was just to let him know that everyone didn't want him dead and somewhere there was someone who believed in him. He appreciated the Filipino master.

"Okay, goddamnit," Chance said, "I'll ride down."

"You're fuckin' kidding?" Dick said dismayed. His gesture was one of pure friendship without expectations.

"You've been after me long enough, and damn it, I appreciate your support. I'll see you in an hour."

Chance hung up and headed back to the house to clean up and grab his riding shit and gym bag. As he walked to his bike, a rush of ease poured over him like a stiff shot of Jack Daniels after a tough work-week. He straddled his only friend and fired it to life. Riding up Harbor Blvd, he heard the screech of tires behind him and looked in his rear view mirror. The black and white spun a u-turn in the middle of the boulevard and screamed in his direction. A stream of fear and disappointment coursed up his spine.

"I don't believe it," he muttered to himself as he pulled to the side of the street and proceeded to dismount. As he stood, the crack of a loud speaker caught his attention.

"Stay on the bike, punk," the voice barked unprofessionally. "And don't move." The young officer slammed the door of his cruiser and headed in his direction.

Chance leaned his long springer front end to the right, slightly, so he could judge whether he needed to run or not, by watching the brisk officer in his rearview mirror. His small mirror came on its target just as the officer noted Chance's movement ; he drew his 9mm Browning semi-auto, holding it in service position and kicking off the safety.

"Freeze!" the officer shouted less than 10 feet behind him.

Chance could hear the crackle of the radio pinned to his uniform.

"Don't move a muscle," the officer snapped as he closed on the unarmed rider.

Chance lifted his hands carefully and began to raise them when the officer shouted again. "I told you to freeze." The officer closed on Chance, tilted the butt of the automatic and popped Chance upside his head. Chance tried to standand dodge, but stumbled, and dazed, lost his footing and fell over the right side of the bike, the custom motorcycle falling on him pinning his right leg.

"Move and I'll cap you right now!" the officer shouted. "I'm taking you down."

The radio on his chest crackled again. The operator was obviously alarmed as she shouted over the lines. Chance could hear sirens in the distance and tried to focus on the action as another cruiser screeched onto the boulevard, burning rubber in his direction. He became fearful. His leg was killing him and his best friend was down. The young officer with the short-cropped haircut was visibly shaking and pinching down on the trigger when another cruiser skidded onto the street, squealing to a stop just a few yards from where Chance lay next to the curb, in the slimy gutter.

A black officer jumped from his car, shouting "Officer Clay, he's cool! We've got the right guy!"

"No, you don't," the young officer returned. "I've known Hernandez for five years. He's not the right guy. This is the guilty sonuvabitch."

"You're wrong, brother. He's innocent."

"Bullshit," the first cop spat, "I'm capping this bastard, now."

"You do, and I'll have to take you down!" the black officer shouted, drawing his service pistol as an unmarked car screamed to a stop and a young female detective exploded from the car with her weapon drawn. She slipped behind the young sprung officer about to pull the trigger.

"Don't do it, officer," Kate Norton said, directly aiming her snub-nosed .38 at the side of the officer's head. "You're out of line and you know it. One wrong move and you have no career, no life."

The young officer, Clay Ayers, was shaking like a leaf. Sweat poured into his eyes, and the burning sensation forced him to lose his target visibility. His respect for an arrested veteran police officer was shattered. Bringing him to this strident reality was one of the toughest chores of his life. He lost his father and Lt. Hernandez had filled the empty void until a few days ago. He couldn't stand the idea of losing another dad.

He lifted his automatic slowly away from his aim at Chance. As soon as the weapon was above shoulder height the black officer ran to his back and yanked the gun out of his hand and spun the officer around. Another plain-clothes squad car pulled up and two detectives jumped out. One ran to the side of the officer and pulled him to their car.

"We will take care of him," the plain-clothes officer said in a panic. The other took the officer's car and disappeared. The black officer helped lift Chance out from under his chopper. The two men righted the motorcycle. Chance bent over and stretched, checked his pinned leg and took the bike from the officer's hand.

"Are you all right, Chance?" the tall black cop asked.

"Should I be?" Chance rubbed his leg and then the side of his bruised head, and tried to calm his nerves.

"You might take a vacation," the officer said. "Get outta this town."

"You okay?" Detective Kate Norton asked, coming to his side. There was tenderness in her voice, unlike the strict lock-jawed professionalism conveyed by most officers. Kate worked long and hard on the murder case and was responsible for much of the investigation and belief in Chance. She was building a history with Chance, one she enjoyed and he sorta dodged.

"I'll be fine," Chance said. "You guys need to clear the air in the office."

"You're right," Norton said. "I'll do what I can. Where are you headed?"

"Not sure I should tell you," Chance said, "I'm headed to IMC dojo for training. I'm outta shape, in more than one way."

"Maybe I'll see you there sometime," Kate said. She was good looking but had that rod-up-the-ass appearance of a woman trained in uniform behavior. She had an athletic build with a narrow waist and a killer ass. Her hair was blond and natural with a wave that would have made a Clairol commercial proud, and she had the face to back it up.

Chance saved her life and her career in law enforcement and had high respect for her, but wasn't in any mood to get close. There was something about her that drove him away. She represented everything Chance avoided, yet she leaned toward Chance as if he was a long lost love.

"I need to get back in shape. You and Sifu were the only two folks who believed in me," Chance said. "I need to give his Zen approach a roll of the dice."

He straddled the bike and punched it to life. She rested her hand on his shoulder. He turned and smiled up at her slightly before he rode off nodding to the other officer.

The dojo, built into an industrial park on Vermont in a commercial section of town, represented Richard's growing empire. The large sprawling dojo mats and walls were lined with 75-pound kicking bags, some old and torn, then wrapped with duct tape. One wall was lined with mirrors and the back wall was adorned with shelves stacked with sacks and pads for training. Dick enjoyed hanging banners and posters from the various events and seminars he was asked to attend.

The front office, adorned with awards and commemorations given to him by local police forces and military special operations units represented Dick's history from his days training with the late Bruce Lee. Another room was filled with weight-lifting equipment. Small locker rooms for men and women filled with old rusting school lockers bustled with young folks preparing for varied workout routines. A large professional boxing ring resided in the final room. The dojo had a 20-year history and the equipment was well worn and rusting. The gym needed a coat of paint and a great deal of detail work, but it was a working gym and dojo—no messing around.

Chance peeled up the freeway, bounced off the interstate, around the block and into the asphalt parking lot and parked in a spot directly in front of the entrance. As he entered the dojo, he was apprehensive. He endured his share of conflicts, but wasn't sure he was ready for another battlefield. Dick met him just inside the door.

"Hey, you made it." Dick was a stout Filipino who came to the states with Bruce Lee 20 years prior. He was a master of the first degree but lacked the slender athletic looks of Lee.

"I just barely made it," Chance said.

"I'll show you where to change," Dick said, taking Chance through the dojo and into the locker room. Chance looked around the sweat-smelling space with tattered indoor/outdoor carpeting and rusting lockers, desperately in need of a new finish. It reeked with a heavy oil field fragrance and the feel of a street warrior's enclave. He changed and made his way back to the dojo, a large room covered in thick matting. In most dojos, it was standard etiquette for the entering student to bow and show respect before stepping onto the mat. Since Chance had taken Tae Kwon Do a decade before, he instinctively stopped at the padded edge, put his feet together and his hands at his sides and bowed slightly.

There were seven students on the gray training surface facing the mirrors and a short anglo man who was introduced to Chance as Brad. He had the look of a street fighter with a trimmed mustache and a sincere smile. He reached out and shook Chance's hand and introduced the other students. Chance took a deep breath as Brad indicated for the class to begin a series of stretches. Then he asked each student to grab two Filipino fighting sticks; yard-long bamboo rods, one inch in diameter with burn stripes around them and then varnished. They felt light and agile in his hands. Chance was unfamiliar with them but grabbed a couple as Brad indicated for them to start running around the mat's edge while spinning the sticks in various directions.

After the 15-minute warm-up, they were told to put the sticks away. Dick, or Sifu, entered the mat while all the students stood at the ready for instructions. Immediately Chance recognized the ability of the man whom he only knew previously as a biker. After 25 years, Dick still rode his first Harley, an immaculately restored 1962 Panhead.

Sifu demonstrated a punch-blocking technique. The blocking hands moved quickly to hook an on-coming punch and draw it down. But with each initial maneuver, there were three more. After they tried the block a few times, he added a punch from the blocking hand and a follow-through jab from the other hand. That move was repeated with a partner 10 times with the other hand, and then rotating.

Sifu added another attacking movement or block. Chance felt his brain exploding with every effort to put the mental awareness with the physical moves. Brad worked closely and patiently as Chance's partner. Sifu continued to hammer new moves until several kicks were added to the blocks and punches, then elbow strikes. For 45 minutes, the class worked on adding maneuvers, punches and additional blocks to the first initial move, including strikes using pads.

"Put away the pads," Sifu said, "and pick up two sticks."

Chance did as he was told and stood at the ready as Dick demonstrated the first maneuver, quickly adding a second and a third, and then pairing the students for training. Chance struggled to absorb another move, but he recognized the level of concentration it forced on him and he enjoyed it.

Finally, Dick indicated for the students to return the sticks and lay in a circle on the floor. For 15 minutes, they performed various types of sit-ups and abdominal exercises. When the class was over, Chance bowed to Sifu and Brad. They showed him a new way of indicating opponent regard, a graceful gesture of respect, like a salute. Chance bowed again, spent and sweatingand returned to the locker room.

"Not bad for your first time in years," Dick said. "I expect you down here every Monday and Wednesday at 10:00."

Chance was drained, exhausted and dripping like a lineman after the Superbowl.

"I'll be here, unless I roll the wrong dice," Chance said.

"Some 50 percent of this shit is mental," Brad said, walking Chance to his bike.

"You're right," Chance said, firing the Harley to life. "Thanks, I'm impressed, but I need a shower."

Chance rode home without another attempt on his life. He pulled the bike into his backyard and shut the gate. As he walked in the door, the phone rang.

"Yeah", Chance said.

"If I could have my way, you'd be dead," the rough male voice said and the phone went dead.

"Fuck you," Chance said into the dead receiver. He hung up the phone and immediately it started to ring again.

"I'm right here motherfucker, come and get me!" Chance shouted.

"Are you hungry?" Kate asked. "Another death threat; sorry about that. How about lunch?"

"I just got back from the gym, need to shower. Then I'm going to get out of town for a while. I don't need to bring pressure on you."

"As you wish," Kate said, "but when you're ready to see the world again, please give me a chance."

"Thank you," Chance said and hung up. Something tender about her touched him. She was hot looking, in a pure way, packed with integrity and the desire to improve the world and walk always on the right side of the street. He was moved, but her way of life was like water in his motorcycle oil. They didn't mix. He lived his life on the edge of larceny. At least he used to.

Chance showered and jumped back on his bike, heading toward Long Beach. Out of a job again, he still had a few bucks stashed away. He didn't need to think about making money. He was lucky to be alive. He needed to play it cool and slink out of sight for a spell. It felt good to ride over the Vincent Thomas expansion bridge for the first time without being chased by someone.

He looked out to sea over the freighters and docks and small sail-boats. He loved the rumble of his loud exhaust against the superstructure of the steel bridge. The powerful motorcycle cracked as he whipped the throttle and the bike jumped forward. He crossed two more bridges on his way into downtown Long Beach. Cruising left on Pine Street into the restaurant district, he rolled into a parking lot across from the Blue Café, shut down the bike and locked it. He sat in the outdoor patio and ate a salad while listening to the band sing the Joe Houston blues. He drank a beer with his lunch and began to relax for the first time in several long, torturous months.

He was surprised at the wide-open feeling martial arts training gave him. He felt invigorated and alive.

As he ate his salad, he noticed that the promenade across Broadway was packed with small, tossed-up kiosks full of vendors. He paid his bill and walked across the street to peruse the various booths and stands, including vegetable sellers, trinket peddlers and arts and crafts vendors.

As he reached the end, he spied a large tent housing a vast array of miniature bamboo plants in colorful, stone-filled ceramic pots. Each one was filled to the brim with water. While he checked the bowls and plants, he noticed an Asian woman behind the table replanting a small bamboo plant into another pot.. She was intent on her efforts until Chance felt he needed to interrupt.

"Excuse me," Chance said, "I just need a price, and then I'll leave you alone."

The girl turned lightly and stood on small, alabaster feet. She was 5 feet 7 inches tall, and although she was dressed in tattered Levis, her hips were well formed and tightly cupped by the faded denim material. She wore a working sweatshirt and her hands were dirty with damp soil. Her chest was large and jutting, but her smile could melt the high-rise buildings surrounding the promenade.

"Yes?" she said.

"I was just wondering about the price of this plant," Chance said, looking her directly in the eyes.

"That's just lucky seven dollars," she said with a smile.

"Thanks, I was just curious," Chance said, trying to hide his grin. "I'm on a motorcycle. I can't carry anything right now."

"Did you ride the chopper I saw earlier?"

"Yep."

"Nice bike," she said and her face flushed slightly.

Chance enjoyed each feature of her ivory white skin and it must have been obvious.

"I'm sorry to bother you," Chance said and bowed slightly, his big frame gracing her with respect.

She watched him curiously, then turned back to her plant project. Chance stood there for a couple of minutes admiring the ceramic designs and the artistic layout of the small gracious plants. There was something completely anti-evil about each one. Each fired clay pot graced the plant it carried as palms of soft hands holding life.

His eyes drifted to the girl again, to her hands delicately placing a fresh plant into another pot. Her touch was all grace and care. Her long jet-black hair was twisted and held at the back of her head with a silver tie, exposing the pure soft curves of her neck. The side of her face was picture perfect, and she cared for each plant as if it was a small newborn child.

Chance stood awkwardly in his worn cowboy boots as their eyes met again. He was embarrassed for staring. Her dark eyes and his emerald vision met once more. He bowed again slightly in a respectful but awkward thankful gesture and walked away.

# -2-

# Adding Ling To His Life

The winter wind blew across the Los Angeles harbor as if God's broom swept the ugly industrial smells out to sea. Chance awoke to the sound of pelting rain against his bedroom window. It was early, too early to be bluesy, but as Chance rubbed his eyes, he couldn't get the memory of the Asian girl out of his mind. The first thing in a month making him smile, she made him believe life could glow again. He was lonely and the hot-looking female officer had called just the night before, but something deep inside him wanted to give the Chinese girl a shot.

Carl Beard offered him a job again running harbor skiffs. His new assistant called the night before to let him know work was available, but he struggled with the past. While he was under suspicion for murdering several girls in the harbor, Chance lost his job and dove underground to find the guilty source. It was all behind him now, except a nasty sense about San Pedro. The town turned on him, and he couldn't get over the dark sensation as the months passed. It haunted him, but he was determined to stay his seaside course.

He still wasn't sure who knew or believed the truth and who didn't. He felt edgy, like a man uncertain if his speeding ticket had become a warrant. He pushed his motorcycle to the curb and fired it to life. He rolled down to the harbor and to Canetti's, the fish and chips joint, where Suzanne worked before she was killed. The middle-aged fat Italian woman still worked there, immediately recognized Chance, popped two pieces of wheat toast in the dented toaster and brought him a cup of coffee.

She was usually as dower and depressed as a prisoner on death row, but for some reason, Chance brought a sense of hope and compassion to her wrinkled features. She'd lost a child and understood Chance's loss. She touched his shoulder as she delivered the stained ceramic mug of steaming java. "How you doing, big boy?" she asked.

"I'm cracking a new deck of cards, I suppose. And you?"

"We're okay. Will life get back to normal for you?"

"Thanks. I still get death threats from time to time."

"You're kidding," she said. "You would think they'd be on the ball better than that."

"Joe may be on trial, but some still think it was me," Chance said. "I'll take some egg whites scrambled and a short stack. I'll need the energy today."

"You're right." She wrote his order down on her crumpled waitress receipt pad. "No more girls will be killed, hopefully for a long time. Hey, breakfast is on us. I'd like you to stick around."

Chance looked up at her big dark Italian eyes and he saw the sincerity in her creamy features. "Thanks," he said and got to his feet and gave the woman a hug.

It was a cold day outside and dark clouds hung over the harbor. As a kid, Chance always connected gloomy days with grueling times when he received negative report cards, too many. He was forced to return home to have it signed by his violent parents. Although it was threatening more rain, he rode his motorcycle down to the end of the docks to the Harbor Taxi landing area.

All he had to his name was that motorcycle and it meant the world to him.

As a biker, that machine was his best friend. It was always there when he needed it. It was his magic carpet to new adventures and his escape pass when times were bad. As he rode to the end of the peninsula, he thought about Rosa in Arizona. Another good woman he almost hooked up with, except for the acts of arson by the evil woman who haunted him a while back.

He loved women and wanted nothing but good for everyone in his life, but his luck didn't deal him stellar hands on love's felt gambling table.

He pulled up to the makeshift building at the end of the docks and the little Hispanic receptionist ran out of her office to greet him.

"Chance!" They hugged and big Carl came out of the office.

"You're still fuckin' guilty and you know it!" Carl shouted. "Maybe not of murdering those women, but everything else."

"You could be right," Chance said, locking his bike to a ring they welded to an old railroad track.

Chance worked around the docks, straightening up when Carl approached. "Another death threat," Carl said.

"Not for a couple of days, but I'm watchin' my back," Chance said, changing the oil on one of the skiffs. "How's business this week?"

"Busier than hell. Good to have you back."

"I appreciate that. So let's get to fuckin' work."

Chance tried his best to let his mind be absorbed by work, but it drifted to his past, to the women who were killed; his buddy Vince, who was killed for greed, to the woman who still haunted him, even though she was in jail for arson and murder. He didn't think about her much except to ask his jailbird connection to let him know if her prison status changed. While he scrubbed the decks and captained the boats out to the oilrigs under the gray skies he wondered whether his life would ever be the same, normal or standard. He saw no kids in his future, no more wives, just the ongoing pursuit for a woman who might understand his need for freedom, motorcycles and an occasional adventure.

He admired friends with long marriages, all the toys they accumulated and the wealth they built. Too many of those relationships were torn asunder by changing desires, other relationships and divorce. During Chance's last divorce, he met with an attorney who explained the make-up of the current marriage and divorce laws. He decided that if he wanted a partner in everything he did, he'd work on a written contract, not a marriage license. Besides, if he wanted to have sex with another woman, he didn't want to lose his house over it. Hell, he wasn't sure he'd ever have a lasting home again, with or without another woman. His San Pedro shack held too many bummer memories.

As the week rolled along, the clouds hung low and gray. Offshore winds blew over the harbor, creating nasty whitecaps on the water. Chance worked hard every day except Wednesday. He rode to the IMC dojo in the morning and trained. He watched his back carefully whenever he was in public. The dojo was the one uplifting experience of the week. He felt invigorated, stimulated and driven as he left, but it was only Wednesday. He worked 12 hours on Thursday, and told Carl he wanted Friday off. Carl could tell just looking into Chance's green eyes, he needed something or someone to brighten his hammered spirits.

Friday morning, Chance crawled out of the sack at the crack of dawn and rode to the gym early. He lifted weights for an hour, then stretched before the class began. He wasn't as limber as some of the younger students and he practiced his kicks on the heavy bag, turning his body to adjust the kick to the correct height. Each move demanded his attention to twist his heel against the mat and torque his torso to launch his leg in the correct position for a powerful thrust and balance. Dick Bondano came into the gym and coached Chance before the class began. Brad, the young coach, arrived with the other students and they went to work through one grueling routine after another.

After the class, Chance rode back to the pad and showered, changed, and then rode the long chopper over the Vincent Thomas Bridge in a drizzling rain, darting in and out of 18-wheelers hauling cargo away from the sprawling ports of Los Angeles and Long Beach. He headed directly for downtown Long Beach. He pulled into the Blue Café parking lot, shut off the motor and chained his bike to the chain link fence post.

Chance walked across Broadway to the farmers' market of small rustic kiosks and headed to the back, where the girl was located last time. His nerves were dancing on edge. With each kiosk he passed, his hopes were hoisted to another level until he made the final turn. A young Hispanic kid stood on the corner of the last row selling roses and Chance bought one. He tried to conceal his rapid footsteps to the end of the aisle where every week, her booth glistened in the sun. As he reached the last display in the row, it was apparent that there was no such booth. He wondered what happened? Every week she brightened his day. He stared at the pavement, disappointed, wondering if the nap of her soft neck was just an illusion.

"Could that rose be for me?" a voice said behind him. The rose hung at his side and he was about to drop it in the galvanized trashcan,when the voice danced in his ears.

Chance spun to face the beautiful Asian girl. He stood over 6 feet but her 5'7" height was comforting. "I actually thought that since you work with plants, you wouldn't want another," Chance said.

"It's the meaning behind the gift that's most important," she replied.

Chance held out the rose to her and the sun seemed to break through the dark clouds above. For the first time in a week, he noticed color in objects around him and warmth on the back of his hands.

"That rose represents more than you can imagine."

"All for me?" she asked.

"And more," Chance said nervously. "My name is Chance. Can I buy you lunch?"

"I can't. I must watch my booth."

"I wanted to check with you before I ate," Chance said.

"Thank you," she said and reached for his hand.

Chance took her hand in his and squeezed it gently. He didn't want to leave. He spoke to her week after week. He was concerned about any involvement but as she got to him, his confidence grew.

"Have you eaten?"

"No." Ling said.

"How about I grab a terrific salad and we share it?"

"That sounds wonderful!", she said.

Chance spun to leave, but then turned back.

"Something to drink?"

"I've got a bottle of water we can share," Ling said.

Chance darted away, but spun back once more. He felt like a high school kid at his first dance.

"Where's your booth?"

Ling smiled at him and his awkwardness. She was fascinated by his tenderness.

"It's just over here," she said pointing. "I'll be there."

She bowed slightly like the students at the dojo. Her hair was pulled back in a silver clasp. She was a thing of beauty with her dark mane lifted off her neck, revealing soft, delicate curves.. What was it about a woman that called to him like a loud speaker calling troops to the chow hall? He didn't want to take his longing gaze from her.

He felt so connected, so attracted and so drawn. He struggled not to run across Broadway to the Blue Café where he ordered the Californian salad. It was one of the best salads he ever enjoyed. It was packed with candied walnuts, crumbled blue cheese, leafy lettuce, spinach, various veggies and grilled chicken.

It seemed to take forever for the salad to be delivered. As soon as he snatched it off the counter, he jogged back across the street and through the various booths, oblivious to the goods for sale. He darted from one booth to the other, ignoring everything, but caught the smells of flowers and the warmth of the fleeting sunlight, until he reached her area.

She set up two chairs in the back with a small table behind her colorful display of Bonsai trees and Lucky Bamboo plants. Chance spread out the salad and dished her a portion into the lid of the container, which he sliced free with his trusty Spiderco knife.

"Thank you," Ling said and took a bite. "Ummm, good." She seemed to beam with each motion.

"Do you live in Long Beach?" Chance asked.

"Excuse me?" she said, swallowing a bite, "Yes, I'm going to Long Beach State."

"Pardon me," said a tall Long Beach Police officer standing at the edge of the marketplace with his stout female partner. "Are you Chance Hogan?"

"Yes, sir," Chance said, getting to his feet. "Can I help you?"

"Can we speak to you for a second?" said the officer, stepping back to signal for Chance to follow him.

Chance stood and faced Ling, "I'm sorry, please…"

"I'll be right here," Ling said and touched him for the second time. Her contact reassured Chance as he stepped away from the kiosk and followed the officers. Out of sight and away from the crowds mingling around the market stalls, the cop turned to Chance.

"Listen, we know about the case and who was busted, but there's still a lot of heat out there who think you did it. I would like for you to keep a low profile for a while. In fact, we think someone is watching you."

"I thought coming to Long Beach would be hanging low," Chance said.

"Not this Long Beach. We're too close to Pedro," the cop said while the other officer looked on and nodded. She was looking Chance over thoroughly.

"Take care of yourself," she said, "We know you're innocent, but the trail to you hasn't dried up."

Chance returned to Ling's booth. He wasn't sure what to do or where to go or how Ling would react.

"Is everything all right?" she asked as he grabbed his seat and picked up his salad.

"Actually, no," Chance said, chewing on a bite of lunch. "I hate to mention this, but…"

"I know all about it." Ling read about it for weeks in the newspaper. "I knew I recognized your picture from somewhere. As soon as the cops mentioned your name, I knew who you were. At least I know you're not married."

"Seems that although they have the guilty guy, I'm still under suspicion in many eyes. I shouldn't be seen with you in public. I don't want you to be influenced by all this."

"I'm surprised you were even suspected," Ling said.

"I'd like to go out with you sometime," Chance said, "after this has all blown over. Enough of me; tell me a little about yourself."

"I'm just a student from China going to school on a student visa. I'm studying art and I love it here," she said. "Are you sure a bad-ass anglo biker wants to go out with Asian chick?"

"Does a smart college chick want to have anything to do with no-account biker who's been in some sort of trouble all his life?"

"You damn right!" Ling said. She smiled, and to Chance, her glistening gaze was a beam from above.

Customers approached as they finished their lunch. Ling left some of hers and offered it to Chance, who finished it. He picked up the plastic utensils and trays and threw them away.

"I'd better leave."

Ling Wu snatched up one of her cards and wrote a number on the back. "Please call me."

"I will, tonight," Chance said, putting the card into a vest pocket. He leaned close to her face and kissed her cheek. She put her hand on his and squeezed.

"Tonight," she said as he walked away.

"Can I help you?" she said to a couple admiring a Lucky Bamboo plant. Then she looked up at Chance, who turned and caught her eye. She waved.

"Can I have a card?" A young military looking man asked.

"Sure," Ling said, handing her card to the young man who seemed tense. "Can I help you?"

"Not right now," he said, looking at the card. "Do you have a shop?"

"No, I'm just freelance. I'm here on Fridays."

Her card only had a website and e-mail address.

"Can I have a number to call you?" the young man asked.

Ling was getting irritated dealing with the stern man who indicated no interest in her plants.

"Just e-mail me. Now, if you'll excuse me."

"You should be careful who you hang out with," the tightly cropped man said, grabbing her arm.

"What's the matter with you?" Her voice raised several octaves, which drew attention from onlookers.

He let her arm go and kept his head down, while moving slowly away.

"Don't forget what I said," he muttered.

# -3-

# HOT DEADLY
# FIRST DATE

Chance couldn't feel the drizzling rain as he rode home on his sweet running chopper. He was gliding on the touch of her soft skin and captivated with wonderment. He wanted Ling Wu and wanted to know her more. At this point, he could only sense her basic desire for well-being, her gentle manner and creative nature. As he flew over the expansion bridge on cloud nine, he relished her touch against the pitfalls of his life.

He was still disturbed by the threats at his residence in San Pedro. He pondered moving to a nearby town and laying low for a while. He had a riding partner in Phoenix who owned a shop and would probably give him a job, but that would take him away from this girl. Part of him reeked of hostility toward any force trying to inflict its will on his life. He enjoyed the coast and wanted to stay.

He pulled up onto the sidewalk next to his house and opened the leaning wooden gate. He could hear the phone ringing inside, but knew he couldn't get to it in time, so he let it ring. He shoved the long Harley inside his garage and looked it over, blew off some of the road grime with his air gun and wiped it down.

He picked up the phone to check messages and had two. One was from the receptionist at the docks. "We could sure use you down here this afternoon," she said. "Give me a call."

The other was vacant at first; then a low, deep voice coughed in front of heavy metal music rumbling in the background.

"They'll find out who really killed those girls, and they're going to find out soon." Then the phone went dead.

Chance dialed the docks.

"Water Taxi Service," answered the receptionist in her sexy voice.

"Oh baby, I want you," Chance said.

"Hey, we've got work for you," Alma said with a giggle.

"When?"

"We need someone this evening to haul a generator to a freighter. Can you be here in a couple of hours?"

"I need to run one errand and I'll be there."

"Thanks," Alma said gratefully and hung up.

Chance put down the receiver and pulled Ling's card out of his vest. He turned it over and dialed her number. He knew she wouldn't be there, but if she had a message machine... "Ling Wu here, please leave a message."

"Ling," Chance said, "I'm working for a water taxi and dock service and just got called to work a late shift, so I may not be able to call you until much later. I'm sorry about the interruption today. Listen, if you don't mind, I'll call as soon as I get home. My number is 521-9900. If you have an emergency and need someone to call..." The message unit cut him off and he hung up.

He put on some work clothes and a heavy, lined flannel shirt with his vest and pulled his bike out of the garage. He rolled down to Harbor Boulevard and took a left toward town. About two miles up the road was the police station and he pulled into the parking lot. Upon entering the front reception area he asked the heavy-set female officer at the desk if he could speak to Kate Norton. The officer looked at him with a sideways glance and picked up the phone. Abruptly she hung up.

"She's not in, can I take a message?"

Chance looked up as two officers entered the lobby. Both glared at Chance as they walked past.

He turned back to the surly desk officer and said, "Yeah, can I have a piece of paper and a pen?"

Without answering, the officer slipped a pen and paper across the desk.

"I'll be right back," she said and walked to a door in the back and disappeared.

Chance sat down at a small table and wrote. *Kate, I stopped by at 3:30 today to tell you I received a threatening phone call and someone was following me today. Just letting you know.*

Chance didn't like the smell of the police station. He didn't care for the military look of the joint. He didn't like the vibe or the power these people could wield over him. He felt like a Jew in a Nazi transit station.

He waited 15 minutes and the officer never returned to her post. He got out of his chair and walked to the door and out to his bike. The parking lot was well lit and visible from the PD building. He jumped on the bike and rode it down to Fifth Street, where he turned up to the local instant print facility. He jogged in the glass door and made five copies of the message to Officer Norton. He signed each one and numbered them.

He rode back toward the station and past it to the next office building, where he parked his bike and walked a block back to the building and into the door.

The desk officer was back at her desk. Chance walked up and put the five copies on her desk.

"Sign 'em," Chance said, handing her the pen.

"I don't have to do anything," Officer Walkins said abruptly.

"If you don't initial each one, I'll sit down here and wait for her to return or speak to your supervisor."

She yanked the pen from his hand initialed all the copies and grabbed them. Chance slammed his palm onto the sheets and retrieved two.

"I'll take two," he said, looking at her directly. "You can have three, so at least one won't get lost. Thank you for your service."

Chance pivoted on the heel of his work boot and stormed out the door.

He rode down to the dock and checked in. He immediately captained a skiff toward one of the offshore oilrigs to pick up a crew. Clouds hung over the harbor and rain continued to pepper the white caps. Outside the breakwater, swells climbedand dipped into the troughs. He wanted to reach out to Ling Wu, but he needed to make a few bucks and ponder his future.

For the first time, he thought about a career beyond being a helluva motorcyclist.

Ling Wu dodged the mist under her makeshift tent until it was time to pack up. Business slowed on the intermittent rainy day in the downtown Long Beach Promenade. She moved to the U.S. after a terrible struggle with her Chinese hierarchal family. As China began to embrace elements of western society, her family became more withdrawn. She loved the freedom, the creative nature and the democracy and attempted to reach toward it in her own life. She studied hard and began to apply for the visas necessary for travel when she was in the Chinese equivalent of high school.

As society expanded the need for students taught in the west increased, her efforts didn't go unnoticed, Finally, officials granted her a visa and a national computer firm even sponsored her trip to America for her first year of schooling. Her family abhorred the notion but her will was strong enough to overcome their objections to seek higher education in America.

After her first year at Long Beach State, she was forced to return to China and work with a sprawling government-controlled computer firm for six months to pay them back for her educational assistance. At the end of six months, she returned to continue her education, against the will of her parents. She fought hard and long, and success graced her with a return trip for her sophomore year.

From time to time, Asian students asked her out, but her parents refused to support her efforts or any dating stateside.

Although she came from a large, established, successful and traditional family, she lived lean and survived on her own. She worked part-time for a restaurant and then a local nursery run by a Japanese couple. She learned how to care for and design Bonsai, cherry trees and bamboo plants. She took to it and as she entered her senior year, she continued to work for the Kadako family, and then built her own sideline business to augment her income. She enjoyed working with the family and their delicate plants. She studied their cherished Zen nature, respecting and honoring all living things, from a blade of grass to a giant redwood.

She lived in a small apartment in a massive college complex and pulled her little Toyota truck around back. She unloaded the plants into her single garage and the small adjacent patio and parked the truck. She was still concerned about the arrogant guy who confronted her, but Chance and his warm spirit took to her. His long hair and almost cowboy look surprised her, with his worn Levis and tattered cowboy boots. There was something artistic about him, from his welded belt buckle to his motorcycle wheel ring and his lean custom motorcycle. Everything indicated a creative, free-thinking soul.

She put down her bag of gear on her tile kitchen counter and checked messages. As she listened to the message from Chance, she noticed a car pull up out front at the curb. It had all the markings, or lack thereof, of the unmarked cop cars rolling around the college campus. She paid little attention until the driver got out; it was the man who confronted her at the Promenade. He had obviously followed her home. She wrote down Chance's number and ran out the back door, down the alley to her girlfriend's condo and pounded madly on the front door.

Alison, a voluptuous redhead, opened the front door. Ling pushed her way in. "What's up, Ling?" Alison said, backing up.

"I've got to use your phone," Ling said and headed for the kitchen. She dialed quickly and listened. It rang four times and then the machine picked up. "Quick, leave a message," Chance recorded.

"Chance, it's Ling. I need your help. I'm at 322 Cerritos, apartment 14. Somebody followed me home."

"What's going on?" Alison asked her brown eyes widening.

"I can't explain it. I met this guy... Well, sit down. You won't believe this."

Chance's skiff, the Molly B, bobbed up and down near the barnacle-laden pylons holding the solid- mounted offshore drilling rig to the ocean floor. The crew lowered a folded set of stairs into the turbulent brine and Chance prepared to toss the first oil worker a line.

"Hey, what took you so long?" Slim hollered, tying off one slippery line and pulling the other in so the other workers could board.

"I'm right on fuckin' time, pal," Chance hollered back over the noise of the motor. "For that, you have to wait for the next boat." Chance razzed him while securing the skiff.

"Hey, gimme a break, will ya," Slim begged.

The others climbed on board and they shoved off. The bounce and the noise of the rig and the gray sky above gave Chance the sense of wild action. He respected the oil workers for their hard work, under tough conditions, and their commitment to the job. He made every effort he could to be on time and hustled to get them back to shore. The swells made surfing past the jetty a life threatening challenge, and Chance studied boat handling in rough seas to make the passage as fast as possible without losing anyone overboard. Often when they broke the offshore current line at the breakwater, the passengers cheered as Chance kicked up the speed a couple of knots for the last smooth half-mile run to the Taxi Service docks. As he pulled up, he tied up the boat and wished the workers well, then jogged inside the office for a cup of coffee.

"Carl, mind if I call home to check messages?" Chance asked.

"There's a message here for you," Julie said, "a girl named Ling Wu called, said there's a problem at her place. She called all the dock service joints in the harbor looking for you. She seems like a nice girl."

Chance stepped to Julie's side of the desk and dialed the number. It wasn't Ling's.

"Hello?" answered a girl on the other end.

"Is Ling there?"

"Is this Chance?"

"Yep."

"Just a second, Chance," Alison said, handing the phone to Ling.

"Baby, after you left the Promenade, some weird guy stopped by and wanted my number. He started to give me a hard time. He followed me home. I locked up and ran down the street to my girlfriend's apartment. Can you come over?"

"I'm on my way," Chance said.

"It's 322 Cerritos in Lakewood, apartment 18."

"I'll be there in 20 minutes," Chance said and hung up. "I gotta hit the road, Carl. That shit isn't behind me just yet."

"No problem," Carl said, "just be careful. Remember the Mexican serial killer who hired the truck drivers to keep killing girls while he was in jail to take the heat off him? There's probably someone trying to get that cop off and lay it all on you."

Chance grabbed his old leather vest and ran for the door. He fired up the chopper and did a wheel-stand down the peninsula onto Harbor Boulevard and onto the freeway. He was one with that motorcycle, flying down the freeway in the drizzling rain at 80 mph at night with his shades on. He tore up the San Pedro freeway; eight miles to the 405 south, another five miles to Lakewood Blvd, off the freeway and slid to the stop at the bottom of the ramp.

Riding on the city streets in the rain was ten times as dangerous and slicker than freeways. He peered around his glasses for better visibility until he found Cerritos Blvd near the college and the apartments. Chugging along the street, he counted the numbers. As he closed on the address, he saw a dark sedan pull away from the curb in a hurried fashion and peel down the street. Chance pulled up to the curb and slid to a stop. He ran to the address and knocked on the door.

Alison, a very hot-looking, 5-foot 4-inch redhead, opened the door in a terry bathrobe.

"Is Ling Wu here?" Chance asked, a dripping mess. "Sorry, I'm a mess. I'm on a motorcycle and I came directly from work."

Ling stepped up behind her. "You ran him off. As soon as we heard the bike, he pulled away."

Ling was three inches taller than Alison, a slender, alabaster thing of beauty. Disheveled in her work clothes, she presented a statuesque classical flair. Suddenly he became very aware of the warmth emanating from the apartment, the glow of the warm incandescent light-tand perhaps the smell of chocolate chip cookies baking in the oven.

"I can't come in," Chance said, "I'll destroy your rug."

"Come on," Ling said, "Let's go to my place. We can put your bike in the garage and dry you off."

"Will you be all right?" Alison asked anxiously.

"I'll take care of her," Chance said, "or die trying. Thanks so much for your help."

"Follow me," Ling said, leading him back to his scooter, where he straddled it quickly and fired it to life.

"Get on," Chance said.

"You're kidding?" Ling stood on the sidewalk in the drizzling rain.

"We're just going around the block. Besides, if he's still around, he'll think I took you away."

She climbed on and wrapped her arms around him, and for the first time felt his muscular torso. Chance revved up the engine and peeled down the street to the corner, leaned left slightly on the wet pavement and made the noise of a motorcycle blasting down the street. At a high rev he shut off the engine and coasted down the alley until she pointed out her garage. He pulled up and they went inside.

"Don't turn on any lights," Chance said. "I don't want him to know you came back." In the garage, Chance took off his wet work boots and his soaked flannel.

"I'll get you something to wear and we can dry your clothes," Ling said.

Chance began to peel off his threads. He liked the way she moved. From what he could see of her pad, she was neat; even her garage was organized. Her oriental décor was handled with class. He peeled down to his boxers and stood freezing until she returned.

"Quick, put this on. Go upstairs and take a hot shower, and I'll make some soup. I have some homemade hot and sour. Would that suit you?"

"Perfect, but I need you to make a call." He pulled his damp wallet out of his soggy pocket and removed Kate's card.

"Call this investigator. Tell her what you said. Will your girlfriend help?"

"Of course," Ling said. "I'll call."

"After you tell her what happened," Chance continued, "ask her to call you back in a half an hour, so I can speak to her."

She showed him upstairs, where he jumped into her shower. It felt like a million bucks. As he showered, he thought about her arms around him, her warm tits pressed up against his back. After a few minutes, there was a tap on the bathroom door.

"Okay if I come in?" Ling asked.

"Sure," Chance replied. Ling walked in, dressed in a long ornate silk oriental robe.

"I told her to call in an hour," Ling said, letting the robe fall to her feet.

Through the tinted glass, Chance could make out her delicate form. She pulled on the door and stepped into the shower. Chance didn't quite know what to do; his body was soaped down and he stepped to the side to let her in, but she amazed him. Trying not to gaze overtly, keeping his eyes focused on her deep amber pools, he pushed her toward the shower head and rinsed her body down to warm her, then lifted her delicate chin and kissed her.

It was as if they were meant to kiss. Everything fit, her lips, her body, like a soft peach in the palm of his hand. He held her hair up to the showerhead and let the hot water soak her long mane. He kissed her cheeks, down her neck and across her sumptuous tits. He kissed around each one and down to her tight belly while running his hand simultaneously down the small or her back, then over her ass. They were beginning to explode in the shower. Chance rubbed his soapy body against hers.

"That's all you get," Chance said teasingly. "Let's get the hell out of here."

"You go first, honey," she said, "I'll be right behind you."

Chance stepped out of the shower and grabbed the towel she left for him on the sink. He dried quickly and brushed his long sandy-blonde hair. As he finished, she shut off the shower and opened the glass door. Infatuated with everything about this woman, he mentally committed to her safety. Nothing could happen to her. He had a towel waiting and another ready for her long black hair. She stepped up to the towel but didn't take it. She leaned against him and grabbed the hand towel to ring her hair while Chance patted her down and pulled her toward the bedroom.

They barely made it down the hall, clawing and pawing at each other until together, they scrambled into the bed, tangled in each others arms. Her large round tits and small hard nipples pressed hard but delicately, against his chest. He entered her slowly and tenderly and she moved like a violinist, touching the cords precisely for just the right notes. She came, shuddering, but Chance kept moving inside her until she came again.

She collapsed on him and he rolled her over, staying firmly inside of her and started moving once more.

"Don't stop!" Ling cried as she neared another climax, bringing Chance with her. He pushed himself up on his fists and looked down at her body as he began to explode. She screamed and they exploded like two singers cutting their first perfect sound track. It was amazing.

Chance rolled to her side and she rolled with him.

"When can we start over?" Chance asked.

"How about after we have some soup," Ling replied, holding him close. "We can get that call out of the way and go back to bed."

"Sounds good to me." They held each other close for a few moments.

"Can we make this last?"

"Only as one blissful day after another," Chance answered.

Ling kissed him again and slipped out of bed. Chance admired the small dimples just above her ass and the dime-sized birthmark on one cheek that he planned to kiss many times. She slipped on a robe and offered Chance a beer. He declined and asked for tea. She headed downstairs and checked the soup. Chance followed and helped set the table. The rich spicy aroma filled the kitchen and made Chance's mouth water.

"Can I turn on a light or two now?" Ling asked.

"Sure," Chance said, "I think it's cool. Do you have a hair band?"

"Sure, in the bathroom," Ling said.

Chance jogged up the stairs and entered the bathroom, where he opened the drawer beside the sink and picked out a covered rubber band. He grabbed a brush and brushed his hair back until all the kinks were out then wrapped the rubber band around his thick sandy hair.

Downstairs, Ling busied herself with preparations for dishing up the soup. She turned on her CD player, kicking off the selection with an Anita Baker tune called *Rhythm of Love*. She pulled two white ceramic bowls from the cupboard above the sink. They were pale white with vibrantly detailed tiny koi fish illustrations fired into the exterior. She had never felt this level of connection in her life. It danced over her like a warm blanket on a cold day. She opened a drawer and pulled out two ceramic spoons and chop sticks, then wondered if Chance would deal with the cultural change. Something in her heart said he would.

The front door of her condo was built to standard construction criteria and officer Clay Ayers was able to jimmy the lock with conventional lock-picking tools. Dressed in all black, including a woolen knitted hood, he pushed the door open slightly. Breathing hard, he peered into the interior and saw Ling, with her back to him, working in the sink. She was an incredibly sexy girl and he could see the dampness from lovemaking, around her neck.

He was a nervous wreck. He had never raped a woman or murdered anyone, but to his way of thinking, a cop, a brother in arms, was going down for Chance's faults. As far as he was concerned, Chance was a no-account biker, a lack-luster individual from the dark side, who deserved to take the fall for the murders, guilty or not. He crept into the living room and quietly closed the door.

The San Pedro murders were uniquely exercised and Clay was trying his best to mirror the original crimes. Without that, his efforts were of no use. The full gravity of the crime were incomprehensible unless he committed one himself. As a cop, he had experience with many crimes, including a couple of the Pedro murder sites, but committing one was another story. Sweating like a stuck pig, he crossed the dining room and lunged at Ling Wu.

He wrapped a cord around her neck and dragged her backwards to the floor, choking her. As she fell, she reached over her head trying to tear at the assailant, desperately grabbing the hooded mask, ripping it from his face, and revealing his identity.

She tried to scream but her strangled windpipe made it impossible. As she lay on the floor, almost passed out, she saw his face. Their eyes met. He wrapped her mouth with duct tape and released the rope.

At that point, he suddenly felt committed.The rush of the crime collided with his years of service training. His integrity clashed with his desire to save a brother. If she lived and recognized him, she'd pick him out of a line-up. He knew he couldn't let that happen. He'd crossed a dire line the moment he broke into her home.

Chance looked at himself in the mirror and thought about things he had never considered, like settling down. Dancing emotionally, his heart was doing the disco in his chest. He was on cloud nine. He put the brush back in the drawer and retied his robe. He was in a euphoric state where nothing mattered. He was infatuated and absorbing everything about this woman, from the sights and smells, to the textures surrounding him, but judging nothing. He turned off the bathroom light and opened the door.

As he turned into the small apartment hallway, he heard a thump. Ayers dragged Ling to a chair, but she struggled free and fell to the linoleum floor. He slapped her across the face and tried to lift her again, but couldn't. He pulled his service revolver and pointed it at her head.

"You're going to get into that chair, bitch, or I'll blow your head off now!"

Chance heard the words as he stepped onto the first step of the descending stairs. He turned and froze. He tore back into the bedroom, but his Levis weren't there, nor his trusty knife. He looked around the room in a panic, opening drawers and cupboards. He had to do something, but what? Her room was simple and clean with a few plants, a very ornate Chinese dresser and a mirror. He opened the sliding door to her wardrobe and cringed. There was nothing. He turned and ran to the head of the stairs.

"Hey baby, can I help you with anything?" he shouted, but there was no reply.

Ayers froze. Chance was in the apartment. He had planned to kill Ling after Chance had been in the home and his fingerprints were everywhere, but that wasn't the case. He stood above Ling and decided that he couldn't kill them both, or could he? Did he have a choice?

"I'll be right down, honey," Chance said, racking his brain for a plan. If the cop shot Ling, he'd kill him, but that wasn't good enough.

"Fuck it," Chance muttered He charged down the stairs and came face to face with the deranged cop standing over the woman he was falling in love with.

"Are you out of your fucking mind?"

"You should have climbed out a window up there and run, you fuckin' scum," Ayers said, the gun shaking in his hand.

As he looked at Chance's long hair and goatee, all the hatred he had for bikers surfaced. It replaced his concern for murdering the girl and the fear of his acts with pure hatred.

"You move one inch and I'll kill her."

"You're going to kill her anyway and now you've got to kill me too," Chance said, moving closer. There was only 10 feet between the two. "Now you've got another decision to make. If you kill her, I'm going to kill you, so you have got to cap me first, then kill Ling and get the hell out of here. You better make your move quick, cop, because if I get my hands on you, you'll wish you were dead."

"Don't move, motherfucker!" Ayers said and started to raise the weapon in Chance's direction.

Chance charged, just as the phone began to ring. Ling was terrified and couldn't move. Chance scrambled toward the gun, blocking it as Ayers attempted to aim, but the gun went off. The bullet shredded a cupboard door.

Terrified, Ling dove toward the sink, while Chance blocked the gun's direction, and yanked Clay to the floor. She scrambled to her feet as the phone rang. If it rang four times, it would automatically go to message. She desperately reached toward the kitchen cabinets as the .38 discharged again. She she dove for the phone, knocking it off the receiver. The gun went off again in the ensuing struggle and Ling tore the duck tape off her mouth as the two men wrestled on the floor. The gunshots reverberated through the apartment interior.

"What can I do?" she screamed at Chance, who was fighting for his life and hers.

"Stab the sonuvabitch!" Chance yelled.

Officer Kate Norton heard the struggle and gunshots over the phone. She was in her car in the vicinity and went on full alert, hitting her siren and slamming the blinker on the roof of the car.

"Can you hear me?" she screamed into the cell phone.

There was no answer.

Ling opened a drawer beside the sink and withdrew a butcher knife.

"Stab him anywhere," Chance pleaded as Ayers tried to roll on top of him. Chance let go of him with one hand and broke his nose, then hit him in the neck below his chin as hard as he could.

Ayers gasped and began to gag. Ling watched but couldn't bring herself to stab the cop.

Chance grabbed the barrel of the S&W snub nose and wrenched it up and back toward Ayers, breaking his index finger and disarming him. Chance continued the move, striking Ayers above the right eye with the butt then drawing the heavy pistol back and striking him on the temple.

Ayers lost momentum, and Chance hit him again with the pistol, knocking him out cold.

A siren screamed outside. Kate jumped out of the sedan and ran to the open door, her weapon at the ready.

# -4-

# SEX AND BROTHERLY LOVE

An ambulance took Ling Wu to the hospital with Chance riding shotgun. She wasn't badly hurt but terribly shaken. Kate insisted that she go and get checked out. She also took their statements, with another officer as witness. Ayers was arrested and taken to the jail section of the county hospital.

Chance sat in the sanitary white interior and held Ling's hand.

"What a first date," Ling said. Her voice was scratchy from her throat injury. She had abrasions across her neck and a bump on the back of her head.

"I don't know what to say," Chance said. "I...

"You don't have to say a thing," Ling said. She tried to roll toward him but the EMT pulled her back down on the gurney and tightened the straps.

"Yes, I do," Chance said. "I've had a problem with women for ten years, bouncing from one relationship to another. I can't seem to find the one and what I have found, has been bad luck. It's like I was dealt one bad hand after another."

"You're not the only dealer in the game," she said, squeezing his hand. "I plan to see you tomorrow night unless you have another surprise for me."

"We'll talk tomorrow night," Chance said, "but I promise no surprises between now and then."

"I should tell you that my brother is coming from China at the end of the week. It will be his first time in America. I would like you to meet him."

"I'd be glad to. We need to see that you're repaired," Chance said. "I'll look forward to it, and if there's anything you need, give me a call."

"I will," she said and squeezed his hand.

Chance looked at her lying there bruised and wounded, and wondered what the hell he had gotten into. She was a soft dream, a thing of beauty. He understood how guys would spend years building the ultimate custom motorcycle and yet still be distracted by a woman when showing it for the first time. He wanted her, but there was something more about her that deserved respect and care.

He decided, as he looked down at her alabaster skin and narrow lips parting to reveal a warm smile, that he had already put her life in harm's way once and that was one too many. He would do anything in his power to see that he was never responsible for anything of that nature again, and that if anything in his life would bring her harm or discomfort, he would stop it, even if it meant he had to leave her.

He stayed with her at the busy hospital, where she was admitted into emergency and wheeled into the examination room. He waited for a couple of hours while the doctors observed her, gave her an MRI, neck test and bandaged her. She finally was released and wheeled to the curb in a wheelchair, where Chance made certain a cab would be waiting.

"How do you feel?" Chance asked.

"I feel good," Ling said. "They gave me a valium and a pain killer and I'm doing fine. Let's go dancing."

"Yeah, right," Chance said, taking her directly home. The kitchen of her house was still taped off as a crime scene, but they went directly to bed. She undressed and slipped on her tattered robe. She gathered Chance's work clothes and folded them on a chair. They both slipped into bed nude and immediately wrapped themselves around each other and kissed.

"Good night baby," Chance said.

"Good night, you gorgeous man," Ling said and immediately slipped off to sleep.

The next day, Chance was back on the job whistling the infatuation tune. The news broke in the local seaside paper and Carl read the front page article as Chance parked his bike and walked in the door.

"Thanks for mentioning the taxi service, pal," Carl said. "Last night must have been wild."

"Never a dull moment," Chance said, "that's for sure. I told you, the shit hasn't stopped flying."

After Ling's classes, she drove her little pickup to the airport and picked up her brother. She spent the afternoon driving him to the beach, Universal Studios, and through Hollywood to give him a taste of Los Angeles. She hadn't seen her brother in two years.

"Are you ready to come home?" Chang asked, his quiet countenance broken. He didn't like her little used pickup, having expected a limousine.

"I haven't graduated yet," Ling said matter-of-factly.

Chang was one inch taller than Ling's 5'7" height and trim. He wore black slacks, soft leather shoes, a black turtleneck sweater and carried a black sport coat. He was his father's protégé and trained well for it, almost too well. He was tough, serious and determined, ala old communist China. He didn't take anything lightly. He ignored Ling's reply.

"I have some business to do while I'm here," he said, as she pulled up in front of her condo in Long Beach. The sun crept out as the clouds dissipated. There was a freshness about the area; the trees looked clean and bright green and the air smelled fresh. Chang couldn't help but notice the openness of the atmosphere in California. Unlike the density of Hong Kong, California was dense, but not as congested.

"This is where you live?"

"Yes, I love it here," Ling said. "You will see."

"Why are you so happy? Isn't school very difficult?"

"Yes, it is, but I'm enjoying myself."

Ling's emotions danced on cloud nine since she hooked up with Chance and she enjoyed every second of having him in her life. Even with the incident with Clay, she felt closer to Chance, as if they had already developed strength and respect.

"Do you need to take care of business tonight? You can borrow my truck."

"Tomorrow," Chang said. "I'll call for a car."

"Let's get you settled into my spare bedroom and we'll have a drink," she said gleefully. "Tonight I want to take you to dinner on the Harbor at the Hilton in San Pedro. I will introduce you to my boyfriend."

Chang's expressionless eyes lit up and he turned in the open door while carrying his bags. "You have someone in your life?"

"Yes, and he makes me very happy," Ling said and opened the door to the spare bedroom, which was just as neat and well adorned as the rest of the apartment. Chang did not compliment her, but he nodded his approval of her accommodations, which made Ling smile.

"Tell me about this man," Chang said as he hung his overcoat in the closet and began to put his clothes in the ornate Asian dresser Ling provided.

"I will show you tonight," she said. "You can ask questions later."

She left him in the spare bedroom and went up to her bedroom and pulled off her gray sweatshirt and her tight denims. She looked in the mirror and popped the snaps off her everyday bra, releasing her large boobs, the shapes of wonderfully soft slopes capped with small but pointed nipples hardening with the slightest touch.

She opened a slim lacquer drawer and pulled out a skimpy pink Victoria Secret bra. It would lift her heavy tits just enough to make them want to spill over any neckline. She wanted her man again. She pulled a long form fitting, jet-black low-cut dress over her head and inspected the slit up the side. She put on fresh hose and paten-leather, high-healed shoes that tied her small shapely feet in place with shinning black straps. She pulled her hair back into a black plastic monster, looking like a sado-masochism fist guiding her lovely head wherever it chose. Very little makeup was necessary, but she touched her eyes and put on a dark crimson lipstick. It made her face dance and glow.

Her brother represented 300 years of tight-knit family history during turbulent political times. She was high on romance, but took each step down the stairs with an air of royalty and respect. Gracefully she entered the kitchen to fix drinks, understanding the delicate situation she faced.

Chang washed his face and went into the freshly repaired kitchen and picked up his drink.

"What happened here?" He asked eyeing the repairs.

"I'll explain later," Ling said.

She glowed as she spun to face him with a white Russian in her hand, clinking it to his glass.

"It's great to see you, my brother."

"Likewise," Chang said quietly. "You know that your family wants you back." He was serious.

"You take this family stuff too seriously," Ling said. "We only have one life. We must fill our hearts with what we believe and trust in."

"Do you know what that is?"

"More every day, my brother. Let's go to dinner."

They drove down through the heart of Long Beach into the hip downtown region to Ocean Boulevard, then north over the bridge, leading mostly to the truck drivers' industrial section of town. They slipped along the stretch once housing the Long Beach naval base on Terminal Island, recently torn to the ground as military bases were closed. More container docks were being built as two of the largest ports in the world continued to expand.

Ling drove over the Vincent Thomas expansion bridge, a smaller version of the Golden Gate. It swayed over an area with equal character to San Francisco, only smaller, with rolling hills and old Spanish homes looking over the harbor and out into the Pacific. She drove north on Harbor Boulevard along the main channel of the harbor, past the ocean-going fire department, the Nautical Museum and a launching pad for wooden Brigandines. Members of the community came to donate time to help build two tall ships for the California fleet of restored replicas.

She drove past Chance's house on Crescent Avenue and honked. It was her signal to Chance. Ling drove down past the sprawling Cabrillo Marina and pulled into the Hilton parking lot and slipped out of the truck. As they walked to the entrance, she could hear the sharp muscular chant of the Harley-Davidson rolling into the marina area, like a dark knight stalking his prey.

Chance pulled up in front of the Hilton on the long tan, metal-flake chopper and kicked the kickstand down. He was in his dress biker uniform, Levis, polished brown cowboy boots, his leather belt and brass wheel Concho belt and a button-down collar, ivy green, khaki shirt and his leather vest. Chang was taken aback by the wild Harley-Davidson and the size of the long-haired man and his machine. Even in this day and age of China, custom cars and bikes were a rarity. Chance immediately recognized the disdain in Chang's look and ignored him to hug Ling.

"I have something for you," Chance whispered in her ear, "and it contains a piece of my heart."

She hugged him back, thrusting her body against his and kissed him like they hadn't touched in weeks. The tenderness was evident in the way their bodies melded to honor each touch, with each caress. Blushing, Ling stepped away from Chance.

"Chance, this is my brother, Chang."

Chance wanted to reach out to the man in good-hearted American fashion, but he could see dislike forming in the young man's harsh features. He held out his hand cautiously.

Chang did not reciprocate, but said, "I'm taking Ling Wu back to our family in China."

Chance looked at Ling who was an hour-glass of loveliness, in her silk, form-fitting dress, and her face an instruction-book on tenderness. Her eyes opened wide and she shook her head. Chance remembered the decorum of the dojo and thought long and hard about Asian respect, hospitality and hostility. He bowed slightly and said, "Whatever she wishes."

He stood up straight not allowing Chang to disturb the shear silken nature of Ling Wu's presence in his life. He would not let the young man disturb his *Wa,* Chinese for a surrounding area and the peace of mind it contains. They walked into the restaurant overlooking the marina and sat at a square table. As the afternoon sun changed, the glistening look of the pleasure boats took on a warmer hue.

Ling sat between the two warriors. Chang's demeanor was slipping away. He was a good-looking man, slick and dressed immaculately, but his jaw was clenched, and Chance could see the rippling muscles twitching in his cheeks.

"You Americans have no future," he said, his eyes becoming set like frozen marbles steered to Chance's rustic look and style. "I cannot wait to take my sister from here."

"Why have we no future?" Chance asked. "Don't you believe in freedom or capitalism? Do you have some false sense of self and believe that through dirty looks you will run China. Don't you believe that your people deserve to be free?"

Chang jumped to his feet. "I will not take a slur from a wide-eyed Anglo. You mean nothing to me."

"You'll have a tough time doing business in this free nation with that attitude," Chance said, and turned to Ling.

"Honey, we're having a helluva start, my love." He got to his feet, and bowed slightly.

"I stand out of respect for your sister. You are her guest, so I will not kick your ass right here, but you need a lesson. I will not leave this table like a whipped dog. I will stay unless you press the issue. It is your decision. You can sit in peace, or we can go outside with your sister's permission and see if through violence we can come to some level of understanding. Or we can meet at the dojo at which I train, the options are many."

Chance turned back to Ling Wu, "I'm falling in love with you and as your friend, I will bend to your will."

"My brother has always been a pompous jackass. What would you like to do?" She asked Chance and glared at her brother.

"My choice would be to go outside right now and take care of this," Chance said.

"Fine by me," Ling said and sat back down, "I'll order you a drink." She turned away from her brother.

"Let's go, pal," Chance said.

Chang backed away from the table and as soon as Chance rounded the corner, he spun and threw a back kick. Chance spun and with his left arm, blocked the kick and struck with his right, throwing his right elbow into Chang's jaw with a swift motion. Chang backed away bouncing on his light leather fighting shoes. Realizing that Chance had some experience, as well as strength and size, he questioned his tactic and repositioned himself.

Girls in the restaurant screamed and guests called for help. Security ran in their direction from the foyer. Chang was light on his feet and moved his small arms around in a flowing Asian fighting regime. He darted at Chance and jumped to form another kicking attack. Again, Chance blocked the first easily but was unable to block the second kick and two strikes to the head. Chance was knocked off balance and Chang struck with another kick to the ribs; moving in closer, he reached under his jacket for a dagger. Chance reeled against a tiled pillar in the center of the room. He blocked another kick, but his lack of years of training was evident as Chang threw a hard jab at his neck as a distraction to allow him the opening for the knife kill.

He was poised, athletic and confident. His moves were precise and purely executed. Chance rocked against the pillar, slamming his head against the thick ceramic surface. He was dazed as the knife move came like a surgeon's blade at his abdomen— a dog's death strike.

Chance couldn't breath; his windpipe was bruised and he gasped for breath. The knife came at him with precise control, directed at the top of his abdomen with the blade parallel to the deck. Chang threw a block to Chance's eyes to insure that his strike was unhindered. It came out from Chang's side directly at Chance, then shifted to a slashing movement, opening Chance's guts and allow his innards to fall at his feet with the utmost disrespect. It was the most humiliating blow he was capable of. His frown suddenly turned upward in the form of glee.

Chance, feebly aware of what was happening, but strong, saw Chang pull the titanium stiletto and cock it into a strike position. He knew what move he was supposed to make, to turn away yet aggressively take control of the blade, but he had trouble moving. He began to implement the first rule, to take his body out of harm's way, but his spin was hindered by the bruising kick to his ribs. He had lost his breath and the strike to his throat prevented any effort to suck it back in.

He gasped just as something seemed to move the knife. It was off course, passing his body. He looked to his left and saw Ling pushing Chang with a chair, just enough that the strike missed its target. Chang attempted to recoil. Chance took a breath, then struck the side of his jaw with everything he had, which wasn't a lot at the moment. Chang looked wide-eyed with surprise.

Chance regained momentum and pushed the weapon further away from his belly. He twisted Chang's weapon wrist and took the blade away, striking Chang harshly with the jeweled butt of the knife. Chang stumbled and fell to the floor. They were surrounded by frightened and curious onlookers as the security guard burst through the crowd with his weapon drawn.

Ling slid up beside Chance. "You should get out of here," she said. "I'll meet you back at your place."

Chance nodded and offered her the knife.

"Don't American bikers have a code for that?" Ling said.

"You're right," Chance said. "The code is 'use it or lose it', but I was offering it out of respect for you. Thank you for what you did."

"One good deed deserves another," she said smiling and kissed Chance.

He wanted to grab her into his arms, but it wasn't the time. He slid the knife in his waistband and backed into the gathering crowd. He made his way to the front door and pushed his bike away from the marble foyer before firing it to life.

The Hispanic security officer pointed a revolver at Chang as Ling helped him to his feet. He disregarded the officer's weapon as unworthy and began to move toward the door with Ling. She said nothing to him or the officer as they walked through the crowd. They could hear the motorcycle fire to life and Chang straightened as the rumble filled the air, leaving in honor but defeated. Inside he seethed with anger.

Ling drove Chang back to her condo in silence until they pulled up in front. She handed him a spare key to the apartment.

"I'm very disappointed," she said. "Listen to his words. You cannot do business in America with your attitude. Go inside, I'm leaving you here. Relax."

"You are going back to him, are you not?" Chang said, his head bowed as he crawled out of the car.

"Of course," Ling said with strength and determination. "I will see you tomorrow."

Chang stood on the curb and watched as she pulled away. He had been slapped and was completely out of his element. In China he was a god, at least he liked to think so. No one questioned his actions or intentions. They obeyed immediately or were punished.

Chance arrived at his pad wrapped in a deep sense of remorse. He felt like he was turning up all the wrong cards with this girl. He wanted her to love him as much as he was feeling for her, but every encounter resulted in a violent experience. This was not the way to develop a lasting relationship. He pushed his bike into the garage and locked the door. He went into the house, fully expecting a Dear John call, or nothing. Perhaps he would never see her again. He pulled the stiletto out of his waistband and inspected the fine lines, the delicate dragon engraved into the ivory handle. He admired the workmanship, and thought about how close he had come to being mauled by this weapon. It represented more than he could possibly imagine.

Chance went to a white kitchen cupboard and pulled down his bottle of Jack Daniels. He remembered what she said at the restaurant and pondered it, as he strode onto the deck at the front of his house and looked out at the harbor. He enjoyed the changing hues of the port as the sun set behind him over the Palos Verdes Peninsula. There was something about a sunset that revealed the humble attributes of humanity on earth.

Most of what any human could ever accomplish would never compare to one glistening sunset on the ocean.

He toasted the amber glows reflecting on the salt water and the white sails dancing along the harbor whitecaps and took a swig.

Whether or not he lost Ling, hopefully another sunset would grace the sky tomorrow. His heart felt heavy; the sunset was a dynamic constellation, but he wasn't sure it would fill the need in his heart.

He sat in his deck chair and watched a massive cruise ship glide through the harbor's main channel at five knots, heading out to sea. Its lights were aglow as it passed and the lights on the myriad of cranes around the harbor snapped on as the sun began to sink and the colors on the harbor changed again to a deepening blue.

He was brought back to reality by a horn honking in quick bursts. He turned to see Ling's small pickup turn onto his street from Crescent Avenue, make an abrupt U-turn and park along side his house. She jumped from the cab as Chance stepped quickly from the deck to meet her. They embraced in the front yard and Chance held her close.

"I didn't think you would come back."

"I said I would, and nothing would stop me," Ling said after a long tender kiss. "My brother…"

"You don't need to say a word," Chance said and kissed her again. They held onto each other as if they would never see one another again. People honked as they rolled by. The sun sparkled its final glimpse of warmth on them as it dipped over the rolling hillside behind them. Another passing couple honked and their lips finally parted.

"Are you hungry, honey?" Ling asked as Chance led her inside the house.

"For you," Chance said and slapped Ling on the ass.

She stopped abruptly and then pushed her ass out some more. "One more time."

"We should go in the house," Chance said, "we don't need to cause an accident."

"Damn," Ling said, "I brought you some food. We better eat it while it's hot."

She trotted back to her car and pulled out a bag of Chinese food. The rich aroma filled her truck cab and she inhaled the smells. She looked out at the harbor and noted just a touch of crimson in the darkening sky. It was as perfect as their kiss and the smell of the garlic soaked, spicy Kung Pao chicken and egg flower soup, enhanced the mood.

Chance left the door open for her and began to set the table. She drove him wild, like the taste of a wonderful peach pie, and suddenly someone yanked the plate away as the scoop of French Vanilla dripped over the edges of the warm crust. He was dripping with desire as he put out plates and fixed her a White Russian.

She placed the brown paper bag on the counter and looked around his pad for the first time. It was scattered with motorcycle memorabilia and art. She liked the simplicity yet masculine artistic details of his work in progress. It was a mess, but she could see promise. Chance sat at the head of the table and sipped his bowl of soup while gazing at her seductive beauty in the tight dress.

"I can hardly contain myself," he said.

"That makes two of us," Ling said, digging into the hot and spicy Kung Pao chicken and vegetable fried rice. The two of them ate like ravenous, lustful animals.

"What are you into, baby?" Chance asked staring into her eyes.

"I don't exactly know," Ling said beginning to blush. Young, and raised in China, her sexual encounters were limited.

Chance reached across the corner of the table, in the breakfast nook overlooking the harbor and brushed the outside of his fingertips against her hardening nipples. She took a sharp breath and they protruded more. "I have never felt free to discuss my feelings before. For some reason I feel safe and secure."

Chance took a man-sized bit of the spicy chicken dish, bit off the point off a red pepper for additional spice and looked deep into her flickering dark eyes. Her words were deeply significant to him. His mind railed with thoughts of his recent past. A light mist of sweat built on her forehead. He sensed her arousal, but he was also flooded with a deeper level of responsibility.

Chance reached across the table once more and this time she set down her fork and sat up a bit straighter in her seat; her breasts were bubbling over the low cut black gown. He reached between her breasts and touched her alabaster flesh at the edge of the dark gown. With just one fingertip, he traced along the edge of the gown over each round swelling boob.

"We may have something very special here," Chance said looking deep into her flickering eyes. He took another bite of his food then pushed his plate away. She looked at him wide-eyed.

His life flash before him. He wanted to toss the table aside and embrace her for an encyclopedia of reasons. Sure, there was lust, but something way more. His heart swelled with emotion, terror, romantic history, and the future. Simultaneously, they pushed the table aside and embraced.

They retired into his disheveled bedroom for a long night of passionate wrestling under the sheets. They could hardly stop. Spent and exhausted, Chance finally blew out the last flickering candle.

"Wow," they both said simultaneously and kissed once more.

# -5-

# NOT JUST ANOTHER FRIDAY NIGHT

The morning started cool on the coast as a dense fog drifted over the harbor until almost noon. Ling Wu worked hard in her art classes studying ceramics. She labored at the pottery wheel before the holiday to better her grades and be clear of school projects for the Christmas season. Ling and Chance brewed escape plans. They enjoyed every minute of sheer bliss during their two-month steamy relationship. They spent every weekend together and several nights during the week, depending on schedules.

Ling's brother, Chang, left the states less than a week after their initial caustic encounter and flew back to mainland China. Chance never heard another word from him and Ling never mentioned him. But he knew something negative would fester from their initial encounter. He would deal with it whenever it surfaced. He was determined to make the most of this relationship. It was rapidly turning into the brightest star in his biker-smudged galaxy.

The two lovers built steadily toward a future together. Although their genes originated from different races they were as compatible as Harley and Davidson. Chance and Ling decided that when she graduated, they would open a bike shop. Chance attended all the nearby swap meets collecting parts and making his garage into a miniature motorcycle shop. It was tight but well-equipped. He performed service for select local riders and worked with a local artist on a concept drawing for his first project bike. Their goal was to build on a shop for five years, while trying to obtain approval to start a Harley-

Davidson dealership in the neighborhood. Chance signed up for retail business classes at Harbor College while still working on the docks part-time.

For the first time in his life, he'd met a woman who worked for him, with him, and was sexually compatible. From time to time, he awoke in a cold sweat. He harbored deep-seated guilt regarding his past romantic life. He never meant to hurt a woman, but he had and he remembered each encounter and each failure; they haunted him like bad Karma. Every girl he'd made cry would come to mind at odd times, and he wondered if he deserved Ling. He splashed water in his face, brushed his teeth and felt blessed by the outlaw god for allowing him to find a woman who enjoyed his lifestyle, loved sex as much as he did and possessed a high degree of integrity and style. She was also a knockout and he was proud to stand alongside her anywhere.

Chance looked at his rugged features in the mirror and shook his head. "You're a lucky motherfucker, goddamnit," he muttered to himself as he pulled on a t-shirt. For once, the cards he drew were nonstop winners. It was Friday night and Ling would dart to his pad after the flea market to spend the weekend. He shuddered with pure pleasure as he imagined her arrival and the first thing she did was to disrobe and dress for dinner. He couldn't wait. As she peeled out of her sweats his hands would roam over her body and ultimately they would make love. On occasion, that would end their dinner plans and they'd frolic in bed all night.

On other weekends, they showered together and dressed for dinner. Usually at dinner, Ling would tease Chance with the thoughts of picking up another girl and taking her home for a threesome. By the time they paid the bill and reached her truck, his hand was under her dress, down her blouse or she gave him head in the front seat. Then they'd rush home for more good times. The rest of the weekend was spent working on bikes and making plans for the future. Ling would even attend occasional martial arts classes with Chance.

Chance spent most of the morning working on his bike after he went for a short run. The bike was his brother. He kept mostly to himself except for Ling and a couple of riders who were customers. His bike was worn, but it handled anything that Chance threw at it with style. While working on the docks, he took special care to manage the harsh salt spray. He moved away from delicate chrome and preferred to powder-coat or Jet Hot coat his pipes. It gave his bike a different bad-ass look and his exhaust never discolored. He wiped down the rigid Harley on the lift and checked the tightness of his motor-mount bolts and the nuts and bolts fastening the transmission and rear fender to the chassis. Vibration to his solid-mounted machine shook fasteners like a band of termites attacking an unprotected small wooden shed left in the elements. It was just a matter of time.

He checked the oil in the engine and transmission and then pulled the plugs just to see how they were burning. At noon, he rode over to see his painter, Phil, about a bike project he was working on and then rode to the Lighthouse Café on 34th street for a sandwich.

As he looked down the street that seemed to run off a cliff to nowhere, he could see the LA lighthouse on the end of the jetty built by WWII Veterans. It was a masterful notion to separate the mighty swells and Pacific storms from the mainland and afford residents and shipping lines a safe place to cruise and anchor. It worked beautifully for everyone but the surfers, who couldn't find a decent wave in Long Beach and were forced to roam south.

Chance ate lunch and then fired up his scoot for the ride back to his pad to work on the shop and a customer's bike. As he pulled up out front, Japanese Jay was sitting on the deck waiting. Jay was big for a Jap, some six feet and wide like a football player. He came from Japan to Hawaii to surf and then to the California coast to keep up his vocation as a biker/surfer. He was a biker-dealer exporter. He made his money building old styled bikes and shipping them to Japan. His career had some benefits, combined with a couple of risks.

Business fluctuated constantly. One week, Jay could take his girl to dinner; the next, he had to borrow money from her to keep the lights burning. He had a full scraggly beard and his hair was thick, black and long. He had one of those faces that was all friendly until his expression changed. Then it became the face of a tyrant, perfect for his biker side. He could be tough as nails when he needed it, unless it was one helluva façade; Chance hadn't seen him in action, so he didn't know.

"What's happening, Jay?" Chance asked.

"Thought I give you first bid," Jay said.

"Whatta ya got?" Chance asked as Jay led him out to his mid '70s baby blue Ranchero. Jay walked to the faded truck and leaned over the bed railing. It was filled with old plastic milk crates packed with motorcycle parts. Two early original rigid frames stood next to them.

Chance surveyed the boxes and estimated the level of parts he had in his sales baskets.

"Two basket cases, huh?"

"Yep," Jay said. "You interested?"

"Don't have the money just yet. Whatta you want for them?"

"We're shooting for $2,000 apiece."

"Damn, I would like to pick up one, Jay, but I just don't have the cash."

"I make deal for you," Jay said, kicking the dust at his feet with his beach sandals.

"What kind of deal?"

"I take three thousand for both."

"Goddamnit," Chance said, "I told you I don't have the fuckin' money, now get the hell out of here."

Ling Wu spent most of the morning working on a college art project after attending one early class, then she blasted home to gather her supply of Bonsai trees and lucky Bamboo plants. She drove past the nursery to pick up some plant food and a couple more ceramic pots. Mrs. Kadako came to her truck to help her load and pack the delicate plants and fragile ceramic pots.

"You doing well?" the elderly woman asked Ling.

"I'm marvelous," Ling said. "I couldn't be happier."

"I have watched you grow," Mrs. Kadako said. "You are good and I'm happy for you."

"Thank you, Mrs. Kadako," Ling said, bowing her head slightly in respect. "If it wasn't for you, I wouldn't have any of this happiness. It is true plants are blessed, or those Lucky Bamboos are truly lucky."

Ling finished packing and closed the tailgate. She drove slowly and carefully. She pondered her arrangement as she packed and prepared for the run downtown to the Promenade flea market, noting that her sales line was anything but attractive. Once her arrangements were fashioned, however, her booth took on a happy air of serenity and comfort. She hoped Chance was drawn by the lovely plants and the comfort they offered.

As a child she experienced the teachings of Buddhism. Mrs. Kadako reintroduced Ling to the Dharma and the notion of Nirvana, or tranquility, through her plants and respect for all living things.

As she drove along Pacific Coast Highway in Long Beach through some of the tougher sections of the city, she pondered her growing romance and its effect on her life. She found it gave her promise and focus for the future. Chance was incredibly good to her and she thanked the spirits for putting her together with such a man and prayed that it would be the beginning of something truly meaningful. She pulled up to the booth on Broadway to pay for her ten-by-ten spot and pulled around in back to set up. The sun shone bright on the harbor and one of the booths housing the Thai Food Factory, The smells delightfully filled the Promenade.

The temperature was perfect and one smiling customer after another stepped up to the well-organized booth, many purchasing her delicate offerings. Her booth was different everytime she arranged the plants and trees, showing off the glistening ceramics and the shape of each plant to its best advantage. She placed them in a multi-tiered horseshoe configurations, highlighting a fountain in the center, with running water from a battery-powered pump hidden behind the arrangement. After she set up her booth, she wandered over to the Thai food booth and ordered some Pad Thai and a Chicken Sate.

Her emotional zeal paid off. Her creative nature expanded. She felt with Chance in her life, she could do anything. For the first time she faced her insecurities and Chance showed her how to deal with them, or raise the bar to allow her unlimited access to her abilities. Doors were opening she never expected. Sexually, he helped her tear the iron gates off the hinges. He encouraged her creativity and her education. She loved every second of his support and companionship. He placed no barriers but released her from hers.

Sales for her Friday were the best she ever encountered and she was pleased as the sun began to set in the mighty Pacific. She started to load her truck with the few remaining plants she hadn't sold. As she drove away from the refurbished downtown art-deco strewn area, she mentally clicked off the minutes before she would be wrapped in his arms. She visualized the seconds it would take her to strip for him and allow his gentle hands to explore every inch of her. She teased herself with fantasies for the evening and almost ran a red light on Atlantic Boulevard. Snapping her senses back to reality, she drove the last five miles home in her little pickup, as fast as she could, without drawing a ticket from a Long Beach police officer.

As she pulled into her alley and up to her garage, she noticed a small Ryder moving truck in the alley and pondered the thought of a new neighbor. She also thought about moving in with Chance. They were discussing prospects for the future, but she still had one semester to complete before graduation and the logistics leaned toward her staying close to school for the time being.

She unloaded her truck and carefully moved each plant to a secure spot, checking the water level on all the lucky bamboo. As she walked in the door to her apartment from the garage, a smell caught her attention. It was something different, something odd, but she disregarded it and headed upstairs to take a shower. As she reached the top of the stairs, she noticed the smell again.

She slid open the door to her closet and was confronted by an all black figure. She tried to slide the door shut but black-gloved hands grabbed the edge of the mirrored door and flung it open. She spun to escape to the stairs but another goon in a black outfit stepped behind her, grabbing her from behind. She learned just enough from Sifu's classes to respond with an elbow strike over her shoulder and immediately another to the man's side. The smell, she thought, was perspiration. The strike broke his grasp and she leaped for the stairs just five feet away, but her assailant attacked her from the side, slamming her against the stucco wall knocking the wind from her lungs.

She collapsed to the floor trying to scream, but a hand with a chloroform soaked cloth immediately stifled her cry. She jerked her head from side to side, fighting the effects. The cloth was removed and replaced with a strip of duct tape. Kicking with her feet, she struck back at one attacker, driving him to his knees. She noted pained Asian eyes.

Dazed, she kicked madly, scuffing the stucco wall in the hall when she lunged to escape. She tore at the carpeting until one attacker hit her like a sledgehammer in the center of her back, shoving her face against the thick rug. With her mouth sealed, her moans came hard and fast as she struggled to breathe. The shorter of the two attackers grabbed her hands and tied them with large hurtful cable ties. One assailant lifted her by her bound arms and her shoulder joints screamed with pain.

"Don't move or you die," the shorter of the two attackers demanded. She felt the other attacker grab her feet, but ignored the warning and kicked furiously.

Ling freed herself of one man, pulling at the shorter of the two men heading toward the stairs and yanked him down the carpeted steps as he tumbled and crashed to the deck butting into her hard wood dining room table. For a second, she was stunned as the taller goon scrambled down the stairs, grabbed her feet and bound them with a cable tie.

As one skinny goon sat on her tender form, the other pulled a large throw rug from behind her couch. They shoved her coffee table aside and splayed it out awkwardly. Hurriedly they grabbed her as if they were under terrible time constraints, tossing her on the rug and knocking the wind out of her again. She was dazed but tried to scramble away. As they shoved her to one end and began to roll her up in the rug, she fought with her knees, thighs and torso jerking until the rug consumed her and a claustrophobic sense engulfed her.

Consumed by this thick dense rug four feet longer than her height, she was invisible. She sensed some level of light until the men stuffed the ends with more rolled rug fragments. They jumped to their feet, ran to the sink, threw open the cupboard below and grabbed a plastic trash bag. Opening it, they yanked out two sets of blue overalls, pulled off their ski masks and donned moving company uniforms. They brushed their hair silently, sharing one brush, hefted the rolled rug onto their shoulders and headed out the back door to the truck waiting in the alley. Without concern, they tossed her in the back and she rolled in the rug against the thick tattered wooden slats. They slammed the roll-up door with a clatter, scrambled into the cab and drove away.

Ling usually arrived at Chance's seaside pad before 5 o'clock and always called before she left her apartment, but he didn't hear from her. He picked up around the house and thought about the evening. They had been together for almost two months and he felt it was time for something special. He changed the bed sheets and put out a few new candles. He jammed to the store and bought a dozen roses, the color of traditional custom painted red and orange flames. He made sure he had enough Kahlua for a drink or two. Stopping at Chin's on the way home, he picked up some Chinese food.

When he rolled up to the house, he noted the time - 4:45 - and congratulated himself on having a few more minutes to put the flowers in a depression era green glass cookie jar and set out the food.

At 5:00, he poured himself a Jack on the rocks, expecting her to walk in the door at any minute. He set out her glass and took the Kahlua and Absolut vodka out of the cupboard. At 5:30, he called her home and got her answering machine.

"Hey baby, you're drink is waiting, get your cute little ass over here."

At 6:00, he became concerned and paced the floor. The phone started to ring and Chance grabbed the wall unit.

"Yeah?"

"What's wrong, your new squeeze has left you already?" Kate Norton quipped.

"As a matter of fact, I can't seem to find her."

"I called to tell you that they released Clay today."

"Oh, that's even better," Chance said.

"What do you mean? I thought you'd be pissed."

"Ling usually makes it over here before 5:00," Chance said. "She calls about 4:30 when she's leaving her place. I haven't heard from her. It's almost 6:15."

"Maybe I should check," Kate said with concern.

"I can't imagine," Chance said, "but since Clay is out, maybe it would be a good idea."

"I'll swing by there on my way home. Call my cell phone if she shows up."

"Thanks," Chance said, his level of anxiety rolling up the terror scale. He hung up, finished his drink with one gulp and wandered around the house looking for something to do. His demeanor changed from sexual tension to outright hostility.

Why would Clay fuck with his girl again? He'd be dead, hung by his own people. The whole law enforcement community in San Pedro would be in hot water.

Chance muttered, "Why would they cut him loose?" He turned and coiled to hit a wall, slapping a door jam with his forearm. A large thump filled the small home. He put on a CD of Luther Van Dross, and listened, hoping for a sign.

He stood in the middle of the hallway and looked around at the photos and art. Suddenly it meant nothing. Where was she?

Kate, in her white plain-clothes car, rolled up to the apartment complex on Cerritos Boulevard and parked. She went to the front door and knocked. There was no answer and no evidence that the front door had been tampered with. It was still locked. She walked to the corner and around back. The garage door was open. She hesitated. Ling's pickup was in the garage. She approached the inside door to the interior and drew her service pistol. Crouching slightly, she opened the door a crack and looked inside.

"Ling?" Kate called through the door. The kitchen seemed normal. A door under the sink was slightly ajar. As she slowly moved into the room, she noticed a chair knocked over in the dining room. She immediately called for backup and moved into the foyer, where a plant was knocked over and the potting soil spread onto the carpeting like a black plague where the ceramic planter had fallen and split.

The living room was okay at first glance, but the coffee table had been moved. She could see the indents in the rug where it was positioned.

"Ling?" she called again and proceeded slowly, cautiously, upstairs, her pistol at the ready. At the top of the stairs, she looked into the bathroom, but at first glance saw nothing ajar. She proceeded carefully, looked behind the door. Her heart was pounding with fear of the worst as she moved the shower curtain aside.

Nothing.

She stepped back into the hall and noticed some marks on the dry wall across from the bathroom door. Then she stepped into the bedroom with her gun extended and surveyed the room quickly to ascertain whether anyone was there.

Nothing. The bed was still made. One closet sliding door was open and off its track. She heard another patrol car pull up out front.

She ran downstairs to meet the officers.

"Don't go in just yet," she said. "Just tape off the front door and across the back door and don't let anyone else in. We need investigators. I think we have a kidnapping on our hands."

She stepped back into the alley and looked around. Nothing was evident, then she remembered Ling's friend who lived a couple of doors down. She walked past a couple of units and up to the door.

"Yes?" Alison said, in a robe with her wavy red hair rolled in a towel above her head.

"Hi, Alison," Kate said. "Have you seen Ling Wu?"

"No," Alison started. "She's stuck on the biker in San Pedro. Don't see her much anymore."

"See anything around her place today?" Kate added.

"Well," Alison thought, "I did see a small moving truck out back a little while ago."

"Do me a favor," Kate said. "Go right over to your desk, sit down and think about that truck. Make notes of anything about it, the color, the make, the company, license plate, anything. I'll be right back."

Kate started to walk back to Ling's unit and pulled her cell phone off her waist and started to dial Chance.

# -6-

## Which Way To Turn?

Chance poured another Jack on the rocks when the phone rang. It was Kate.

"Are you sitting down?" Kate asked.

"What the fuck is going on?" Chance snapped.

"I'm not kidding," Kate said trying to punctuate her words. "You need to sit down."

Chance was silent as he took his drink to the breakfast nook and sat down. "Okay," he said solemnly, "Shoot the dice."

"We don't know exactly what happened yet, but we're guessing she's been kidnapped," Kate said and held her breath tentatively, waiting for Chances to respond.

Chance looked at his drink, then at the tile on the counter under the glass doors of the cupboard above. On the tile was a fired ceramic vase, with glazes that always lit him up; they were that beautiful. In the vase was the Lucky Bamboo Ling gave him. It was the best one and represented more than pure natural beauty, luck and artistic strength. She had picked it out and given it to Chance with a card. It told him just how much her love for him was growing. He could smell her Eternity perfume and see the constant joy in her eyes.

"Goddamnit!" Chance said, gulping hard on his drink and slamming his favorite glass against the dining room table. "I'll kill anyone who harms her, Kate. I want you to tell me what you know. Everything."

"Not much right this second," Kate started. "There was some sort of scuffle in her apartment, no blood, but it looked like someone was fighting. Other than that, the place is clean. I've sent for the kidnap team and they're going to pull Clay back in for questioning. That's all I know."

"I need to know everything, every fuckin' detail," Chance said, "and make it Wyoming lightening fast!" His voice was warrior strong, unrelenting and as direct as the rattle from a diamondback. "Anything and everything. We need to find her, alive. I'm in love with this chick, and will do anything to get her back."

He was assured and strong and although Kate wished that dedication was directed at her, she respected him. She ran down every sketchy detail including Alison's report of the Ryder truck.

"Let's stay in direct contact," Chance said. "If you can get me a cell phone, that would help a lot. I'm going after the truck. I'll call you back."

Chance hung up and grabbed the phone book. Then he tossed it across the room and went back to the tall cupboard to the left of the sink and opened it. He pulled out the fifth of Jack Daniels and spun the cap off and started to take a swig. With the glass ring against his mouth he raised the bottle, then stopped and said, "No time to lose, motherfucker."

He recapped the bottle, put it away and picked up the phone book. He scrambled through the pages as a tear crept down the side of his cheek. He turned each page as if something on the interior would tell him where she was. He called the 800 number for Ryder and got a smooth southern female voice after five minutes of wading through an extensive voice mail system.

Ryder Customer Service, this is Alicia, can I help you?"

"How can I find a particular truck that was probably rented yesterday?" Chance asked.

"Do you have the invoice number or the plate of the truck," She replied.

"No," Chance, said his frustration with his own ignorance expanding. "It was rented from somewhere in Long Beach."

"Sir, we have six locations in Long Beach and 24 on the west side of Los Angeles."

Chance started thinking fast. What information could he use?

"Can you give me a list of the locations in Long Beach?"

"Yes sir, do you have a Fax machine?"

"Fuck!" Chance exclaimed.

"Excuse me, sir?"

"I don't have a goddamn Fax machine," Chance said. "Could you read them to me?

"Certainly," she said, sighing, then began to read. Chance grabbed a pad of paper and started to jot down each address, "3209 Atlantic; 17434 Pacific Coast Highway; 9482 4th Street; 24850 Spring Street; 4375 Redondo Blvd.

"Here are two in Bellflower," she said. "Would you like them?"

"I better take them, thanks," Chance said and she gave him an address on Lakewood Blvd, and one on Cerritos.

"Do you have one out by LAX?" Chance asked, trying to get whatever info he could from someone who was helpful.

"Of course," she said. "That's 3250 Aviation.

Do you want phone numbers for each?"

"Nope," Chance said. "I'll pay each one a visit, until I find out who rented that truck, thanks. I've got to go."

He hung up, wadded the note pad up and stuck it in his vest, along with a Wather PPK. He pulled his trusty brother out of the garage. He felt as if he was on some strange drug, grinding his teeth and focused as if he was taking out a Taliban leader with a sniper rifle.

He jumped on his scooter and fired it to life, taking off immediately. He hit the freeway like a crazed maniac, cutting traffic toward LAX, up the San Pedro Freeway to the 405, San Diego Freeway and headed north to the 105. He rode as if every vehicle was programmed to miss him completely. He pulled up in front of the small Ryder shack, shut off the bike and ran in the door. A large black woman was the receptionist. "Can I help you, sir?"

"Did you rent any box trucks yesterday?" he asked.

"Of course sweetheart, o' we be out of bisnus," she said.

"Look, I'll be straight with you," Chance said, beads of sweat on his forehead, "My girlfriend was kidnapped yesterday and the officer said she may have been taken in a Ryder truck."

The hefty woman suddenly stopped everything she was doing and moved to another desk. She carefully went through each invoice.

"Some 90 percent of our business is regular customers," she said. "I'm looking for anything that might be different."

"I can't tell you much more," Chance said.

"You already have," the big woman said; then she shouted, "Charley!"

A tall kid wearing a business suit and tie came into the room from his office. "Yes, ma'am?"

"Anybody strange come in here yesterday?" she asked.

"Two guys," Chance said, but he was guessing as he tore through his own mind, reaching for more questions.

He thought for a second and said, "Nope, just a regular day."

"I'm sorry sir, but we don't seem to have what you need, but I'll keep watching," she said, as sadness filled her eyes.

"Thanks," Chance said heading for the door, then returned, "If anything comes up, anything at all, like two cops renting a truck or maybe Asians, call me." He scratched his name and number on a slip of paper and handed it to her.

"Good luck," she said as the glass door shut behind him. He jumped on his faithful scooter and aimed at Long Beach. His first stop was in a rough section of town at 3209 Atlantic. It was a corner lot fenced in with chain link. Trash and graffiti lined every building in the neighborhood. Several drunks made the corner of Atlantic their home. The area smelled of old cigarettes and sweat.

Chance pulled up to the small pre-fab building and ran up the steps just as two blacks bursts out of the front door packing a small bag and guns. Chance tripped the first one and as he fell over backwards, he took his gun away and stuck it in the pocket behind the other man's right knee. "Drop it quick, if you want to walk away," Change said.

"I ain't dropping shit." The tall black spun as Chance pulled the trigger. The crack was ghastly, like the slam of an ax hitting a railroad tie. The bullet went into the hype's filthy denims, cutting through the cartilage and tendons at the back of the knee and exploding through the kneecap on the other side.

The man was thin and evidently reeling on drugs. He grunted; the drugs prevented the pain switch from being thrown and he collapsed down the steps. His partner jumped to his feet as Chance collected the other weapon.

"Take your partner," Chance said as he reached for the shopping bag that recently held a bottle of wine and now contained a small bundle of cash, "and get-the-fuck outta here!"

The black turned and looked up at Chance's tanned features as he lifted his crying partner under the man's arms and started to pull him backwards toward the alley.

"I need dat money, man. I got to have a fix."

Chance look at him directly in his dark eyes, "Each business deal has its risks, partner."

He turned and walked up the stairs with both guns in his hands. He pushed the door open and walked in. Three employees huddled together.

"Have you called the cops?" Chance asked them.

The black gentleman behind the counter said, "The women won't let me. Those guys said they'd come back if we did."

"You can call them now, if you want," Chance said and looked at the women. "They no longer have guns." He stepped behind the counter and asked, "Is anyone hurt?"

"No," the black gentleman said, helping one shaken girl to lie down.

Chance went to the back of the building and looked for a window. He could see the bigger of the black men pulling his partner down the alley. They didn't have a car, so no additional weapons, at least not nearby. He looked over the two pistols and set them on the counter, then thought better of it and set them out of site on a coffee table. The other employee was a fat older black woman who looked at Chance with relief, not fear.

"Can we help you sir?"

"I hope so," Chance said. "My girlfriend was kidnapped a couple of hours ago and they may have thrown her into the back of a Ryder truck. I don't have much to go on, but it probably took two people minimum and the only info we have is that it could have been cops, long story, or Asians, or I'm barking up the wrong tree. All I can do is try to find out where the truck is due to be returned."

"Cops will be all over this place in a second," the woman said, flipping through the day's invoices. "I can't think."

"Listen, do me a favor," Chance said. "How late do these offices stay open?" He was writing his contact information on a slip of paper for her.

"Between 7:00 and 9:00 p.m. on weekdays," she said still flipping through invoices.

"Call the ones on PCH and in Redondo and tell them to stay open until I get there," Chance said. "Oh, and here's your money. I need to get moving, or these cops will hang me up. If you think of anything, call me."

"Can we tell the cops about what you did?" She asked, concerned.

"I'd rather you didn't," Chance said heading for the door. "No time to lose."

She picked up the phone and then thought better of it and turned to her computer. She went on line and was able to send an e-mail to every Southern California Ryder outlet.

Chance slipped on his worn tan gloves and threw his leg over his black solo seat and screamed up Atlantic to Pacific Coast Highway. Long Beach was a beautiful city perched on the blue Pacific with the harbor on the west end and wonderfully wide beaches all across its coastline until, on the east end, there was a community filled with bays and canals. But each city seems to have an area that slips into drug or wine induced depravity and that was the north end of the downtown corridor.

Chance didn't care how he rode. He was on a mission. The area took on a deepening sense of evilness in the dark. The buildings were in disrepair and covered with scattered graffiti. The concrete curbs in front of each building became a depository for used rubbers, broken bottles, cigarette butts and trash. The gutters were cleaned once a week with street sweeping trucks, but no one swept the chewing gum stained sidewalks.

Chance focused on the neon until he found the Ryder Truck sign. He pulled into the parking lot and kicked out his kickstand. The office was open. He ran for the small stucco building in the center of the old gas station lot. He pushed open the door and found a neatly dressed Iranian at his desk.

"Hello sir," the clerk said, looking at Chance skeptically. "Can I help you?"

"Tough area," Chance said.

"It's my home," he said in a matter of fact tone. "I adjusted. Much better than my homeland."

"My girlfriend was kidnapped..." Chance started.

"Debbie called from Atlantic store. She explained," he said. "I have looked through my records for the last couple of days. I have nothing."

"Are you sure?" Chance said.

"I'm sure, sir. Cops don't come in here."

"Did she tell you that my girlfriend was kidnapped?"

"Too bad," the gentleman said in a tone that indicated little concern as he put his paper away for the day and prepared to leave.

"But did she ask you if any Asian guys came in here?" Chance's frustration level was obvious.

"She mentioned it," he said, putting some files in a cheap brief-case.

"Goddamnit, I need some help with this. I need to find my girl! Chance shouted at the man.

Mr. Surkie was short and thin as a rail. He appeared to contain no emotion whatsoever and he moved around the office turning off the lights.

"My wife was raped and murdered trying to get to her car one evening, sir," he said, his voice lowering. Then he held the door open for Chance. "I must go home to my children."

Chance bowed slightly and without another word left the office. He rode to Spring Street only about five miles away and found the next office, but the lights of the sign weren't lit and as he pulled up to the gate, discovered that it was locked. A closed sign hung crookedly in the office window.

Chance hurried to his bike and was on the road in seconds, heading toward the last location in Long Beach on Redondo Blvd. Redondo was a major street, but not designed that way, with residents scattered among small offices, shops and dental buildings. He spotted the Ryder office right away and snapped the throttle. The lights were still on in the small lot. There were only a couple of trucks on the corner pad of asphalt. The business stuck out like a sore thumb in the middle-class neighborhood.

Chance could smell the fresh scent of the ocean as he pulled in and shut off his motor. Jumping off the bike, he ran to the small trailer office. The Open sign was still in the window. He came face to face with the strained looking appearance of a 35-year-old white clerk.

"Can I help you?" the man asked. He was not 6 feet tall, maybe 5'9". He wore a neat tie and white button down collar shirt, but the collar seemed too snug and his face reddened at the site of Chance towering above him.

"Yes, hopefully you can help. I'm not having much luck," Chance said.

"Excuse me, but we kept the shop open for you," he said raising an eyebrow,."What size truck would you like to rent?"

Chance spotted a young blond in the corner, peaking out from behind a computer. "Did she explain my problem?" he asked.

"Sue took the call," the supervisor said. "Look, I've only got four trucks. Let me know which one you need."

He slid a plastic laminated card at him that listed the various Ryder truck sizes and accessories on each truck. Chance slid it back across the counter.

"Listen pal, someone kidnapped my girlfriend and they may have used a Ryder truck. They may have been cops or Asians, and I need...

"You don't need a truck? "I'm running a business here, not an investigation service. You'll have to call this 800 number..." His attitude was all over his face like bad make-up on a woman.

Chance snatched his tie and pulled him across the counter. With his other hand, he reached up to his neck and tightened the tie until the man could hardly breathe.

"Sue," Chance said, "did she explain my problem? My girlfriend is gone and I'm looking for anything that could help me find her."

"All our clients in the last couple of days have been regulars or couples moving and returning the trucks to us, but here's one that was odd."

She held a copy of an invoice in her hand. She was young and skinny, but cute with long wavy blond hair. She was obviously intimidated by her barking boss, whose face was changing from pasty white to crimson.

"I'll keep looking, but that one was rented to two off-duty, Long Beach police officers and they were going to drop it off in San Pedro."

"Thanks much," Chance said as she set the piece of paper on the counter. "Are you married?"

"No," Sue said, blushing, her eyes darting to her boss's red face.

Chance looked at the man's name tag; then his eyes centered on the man's crimson features.

"Rob, if I can't find my girl, I'm going to date Sue, and you don't even want to upset my girlfriend, motherfucker."

Chance abruptly pushed Rob against the desk behind the counter hard. He crashed into the prefab metal desk, grabbing at his neck and falling to the floor. Chance wrote his number on a post-it and handed it to the girl.

"If you have any problem with him, let me know, and if you discover anything else, please call me." Chance grabbed the invoice and headed for the door while Rob squirmed on the gray industrial carpeting.

The Ryder truck rumbled out onto the 10 freeway, heading east. Ling was tossed along the rough-hewn deck planks, then slammed into the separated rails along the walls of the aluminum truck body. Breathing in small spurts, she lumbered in and out of consciousness in her tubular coffin. She tried to press her body against the rug to give her just an inch more of flexibility. She squirmed until she tired and gave into captivity, until she rolled into another plank and was awoken again. She mentally cried out for Chance to find her and release her as the truck lumbered along the interstate.

In Palm Springs, the two Asians pulled the creaking truck off the freeway at a truck stop, gassed up and found a quiet, dark location to back into the curb, out of sight. The taller of the two got out of the cab and opened the roll-up door. He crawled in and rolled the door down. He untied the Indian throw rug and unrolled it until Ling lay there kicking in the darkness against the rough wood deck. He turned on a small flashlight and stuck it between two runners to illuminate the dusty box interior. For the first time, she could see one of her captors. He was young, slender and Chinese.

He had a canvas bag and opened it to grab several pairs of hand-cuffs. She heard the clinking of metal as he rolled her on her side against the harsh surface. She kicked with both feet cable-tied together. The cables cut into her skin and hurt like hell, but she fought anyway. Suddenly she could feel small smooth hands grabbing her shoes and twisting. She felt a pair of handcuffs spin around her ankles and click into place. Then she heard the snap of side cutters cut the cable ties away. She felt a soft cool cloth against her skin until it came in contact with her ankle wounds and then she flinched as the alcohol splattered cloth touched torn flesh.

He cleaned her wounds and dressed them, then did the same to her wrists, replacing the cable tie with handcuffs and clamping her hands together at her lower back. She heard him moving a length of chain behind her and felt him jerk the handcuffs on her wrist and link them to the chain. He attached the chain to an anchor loop on the deck. She yanked on the chain with a tear running down her cheek.

She tried to speak to her capture to no avail. He was young, thin, and seemed scared. He said nothing, just worked quickly. The duct tape sealed her mouth and he wrapped a rag securely over her eyes. She groaned, pleading with the man in the truck. He folded the rug in half and moved it so she could lie on it. Then he opened the door and she could feel the cool evening air fill the box. She groaned against the tape, jerking on the chain.

She pleaded, "Chance, Chance, Chance, Chance. Help me." The words were there without sound. The truck started and rolled back onto a freeway. She lay down on the rug and tried to sleep.

Chance stepped out of the tiny office and looked at the paper form under the lights. He knew that this was a remote lead, but he would follow it to the end of time if necessary. He jumped on his bike and headed toward Ocean Blvd on the coast. It was dark and the lights of the harbor danced on the water as he neared downtown where Ling set up that day to sell her Lucky Bamboo.

He swallowed hard, thinking about her smile visiting every customer who was fortunate enough to meet and converse with her loveliness. He thought about their plans for the future, while his chopper rumbled quickly over the Darryl Desmond Bridge out of downtown, heading west across Terminal Island for five miles to the expansion Vincent Thomas Bridge, over the main channel and into San Pedro. He looked out at the light-strewn Palos Verdes hill in front of him; the cranes lit up to the south along the shipping channel. A container freighter, loaded down, moseyed out of the harbor at 5 knots.

Generally this was a sight he waited for and enjoyed, including the salt air smell as he hauled-ass home.

He rolled off the freeway and leaned his handlebars onto Harbor Blvd, where he found the Ryder yard. He pulled up to the closed and locked gates and wandered into the alley behind the building. It was after 9:00. He pulled out the invoice and found the license number under a 1940s street lamp. He looked at the trucks in the yard to see if the truck had been turned in. Chance move around the yard peering at each truck, until he confirmed it hadn't been turned in yet.

He straddled his stretched motorcycle and headed home. His mind whirled to a myriad of feelings. He wanted to be dead, gone or taken like Ling. He'd never felt this sensation and there was the sense that he deserved what was happening. He looked at punks on the sidewalk, with pure disdain, looking for a fight. Then it hit him, the dojo. He pulled up to the house and ran inside, nothing, no messages. He grabbed his gym backpack and headed back to the bike. It was late. Kate was standing beside it.

"How you doin'?" she said stepping up to him.

Her hair was pulled into a bun behind her head and she was wearing a professional dress suit. She looked good, but Chance didn't see anything except her concerned blue eyes.

"I'm not doin' worth a damn," Chance said. "I thought I would go to the gym and spar before I kill someone on the street."

"We've had a few calls," she said, handing him a box.

"What's this?" Chance said.

"The cell phone," Kate muttered quietly. "I was having a problem getting it through until you popped the two thieves at the Ryder on Atlantic. They've been responsible for a multitude of recent store hold-ups in Long Beach. Did you find anything?"

"One weak lead," Chance said. "Two Long Beach cops rented a van in Long Beach to be delivered to San Pedro. I've been by that yard and it hasn't been turned in yet."

"Let me know if I can do anything," Kate said. "I've got to go. The number is in the box. Charge it while you're at the gym, then we can reach each other anytime."

She stood on her tip-toes and kissed his cheek and scooted to her patrol car.

Chance watched her pull away and returned to the house to charge the phone. Then he was back on his bike for the short ride up the Pedro freeway to the IMC dojo. The gym was still open. He changed and jogged to the sparing room housing a professional-sized boxing ring. Brad danced around a student throwing jabs at him. The warm gym smelled of sweat. Chance pulled himself up by the ropes and kicked between them until he was in the ring.

"Hey," he yelled at the two. "I need to fight right this fuckin' minute."

Brad, the instructor, stopped mid-swing and bowed to his student, who looked at Chance, dismayed.

"This is my round," he said to Brad.

"Would you like to have a real go at the big guy?" Brad asked his student quietly.

"No sir," the kid said, bowing back.

"Then give us a few minutes."

He turned away from the kid, who could sense the severity of Chance's gaze and stance. He backed to the corner two steps away and crawled out of the ring. Brad faced Chance and bowed.

"I heard something on the radio. That your girl?" He looked into Chance's eyes and could see that it was. "I'm sorry." He turned to the corner of the ring and motioned for another set of fighting pads. He tossed the helmet to Chance.

"Put it on."

Chance pulled it over his head as another kid crawled into the ring with a set of gloves. Chance tugged them on and laced them up.

Chance looked at Brad in a somber gaze and said, "Just beat the living shit out of me."

"You're a big boy," Brad said, "let's see what you're made of." Brad was an anxious scrapper most of his life. He loved to fight anyone, anywhere. He was good and trained constantly.

Chance charged him like a bull. He hadn't been training for that long, but enjoyed every challenge. Tonight he was lost in pain and he tore at Brad like a Brahma bull at a pen. He wanted vindication, justice and Ling back in his arms. His swings were wild and without poise and Brad ducked them easily, landing a couple of body punches in return.

The errant punches that Chance landed were hard and full of aggressive power and strength. Brad went down behind one right hook, but quickly leaped to his feet and side-kicked Chance, knocking the wind out of him.

He moved in for close quarters combat and the two men leveled a volley of punches into each other. Then Chance threw an upper cut that lifted Brad from the mat. He was dazed but kept fighting, as if he was asleep and his punches were on automatic. They went at each other like two mad dogs, punching and kicking until Brad threw a round house, spinning Chance against the ropes. He bounced against the spring-loaded line and came back with even more aggression. Brad threw a direct shot into Chance's solar plexus just below the rib cage, but Chance blocked it and kneed Brad in the ribs.

Brad turned slightly to dodge the blow and struck Chance in the neck. Chance gasped but spun to kick. Brad blocked the kick handily and struck Chance solidly in the jaw. Chance went to the mat, rolled and used the ropes to pull himself to his feet.

The kids watching ducked and cringed with each blow. Chance was a powder keg full of hostility, whereas Brad was a true scholar of hand-to-hand combat. He enjoyed every nuance of the moves. The punches never bothered him. It was as if he was playing his favorite game of cards. If he made a wrong move, he took his lumps and improved his defensive maneuvering form.

Again they clashed in a barrage of fists and feet when suddenly each fighter felt something at their backs. Sticks were hammering their spines and they were driven to the mat. Fatigue and pain ended the fight, but they rolled away from the attacker and struggled to their feet to face the Sifu.

"Style and grace always," the man said and bowed to them. He had one Filipino fighting stick in each hand.

"You have felt great loss today, but your time is precious and each move must be handled with mental agility and not random violence and anger. I want you both to come at me."

Brad's gloves dropped to his side. He had faced off with Sifu in the past and it was like nothing he had ever seen or experienced. Sifu looked relaxed, almost at ease. Brad raised his gloves with Chance, because he knew the code and had broken it. He must face his lesson with poise. The two men approached Sifu and Brad took the first shot at the master with a roundhouse side kick as Chance charged like a drunk in a bar, swinging madly.

For the first time since Chance had trained with Dick Bondano, he saw the Jackie Chan/Bruce Lee abilities. Sifu danced on the mat as if he was on a cloud, blocking their thrusts with ease and striking with deadly accuracy. Both men were slammed to the mat with terrible blows from the Filipino sticks.

"Do you understand?" Sifu asked as they rolled to their respective corners. Unable to get to their feet, they rested against the padded poles and nodded to the master.

"Brad," Sifu said, "You should know better."

"He needed release from great pain," Brad said between his gasps for air.

"I understand," Sifu said, "but he must learn not to just scream into the wind. He must understand his 'ri' and reach for solutions." Then he looked at Chance,."We are here for you, brother. We won't beat up people or act like a gang, but help you find your way and your girl."

Chance nodded panting, like a pack mule at the top of the Grand Canyon. "Thank you. I will need your assistance and advice."

They got out of the ring and Brad and Chance went to the locker room to change. "Wanna get a drink?" Brad asked.

"You goddamn right, but I have no time. I must find her," Chance said. "I appreciate the beating and I will work on my form."

"My fault," said Brad, "I should have never allowed it to go in that direction. My mistake, but you must eat something. Let's head back to the harbor."

Brad mounted his '63 Panhead and the two of them rode to the 22nd Street Landing and ordered drinks and a side of Calamari.

"Do you know anything?" Brad asked between bites.

Chance told him what he knew. "I'm chasing Ryder trucks. But there's a remote chance she's headed back to China. Her brother wants her home bad."

"Not much of anything, including kidnapping, can leave the Los Angeles Harbor. I've been working these docks for 15 years," Brad said. "The worst harbor for that kind of crap is Houston. The quicker a ship can get out of the states the better. If they can get through the Med and into the Suez, it only takes a case of Marlboros to get through. Sifu will be your connection in the Philippines, China, Korea and Hawaii. He knows them all."

Chance rode home, beat and dejected. He felt lost as he pulled onto the sidewalk and into the gate. He permanently bolted the old wooden slat garage doors closed and took his bikes in and out of a small side door. He secured the door and walked, dejected, into the house. It was a cool evening, but a dense fog rolled in over the harbor and took out the lights of the cranes like some mystical giant. His depression, like the fog, threatened to engulf Chance. He poured himself a Jack on the rocks, in a ceramic cup this time, and headed for the living room, then thought about checking his messages.

Nothing.

# -7-

# WHICH ROAD LEADS TO LING?

Ling tried to sleep, but she was hungry and sore. The cuffs on her ankles irritated the wounds from the sharp plastic cable ties. She could sit up but she leaned against the slats bolted to the aluminum side-walls and it wasn't comfortable for any length of rattling road time. Besides she needed to go to the bathroom.

Seven hours passed as the lumbering box truck headed through the cool desert at night beyond Phoenix toward Tucson. At 2:00 in the morning, the truck pulled into a rest stop. Again the man on the right, in the passenger seat came to the back and opened the door. Without a word he unchained her from the bulkhead and pulled her to her feet. Then she heard rustling in his bag again and heard him dragging more chain free. Fearful he intended to harm her, she attempted to jump around, but he grabbed her by the wrist and lifted her hands until the pain was too great to fight back. She slumped and he attached another chain to her handcuffs. He uncuffed one of her wrists and one of her ankles and ran the chain between them.

"I'm going to let you pee," he said threateningly, "then I'm going to give you something to eat, but if you attempt to lift your blindfold, remove the gag or cause a problem, I'll beat you and you'll never hear from me again."

The man hissed the words as he yanked her down from the truck bed and led her into the desert, where she was forced to pee between the brush and creosote in the sand. It was cool and she could smell the clean desert air and the scent of trucks as they roared past on the freeway.

This was her first inclination that these men were not destined to hurt her, at least not on the road. She was being delivered, but where? When she was finished, he hefted her onto the tail gate and gave her a sandwich and some juice. She ate heartedly and then he handcuffed her wrists and ankles once more. He rolled her in the rug this time and tied it securely.

She could tell when the truck started and pulled onto the freeway, but a half hour passed and they pulled off the freeway again and she noted the sounds of a gas station and refueling. Then immediately the truck headed back onto the freeway. She was terrified that she was being taken to be a slave girl in some foreign country, or she would be forced into prostitution.

She prayed that Chance would find a way, a clue, something.

Chance woke with a start. It was 5:00 in the morning and the phone was ringing. "Yeah?" he mumbled, half asleep.

"Is that your girl who was taken?" Julie asked. "Carl has a job for you, but if that's the case, I know you can't make it."

"You're right," Chance said, "but thanks for calling. I need to get moving."

"Good luck," Julie said. "If I was in a fix, I'd like you to be the one searching for me."

"Thanks," Chance said, "I'll report in."

He hung up the phone and sat up and grabbed his knees. He hadn't slept worth a damn. He rubbed his eyes and tossed his legs over the edge of the bed. Something unreal was bouncing around in his mind; he couldn't get it straight. Ling didn't come over, Kate called Ryder truck rental joints. What the hell kind of joke was this? He pondered the notion over and over. It couldn't be, it couldn't be happening to him. He found the girl for him. Through her he had direction, then suddenly nothing.

Chance stood up slowly and headed for the bathroom. He ran the shower. While brushing his teeth he could smell her perfume in the bath. He looked into his own green eyes and choked. His cheeks were reddening and he sensed he was nearing a breaking down. He tossed the toothbrush in the sink and jumped into the shower, letting the warm water splash him in the face. He had to find her, quickly. As he showered, he ran through a litany of scenarios, obstacles, reasons and motives. It dawned on him that he would have to find her brother's phone number and speak to him. He showered quickly and didn't shave. He had a full mustache and generally a couple of day's growth on his face until Ling came along.

He brushed his shoulder length mass of hair and ran back into the bedroom to dress in Levis, a sweatshirt, his vest and roughed out brown cowboy boots. He called Kate's cell number and just as he thought he would catch her answering machine, she picked up the phone.

"Good morning, Chance," Kate said.

"Not so good, in fact." Chance said.

"What can I do for you?"

"I've got to get back in that apartment. I need to find her phone book. I need to contact her brother."

"Let's do it," Kate said. "I'll meet you at Curly's on the hill. Then we'll head over there."

"Thanks," Chance said and hung up.

Curly's was a long-standing oilfield workers' restaurant and bar on Signal Hill overlooking Long Beach. It still had two oil wells pumping away on the corners of the lot. The exterior was covered with old rotten planking and enameled oil signs from the past.

Chance jumped on his trusty chopper, shot up to the gas station, refueled and flew across the bridges at 20 mph over the speed limit. He pulled up to Curly's, walked in and ordered coffee, egg whites scrambled and wheat toast. Kate came in, ordered just wheat toast and coffee and sat besides Chance.

"What do you have in mind?" she asked.

"I just want to get a feeling whether he might have anything to do with it or not," Chance said. "I have another Ryder joint on Cerritos to hit and one on Lakewood. What about that cop?"

"They haven't caught up with him," Kate said, shrugging. "He should be questioned today. We're still waiting for lab reports. They'll be ready first thing this morning. We tore that place apart looking for clues. I think they wrapped her in a rug and took her in the truck, so you're heading in the right direction, if you can find something. If you do, we've got to move on it instantly."

"Show me how to work this thing," Chance said, pulling the cell phone out of his vest.

"Sure," she said, taking it from him. "I have it set up for you. Here's how to call me quick. I put your number in here under 'Home' so you could check messages." She demonstrated how to make calls and call the operators.

The restaurant smelled of old flapjacks and the warm aromas were comforting, but they finished their meals quickly and scrambled out to their vehicles. Chance blasted ahead of Kate to the apartment and pulled up in the back in the sloped alley designed for rain run-off. He pulled to a stop on the asphalt incline and kicked out his side-stand. She pulled up beside him in her plain white sedan and jumped out, opened the garage and they went in the rear entrance, since the front was still taped off with crime scene tape that fluttered in the mild offshore breeze.

Entering the apartment, Kate looked around, "Do you know where it might be?" she asked.

"You're the goddamn investigator," Chance grumbled, going to a drawer in the kitchen next to the phone. He pulled it open and pulled out her small leather-bound directory and began to flip through it.

"Here it is," he said. "Can I make the call here?"

"Sure. Actually it would be positive if our conversation showed on the records, but what time is it in China and where does her brother live there?"

"Hell, I don't know. It's probably some 15 hours ahead, but I'm calling. I need to get a feel for his involvement."

Chance started to dial. Fortunately the country code was listed and the phone buzzed and bleeped in Chance's ear. As he looked around her kitchen, seeing the signs of Ling's style, his level of anger grew.

"Hello (in Chinese)," the small female voice muttered.

"Is Chang Wu there?" Chance asked.

"Yes," she said in a voice as soft as silk, "can I tell who calling?"

"Chance," he said.

"One moment, sir," she said and Chance could tell the phone was set down.

Ten seconds passed when the phone was snatched up, "What is it?"

"You know what it is, asshole," Chance said.

"What do you mean?" Chang said. "I don't need any of your American shit. Why you call me?"

"Where's your sister?" Chance said.

"What?" Chang said.

"You heard me," Chance said. "Where's your sister?"

"She's there with you," Chang said bitterly. "She better be."

"She's not," Chance said.

"What do you mean?" Chang's voice changed to desperation. Chance surmised from his tone that he wanted to say something. "She's been kidnapped," Chance said, "And I want her back."

"I have nothing to do with it," Chang said abruptly, his voice turning cold as ice with defense. "You find her, or I come to America and find you." Chang hung up.

Kate listened on the upstairs phone. She set the receiver down and bounded down the stairs. "I don't think he did it," she said, "but I do think there's more. I wish he was here and we could question him."

"I'm going to the last couple of Ryder joints in town," Chance said, "Let's talk later."

Chance rode up Cerritos as the Ryder shop was opening. It was the most lavish Ryder franchise with more than just trucks, but fork-lifts and cranes. It was located on a 2-acre corner and Chance pulled up as they pulled the chain-link sliding gates open. He pulled up to the office and shut the Harley-Davidson off. Inside was a large counter with several clerks. He picked one and stood in front of him as he set up his station.

"I'm sorry sir," the young dark haired man said looking up. "Can I help you?"

"Yes," Chance said, "my girl was kidnapped in a Ryder truck and I need to find out where the truck was headed."

"Hey," the kid shouted to the other crew, "this is the guy." All the clerks huddled around. The taller of the bunch stepped up.

An older guy with a potbelly and a closely trimmed full beard approached. "We all came to work early," he said. "We went through every file and pulled out anything that might have had the slightest connection with your problem. Come around the counter and I'll take you into a room and you can review them. None of the guys remember any Asians or cops coming into rent trucks, but take a look."

He led Chance into a conference room with a glass window looking out to their counter and displays of shipping and packing materials customers could buy or rent.

The conference table was Formica surrounded by metal chairs. At one end against the wall was a framed motivational poster. Chance sat with his back to the wall so he could look out the window, an old habit. Several of the salesmen murmured to each other as they watched Chance take his seat. He looked through every invoice and studied the drop-off locations. Most were within the state, one was in San Diego and one in Arizona. In some cases, women had signed the contract and he eliminated those. He kept thinking about the Pedro drop-off and wanted to get back to town and check out that lead. He called Kate on the cell phone and gave her a couple of addresses to check out, but had little hope that any would lead to anything.

As he left, he asked the big guy to make copies of several of the invoices, "Thanks," Chance said, "I can't thank you enough."

The big man smacked him on the back with a thick palm, "Anything," he said. "While you were in the conference we checked out your bike and I had a couple of the guys keep an eye on it."

"Thanks, brother," Chance said leaving. As he rode out of the city toward the coast he began to feel helpless. There was no contact, no message for ransom. He wanted to hear something, feel something. He was beginning to feel like he could chase Ryder truck leads for the rest of his life, and the one he wanted was just out of reach, but he knew he had to check out the Pedro drop off lead with the cops.

San Pedro PD still hadn't picked up Clay, and he was a prime suspect. He pondered the acrimonious conversation with Chang and couldn't draw any conclusion. Nothing was clicking. He rode over the expansion bridge into Pedro and pulled up to the small Ryder office. The office was a tiny clapboard building in the back of a small lot. There didn't seem to be any new trucks in the lot as he approached the building. Two small Japanese people were behind the counter and appeared to be a husband and wife team. The middle-aged woman approached him immediately,

"Can we help you, sir?" she asked timidly.

Chance pulled out the copied invoice and handed it to her. "Has this truck been turned in?" Chance said anxiously.

The woman took the invoice and compared the plate numbers to the chart on the wall. She turned back to Chance and shook her head sadly returning the invoice. Chance grabbed a slip of paper and wrote both of his numbers on it. "Please call me when it's turned in," Chance said.

"Yes sir," she said.

Chance rode home in a hurry, jumped off the motorcycle and ran inside. He called Kate.

"Hey, let me give you a name. See if there's a San Pedro address attached. It's a Long Beach cop."

"Sure," she said. "Anything else?"

"Have you heard anything?" Chance asked. "What about that fuckin' maniac cop?"

"They're still looking," she said. "It pisses me off that they cut him lose. He's going to be on the nation's most wanted if they don't find him in an hour."

"Jesus Christ," Chance said a chill running up his spine, "How could this be? I've got a message. I've got to go." Chance hung up and listened to his messages.

"Chance, this is Roberta from the airport Ryder office," she said excitedly. "I found an invoice for a box leaving here and going to be turned in somewhere in Houston. I checked it out and the location is near the Port of Houston docks. I wouldn't have thought of it except the two guys who came were strange. I remember them. One was Asian and the other looked like a cop, but acted like some sort of mercenary. They met at the office; they didn't know one another. Here's the number for the Houston location, 817-432-5673."

Chance hit the replay number to listen to the message again and wrote down the phone number in Houston. He was intrigued and remembered what Brad said about smuggling out of the Houston Port. He pressed the button to listen to the next message and waited.

The phone clicked and recording started, but there was no voice, then it went dead. Chance listened to the message again. "Ling, are you there?" he said and hung up.

Kate returned to the office where the tone of acceptance had changed. She was still an underling who immediately faced a case involving an officer, so it appeared to other officers that she was a turncoat, or she worked in the Internal Affairs department. She ducked the disquieting stares and behind-the-back hurtful comments and moved ahead with her assignments.

When Officer Ayers was arrested, and finally when Ling Wu was kidnapped and officer Ayers turned up missing, the attitude changed. That was the iron straw that broke the camel's back. Suddenly she received support. As she returned to the office, she confronted several officers who offered to help with any information they had, but nothing fit. A junior female officer came to her cubicle and sat down.

"How you doin'?" Heather said. "I don't know if I have anything but we should check it out." Stocky and Hispanic, Heather's uniform, bulletproof vest, and polished gear seemed to engulf her.

"What is it?" Kate said directly, since Heather was one officer who scorned her heavily during her initial investigation.

"I once had a thing for Clay and he took me to a favorite spot below the border. It's in Rosarita Beach. He has a little cabin there. Here's the address."

"Why are you telling me this now?"

"I'm sure he didn't kill that girl or kidnap her," Heather said, rolling a pencil back and forth nervously in her fingertips. "I spoke to him after he was arrested. He told me that he wanted to help Joe, but couldn't harm the girl. He was a wreck. Joe convinced him that your biker was the bad guy. He knew when it was over that Joe was the one. I know that this won't look good on Clay, but they will at least find out he didn't intend to harm the girl."

"I hope you're right, for his sake," Kate said reluctantly and made some notes. She made a call to San Diego and put the word out, and then she called Chance. The line was busy.

Detective Louis from the San Diego Police department was dispatched to the Mexican Embassy to pick up the required forms to go to Mexico and serve a warrant. He drove across town as the sun glistened directly overhead and south on the 5 Freeway toward the border and Tijuana. He stopped for lunch at the marina overlooking Coronado Island.

The Ryder truck stopped outside Tucson and one of her abductors jumped out and ran to the back, lifted the roll-up door and shut it behind him. He flicked on a lamp and hung it from one of the slats against the wall and unwrapped her from the rug. She sensed that it was the other man. He was wearing an interesting fragrance and touched her uncomfortably, massaging her ass and tits, but not saying a thing. She jerked and recoiled against his touch. He chained her to the wall again. When he finished he kicked her in the thigh deliberately and didn't put the rug underneath her but slammed the roll up door and left. As the truck jolted and began to move again she struggled with her feet to reach the rug and pull it toward her.

As the truck rolled down the freeway, she grappled with the heavy material and tried desperately to shove it under her ass so she could rest. It was almost noon before the truck stopped outside a small town, a 100 miles from San Antonio. It was 2:00 p.m. in Texas when one of the men rolled her in the rug again, so she couldn't make sound when they refueled and changed drivers. They grabbed some food and continued east toward Houston.

Kate pulled up to Chance's pad and slammed on the brakes. She ran up to the door and banged on it. Chance came to the door.

"I tried to call you," she said. "You were on the line."

"We've got a lead on where Clay is," Kate said. "He may be in Mexico. We've sent a San Diego officer down to find him. My contact said that he wouldn't kidnap Ling after what happened."

"Yeah, right," Chance said. "I got a call from one of the Ryder joints. Seems a couple of odd sorts met at the airport lot and picked up a truck. They're taking it to Houston. Brad from the dojo said that Houston is the best port for smuggling. Whatta you think?"

"I don't know what to think," Kate said. "I want to hear about Officer Ayers. If he has her, well…"

"What if they smuggle her on a ship," Clay said, "What the hell can I do?"

"That's a tough one," Kate said. "You need a passport and a visa for China."

"Can we move on that stuff, in the event that Clay doesn't have her?"

"Let's go," Kate said. "Put that motorcycle away and come with me."

Chance rolled his bike into the garage and bolted the door. They headed downtown to order the passport; with Kate's badge the passport would be ready in 24 hours. They drove to the Chinese embassy in Los Angeles after grabbing some Popeye's chicken and munching along the way. With the receipt for the passport and additional photos, he was able to get the paperwork flowing toward a 24-hour deadline. On the way back from downtown, Kate's cell phone buzzed.

"Hello?"

"This is Heather. Officer Louis picked up Clay. He doesn't have the girl," Heather said. "That's good news from my standpoint, but it doesn't bring the girl back."

Kate hung up. "Clay doesn't have Ling," she said, "If you're going overseas, you need shots. Let's get over to the Health Department in Long Beach."

Chance pulled his cell phone out of his leather vest and punched in the code for his home number to check messages. There was one: "Chance, this is Chang. My sister gave me your number to apologize for my behavior. I'm glad I kept it," Chang said. The long distance message was sketchy. "My sister means the world to me. Nothing I have can ever replace her. Much of this is my fault and now I apologize for much, but we must work together. My family has a problem here and another family may have done this. Call me soon."

Chance looked at Kate. "I'll need the shots. That was Chang. He apologized. Seems there is a problem between families. Someone may have snagged Ling as a negotiating tool."

# -8-

# THE BORDER RUN

Just after 6:00 p.m. central time, the Ryder truck rumbled into Houston and turned south on the US 90 Alt highway and onto Wayside Drive heading toward the docks. The jarring turns awoke Ling and she struggled in the rolled carpet. She hurt everywhere and her stretched tendons tore at her shoulder joints. The darkness deprived her of any connection to time and a deep depression set in as she fought not to cry. She'd never encountered anything of this sort. Although she read books about Chinese history and abused women, she never actually encountered such pain, seclusion and fear. She had no notion of what was happening to her or why. Her wrists were bleeding from the jarring truck rumbling over railroad tracks. She twisted in the rug to prevent the wooden deck splinters from piercing her skin. Her face ached from the duct tape across her mouth. She was hungry and missed Chance.

The truck bumped over more train tracks, reaching Garcia Street, then turning into the city docks. There was an old wooden guardhouse at the entrance, but it wasn't manned. The driver turned onto Foster Street and followed a line of cargo ships moored with massive hemp lines along the concrete docks on the narrow channel in the dark. The street was unlit.

Rat guards on the ships' lines rattled against rusting hulls. Desolate and damaged buildings and rusting corrugated tin shed warehouses lined the docks. Starting with Warehouse 25, they passed 24 and 23. The galvanized steel buildings were dented and worn, but large, white chipped numbers were painted on each corner. The ships seemed invisible behind the sprawling buildings silhouetted against the sides of the hulls. Only a rusting superstructure or cranes stood taller than the corrugated sheds. At Warehouse 16, the driver pulled up to a loading ramp and into the open warehouse. It was empty and deserted like some teetering, abandoned building in the middle of the desert. It smelled of past cargos, produce, cotton and rotting wood. In the corner was a new wooden crate standing open, and a single bulb glowed above it. It was the only light in the building that was 500 feet long and 100 feet wide.

The truck pulled up to an open crate. The drivers inspected it through the windshield, then turned around and drove the length of the building in a perimeter until they were sure no one was inside. Returning to the open box, they stopped and the passenger departed. He inspected outside the building and around it looking for anything suspicious, then returned to the cab. "Okay," he said to the driver.

Ling could hear them, but couldn't tell what was happening. One of the men opened the roll up door at the back of the truck.

"Time for your transfer, baby," he said. He kicked her through the carpet and unlocked the chain from the side of the truck. The driver shut his cab door, rounded the back and jumped up into the box. He grabbed one end of the coiled rug, like a massive cigar, while the larger of the two pulled at the other end. She jerked and kicked out with both feet, but the taller of the two dropped her on the hard wood. She had no choice but to succumb or be dropped again. Slowly, they let her down from the truck until she rested, encased in the throw rug, on cold concrete, her chains dangling from the carpet end. Suddenly she felt the cold cement penetrating the fabric, and then she was being lifted and dropped a short distance. She clamored against another foreign surface. It flexed, she panicked and jerked.

"Relax," an Asian accent spoke for the first time. "It won't be long."

Sensing she was someplace forbidden and unnerving, she fought anyway and someone punched her through the layers of rug with something like the handle of a rake. She doubled up like a snail recoiling into its shell.

"Hold still or die," the rough voice muttered.

The two men grabbed the top of the 2 by 6 framed crate and dropped it over the remaining box. One of the agents ran to the cab for a hammer. He pounded the supplied nails into place, then opened a cell phone and dialed.

"The package has been delivered," he said. He listened for a few seconds then hung up. Suddenly vehicle headlights flashed at the opening of the building.

The two hijackers backed into a corner as a dark limousine rolled into the warehouse and stopped. The limo driver emerged and opened the back door. The truck agents walked cautiously to the door and leaned in for instructions. The shorter of the two, an athletic Asian, jogged to the truck, got in and drove it to a remote corner of the warehouse and parked it as deep into a dark corner and as far away from doors as possible. A tall, thin man opened the trunk of the limo and pulled out a large tarp. He climbed on top of the Ryder truck, pulling the tarp over it and strapped it down to conceal the vehicle.They both jumped into the limo, as the car pulled away.

"What's happening to the crate?" the tall, narrow white truck driver asked.

"Watch," the Asian riding shotgun said as another Asian drove toward the warehouse doors. He turned and saw a forklift rumble into the warehouse and slide its heavy tongs under the box, lifting it slightly. The smoking forklift spun and motored down the loading ramp toward a tramp freighter moored at the dock. A ship's crane swung around in front of hold number two, and two dock workers ran up to the box as the fork lift backed away.

Ling tried to kick against the crate sides, but the noise of the forklift and crane was too distracting. No one noticed.

They tossed two fiber straps under the crate, between the wooden 4-by-4s and hooked the four bulky stitched eyes over the rusty crane hook. Standing back, a black dockworker wearing a florescent hardhat, looked up at the union crane operator stuck in a small glass dome on the side of the 20-ton crane, and gave him a thumbs up. The crane boom lifted slightly, pointing at the dark sky; then the steel cable rolled inward, taught, drawing the crate off the dock and into the night air. It spun to line up with the hold as the metal cable retracted over the hull of the ship, until it was poised over hold number two. Then it descended into the steel interior of the ship, to the cold second level.

A small Filipino boy, standing on the steel moveable deck, signaled to the crane operator, directions and placement between two mast-less sailboats and a generator shell weighing 40 tons and worth over 4 million dollars. The crate clunked against the steel plate deck and another Filipino crewmember unhooked the cable, signaling to the crane operator to lift the cables from under the crate.

Ling was jostled violently as the crate met its fate on the chilly steel decking. She could hear the crane above whirring and the terrible sound of metal against metal as the massive doors over the hold slid closed. She could hear noise all around her and suddenly realized she was not sitting still. There was some movement beneath her. At first she thought the smells were coming from the crate, but then with the shifting deck, she was terrified. She sensed motion and the vibration of the ship's generators. Where the hell was she?

Ten minutes passed and she heard the signal horn of a ship nearby. Then she felt the bump and grind of a tugboat finding its spot against the steel hull of the ship.

Suddenly she sensed her surroundings were moving.

Kate picked up her cell phone off the seat of her sedan and called her office. "Get me a number for the PD in Houston, kidnapping department." She waited, then said out loud as Chance frantically wrote the number on a pad of paper, "817- 653-2283, Officer Tinney, thanks." She hung up the phone and began dialing the number as Chance read it back to her.

"Officer Tinney," she started, "We have a kidnapping in Los Angeles. We are e-mailing you the report and description. We believe a Ryder box truck was used to transport the victim to the port in Houston. Can you check the area for Ryder trucks?

The response was an affirmative as they pulled into the Long Beach Health Department parking lot. As Chance sat in the waiting room, he filled out forms for an International Certificate of Vaccination, as approved by the World Health Organization. A nurse called his name and he was lead into a small sanitary office operated by a Korean woman who could speak English, but her accent was difficult to understand. Chance was forced to ask her to repeat herself constantly.

"Missers Hogan," she said, "Where you going?"

"I'm not sure," Chance said, "to China if I have to."

"You Chinee visa?" She said.

"I'm not sure I understand?" Chance asked, leaning in her direction.

As she explained, she gave him a polio shot, a yellow fever vaccination and a hepatitis A shot and a couple of others in his left and right arms alternating. She filled out a form from the U.S. Public Health Service and turned it over to him. He stood abruptly and pivoted his arms in long arches as instructed, then quickly returned to Kate in the waiting room.

"Any word?" he asked.

"Not yet," she said. "You need to get home to call her brother and pack. I'll pick you up in the morning. We'll go after that passport and visa.'

"We need a break. Get those cops to find her before anything else happens," Chance said, pounding the dash of her car. "I don't know shit about commercial ships. I'll call Brad for some pointers. I want to take my bike. I want it on the ship with me, if that's the deal."

Chance headed into the house and poured himself a drink and dialed Chang in China. The phone rang for a long time before someone picked up the jangling receiver. "Hello (in Chinese)," the soft-voiced Chinese girl said.

"Is Chang there?" Chance said.

"Yes, right away," the voice came back. It was like a flower and relaxed Chance for a few seconds.

"Chance," Chang said, "Thank you for calling me back. You don't need the whole story, but we have a large family here with large holdings and a dispute with a family who I fear is in the opium business. They have threatened in the past, but my over-confidence has disputed them. They have been desperate to find a way to break us. I'm sure this is their doing."

"Rumor has it that they have taken her to Houston," Chance said, "and they may be putting her on a ship."

"Once they have her on a ship, they will be in control, and my family may be in danger of losing everything," Chang said. "They want our land for growing opium poppies, the sleep-bringing poppy."

"I'm going after her," Chance said. "You'll have to hold on until I can get to her."

"What can I do?" Chang asked.

"I need port contacts," Chance said, "I need to get on a ship heading your way."

"I will see to it," Chang said. "I will send a package overnight. Don't leave without it."

Chance hung up and darted around the house, collecting things that he might need to take. He packed his bedroll. Then he jammed back to the kitchen and called Brad.

"Hey brother," Chance said, "I need your help. I'm going to be on a ship heading for China; who do I call? And I'm taking my bike, goddammit."

"Take it easy," Brad hollered in the phone. "You're most likely going to need a tramp freighter out of that canal. Not a lot of container ships in that port. Call this number and ask for Cliff, he's a port agent, 817-568-6623. He can get your bike on board. He'll get you passage on a ship. It may not be pretty, but it will get you any place in the world. You can get off in any port and do what you want. They won't blink if you don't get back on, but if you miss the ship, you'll be on your own. Did you ever spend time on ships?"

"Yep," Chance said, "When I was in the Navy."

"Do you have a passport and Chinese visa, oh, and your shots?"

"Yeah, I'm in good shape there, but I needed the contact to get on a ship," Chance said. "Not any ship. I need to try to find the one that's got Ling."

"That's his cell phone number, so go to it," Brad said. "Call him now."

Chance hung up. He picked up the phone and set it back in the cradle. He could smell the Jack Daniels wafting out of the ceramic mug. He looked at the phone number on the slip of paper and pondered his next move. He had been in a couple of spots in his life, but this one took the cake. He swore to himself that once he got Ling back, he was moving away from this god-forsaken harbor town forever. He picked up the phone and dialed Kate's number.

"Chance," she answered, knowing and hoping it would be him.

"Here's the deal," Chance said, "Seems there's a family dispute in China and Ling is the pawn. She may be on a ship already and I've got to go."

"Do you need anything?" she asked.

"Just you," Chance said. "I'll need your help every step of the way. Chang is sending me a care package and Brad has given me a port agent's number for help with a boarding pass and assistance with shipping my bike. I need to roll. I need to be on the road as soon as possible, tomorrow. There's one major problem, which ship?"

"Curly's at 7:00 a.m.?" she said. "You need anything tonight?"

"I'll see you in the morning, babe," Chance said. "Thanks for everything."

He hung up, kept packing and finished his drink. He was more determined than ever to reach Ling's side. How could anyone dare use her this way?

# -9-

## CHANCE ROLLS HOUSTON DICE

Ling's legs hurt like hell. Everything cramped. She was starving and could hardly breathe. She knew she was on a ship and that it had pulled out of a harbor somewhere because it seemed to drift along for hours slowly at first. Then she sensed another boat was along side and the ship nearly came to a stop. After that encounter, she could feel the vibration increase as if it was running along rough surf.

Her entire surroundings shook and rattled, then another sensation mixed with the rattling vibrations; the ship began to rock back and forth. The sense was almost sensual in a fearful sort of way, as if she was captured in large ominous hands and being rocked. The crate, locked and nailed, slid from time to time, butting into some other object. She prayed it would split her coffin, but she knew she was still cuffed and bound. She didn't care, any escape was better than nothing.

There was a sense that she was somehow on a long mission and she prayed that someone would let her out of the box.

Chance set his alarm at the crack of dawn and dressed in grubby clothes and jammed to the garage, like a city worker sent to repair earth-quake damage. He hustled out to his stucco shed and inspected his motorcycle stem to stern, checking the air pressure in the tires, the cable adjustments, the fluids, including brake master cylinders, and his transmission. He tightened all the bolts he could reach quickly and prepared a set of tools to haul along in his bedroll. He ran back to the house and grabbed the packed roll and returned to strap it to his handlebars.

He was forced to pack for winter and summer months as best he could, and he racked his brain for a list of necessary items. The bedroll contained the small stuff, tools on the outside and clothes inside. He packed a few knives in an old tank bag that he strapped to his gas tank and stuffed a tight 9mm Walther PPK in his vest. He took virtually all the money he had and his bath items, in the tank bag. He grabbed aspirin, vitamins and his cell phone, which rang at 6:00 a.m. sharp.

"Want me to pick you up?" Kate asked.

"Sure," Chance said. "I'm ready."

"I'll be there in five minutes," she said and hung up.

Not wanting to waste one second, he continued to pack wire ties, shrink tubing, and a set of European plug adapters. He found a pair of small binoculars and stuffed them into the bag. Digging through the house, he found a small atlas, twisted it and stuffed it into the bag. Brad, a dojo master, told him to take trinkets as gifts for people who helped him. He dug through his drawers of crap, left over from rides, like pins, decals and key rings. He put them in a Codera pocket, with a pair of tennis shoes in the top of the tank bag, along with a wadded up backpack in case he needed something to carry stuff in while on shore.

He felt like he was going crazy with desire to get on the road and find a ship. He had only one mission in life, to hunt down Ling and the bastards who took her. He threw on a clean sweatshirt and heard someone tap on a car horn out front. He ran to lock up his garage, then the house. As he stepped out to the curb, he saw Carl's classic pickup next to Kate's white sedan.

Carl rolled down the window. "Hey, I read about your girl. I suppose you're going after her," Carl shouted out the window. "I've got friends at sea and in ports all over the world. Call me if you need anything!"

He handed Chance a stack of business cards, and in it was a wad of bills. Carl's rustic seagoing face was as stern as a bull's preparing for a fight. "Bring her back."

"Thanks," Chance said. "You're goddamn right I will. I'm riding to Houston to catch a ship today."

"Stay in touch," Carl said and revved up his twice-pipes on the '55 Ford truck.

"Wait," Chance said, peeling the number for the port agent, Cliff, out of his pocket. "Give this guy a call, will ya? He's at the Houston Docks. I need a ship heading to Europe and China through the Suez Canal that will allow me to keep my bike on board. And if you can find a Captain who is cool, I'll need all the help I can get."

"I'm headed to the office this second," Carl shouted. "I'm all over it."

He peeled down the street and around the corner. Chance looked out over the harbor with a whole new perspective. His eyes peered out at ships lounging against piers and motoring in and out of the harbor, with a sense of a man looking for the right tool to get the job done. He jumped into Kate's cruiser and they pulled out for Signal Hill and breakfast, then to the Passport Office downtown.

For six hours, Ling, trapped in the crate, smelled damp wood all around her. Then she heard footsteps. There were maybe three or four people surrounding the box and she heard a lock snap open, followed by the harsh, ear shattering clatter of a hammer against some sort of wedge being driven between the lid of the box and the base. She instinctively ducked. The noise was loud and terrifying. The squeal of nails being pulled from wood rang in her ears as she waited, trembling. Gloved hands tore at the lid and peeled it back until the lid banged against the wooden crate at her back, startling her. Then small hands lifted the coiled rug, unrolled it, covered her eyes with a blindfold and lifted her up by the shoulders, pulling her to her feet. Her legs hurt badly from cramping and she could hardly balance, but it felt good to feel the air on her skin.

There was some discussion around her and she guessed it was in Tagalog, the Filipino language. Then someone pulled her back until she took tiny steps and was standing at the back of the box. They beat at the front of the box again with hammers and wedges, shaking her foundation. She tried to balance against the sway of the ship and her narrow stance. Small hands held her until the front of the box was torn away. Someone knelt at her feet and removed the cuffs around her ankles, and several men led her out of the box. She could sense she was standing on damp steel. She stepped carefully, testing each movement, each area, for a base or a hazard. Her legs felt weak and shaky.

She was led through several steel hatches, her head pushed down to prevent a head injury against the heavy steel frames.

Someone touched her shin every time she had to lift a foot to pass through a hatch until she sensed she was stepping onto some sort of mat or carpeting. She was lead down a tiled hallway for a few steps, around a corner and then stopped. She felt someone in front of her, perhaps looking at her. She could smell cologne. A hand carefully uncuffed her and she suddenly felt a wave of relief.

"Remove the blindfold," the voice said, and she felt several hands lifting the rags from around her eyes. She blinked and squinted, fearful of brightness, but there was none. She was standing in a ship's corridor or passageway. It was narrow and dark. The floor was covered with a bristle mat that was black with grease and grime. There were greasy fingerprints on the steel walls, painted white a long time ago. She seemed surrounded by small Filipino men in filthy overalls. They were tremendously inquisitive looking. They were young and seemed in awe of her height and stature.

The man in front of her was Chinese, and perhaps 5 foot 6 inches tall. He stood shorter than her by two inches. He had a soft face and the remnants of a wispy mustache running down either side of his mouth. His hair was jet black and short in the front, with some sort of ponytail at his neckline. He was nasty looking in all black, wearing black leather running shoes. He reached up to her face and took hold of the corner of the silver duct tap and yanked it off in one painful blistering movement. Ling bent and grabbed at her face, tears rolling down her cheeks. The sailors around her cringed at the torturous motion and looked away.

"Take her away," the young man snapped, turning and disappearing up a set of stairs.

Too startled and afraid to speak, Ling peered at the evil looking Chinese man fearfully. She knew he was someone's soldier, a nasty one.

They led her to a very small elevator, with a steel door on hinges on the outside and a linked sliding cage on the inside. It pulled open to the side. The floor of the 3-by-3-foot lift was diamond plate. Brass plates were riveted to the front of the doors and etched with Japanese letters. It indicated either the manufacturer of the elevator or the ship. She stepped onto the plate tentatively and two of the crew stepped in with her. They pressed the button for the D deck and the elevator rose slowly four levels and stopped. There were no buzzers or bells announcing the floors. She stepped out onto a polished linoleum floor and was led to a cabin with a latch and lock on the outside.

A crew member unlocked the cabin and showed her inside. It contained a small sitting area, a bed and a bathroom. The crew members showed her some clothes left for her, plus, in the head, soaps and shampoos. As they left her they bowed slightly, watching her inquisitively. They locked the door behind them. Ling looked around the room in a daze, then ran to the large porthole facing the port side of the ship. It was bolted shut permanently, but she could see out. Unfortunately, there was nothing to see except open gray ocean. She looked around the periphery of her view from the porthole and could not see anything indicating the name or origin of the ship. A tear ran down her dirty face.

She ran to the head and looked at herself in the mirror. She looked tired, drawn and red around her mouth where the industrial tape was ripped away. She was relieved to be alive, but she missed Chance. The fear of the unknown engulfed her. She had never been on a ship and didn't understand the reason for her capture. She tore her clothes off and showered, hand-washing her clothes as she did.

The city hall opened on time and the passport was waiting on the top of the pile. Kate handed it to Chance.

"Let's get over to the embassy," Kate said, "and see if they won't give us the seal we need for your papers."

Chance and Kate sat in her car in silence waiting outside the Embassy until the gate opened and they were allowed inside. Kate marched up to the information desk and flashed her badge. She was led to the visa clerk and a Chinese visa seal was stamped in his passport. Cognizant of alarming the officials, they wanted to run to the door, but instead walked carefully over the polished marble floor and through lavish interiors with their hint of communist rule and power.

"It's like a free man walking into a prison," Chance said. "You're just not sure they won't close the gate behind you."

"You're right," Kate said, heading to her car. "How's packing?"

"I'm ready," Chance said, "I'm itchin' to get on the road."

"Keep the passport, the visa application and shot record together and you're ready to go," Kate said, starting her car and speeding quickly back to the harbor. Chance looked at his old Harley watch and estimated that if the package from Chang arrived at 10:00 from FedEx, he could be on the road by 10:30. He scrounged through his mind, testing for anything he forgot to pack, or failed to check on the bike.

They pulled up to the house and Chance turned and looked at Kate. "Stay in my place if you like. I'll give you a set of keys."

"I might take you up on that," she said. "I'm going to stick around until you're on the road, if that's all right. We might think of something."

"I'd appreciate that." Chance turned and looked at her blue eyes looking so hopefully at him. He leaned close to her and kissed her lips lightly.

"Oh, Chance," she said and raised her soft hands to his face for another kiss, but he was interrupted by the honk of the FedEx truck pulling up beside him. The driver jumped out and rounded the front of the step van.

"Hey, glad I caught you," he said holding a package the size of a couple of shoeboxes. "Sign here."

Chance signed it and they scrambled in the back door of the house to open it. The box contained several items and a handwritten note from Chang. A separate box contained an Iridium satellite phone, antenna and instructions. A Garmin hand-held GPS was also in the box and two magnetic buttons about the size of a silver dollar. He didn't know what the hell they were for. He opened the note and read it aloud to Kate.

"Chance. I'm the young angry sort and it has cost my parents dearly. Our farm is now challenged due to my own stupidity, but I don't want to sell our farm to drug dealers. On the other hand, if I had released it, we could have moved anywhere and my sister would not be in this danger. Just like my handling of your kindness, I have ruined everything.

"I'm not sure how we can do this," Chang's note continued, "but here are some tools. This phone will allow you to reach me anywhere on the planet. The GPS will allow you to track yourself and ships. If you can attach a button on the ship she's captured on, we can trace it. It is important that we find her and take her back before she reaches mainland China. I have also enclosed some cash and two credit cards to keep you moving. I will be happy to celebrate with you and Ling here. Sincerely, Chang"

"Good stuff," Kate said. "Let me have the number to the phone so I can reach you."

Chance opened the box and found the paperwork. He noted the number on a small notepad and gave it to Kate. He took the package out to his bike and carefully found places for everything. He backed the long chopper out of the garage and parked it beside the house. One final time inside, he gave Kate a set of keys and looked around. For the first time, he realized the severity of his mission. He was angry at Pedro. On the other hand, it was home and his little house had allowed him to meet Ling.

"If you live here," Chance said, "this will be my home base."

"Hopefully it will be your base always," Kate said and put her arms around Chance, pulling him close. His mind considered her thought, as he looked at her deeply and hugged her small form against his body. He had to move. He faced a 24-hour run ahead of him. Kate was cute in an official sort of way, yet her soft features were a book of concern and love when it came to Chance. She held him for all she was worth. He leaned down and kissed her.

"I will be in constant touch," Chance said and pulled on a lined flannel shirt and his brown leather vest over it, then finally his gloves. "I hope I haven't forgotten anything."

He swung his leg over the seat and fired the bike to life. He pushed the tank bag back and forth to ensure that it was fastened securely, then tested the bedroll, kissed Kate once more and put the bike in gear. The tank was full and capable of nearly 150 miles before needing fuel. He waved over his shoulder as he headed east on Crescent Ave. toward Harbor Blvd.

He caught the Pedro freeway north to the 91, then east to the 605 north, then to the interstate 10 east. He locked his sights on Houston. He kicked the bike into fifth gear as he rounded the freeway on-ramp and waved at a trucker who honked his support. He pushed the speed up to 80 and held it firm. His plan was to at least, seek out 125 mile distance locations for refueling. Riding a rigid frame could be abusive, although he wasn't thinking about it much. He thought about Ling Wu and the terrible situation she was in, and about her brother, as he pulled into Palm Springs and refueled, ate a protein bar, drank some water and kept moving. He was in a daze darting between slower traffic. His mind swam with confusion, hatred, fear, the unknown, the adventure, and every cell was laced with Ling and his desire to find her.

He ran through another hundred miles to Blythe, thinking about the wonderful sex he was having with Ling and her future embraces. She drove him crazy with passion. He could hardly keep his hands off her. He imagined every inch of her, his fingertips delighting in each touch. It gave him chills and made him mad that Chang and his people could interrupt such non-stop bliss. It wasn't fair and someone had to pay.

Chance pulled into the small desert town of Blythe on the border of California and Arizona and rolled into a Shell gas station. He marveled on how bad a town could look, yet how shiny the station was. He refueled and hit the road. Next stop Phoenix or as close as he could get without running out of fuel.

There was a light tap on the door to Ling's cabin. She was sleeping soundly for the first time and had rested for several hours.

"Hello," she said in a sleepy voice, sitting up to the sway of the ship.

"Can I come in?" It was a woman's voice and Ling responded with glee. She was glad to finally hear the voice of another woman.

"Of course," Ling said. "I can't let you in, though." She heard the lock snap open and the hasp pulled from the lock tong, and recognized that although there weren't bars on the steel door, this was her prison cell.

The door opened slowly and another tall Asian woman stepped into the room. She had many Anglo features and Ling couldn't seem to make out her origin. Her eyes were rounder than hers and her face narrower, perhaps Korean.

"Hi, my name's Kim," the girl said, standing almost the same height as Ling, maybe an inch taller. She wore tight Diesel denims and a low-cut black blouse. She was well endowed and the tops of her tits spilled over the top of her blouse.

"What the hell is going on with you?" she asked.

"I wish I knew," Ling said with apprehensive eyes scrolling the length of the tall woman. "What are you doing here? This isn't a floating whorehouse, is it? Where are these people taking me?" Ling suddenly stood up and grabbed the woman. "Do you know what I've been through? I need my man, I want to go home." She burst into tears shaking Kim's shoulders weakly, desperately.

"I wish I knew," Kim said. "I just work on the ship in the kitchen and they gave me the key to see you and get you some food."

Ling slumped to the bed and buried her face in her hands crying. "I don't believe this," she said, and then jumped to her feet again heading for the door, and began to push Kim to the side. "I'm going to find out. I didn't attend all these years of college to be forced into prostitution."

Kim stopped her. "There's no place to go. We are at sea heading to Savannah. That I do know. I'll see if I can find out more."

"Please," Ling said sitting on the edge of the bed again. "If only I could get word to my boyfriend. He'd find me."

"Getting word anywhere on a ship is tough," Kim said. "Let me get you some food."

Kim stroked her freshly shampooed hair and touched her shoulder. Ling grabbed her hand gently and looked up at her. "Thank you."

One the east side of Phoenix, Chance's scooter sputtered and ran out of gas while screaming along at 85. He reached under the tank and turned the petcock to reserve. The bike coughed, as traffic began to surround him, but he was confident that his motorcycle would find its spare supply and roll again. A second passed and the engine caught the flow of fresh fuel and he sped up to speed once more. Another 10 miles and he pulled off the freeway and into a gas station for refueling, stretching, checking over the bike and rolling out again. He only had 90 miles to go to get to Tucson. It would be nearly 5:00 p.m.

He felt the sense of mission mixed with desperation. He held his chrome handlebars taut, and muscled his way through Phoenix traffic.

# -10-

## OUT TO SEA

Chance pulled out of Tucson as the sun set, with a full tank of gas and nothing in his stomach. Next door was a burrito joint and his stomach growled, but he needed to keep moving. If he was later than he planned, the ship could be gone and he would be shit outta luck— for life. He jumped his motorcycle and careened back to the freeway. El Paso was another 275 miles and he bit off another 150 miles before stopping in Lordsburg, New Mexico, for fuel. The desert was flat and hot, even as the sun disappeared in the west behind him.

The Harley flew along the narrow asphalt strip like a rumbling locomotive locked to its tracks. He focused on nothing but his woman, miles and time. He knew the toughest slot in the trip plan would be the flatlands between El Paso and San Antonio, which was nearly 500 miles of Mexican borders, Davis Mountains and flatlands. He prayed he could push through without encountering any major mountain ranges complete with 30 mph twisties. The boredom of desert highways over long straight stretches of flatness was dangerous on the eyes, so he started drinking diet cokes and taking supplements to maintain his alertness through the night.

There was also the threat of small wild animals, attracted by the single bouncing beam of his headlight, darting into the dark highway at night, but he had no choice. He needed to keep moving.

At 11:30, he left El Paso on his first jaunt along the border and into Texas. Mileage signs indicated that he couldn't get to Del Rio on his gas tank, so he pulled off the freeway in Van Horn in the Davis Mountains and topped off his tank. The bike was running as sweet as the open road smelled, and he avoided thinking about it in case it would jinx his mechanical track record. Leaving Van Horn, riding through rolling hills, three deer lingering beside the road caught his attention. The adrenaline rush kept his senses keen for another 100 miles into Del Rio, but he could tell fatigue was setting in. He pushed on.

Kim brought Ling Wu a plate of curried beef and a bowl of rice. On the side were orange and apple slices. Ling, emotionally and physically revived as Kim entered her cabin, decided she would request information, but first she needed to build a positive rapport with the tall Korean woman. She was afraid that their first meeting may have given Kim a weak impression of her emotional state.

"Hi Kim," Ling said holding the door open. "I'm sorry about my outbursts earlier. I'm sure you can understand."

"Absolutely," Kim said. "I will find out anything I can."

Kim set the tray on the small desk where Ling could pull up her chair to eat. She sat down beside Ling and touched her hand gently.

"The men haven't come to dinner yet, but if I hear something I'll fill you in."

The first time Kim came to her room, Ling assessed her appearance but missed something. She saw a woman in denims and a low cut plain form fitting black blouse. She was good looking, but not sexy then. This time, something was different. Kim seemed to lean toward her, revealing more succulent cleavage. She was wearing make-up now, her lips a deep red and outlined perfectly. Her eyes were framed with eyeliner and she wore glistening diamond earrings unlike before. Ling wasn't sure what to make of it. Maybe the woman dressed more for dinner? She was hot looking from her narrow waist and long legs to her full breasts and ivory oriental features.

"Thanks for the lunch," Ling said, "You mentioned that we are going to Savannah?"

"Yes," Kim said, and Ling could swear she wore a costly perfume. "It will take us another day and a half, and we should be there for two or three days."

Kim stood very close to Ling as she got up to leave. "If you need anything, let me know."

"How about something to read," Ling said, "maybe a book and a newspaper? Could you make a call for me? My boyfriend will be worried sick."

"I'll see to the reading material, but something tells me they're watching me," Kim said, and touched her cheek as she stepped out the door. Ling looked after her but only saw some ship fire alarms in the passageway along the bulkhead.

She sat down to eat and ate heartedly. Although she wasn't sure how to read Kim's hot looks, she liked the girl and it was comforting to see someone with a friendly face and not handcuffs. She ate everything but the fruit and stashed it in a gully that ran under her porthole along with half of the jug of water Kim brought her. She still didn't have any notion of the crew's intentions and was afraid if something went wrong she better save some food.

She started to look around the cabin for something she could use as a weapon.

While riding at 90 miles an hour through the flat Texas plain, Chance thought about the road ahead and what provoked the kidnapping. He had to call Carl and find out if he got him hooked up with Cliff and a ship. He quizzed himself on some way to determine what ship Ling was on and how to find the sonuvabitch who took her. He pondered and daydreamed about his actions once he snagged the throat of the perpetrators who hurt his girl. He pulled off the freeway on the outskirts of San Antonio, refueled and called Carl.

"Julie," Chance said, "Is Carl there?"

"How you doin'?" Julie said. "Carl's on a run, but he said to call Cliff. All is in order. Do you still have the number?"

"I'm doin' alright," Chance said. "I'm in San Antonio and tired. Only another couple hundred miles to go. Then I just need a ship and need to get movin'. Let me have that number again."

He wrote the number down in a small spiral bound note pad where he stored all the numbers and any information he needed. He dialed Cliff.

"Prime Maritime," the answer came.

"This Cliff?" Chance asked.

"You bet," Cliff said. " Chance?"

"Yeah," Chance answered. "You know, we can't reach out to any authorities. It might endanger her."

"We got you set," Cliff said. "I know the overseas treachery. It's cutthroat, and I've been riding scooters for years. I'll look forward to checking out your bike. Head toward the Port of Houston City Docks. You'll need the Port of Houston Exit off the freeway, and the signs will take you directly to the port. Just ask the guard how to get to Dock 19. You'll be looking for the Leon. It's a ratty tramp freighter, but they'll be glad to hoist your scooter into one of their holds. I picked this ship because it's a general cargo ship based in Hamburg. The only ship that left yesterday was also a general cargo job with the same line based in Hamburg. This one's rusting and ugly, but it's your best shot.

"You may have to pay to get the bike loaded in the states, but out of the states it won't be a problem. My guess is that even in the states, if the guys know what you're up to, one or two of the dockworkers will be Harley riders and they'll take care of you. Just get on board. They're waiting. Call me if you need anything else."

"How the hell can I find out where the other ship is going and what the name is?" Chance asked while jotting down notes.

"It's called the BiBi, but you won't have a clue of ports-of-call until you get to Hamburg. Even then it will be iffy," Cliff said.

"Thanks much, buddy," Chance said.

"Anything I can do," Cliff said, "I hope you find her."

"I will, goddamnit," Chance said, "And fuck anyone who gets in my way."

Chance hung up and jumped on his scooter for one final 190-mile stretch from San Antonio to Houston. As the sun came up dead ahead of him, the night cool began to lift as he rolled toward Schulenburg for a refill. It was a dewy morning in the Shell station as two rough-looking kids approached.

"We need some cash, man," a stout kid said slapping his hand with 2-foot length of 1-inch pipe. "We know you Harley riders are rich."

Chance didn't look up past the piece of pipe, but spotted the other kid trying to creep up behind him. He still had the .380 caliber stainless Walther PPK in his vest. Nothing was going to stop him from getting on that ship.

"Get a job motherfucker," Chance said and pulled the spout out of the tank and pointed it at the kids face. "How about some free gas, will that work?"

The kid froze as did his partner.

"I'd rather kill you than look at you," Chance said and his face glazed over with a haunting devilish grin. His top lip rolled under, his teeth sparkled and the kid stepped back carefully as Chance reached inside his vest. The two punks took off running like mad dogs heading for the hills.

Chance put the pump nozzle away and hurriedly jogged to the station to pay his measly bill. The girl behind the counter wouldn't take his money.

"Thanks," she said. "They've terrorized a number of my customers."

"At least they'll leave bikers alone," Chance said, heading back to his bike, firing it up and jamming back to the freeway. Houston was like most big cities with freeways running everywhere, but shortly after riding through downtown, he spotted the 90-off-ramp to Wayside and the port.

He slid off the freeway and followed the signs on Wayside Drive to the City Docks. It was almost sunrise but still dark. Few lights illuminated the street as if he was rolling through some dank backwoods. Suddenly in the dark, the road turned and a small, unlit gate appeared. The guard in the small shack directed him to dock 19, and he followed the narrow canal past one dilapidated building after another until he found the Leon moored against the dock. He had never seen a grungier ship.

He pulled up on the dock beneath the ship's cranes and stopped. Several Filipino crew ran to the edge of the hull and leaned over, pointing and talking. Out of nowhere, two dockworkers pulled up in a pick-up with the bed full of cables that had been carefully covered with padded Cordura sleeves for lifting delicate objects. They pulled out two of the cables while one of the longshoremen crawled into a 20-ton crane shell and manned the controls.

"We got the word, buddy," one of the union stevedores said, slipping the padded cable under his frame.

Chance unstrapped his bedroll and tank bag, both stuffed to the gills. He watched intently as the cables were lashed together to insure that the bike wouldn't flop over as it was hoisted. The big black longshoreman looked at Chance as the bike was hefted into the air.

"Better get on that ship and make sure they put that pretty puppy where it will stay in good shape."

"Thanks," Chance said, and headed for the gang plank.

As he neared the ship, he took a hard look at it for the first time. It was a rust bucket and even the gangplank was a slimy strip of scrap iron and wood cobbled together. The rope railing was backed with old netting. Two Filipino crewmembers met him at the top of the plank to welcome him on board and take his gear to his cabin. Everything Chance touched as he stepped on the ship was grease-soaked and he noticed the deck was coated in some sticky substance. The crewmen wore orange overalls, but the color was only visible at the shoulders for the grease and grime stains.

"I've got to get into the hold where they're putting my bike," Chance said. One of the crewmen indicated for him to follow. The other took his bags topside.

Chance followed a small Filipino sailor below decks to hold number 3, two levels of steel below the slippery main deck. Chance was surprised with the ship's level of disrepair. Railings were rusted to the point of being sheer skeletons of razor-sharp deteriorating metal that wouldn't support a small dog's leash. The bottom deck of the ship, constructed in Japan, was basically a plate of steel welded to the I-beam girders that supported the hull of the ship. Between the girders were plates of steel fastened to the 1-inch hull of the 10,000 metric ton vessel. If any portion of the hull was rusted to the extent of the topside railing posts, one wrong step would send Chance swimming in open ocean. He watched as the crane operator visually followed the motorcycle, lowering it carefully to the slippery deck deep in the hold.

Surrounding the motorcycle were bars of lead strapped together in bundles, some 30,000 tons in one hold alone. Each bundle weighed one ton. There was just enough space to lower a forklift to assist with the loading and unloading of the lead bundles.

The crewmen were experts in tying anything down except custom paint and chrome. Chance worked with them to secure the bike without ripping the paint from the frame rails. He wrapped the handlebars in rags before they were lashed in place with gnarled hooks attached to shipping straps. With the bike secured, the crewmen showed Chance to his quarters on E- deck. He ran into the Polish captain in the passageway. His cabin was next door.

"Captain," Chance said. "Good to meet you. Name's Chance."

"Welcome," the Captain said. "Lunch at noon, dinner 1730. Breakfast is always at 0730. Need anything find me."

"There is one thing, Captain," Chance said. "When are we leaving? I have a satellite phone and a couple of antennas. Can you help me install the antenna?"

"Soon. And of course, regarding antenna," the Captain replied. "If my door is open, feel free to come in. Usually on the bridge one flight up. We can probably connect to one of the antenna posts above the bridge on the antenna bridge."

The captain, a young 38-year-old experienced Polish skipper, spoke broken English and was most helpful. All the officers on the German-based ship were Polish and the crew Filipino. The captain decided to become an astronomer in college, but discovered that all such classes were taught in Russian and he was horrible at Russian, so he went to merchants' schooling after gaining a masters in metallurgy. His first experience on ships was as a third mate on cruise ships, but his lack of patience for drunken Scandinavians turned his taste for tourism sour. He returned to seaman's school for a Captain's license on a request from the owner of the Leon and Bibi, sister ships.

Chance's room faced the bow with a separate bedroom, bathroom and lounge. Tired to the bone after riding for nearly 24 hours, he unloaded his bags and sat down at his small desk, checking his papers and notes. Then he walked next door to the Captain's cabin and tapped on the open door.

"Yes," the Captain said, "Can I help you?"

"Can you tell me where the BiBi is going?" Chance said. "And when are we leaving?"

"We are pulling out in six hours at 1800, if all goes well," the Captain said. "I will try to find out about the Bibi. It was the sister ship to the Leon which was originally Mexican and named Gina Louisa. The company never changed the name of the Bibi, because it's an easy name to remember. It was named after the Mexican owner's girlfriend."

"I'll check back with you in an hour," Chance said and jammed back to his cabin. He was dead tired, but had to see that a couple of items were accomplished before the ship pulled out. He called Kate to check on the cell phone and check in. Unlike the past, the operator put him right through to Kate's desk.

"Officer Norton," Kate said, "can I help you?"

"No fuckin' way," Chance said. "I made it. I'm on the Leon heading out of here in six hours. Have you heard?"

"Yes," Kate said, "the Ryder truck was discovered this morning at dock 16. But they found no evidence of Ling, and once a ship is in international waters, all the jurisdictions change. It's not like we can just call someone to pull over a ship and search it."

"Can you check something out? The only ship that pulled out of Houston yesterday was the BiBi. See if it was moored at dock 16. I'm on the sister ship, the Leon, and we're headed to Savannah tonight. I'll look for the Bibi there. I've got to find her before the ship goes to Europe."

"I'll see what I can find out," Kate replied, "but I'm sure glad you made it to Houston in one piece. Let's stay in touch."

Chance hung up and broke out the Iridium box and began to read the instructions. It came with two antennas, one was meant for the roof of a car with a magnetic washer on the back. The other was a fixed antenna and he needed coaxial cable and a couple of connectors. He found the charger and installed the new battery, then walked down the narrow polished passageway to the captain's cabin and stuck his head in the door. The level of grease and grime on the ship was extreme, so much that the Captain put plastic sheeting on the floor of his entry way, and at one time he took his shoes off in this area to keep the carpeting clean in the rest of his cabin and office. The shoe ritual only lasted so long before the Captain could no longer take the time to don his shoes every time he was called to duty. In short order, his rugs were strewn with grease-soaked paths.

"Yes," he said, getting up from his desk, "I can help you. We go up to bridge."

"Thanks," Chance said, following the Captain, who was badly in need of a haircut, up another level of stairs from E deck to the bridge, a sprawling room adorned with an entire wall of windows over-looking the bow and doors out either side to outside wings on the superstructure. They walked out a door and around behind the bridge on a large open steel deck and up a set of stairs to the roof above the bridge and the highest view point on the ship, except that the area was strewn with antennas and in the center was a steel angled mast holding the radar antennas and additional communications antennas.

On the deck, several antennas were removed at one time and Chance and the captain went through them, looking for spare parts. There was an area on the bulkhead containing two 5/16-inch holes drilled horizontally and below it about three feet, another set of similar holes, evidently for clamps to hold a past antenna. It looked like it might work.

"I send someone up," the captain said. "It is good you have two antennas. When one doesn't work, you have another."

Five minutes later, a stout Polish man came onto the steel deck dressed in grease-soaked overalls, a flannel shirt and a knit cap. He was the ship's repairman. Together, Chance and the repairman cut an 8-foot length of an old fiberglass antenna and clamped it to the bulkhead to support the fixed-mast antenna. Chance ran the coaxial cable to his room and tied it along the railings and out of site of the bridge with cable ties and snipped them off for the detailed touch. He thanked the repairman and gave him a Harley-Davidson key chain. Chance returned to his room and connected the phone. It still needed to be charged completely and it was noon. He found his way to the A deck and the mess hall for officers.

Adjacent to it was the officers' lounge scattered with some shots of semi-nude Japanese girls taped to the steel walls and outside, a small liquor bar. There was a television but no hookup except to a VCR. A couple of old newspapers lay on the corner of the couch. Chance decided that unless the crew knew what his plight was, that he would keep it to himself, but he sure wished they would get underway.

The dining room was clean and neat with a table 15 feet long and enough seating for four passengers and 20 officers. The rest of the Filipino crew had their own separate rec room and dining area. The officers' table was covered with white tablecloths and a narrow path of rubberized white sheeting ran down the center to hold glasses and utensils from rolling off the table in inclement weather. Each sitting had rubberized place mats. It was noon as Chance sat down and Clemet, the steward, brought vast plates of food. Chance introduced himself to Clement and the officer who came to dine but declined to talk much. He was dirty, tired and wanted to see a tugboat assisting this ship to sea.

# -11-

## Sᴀᴠᴀɴɴᴀʜ Hᴏᴘᴇ

The second day out from Houston, Kim continued to bring Ling her meals and chat with her. It was dinnertime and there was that familiar delicate tap on the door.

"Dinner," came Kim's voice through steel door.

"Have you heard anything?" Ling asked as Kim opened the door. She tried to remain calm around the quiet Kim, who she was sure was becoming her friend. Something she needed more than life itself, some hope that there would be a future.

"Only that it's none of my business and to stay out of it," Kim said. "They are nasty men and there are several on board. Do you know why? It's not prostitution as far as I can tell."

"I don't know a thing; I'm lost," Ling said, her eyes filling with tears. "I'm sorry," she said, wiping her eyes.

Kim looked around her room. "Let me have your clothes," she said. "I'm doing some laundry tonight and I'll try to find you a couple of extra things to wear."

Ling gathered her sweats and the Long Beach State College sweatshirt she was kidnapped in.

"That's it, except for what I have on and I've worn it for two days."

"Here," Kim said, handing her a towel. "Peel out of everything and I'll be back in an hour."

Ling stood up and took off the t-shirt Kim loaned her and the denims, then unsnapped her bra, releasing her beautifully sloped tits and uncovering her plump ass as she peeled off her narrow panties. Then she sensed the same feeling she had picked up a couple of times before. Kim was looking at her body in a sensual way. Her eyes seemed to stroke her longingly.

Ling wrapped the plain white bath towel around herself as Kim quietly picked up all the clothes.

"I'll be back in an hour," Kim said, bowing slightly and leaving."

Inquisitively, Ling watched her shut the door. She had an attraction for women, but her level of anxiety and fear had erased any notion until Kim looked at her that way. Ling sat on the edge of the thin ship's bed and wondered if she was crazy or if something was happening, then thought that she had no time to consider it. She had to find out what was happening to her. She ate her humble meal, which was usually about the same, buttery rice with chives, a meat in a delicate sauce, salad and something to drink. She was so grateful that Kim wasn't leaving her condition to the men she saw when she was pushed aboard. Just the thought of their features and seething demeanor sent a terrifying chill up her spine. As she ate, the rocking of the ship seemed to sooth her.

An hour passed and there came that delicate knock on the door.

"It's me," Kim said and opened the door. She was carrying a large load of clothes in a basket, which she placed on the bed. Ling sat on the edge, her face filled with worry.

"I wish I could do more," Kim said. "I'll tell you what, roll over on your belly. Let me give you a little rubdown, then I'll leave you to try on these clothes. You can keep anything you need to wear."

Ling rolled over reluctantly. She was completely naked except for the towel, which Kim pulled from her back and gazed at her nakedness and the curve of her breast protruding from the sides of her body while pressed gently against the bed.

Kim started to massage her neck and along her traps with gentle but firm hands. She worked slowly down her back, around her ass and down her legs, one leg at a time. To Ling it felt so good, as if she wasn't there at all, but getting a massage at a resort while Chance waited outside. She liked the touch of a woman and wanted to explore it sexually, but…

She felt Kim's hands wander up the inside of her thighs softly then touch her outer pussy lips. She jerked and rolled to face Kim. She was close to her and their eyes met. She could feel Kim's breath hot against her neck.

"Thank you," Ling said. "I better put something on." Kim's eyes were bright, her hand resting on the cheek of Ling's ass. She looked hungry yet disappointed, there seemed to be even a glint of anger in her eyes. The kind of selfish anger she often saw in her brother. Kim lifted her hand from Ling's soft as satin skin slowly and got to her feet. "I'm sorry," Kim said. "I hope you find some things to fit you."

It took three days for the Bibi to reach the outer harbor near Savannah, Georgia. The ship bobbed up and down the eastern seaboard until taking on a pilot at the mouth of the Savannah River for the narrow passage inland 15 miles and mooring at Port Wentworth. Ling was looked after by Kim, but not allowed out of her room. Given books and old magazines to read, Kim spent a few minutes with her every meal. As they pulled into the narrow river and passed the historic town of Savannah, Ling looked longingly out the porthole at the town, praying that she would see Chance standing on a dock waving to her.

Kim tapped on the door. "Lunch time."

She brought in the tray and set it down on the small cubicle desk.

"We're pulling into Savannah; I'll try to make that call for you. Give me the number and tell me what you want me to do."

Ling jumped to her feet and embraced Kim. "Thank you," she said. "He'll find me. I know he will."

Kim held her close, feeling her breasts pressed against Ling's. "If I reach him, let's celebrate," Kim said and kissed her gently.

"Anything," Ling said and turned to write the information on a sheet of paper.

Lifting and moving the 1-ton bales of lead out of the Leon took the stevedores longer than they anticipated. They still had hold number one to empty before they could depart. The forward hold didn't have the deck space to lower a forklift into the cold steel dungeon. In the sixth hold, they started by lifting two bales wrapped with cables. Once they cleared enough space, a fork lift was lowered into place, then a platform that could carry up to six bales, and finally a dual platform program was developed so one platform was loaded while another was hoisted to the dock.

The forward hold prevented use all of the other quick unloading measures, yet 860 tons had to be removed before they could depart Houston. The pilot stood by on the dock as they unloaded the last of the bales at 9:00, three hours behind schedule.

Chance, a nervous wreck, didn't want to tell the Captain why he was on board for fear he would contact the Coast Guard and jeopardize Ling and her family.

He went to the bridge and conferred with the helpful Polish officer, while continually reminding himself that he wasn't sure which ship she was aboard or where the BiBi was going, or if she was aboard, or okay. He watched outside his forward porthole as a series of forklifts moved the heavy lead bales from the dock alongside the ship to the warehouse on shore. They buzzed back and forth like bees to a honeycomb, while the crane lumbered back and forth to the queen's nest.

Finally, the last one was removed and the longshoremen disembarked the ship while the crew hustled around to clean the hold and lower the deck plates into place. The massive top doors over the hold creaked and slammed shut violently. The pilot came onboard, a tug pulled up on the starboard side and another idled near the stern of the ship. The Houston channel was so narrow the Leon was forced to travel up the canal another half mile to the end where it could slowly turn around for its departure.

Chance watched every move as the ship steamed at just over 5 knots, past gypsum docks, container docks, the old battleship Texas, collapsing buildings and oil refineries, as they steamed toward Galveston and out to sea. Chance sat on his bunk and looked out the porthole and prayed that Ling would be in Savannah and he could end this nightmare.

The first evening in Savannah was slow. The Bibi needed repairs and cargo was unloaded. Kim stayed on board until dinner and brought Ling her food.

"I'm not going to town tonight. I'll be in town tomorrow," she said.

"Thanks for the efforts," Ling said. "I really appreciate the clothes, but I didn't get my sweats back."

"Oh, hell," Kim said, "they must still be in the laundry hamper. Are you in a hurry?"

"Oh no," Ling said, "not at all." She was beginning to suspect this woman. She was older than Ling, and ever since she touched her, Ling noted a slyness about her and a controlling edge.

"I'll get them back to you in a couple of days," Kim said and the two hugged. Kim kissed her gently on the lips and left.

Every meal Kim reported to Ling about the Chinese on the ship. They were just hanging out while the ship was being unloaded and readied for its next stop in Baltimore. Two more days passed and Kim had not made the call. It was getting close to the weekend.

Saturday morning, Kim brought Ling's breakfast. As Ling opened her cell-like door, Kim began to enter, but a short menacing Chinese man stormed past in the passageway shouting and pointing a threatening finger.

"Are you all right?" Ling asked, concerned for Kim and her relationship with her supposed protector.

"He's upset that the ship hasn't finished its business here so we can move on," Kim said, setting her tray and a local newspaper down.

"Are you going to town today?" I hate to add anymore pressure on you, but…"

"That's okay, honey," Kim said, "Yes, I'm going today. I'll make the call. I should be back by noon, so I can see you then."

"I know you have other shit on your plate," Ling said, "so I won't hold my breath."

"Remember your promise to celebrate," Kim said.

"Yes, of course," Ling said, blushing.

Kim returned to her room, picked up her satellite phone and called the number Ling had given her. It was early in Los Angeles with the three-hour time difference. Kate answered the phone, looking at the clock, 5:00 a.m. "Hello?" she said.

"Is Chance there?" Kim said.

"No, he's gone; who's this?" Kate said in a daze.

"I'm a girlfriend of Ling's. I go to Long Beach State. Did he go after her?"

"Yeah," Kate said, "He's on the Leon heading into Savannah."

"I hope he can find her," Kim said. "Thank you."

Kim took off her form-fitting denims and low-cut blouse and picked up Ling's sweat pants and college sweatshirt and put them on.

She went to the head and softened her make-up then put her hair in a bun at the back of her head with a plastic claw she picked up in town the day before—just like Ling's. They were similar in stature, hair color and skin tones. Then she called the short Chinese man named, Chee.

"He's on the Leon and coming this way. Check it out and meet me on the dock."

She messed with her hair for another ten minutes, donned running shoes and headed down the internal stairwell to the main deck. At the gang plank, the short Chinese gangster waited. He was stout and menacing but appeared intimidated in front of Kim.

"You ready?" he said.

"Of course," Kim said. "Bring around the car. Are you sure the Leon is pulling into the Newport Terminal?"

"That's the report I got," Chee said, trying to hand her a slip of paper. She glared at him and made no motion to take it.

"Is it docked yet?" Kim said.

"Just pulling in," Chee said, and opened the door to the sedan for Kim to get in. He went around front and got in the passenger side of the car. The driver, another Asian but a smaller Chinese man, drove to Chee's directions.

"Turn here on Main, then a left on Crossgate."

They drove up to a guard shack on a gravel road at the Newport Terminal entrance and a woman wearing a fluorescent yellow parka with Security in large letters on the back, emerged from the guard shack.

"We have business with the Leon," the driver said, handing her a card. She jotted down his rental license plate number and flagged him on through.

They drove into a nearly empty corrugated warehouse in front of the concrete docks and stood in the shadows as they watched the Leon rumble slowly toward the docks. The ship and its assortment of mighty cranes had a low sleek look like some rusting nightmare released from an evil fog. The afternoon sun shinned on the port side and made every rusting hinge, every broken rail, each chip of layered paint, stand out like wounds on a dying soldier.

Little hardworking Filipino sailors in grubby overalls soaked with grease threw lines to the American dockworkers. They stood in the setting sun as the port agent strolled aboard. Soon, a platoon of dockworkers approached and began setting up cranes and pallets to remove more lead. The first item to be hoisted from a hold was Chance's motorcycle. Chance walked briskly out onto the dock and moved the bike toward the warehouse. He was a big man on a mission, and the chopper added a sleek weapon to his arsenal. Kim and her men were startled, scrambling for the car. They jumped in and pulled out just as the narrow tires and glistening chrome spokes rolled into the hollow shell of the warehouse. Chance kicked the kickstand out, locked her down and jogged back toward the ship to collect his gear, which consisted of his vest and a couple of maps of the city.

Kim pondered the big American biker moving around his chopper in the sun. He could be a problem, she thought.

"Return to the Bibi," Kim barked. They picked up another member of their team and jammed to the road just outside the Newport Terminal gate.

Kim slid over in the seat near the window. They waited in the shadows behind an adjacent building to the right of the warehouse. They carefully watched the gangplank until they saw Chance nod to the Filipino crewmembers on the Leon and departed down the narrow plank. Kim could only surmise Chance's intentions. He might be looking for the Bibi, and she needed to pull him off track. As Chance threw his leg over the motorcycle, they rolled.

He looked up as he saw the car screech to a stop outside the gate. It looked like Ling in the back seat. His bike fired immediately, like a battery of machine gun ammunition at a dark foe. He slammed it in gear and peeled to the gate.

The guard meandered out of the shack and rounded Chance's bike, noting the license number and eyeing the long low lines of the wild machine.

"I'm a passenger on the Leon," Chance shouted. "I need to move." The girl worked the guard shack since high school. Not half bad looking, the progress of her existence ended when she found a place where she could smoke dope, listen to country music and be left alone, while making a meager living. Her hair was dark and pulled back into a ponytail. She had no form under the big floppy parka. She ate all she wanted.

"Which way is that?" Chance asked, pointing after the sedan.

"That's the way to River Street," the guard said. "That's where all the action is."

Chance sizzled with anxiety in the smoldering southern humidity. She made a note on the clipboard, smiled with broken teeth and waved Chance on.

"Take Crossgate to Main and go left," she said, but before "left" departed her soft southern lips, Chance's rear wheel spit a shower of dust and gravel in his wake. The bike slide sideways as the front 21-inch wheel reached paved asphalt and he yanked it into a straight line. He sped up to the light at Main just a block away, surrounded by a small residential area called Garden City. He pulled left running the red light, trying to make up for lost time.

River Street was once a whorehouse district until 25 years ago, when a revitalization plan was implemented. The town of Savannah contained a myriad of historic landmarks and mysteries, some contained in the recent best seller, *The Garden Of Good And Evil*, but River Street, lined with squared cobblestones that once served as ballast for European ships in the 1800s, had it's own history below the cotton market buildings, and Chance needed to find it and Ling. He entered the old town area as the sky darkened, making the Live Oak trees and the Spanish moss hanging from the trees look like ghosts escaping the old buildings surrounding them. Chance's motorcycle screamed to be released as he floundered in the inner city, trying to find his way to River Street in the dark.

Nightlights followed the bustling evening action. Finally, Chance found the city hall with its golden dome and discovered a rough narrow cobblestone street leading him down to the river's edge, where his motorcycle coughed and sputtered. He pulled it to the side of the street near a pub and parked it on the rough surface. A darkness engulfed him. No cars filled the street, no sign of Ling. Was it just a false alarm?

Kim returned to the Bibi as darkness swallowed the area, but another shift of workers scrambled up the docks to continue shipping tasks into the evening. She went to her cabin and changed, leaving the sweats on her bed. She washed her face, changed her makeup and the way her hair was pulled into a bun like Ling's, and returned to the galley to get her tray of spaghetti with an oriental touch, salad and a slice of jiggling custard. Assuming her quiet demeanor, she knocked on Ling's door lightly.

"It's me. I have your dinner and news."

Ling opened the door immediately as Kim unlocked it and entered.

"Did you speak to Chance?" Ling asked hopefully.

"He wasn't there, a girl answered the phone," Kim said, avoiding Ling's desperate gaze by focusing on the tray of food. "You were right. He's on a ship somewhere coming this direction." Kim didn't fully understand her level of honesty. Could it be her desire for Ling's body? She had no concern for Ling's emotional well-being or her future, but a fleeting notion of compassion slipped into her thinking, and pushed a button. The evil Kim slipped off course.

Ling stood up proud and embraced Kim. A surge of hope and confidence enveloped her.

"Thank you," she said softly. "I'm ready to celebrate, whenever you are."

Kim noted the confidence in her tone and her willingness to do as Kim pleased, delighted her. But she needed to finish her Savannah mission first, then she would have two things to celebrate. Her evil intentions returned.

"Maybe tomorrow night," Kim said and left the cabin abruptly.

Chance grabbed a quick Jack on the rocks in a seaside saloon and quizzed the bartender. The pub, built in the middle of the 1800s with old ships' planks, smelled of 150 years of stale beer and piss. He listened to new and old tails of Savannah's legacy. He wasn't sure what to do. His motorcycle had quit on the street and he didn't know where to start looking for Ling. Pumped full of anxiety since his glimpse of her, maybe, he knew she couldn't be far, yet her presence didn't jive with Chang's kidnapping concerns. Nothing made any sense.

The bartender told a patron about indentured servants. The man, Oglethorpe, who established Savannah, brought men from the debtors' prison in England to save them from assured small pox death in the dank cells. They took a print of a man's teeth when he arrived in Savannah as an identity card to use to monitor his bill-paying progress. Once paid off they were given a cow and 50 acres to make an attempt at life in America.

Chance wished he had a similar way to find Ling in a time when escaping would have been on horse and buggies.

"Bartender," Chance interrupted, "Is there a Harley shop nearby?"

"Sure, buddy," the tall bartender said, wiping the bar with a moist towel. "It's just down the street on the right, Savannah Harley-Davidson. Better hurry, they'll only be open another half hour."

Chance gulped down his drink, slapped a bill on the dark wooden bar and ran for his bike. Unlocking it, he pushed it down the street for two blocks until he saw the small bar and shield outside the old building. It wasn't a full-blown dealer but more of a small boutique, selling licensed Harley-Davidson doodads to the general public. Chance ran in the store and looked around, disappointed. A tall red-head stood behind the counter and eyed Chance.

"What's a matter with you?" she asked "Someone steal your birthday present?"

"Much worse than that," Chance said. "My bike quit. Do you have any tools?"

"We may not look like a dealership," she said, "but we have some tools and parts in the back. Push your bike around back."

Chance went outside and hurriedly pushed his bike around to the back of the old stone building, painted white a hundred times over, but time still turned it pale. The bouncy redhead came out into the area where civil war cotton brokers took stock of loads of cotton and decided whether to buy or not.

"You're from California?" she asked, pushing her long full mane of redness over her shoulder.

"Yep," Chance said. "I'm sure I just knocked a wire lose on the rough streets. I may need a place to sleep tonight. Is there a nearby motel?"

"Our new loft upstairs is warm," she said. "There's a restroom downstairs. Just push your bike in here."

She opened the door and he pushed his bike inside. A small toolbox stood in the corner of the storage area. She turned on an overhead fluorescent.

"I've got to lock up and go take care of my kids. I'll be back in the morning. You can come and go from this door. There's a big Christmas parade in the morning. I'll be back early and we'll have some breakfast."

"Thanks," Chance said and nodded as she locked and alarmed the front of the shop and slipped out, straddled her Softail and rode away.

Chance looked after her gratefully and returned to his bike. A screw on the back of his ignition switch vibrated loose. The brass screw fell and it disconnected his coil wire. He dug around the bike until he found the screw and replaced it. The bike was good to go, but he didn't know where. He wandered up and down River Street in the warm, mosquito-swarmed air, along the Savannah River. He looked in every building, upstairs and down, watched ships meander up and down the river. Then he stopped in another pub and ordered a drink and a bucket of steamed clams. He dipped French bread in the soupy clam-flavored liquid, ate the clams and wondered what the hell was going on.

Through the night, he searched the streets of Savannah; every bar, pub, saloon, and strip joint, until he doubted she was ever in the downtown region. He grabbed a fast-talking horse and buggy tour guide and scoured the side streets, old buildings and alleys. Tired and with sore feet, he returned to the shop and climbed stairs to the new wooden loft. He pulled a Harley-Davidson sleeping bag out of a corner and laid it out. Everything didn't jive. He slept until the bars closed and got up and hung out in the streets, listening to drunks and bartenders for a clue, anything.

Ling woke up feeling buoyant for the first time since her kidnapping. She got up and showered and donned fresh clothes Kim brought, including some very tight jeans that revealed her flat stomach and a short t-shirt top that just covered her large buoyant tits. She felt a little vulnerable, but since she was imprisoned and no one would see her, what the hell? She combed her dark hair and pulled it up in the back, then heard a musical tapping on the door.

"Kim here, can I come in?"

"Please," Ling said.

Kim had a particularly bright smile as she walked in the door carrying Ling's tray of scrambled egg whites, a slice of ham, toast and a side of yogurt. As her eyes danced along Ling's attire, they brightened even more, crawling along Ling's form like a satin pillowcase slipping over a down pillow. Ling looked at the food then at Kim's gaze. She could sense her eyes dancing along her flesh and for a second wanted to lift her top to reveal her nude breasts and hardening nipples underneath, but thought better of it.

"I better get going," Kim said. "I've got some errands to run before our celebration tonight. What do you drink?"

"I like White Russians made with Absolut," Ling said, sitting down to eat, "or a nice merlot. You're not going to stay and chat? Is there anything I need to know or do for tonight?" Ling thought the dialog strange, and hoped Chance would find her first.

"Find something sexy to wear," Kim said, squeezing her shoulder and letting her hand slide down the front of her T to the curve of her breast as she leaned to kiss Ling on the forehead. Ling did not move away, and Kim wanted to linger and let her hand slide down farther and over her nipple, but she could feel her knees begin to buckle and she knew she wouldn't want to leave. She turned quickly and grabbed the cold steel door handle, bringing her back to reality from the edge of blissfulness.

"See you at lunch," she said, opening the door.

"Bye," Ling said, taking a bite of egg whites.

Chance woke with a jerk. He jumped to his feet. Although it felt good to have a couple of drinks the night before, he had to find Ling this morning, call Kate and get this nightmare over with. Just as he was going to run down the stairs, he noticed a commotion outside the shop and heard Red coming in the back door.

"You here?" she hollered.

"Yep," Chance said. "Thanks for letting me stay." He rounded the corner into the head and cleaned up. "What the hell is going on out there?"

"They're getting ready for the Christmas Parade," Red said. "They're starting any minute, now. The street is crowded with locals and tourists."

Chance stepped out of the restroom, pulling his vest on over his shoulders and bumped into the freckle-faced redhead.

"I would have come back to party with you," she said, "but I could tell that someone is pulling at your heart and you needed to deal with it."

Chance leaned down and kissed her lightly on the lips. "You're right," he said, "but I appreciate everything you've done. I don't know what to do now. I thought I saw her in a car yesterday coming through the port, but where the hell would they take her?"

Chance looked out the front of the small shop. Its arched stone doorway was lined entirely with glass. He moved his chopper just out the back of the shop and around front to park it beside her late model Harley. He came around back and put a few tools away.

As he looked out the door to the crowds searching for places to sit on either side of the street, a girl jogged past.

"Is the front door open?" Chance snapped.

"Yep," Red said turning to look after him. "Why?"

"That was my girl," Chance said, bolting for the door. "She was kidnapped."

Just then, Chance noticed a couple of Chinese guys run past the door. He was outside in a second. He could see her running toward what looked like the parade. Fortunately, he was wearing running shoes instead of his cowboy boots, and he took off.

On either side of the street, little kids and their parents sat waiting for the parade to reach them, anxiously pointing at the oncoming banners, bands and dancers. It was a locals' parade with the floats meandering along the harsh cobblestones, bouncing and shaking over the rough surface. He saw Ling run around a reindeer float sponsored by some real estate agency as the kids onboard tossed candies to their buddies in the crowd.

Chance ran as fast as he could, his vest flapping in the cool morning December air. Paddlewheel boats were tied to the river's edge and decorated in the Christmas spirit. He ran between two high school bands, whose players were uncomfortable in their uniforms, pulling on them between notes. Ahead of him was a series of girls dancing and twirling batons. For a second, he lost sight of Ling and the two Chinese were gone.

As he crossed an intersection, the two Chinese runners came up on either side of him snatching his vest hem and jerking him onto the side street, cutting behind the cotton merchant buildings.

Chance struggled to turn but was yanked away, until he rounded the corner and ran right at a block wall. He carried one man directly into the stone wall. Chance spun free and punched the other. He scrambled intothe alley, grabbed an aluminum trash can lid and slammed one man who lunged at him with a knife.

Panting, Chance ran around the corner into the parade again and was stopped by a large lumbering float carrying Miss Savannah. She saw him running at her and looked concerned, until he stopped, jogged around the edge of the bouncing float and ran, for all he was worth, down the street again.

He couldn't see Ling through the crowd, but at least she was getting away. He ran with all he had through another baton demonstration, where teenage girls looked hot in their outfits, but with each row, the outfit got larger and the girls were younger, until mothers walked beside their diminutive daughters stumbling with batons.

He passed a series of custom cars bouncing against the uneven stones and stopping to talk to their buddies in the crowd. Chance ran around them and under the Hilton Hotel archway over River Street and thought he spotted Ling turning ahead. He passed the hotel, where another narrow walkway intersected the historic district. He quickly rounded the corner. Ling was running up the steep black stairs ahead.

"Ling," he hollered, running up the concrete stairs after her. He started to cross the alley at the middle of the stairs when he stumbled and went down. He could see Ling was slowing at the top of the steps as someone kicked him in the ribs. He tried to get to his feet, but he was hit with a 2-by-4 across the back and he went to the pavement again.

Chance tried to think. He wanted to reach Ling, but if he could stop these men, she could escape. He rolled on the 150-year-old alley cobblestones directly at one of his attackers, kicking him in the shins and punching his balls. The man fell backward while raising the 2-by-4 above his head. Chance jumped to his feet and stepped forward, stomping the attacker's knee and snatching the lumber from his hands.

He spun to catch the other attacker with the beam to his side, driving him into the wall. Chance turned back to the man on the ground and drove the end of the 2-by-4 into his chest, snapping ribs. The other attacker pushed off the wall, blood pouring from his broken nose, and reached under his black sport coat for his pistol. Chance stepped up to him, twisting the weapon in his grip until he broke the small man's trigger finger and yanked the pistol free, turning it in his own hand and stepping back from his assailant.

A bullet ricocheted off the bottom step. Chance recognized the hiss of a silenced weapon and looked up the stairs. It was Ling, he thought, recognizing the general figure and clothes, then upon closer analysis discovered the features of someone completely different holding a semi-automatic handgun aimed at him. He dove behind the wall at the base of the stairs as another bullet zinged passed, and another round pierced the flesh of his left leg.

Confused and wounded, he rolled and struggled to his feet before diving down a narrow set of steps running into the back door of a shop selling model tugboats and seaside trinkets. He fell into the store and drew the attention of every patron.

"Never mind me," he said, scrambling to his feet, blood running down his leg. He ran out the front of the shop directly into the parade, across the street and into a series of white vendor tents selling local crafts, including lighthouses painted on bricks as gifts. He stumbled, catching his breath and wondering what the hell had hit him. His heart so wound up in his girl, it broke at the sight of another woman. He stumbled into a fountain in the center of the arts area along the edge of the river.

Chance grabbed two handfuls of icy water and splashed it into his face to the dismay of kids and parents watching him. He sat on the edge of the heavy Ship's Anchor fountain with his back to the parade and tried to assess what had just happened, but nothing seemed to make sense, like a puzzle of a picture that didn't exist. He whipped out his bandana and tied it around the fleshy bullet wound in his calf. His heart sank once more, but this time he was mad. Someone was playing with him and his girl.

# -12-

# THE WINE OF DESIRE

Ling read a book in the morning, looking out her window from time to time. She could see a large flat warehouse and stevedores driving fork-lifts from the tin buildings back to the dock to pick up large bundles of lumber. She watched as they filled a portion of the warehouse, and then began to stack the lumber outside until there seemed to be an extraordinarily large stack of lumber. As quickly as they moved, they quit, loaded the forklifts on trucks and disappeared. She could smell the lumber and it felt good to see the sun beating on the dock. Then she realized that preparations were under way to pull out. It was nearly noon and she was concerned and fearful that perhaps Kim was still in Savannah and might miss the departure. Who would take care of her? She checked the clock on the bulkhead that had been advanced one hour automatically as they meandered from one time zone to the next.

She sat down on the edge of the bed and picked up the book she was struggling to read and relax with and tried to read a page, then returned to the window. It was 12:15 when a black town car pulled up to the dock and three men from the ship, ran to it. They helped two men out of the car and one opened the back door behind the driver and Kim got out. It was warm out there; Ling could tell by the increasing temperature in her cabin, the intensity of the sun on the docks and what the dock workers were wearing, yet Kim was wearing an over-coat and she could see below the coat were running shoes. She made angry motions to the men and came aboard by herself while they dealt with injured men from the sedan. One man was carried quickly aboard and the other's hand was bandaged and it appeared that his nose was broken.

Immediately thereafter, a tugboat arrived. The ship was hauled away from the docks and began to make a U-turn in the narrow river, gradually heading out to sea.

Ling went back to her book, relieved that Kim was back, but images bounced around in her head from the scene on the dock. Had Chance attacked those men or visa versa?

Then at 12:45 the familiar tap was at the door. "May I come in?" Kim asked.

Ling stood up as Kim opened the door. Kim wasn't as joyous as she had been in the morning. A tinge of tenseness showed in her features and movements as she dropped the tray on Ling's desk.

"How'd it go in town this morning?" Ling asked.

"Not so well," Kim said. "I suppose you saw us out the window?"

"I don't have much else to do," Ling said. "I could tell the men on the dock had quit loading lumber and became concerned that the ship would leave without you."

Kim stood abruptly bolt upright. "They will do nothing without me!" she said abruptly, caught herself and calmed. "At least I hope not. Savannah is a nice place, but I would hate to be stuck here."

"Whatever," Ling said. "I'm just glad to see you."

The expression in Ling's warm eyes soothed Kim and she relaxed. "Enjoy your lunch," Kim said, "I have some things to deal with in the kitchen. I'll see you at dinner, and tonight we have some fun, right?"

Ling blushed slightly. "Yes, as I promised."

Chance pulled his bandanna out of his back pocket next to his Elishewitz black folding 3-inch knife which Edge, a customer, gave him with good wishes for his trip. He wrapped his leg with the bandanna and stumbled toward the Savannah Harley shop. He needed to get back to his bike and back to the port. He knew Ling was somewhere at the docks for sure and that drove him to hobble as fast as he could toward the shop.

He was also aware of evil forces between him and Ling and his thoughts were of Ling's comfort first, and the battles he must face in the future with these people. The woman who disguised herself as Ling was armed, had silencers and trained bodyguards who were also armed. It was not going to be a walk in the park to find the ship, get aboard and get her back. Then he stopped, was she still alive?

He could see the shop ahead as the parade ended at the crowds commenting about the floats, while entertainment dispersed. He stumbled into the shop and leaned against the counter. Red ran around the counter and helped him to a small sofa.

"What happened?" she anxiously asked. "Did you find your girl?" Then she stopped herself. "I suppose not?"

"I did and discovered that it wasn't her," Chance said. "I think I'm just grazed. Do you have a first aid kit?"

Red grabbed her Red Cross kit from the head and opened it as Chance cut his pants away from the wound.

"I've got to get back to the ship in a hurry," Chance said. "She's in the harbor."

The bullet pierced the skin on the outside of his calf, sliced through three inches of skin and exited out the back of his leg. Red doused the wound as best she could with alcohol and swabbed it, then carefully applied an antibacterial lotion and wrapped his leg with a gauze bandage.

"Why did they shoot at you?" Red asked, wrapping his leg.

"They don't want me in the picture." Chance pulled his pant leg back together and Red stapled the material to hold it in place for his ride back to the ship.

Chance struggled to his feet shaking slightly from the pain. Red ran into the back of her shop and dug through her purse for a painkiller. She returned to the front with a glass of water and the pill.

"Take this," she said, giving him the tablet. "It will help you get back to the ship." Chance took the Vicadin gladly, and straddled his bike with a cringe.

"Your girl's got a good man," Red said and leaned down to kiss him goodbye.

Chance kissed her and peeled out through the myriad of historic plazas leading out of the downtown district and into the area that was once considered modern and now simply was the ghetto, on his way toward Garden City, until he found Crossgate and turned right, back to the Newport Terminal. As he rolled up to the dock, a crane swung out to meet him, but he saw another ship leaving, rounding a bend in the channel. He raced to the end of the dock to see the stern of the Bibi disappear around the bend.

The Bibi, a 584-foot, 10,000-ton freighter, slowly lumbered out of the harbor past Savannah. The ship was built 20 years ago in Hiroshima, Japan, at the Hatachi Shipbuilding & Eng. LTD. and had been through a number of owners while shipping cargo around the world. Kim and her crew of Chinese gangsters arranged passage on the BiBi for one purpose, to deliver a 1952 Bentley packed with opium to a port in Italy. That one delivery would net them over ten million pounds sterling, worth almost twenty million U.S. dollars. With that money, the family she worked for on mainland China would expand their crops to become the largest, most influential opium source in the world. It was Kim's notion to introduce street priced, quality opium to the US market through an Italian mob connection.

With the kidnapping of Ling Wu and the pressure it brought to bear on Chang Wu, she fully expected the time spent on the ship to garner her with success in several areas. Kim wasn't Chinese. She grew up in a concrete whorehouse in Pusan, Korea. She didn't know who her mother was, just one of the prostitutes who lived in blocks of rooms built in cement steps up a hill overlooking the Pusan Harbor. Sailors and US naval ships tied up at the dock. The seamen were delivered to them for sex but little else, due to the poor quality of life in the area. There was no glass in the windows and open fires in the floors warmed cold rooms. There was no running water, only holes in the concrete floors for toilets. Men who came from other countries were often turned off by the grizzly, dank, nature of the place.

As Kim grew, she became despondent and disillusioned towards the older, nasty whores and the Korean lifestyle. When she was a teen, she stowed away on a freighter, taking care of the crew until it reached Hong Kong, climbing the prostitution ladder as she grew taller and more sexually marketable. Her rounded Anglo features and height made her a hot property amongst the high-end houses of ill repute, and she moved uptown until she was discovered by Lee Wong, who paid her handsomely for her services, which she performed admirably.

He was so taken by her ability to give head and be fucked in a number of awkward positions while enjoying every thrust and manipulation, that he bought her a set of tits and skyrocketed her to the elite in her profession. She began attending various luxury events in Hong Kong society and studied hard to be well-read and educated. She learned of the opium business and decided two things: she wanted to step away from prostitution as quickly as possible and get into the drug trade, and she liked women and wanted access to the cream of the crop. It was her turn to be the dominate one.

If she could break out and into the drug trade, her level of acceptance and power would be elevated substantially. Besides, age was a consideration. She needed to move quickly. She convinced Lee to let her play in the drug field, and he quickly discovered her devilish, seductive nature, while being notorious and unafraid of violence. She wielded the sense of power he needed to control his dealers and the competition.

With the changes to Hong Kong returning under Chinese rule, she understood the melding of the connections to the west through the port of Hong Kong. All she needed was a way to move her product outside the confines and poor economic atmosphere of mainland China. Much like communist Germany and Russia, China discovered communism did not work, and with an open market they could lead reasonable lifestyles. The society, tired of financial ruin, could adjust to an open market successfully, especially with Hong Kong as a guiding light.

Besides, somewhere along the line, she wanted to be totally free and wanted to ultimately live in America. She figured that Lee was easy and weak; his brother and father formed the original Chinese cartel. They were once most powerful and dangerous. She took over most of Lee's duties, to his glee, and the family built trust in her. Lee could sit at home, count the money, have sex, eat and drink to his destruction and merriment. Once she was trusted beyond reproach, she could set up a deal to net her a couple of million and escape to the US. Her goal was to walk away from the drug business once in the US, but she might keep the door open and become a distributor for fine opium in California if need be. She had options.

She wasn't aware of her desire for women until being fucked by men while watching girl-on-girl porno movies. She was surprised, then enticed, until her first experience, which was professional. She was contacted by her pimp and told to go to one of the most lavish hotels in Hong Kong. In the magnificent marble foyer, she approached the reception desk and asked for her contact, who gave her a polished brass key with jade accent and told her the directions to the room. She took ornate elevators to the suite indicated on the key and walked in to find a blond English woman wearing a robe.

The woman was an English television actress in Hong Kong on a public relations mission for the BBC. She poured Kim a drink then told her to strip and take a shower and put on the robe in the sumptuous bathroom. Kim did as she was told, expecting the girl's husband to show up and fuck her.

While in the shower, the door opened and the woman stepped in with her and began to wash her back and run her hands down over her tits. She turned to face the beautiful face of the English actress and for the first time kissed a woman. The sheer softness of the kiss drove her wild and when her tits came in contact with the unbelievable softness of the white woman's boobs, she thought she would collapse.

After the shower, the woman went into the bedroom while asking Kim to get her another drink. When Kim came in the bedroom the woman was naked on the bed with her legs spread and she was told to make love to her. She discovered just how sexy, sensual and seductive a woman's body could be, and she could hardly stop touching her. They became good friends and her career vaulted to another level. She searched to meet her goals and occasionally touch other women.

She found that she was turned on by the slightest contact with women and as she became more powerful, she awarded herself with the purchase of a woman for her enjoyment. But since this trip had begun, she was getting hornier by the mile, until Ling was kidnapped. She was comfortable with telling a prostitute to go down on her, but this was a completely different situation.

In China, she could be the dominant one without the slightest consideration for her paid consort. She took joy in making a young little Chinese druggy lick her from head to toe for a taste of an opium high. She was having a tough time in the submissive roll on the ship with Ling. She wanted her desperately, but didn't feel comfortable giving her $200 and telling her to strip and climb on the bed. She knew the prostitution tack would never work, yet. Her relationship with Ling was having undesired effects on her. She was in the position initially to assassinate this woman, if need be, but she was becoming attached and Chee, a soldier of Lee's brother, could see her softening approach. It pissed him off.

She knocked on the door to Ling's cabin to bring her dinner.

"Hi," Ling said as she opened the door. "You feeling better now?"

"Much better," Kim said, "And you?"

"I'm doing okay," Ling said.

"I have got to clean up in the galley, then I'll be back," Kim said motioning to the drink she had brought. "I made you a White Russian to warm you up. I'll be back with another one in an hour. Does that work for you?"

Kim was standing two feet from Ling and about 1-inch taller. Her tits pulsed in her bra. She just wanted to reach out and pull Ling toward her and feel her lips meet hers.

"We'll play around a bit."

"I'm going to eat and take a shower," Ling said. "I found something that might not be too bad to wear."

Kim reached out and touched Ling's hand.

"I'm sure it will be fine," she said. "In case you're concerned, it will be just you and me."

"Thank you," Ling said. "That had crossed my mind."

Chance spun the motorcycle in a circle, burnt rubber back to the ship and slid to a stop under the crane. He stepped off the bike carefully, the stevedores took over and Chance jammed on board and took the elevator to the E deck and the stairs up one more flight to the bridge. The captain was busy single-finger typing a message on the tele-type communication machine to Hamburg.

"How long will it take to get the fuck out of here?" Chance asked hurriedly, interrupting him.

"Please," the Captain said, "I busy."

Chance's leg hurt like hell and he realized that if the Captain saw the torn leg of his pant and the blood on his Levis, it might take him a long time to explain his wound.

"I'll be back," Chance said backing away.

He walked quickly to his cabin and changed clothes and immediately returned to the bridge. The Captain saw him enter the door and peeled a sheet of copy paper out off the tele-type.

"I have answers," he said, "we leaving in one hour and it will take us 48 hours to get to Baltimore, if they have mooring for us."

"What?" Chance said exasperated, "You mean we might not be able to get into port?"

"Yes," the Captain said and began to smile. "You must relax. Many things can delay our movement. If no dock, we anchor in Chesapeake Bay. I won't know until we are in bay."

Chance could feel his leg throbbing. Moments ago, he could see the ship that stole the love of his life, and now he was face to face with maritime delays before they even happened. He shook his head and turned to leave.

"Thanks," he said, and started down the stairs for his cabin to check his wound and call Kate.

The ship ran smoothly down the Savannah River while Ling showered. She didn't know what to expect from Kim, but was relieved to know that it would be just her and a beautiful woman having a couple of drinks. She still pondered the meaning of the celebration and how the party would take its course. She cleaned up, washed her hair, and put on fresh make-up in the narrow little cabin head.

Kim gave her a wild selection of clothes to wear, including spandex pants and a shear white blouse that tied in the center above her navel. She had never experienced another woman before, but had been intrigued for years. Women were a turn-on for her and occasionally she felt the urge to go beyond looking to touching. Once while having her hair done by a woman in Hollywood, she could sense the desire this woman had as she washed her hair and leaned over her. She had a low cut loose blouse on and Ling stared at her bra-less chest, her tits hung gently like soft clouds of sensuality dangling before her. She could smell her perfume and it drove her crazy not to reach up and cup one breast and feel her nipple harden in the palm of her hand.

Ling tugged on the tight spandex and tied the blouse around her waist without the use of a bra. She could sense that her nipples hardened at the touch of the soft fabric. She pulled her hair up in the back and put a plastic claw around it, lifting the hair from around her soft ivory neck. She was beautiful from her small well-formed feet to her strong shapely legs and narrow waist to large ample breasts with small sensitive nipples. The curve of her undisturbed neck lead to a face with classic Chinese eyes and a small pert mouth with ruby lips and cheeks so soft she should pay herself to touch them.

She admired herself in the mirror, and as the White Russian had its effects, she thought again about close calls she experienced with other women and some of the women she had watched make love on videos. She took a deep breath and for a second tried to cease the warmth tingling in her crotch. There was a light knock on the door.

"It's Kim, can I come in?"

Kim unlocked the door and Ling pulled it open to the inside. Kim gasped with the shear ecstasy Ling's appearance created. Ling had turned out all of her cabin fluorescent lights except for one amber bulb against the bulkhead. It glowed in a warm candlelight tone hiding the stark interior.

Likewise, Ling eyed Kim from the mini skirt and tanned legs to her shapely waist in a black top that contained a series of stainless steel zippers of which she had one open over the shoulder and the one just over her nipples was also revealing.

"God," Ling said, "you look like a million bucks."

"It's a celebration," Kim said, entering the room with a silver tray adorned with a small crystal vase containing a rose, a tall White Russian and a bottle of port and two glasses. She set the tray on the small coffee table in front of the narrow couch across from the desk.

"I have another surprise," Kim said, "but first let's have a toast."

Ling finished her drink and Kim handed her a fresh one and poured herself a short demitasse glass of port and stood up.

"Oh, wait," she said and turned to the radio on the desk that didn't seem to work, but Kim had a CD for it and installed a Barry White track, pressed the play button and turned the volume down so that it simply filled the room with a warm atmosphere. Then she picked up her glass and reached out to Ling.

"Let's toast the fact that your man is not far from here looking for you," Kim said, and they softly touched their glasses together.

"You don't know how wonderful that made me feel," Ling said. "We've only been together a couple of months, but I knew he would find a way."

"Do you have any notion as to who did this, who these Chinese men are?" Kim asked concerned as she sipped her wine.

"I don't have a clue," Ling said, looking down at her glass and feeling the warmth of the liquor spread throughout her. "I thought I was going to be raped and killed initially, then I had some notion about a crime Chance saved me from, and I know my brother wants me to come back to China. I sorta blew out of there without my family's approval."

"What was the crime you mentioned?" Kim asked.

"A few months ago a serial killer was raping and murdering women in San Pedro, California. He was a brutal sonuvabitch and

Chance was accused of the crimes initially because he's a biker and was going out with some of the girls. He went through hell, working with an investigator he knew, to dispel the rumors. As it turned out, a Hispanic cop was the guy, and Chance helped solve the crimes. Unfortunately, the cops still wanted to stand by their brother and an officer tried to attack me, mimicking the crimes to get his buddy off and point the guilty finger at Chance. Chance was with me when he made his attempt and this cop really didn't have the balls to kill me when it came right down to it."

"Men," Kim said, "'they can sure cause us problems. Have you ever thought about doing it with a girl? Oh, before you answer that, look what I brought."

Kim dug a joint out of a small silver purse and a lighter. "What do you think? Want some?"

"Why not," Ling said.

Kim lit the joint and passed it to Ling, who took a hit and passed it back to Kim.

"I've thought about it a lot. Women turn me on," Ling said. She took another hit and a swallow of her drink. She could feel the buzz of the liquor loosening her inhibitions. "I thought you had the hots for me."

They both giggled and took another hit. "I gotta tell you, you're looking hot," Kim said.

Ling stood up and began to dance in a circle in front of Kim. Kim reached up and ran her hands down either side of her hips over the slick spandex pants accentuating Ling's ass.

"Oh, I'm getting buzzed," Ling said, sitting on the desk. "Damn, when you massaged me the other day, I thought I would go crazy."

Kim stepped up in from of Ling, who was sitting on the corner of her desk. She set her port glass on the desk and pushed forward, parting Ling's legs slightly. Her tits were in Ling's face and she felt as if she was slipping into sensual overload. The feelings were crazy, her perfume, the slope of her boobs and the flesh peeking out between the zippers. Ling breathed a heavy sigh. Kim felt the warmth on her chest and she moved forward parting Ling's legs some more. She leaned forward until her hand caressed either side of Ling's hips, then kissed her on the lips.

Ling never felt anything so soft and tantalizing. Their lips went beyond satin to something as heavenly as a child's touch. Ling reached up and touched her cheek and their kiss became more anxious, more foreboding and more ecstatic. Kim parted the kiss and stood, pulling her blouse out of the waistband of the miniskirt.

"I'll be right back," Kim said as she stepped away from Ling and into the head.

Ling's mental state was a maze of liquor, smoke and sex whirling around like a traffic jam of euphoric jewels. She stood up from the edge of the desk and kicked off the high heels Kim gave her and lost her balance as the ship entered the Atlantic and began a gentle roll. She stumbled and fell on the bed, her legs parted slightly.

Kim went into the bathroom and removed her top, the miniskirt and her pantyhose. She had on a pair of silk panties and a low cut bra. Letting her hair down from being tied in a ponytail, it fell around her soft shoulders. Her boob job was perfect and they stood out from her body, strong and firm. She stepped out of the bathroom and discovered Ling passed out on the bed.

Hot red anger swept over her frustrated body, but the more she looked the more she felt for the girl asleep on the bed. She knew that in due time she would have her. She leaned over and kissed each nipple gently, dressed and left her to sleep.

# -13-

# BALTIMORE BLUES

The long 48 hours passed as if Chance's watch was filled with mud. Each second was a year, and each minute a failed deadline. He changed the bandages on his leg and worked with the ship's machinist to make some weights to train with, but it didn't move time quickly enough. The chef, a middle-aged Filipino who wore bifocals and had a pockmarked face, but a wry smile, fixed wonderful dishes, odd combinations like a dinner of French fries, pizza and Creole beef. The evenings were the worst. He endeavored to bury himself in a book by W.E.B. Griffin, on the Marines, but would just as soon eat the pages. Plus there was tremendous vibration in his room, as if the shaft driving the single screw was terribly out of balance. Relating to his experience with motorcycles he assumed that the ship would tear itself apart under these conditions. He constantly set the book down to run to the bridge to check on progress and question the Captain.

"We pushing speed against current," the Captain explained, "and the bottom is shallow leaving the harbor, causing vibration."

The bridge had a 16-mile line-of-site view of the sprawling Atlantic around them. Chance watched the radar system read-out on a large screen. There were two radars at opposite ends of the bridge guarded from blinding sunlight by plastic shades. The radar screen was also coupled to the GPS system indicating the position of the ship and the speed. Chance cringed at the slowness of the craft when they were doing 13.4 knots on the open ocean. He was forced to test his sea legs against the strong swells the ship endured before it pulled into the Chesapeake Bay, past the Newport News Naval Base that housed the aircraft carrier USS Enterprise.

A harbor pilot skiff pulled alongside the Leon swaying at the entrance of the Bay. A slender middle-aged agent climbed on board, up the stairs and stood on the bridge, giving instructions to the mate at the wheel on harbor navigational warnings as they cruised through the Chesapeake Bay. The ship smoothed to an easy jaunt up a posted narrow channel where they passed several Navy war ships, while heading deep into the bay to the Baltimore Harbor. Darkness befell the rusting freighter as they neared the Baltimore region and were surrounded by the lights of the 90-square mile city. Studying the harbor for similar ships, Chance couldn't see anything but an occasional silhouette interspersed around the harbor.

He jammed to the bridge for a better look and the Captain approached him.

"The Bibi is here, but I don't know where yet," he said. "Should I call them?"

"No," Chance said, "I'll find them."

"We will only be here four, maybe six hours after they start work in the morning," the captain said. "We had a fire on board. We need the hold power washed. Also taking off remaining lead."

Chance was stuck on board until daylight. He had no way to get around or to get his motorcycle off the ship. Frustrated, he called the Yellow Cab service.

"Yellow Cab, gimme your phone number," the black woman said directly.

"818-398..." Chance began.

"We need a local number, sir," she said.

"I don't have a local number," Chance said his frustration growing. "I'm traveling."

"Where are you located?" She dropped the sir.

"I'm at the docks," Chance said.

"Do you have a street address?" she said, getting short with him as if she had no interest in sending a cab his way.

"I'm at the Newgate docks, berth A," Chance said.

"I'm sorry sir, we can't help you." The phone went dead.

Chance couldn't believe his ears. Taxi services should know the entire area like the back of their hands. He paced his room, the corridors and ran up and down the stairs to burn time. He showered and sat in a chair looking out the window as the sun came up over the gray city. Rain was forecast as the Captain knocked on his cabin door.

"I have information for you. The Bibi is at the Lazaretto Wharf, Berth B, portside," he said. "Here's a small map of area."

Chance nodded and looked at him as if to communicate his frustration.

"Longshoremen due here in one hour. We unload your motorcycle first. Impossible to get cabs out here."

Chance shut the door as the Captain left. Although the man's English was broken and he giggled as he talked, as if everything was a joke, he was a font of knowledge about anything Chance needed and was always willing to help.

Chance showered and dressed warmly. The rain began to drizzle over the cool 40-degrees harbor. Chance looked at the Xeroxed map the Captain brought and determined the BiBi was less than a half hour away, a short jaunt. He waited for the longshoremen to arrive as he collected his scattered thoughts. All he could do was try to get close to the ship, then he would have to wing a plan to get aboard and find Ling, if she was there.

Ling woke to tossing seas and a tap on the door. She was hung over and dragging her ass. She got up and went to the head.

Without asking, Kim came in the door and set her tray on the desk with a clunk.

"Kim," Ling called from the bathroom. "I'm sorry I passed out. I haven't had a drink in a while and the smoke sent me over the edge."

Kim said nothing and left the cabin, locking it behind her.

Ling stuck her head out of the steel bathroom door held by a bracket that wouldn't allow it to swing back and forth in heavy seas if the door wasn't closed.

"Kim?" she called, but there was no answer. She closed the door and continued to shower, while the seas rolled outside.

Between shampoo and soap, she had to grab the railing against the bulkhead several times. The shower was quick, but made her feel a little better. She combed her hair and put away her clothes and made the small bed. After eating breakfast, she looked out of the window to an open ocean.

When lunch came around, there was a knock on the door unlike any she had heard before. It was hard and masculine. The door opened and a Chinese man stood at the door with her tray. He had a crooked smile as he looked at Ling and handed her the tray without a word.

"Don't you want the breakfast tray?" she asked.

"No," he said as if he didn't want to say anything to her. "Set it outside door now."

Ling stepped over to the desk and exchanged trays. She had to get down on her knees to reach over the ledge and put it carefully on the floor. As she did she looked up at the young Chinese man in all black. He smirked again.

"You should be on your knees," he muttered and slammed the door, forcing Ling to dive out of the way. He operated the flange for the padlock aggressively and shoved the lock in place, walking away. A half hour later, she could hear someone outside her door pick up the tray and leave without a word.

Ling sat on the edge of the bed and replayed the following night as the ship swayed back and forth. She wasn't completely aware of Kim's intentions and thought that since… well, she just didn't understand, and had no way to contact her.

Dinner came in the hands of a Filipino steward. He was instructed not to talk to her and although she attempted to say something to him, and left without a reply. He handed her the tray and waited for her to bend down and put her previous stainless steel tray on the deck before he closed the door. For the next two days, she received the same treatment, and noted that she was in some level of solitary confinement.

The second evening when the young steward arrived, Ling met him at the door, "Please take this note to Kim," she said and placed the note in the tray to be returned to the galley.

Kim picked out the note scrawled on a piece of scrap paper and unfolded it as the wounded Chee came up beside her. "A note from your lover?" He said, sneering at her.

She knew the feelings she had for Ling were compromising her unique power over her men. It showed weakness on her part and she couldn't let anything sacrifice her will, or her goals could possibly be compromised. She would take a different tact with Ling in the future and show her who was the powerful force behind this mission.

The Bibi pulled into Baltimore early in the morning and Ling piled up pillows on her bunk so she could sit and watch as they coasted quietly along the glassy harbor. She didn't understand why industrial harbors had to be so dismal. They looked like hell, but some far worse than others. Harbors along some of the most costly property on earth looked like the worst dilapidated industrial neighborhoods on the planet. The buildings were bland and terribly run down or even falling down.

Savannah and particularly Baltimore had come to realize the retail value of the harbor and redeveloped some of it, but there was still a long way to go.

The longshoremen hurried to work on the ship immediately. On the dock was a train track and a car was backed to the side of the Bibi to pick up a $4 million generator lifted off the ship. Several representatives of the utility company stood on the deck to make absolutely sure their costly products were being handled carefully. They worked throughout the day and into the evening. The next morning at 7:00 a.m., they returned in the drizzling rain, and the single crane began to hum as Ling watched from her vertical rectangular porthole.

Chance stood in the rain at the bottom of the Leon gangplank wearing a ball cap and fully padded attire, ready to roll before the crane operators came on duty. The crew carefully lowered his bike and Chance tried to jump on it before the cables were free.

"Hey buddy, step back," a big black stevedore shouted as Chance tried to jump ahead of the procedure. "You may want to ride in this ugly snot, but we want you to get away safe."

Chance stepped back and paced up and down the docks while the dockworkers removed the straps and pulled them clear of his chopper. The second Chance received the thumbs up from the supervisor, he ran to the scooter and straddled it, wiped the tank clean and taped the map to the polished surface. He turned on the gas, fired it up and peeled down the dock, sending a rooster tail of spray into the air behind him. He jammed out of the yard and up the street to Boston Street and turned left. From the melting map he didn't have far to go. Just under highway 95 to Fort McHenry and left again on Clinton right down to Keith Street where the Lazaretto Wharf was located.

He slammed on his brakes, almost missing Clinton and caught the left. The mud on either side of the road sloshed into the street and he became more agitated. The mud on the asphalt made the ride more treacherous. The long custom bike slid and slipped, but he could see what appeared as docks a couple of miles ahead. As he headed under an overpass, he noticed barricades ahead. The street was blocked off with concrete barriers from gutter to muddy gutter. Chance could not get around, so he spun around and jammed back to Boston Street turning left again. He tried the next street into the harbor and it ran into a guard shack.

He skidded to a stop at the shack and jumped of his bike. The office was fully equipped with communications equipment and decorated for Christmas. A uniformed guard sat stoically at the console and looked up at Chance with disdain. "Can I help you?"

"I certainly hope so," Chance said. "How do I get down to the Lazaretto Wharf?"

"The what?" the guard said, scrunching up his face as if Chance had asked the question in a foreign language.

"The Lazaretto Wharf at the end of Clinton," Chance said again.

"I know Clinton is around here somewhere," the guard said, "but I don't know where."

"Look, I was told to go to Boston and turn left on Clinton, but Clinton is blocked off," Chance said, his frustration skyrocketing. "Is there another street to the dock from here?"

"This is just the street into this refinery," the guard said looking as if Chance was asking him questions for a test he wasn't prepared for.

"I got to get to that dock," Chance said

"Sorry, I'm not a driver," the guard said and slid his glass window shut on corroded aluminum tracks.

Internally Chance was screaming. He spit on the ground and straddled his bike firing it to life, while grinding his teeth. He circled the guard shack and rode back to Boston, turning left again. He rode along Boston to Fell's Point where some of the row homes were built as early as 1730 when the area became the center of Baltimore's clipper ship business. The narrow homes had even narrower alleyways between them, built as access for taking game and vegetables to storage areas behind the old buildings. The area had long since become one of the hottest of 200 ethnic neighborhoods in the region.

Chance pulled up along side a Diamond cab and asked directions, but the man could not speak English. Then he spotted one of the many bars in the refurbished area and a Harley-Davidson parked out front.

He was dripping wet as he entered Mother's. He found the biker amongst the yuppies and headed directly for him.

"Say, could you help me with some directions," Chance asked.

The rider spied Chance pulling up outside and eyed his long chop. "Sure, man," the rider said, "Where you from?"

"Los Angeles," Chance said. "Can you tell me how to get to the bottom of Clinton? The street is blocked off. It's like where Clinton and Keith Street meet."

The rider was dazed by Chance's statement and his Southern California accent. "Ah, yeah sure," he said. "Just take Boston back the other way and get on 95 south and get off the next off ramp, which is Keith. You're right there."

"Thanks, brother," Chance said and ran out to his bike, climbed on and got to the corner when he heard a loud emergency vehicle blurb. He made the turn and the blurb turned into a siren. He pulled over. The cop got out of his car and approached him cautiously. The pouring rain flooding the streets, Chance stood above his seat and pulled out his bandana from his hip pocked and wiped his glasses clean.

"What the hell are you doing?" the cop said. He was wearing his winter jacket and a plastic covered hat, but the rain was still uncomfortable. "Gimme your license and registration."

"I'm sorry officer, but I don't understand," Chance said, going through his wallet and pulling the information card.

"This is a helmet state," he said, "how the hell did you get here without a helmet. Isn't California a helmet state?"

"On a ship," Chance said. He hated helmet laws. "I hate to rush you, but it's damn uncomfortable in the rain and if I don't get back to the ship soon, they'll pull out without me."

"You're on a ship?" the officer continued, not sure he believed the long-haired biker. "There aren't any American crew on freighters and we don't have any cruise ships in port."

"I'm a passenger on the freighter Leon," Chance said, reaching for his wallet again. "They take my bike in and out of the holds." Chance opened his wallet and produced Kate's card. "Do me a favor, call this investigator and check me out, but do it in a hurry."

The officer looked at the card then at Chance, "Don't move a muscle," he said and returned to his cruiser.

"If I don't soon, I'll die of pneumonia," Chance said sarcastically. The rain was filling his tennis shoes as he looked around at the historic area that once was going to be shredded for developments, but due to a few citizens, was saved and renovated. The officer was back in two minutes.

"I apologize," he said, "but this is a helmet state."

"Merry Christmas," Chance said, noting the Christmas decorations around town and thinking of Ling. He returned the card to his wallet, wiped off his soaked black seat, sat in the cold mush and lit up the bike. He headed back down Boston until he found the highway 95 on-ramp. Slipping and sliding and having a difficult time seeing through his dripping glasses, he hit the freeway. It turned into a tunnel under the Northwest Branch Inlet. He paid the toll lady and jammed off the first off-ramp on Keith Avenue before the tunnel.

When he pulled to the bottom, there was a sign indicating a Clinton detour and he took it for less than a block when he saw a ship over some tin warehouses through the rain. He looked for a street sign or an entrance to Lazaretto Wharf, nothing.

He rode in the direction of the ship for another long block and came to a corner. There was a white vinyl banner clipped to the chain link fence that read, 3901 Merten Street, Lazaretto Wharf. He jammed, sliding sideways into a left-hand turn and into a factory parking lot full of grain silos. Wrong move. He pulled out and through the gate next door, past a guardhouse, ignoring it, and between various stacks of plates of steel and massive crates taken off ship, then past a corrugated warehouse. As he rounded the building, he slid up behind mountains of bales of lead bars on the dock and parked his bike. As he shut it off, he could hear the sound of tugs and their horns. He peaked around the corner to discover the Bibi pulling away from the dock.

He jumped back on the bike, fired it to life, and slid around the building on the slick pavement revving the engine and burning rubber. He flew right up to the edge of the dock, guarded with railroad ties and tires strapped to the structure, and revved the pipes for all they were worth a couple more times and shut off the bike. He jumped off and screamed at the top of his lungs, "Ling, Ling, I love you!"

Kim and a couple of her men ran onto the external wing beside the bridge of the 600-foot freighter identical to the Leon. One of her men reached for his gun, but Kim held him off. They had a pilot on board and could not move to fire or break any law. Chance recognized the woman imposter on the bridge and lifted his middle finger to her and her crew. "There's nowhere to run to, nowhere to hide," Chance shouted, got back on his bike and rode away.

Ling's cabin was on port side facing away from the docks, but she heard the rumble of the motorcycle and prayed it was Chance.

# -14-

# Atlantic Crossing, Escape From Baltimore

Ling spun away from the porthole as the door of her cabin/cell opened and Kim stood in the doorway. Ling bolted at Kim with all she had. The steel door opened toward the inside and Kim tried to step back and pull the door shut, but Ling yanked the door out of her grasp and tackled Kim into the hallway, scratching and clawing her way over the woman. She suspected Kim had something to do with her abduction but didn't care what, now. Their relationship was obviously over and her man was on that dock. It was her chance to escape. Chance might be on the dock. He was there and found her.

Kim, on the other hand, felt over-confident due to the ship departing the dock before Ling's man could scramble onboard. Kim had nothing to fear from Ling. She was a pawn, and Kim would implement another devious strategy and take her with power, since kindness didn't work. Overcome, Kim went down hard against the linoleum, over the steel deck, her head hitting the steel base with a thud that jarred her teeth. Ling was on top of her with her knees on either side. She punched Kim in the neck with the web of her right hand and jumped to her feet. She didn't know which way to go.

Her cabin was located on the D deck, which was shaped like a horseshoe with the open end facing the stern of the ship. She saw an aluminum door with a porthole in it and grabbed for the door handle to the outside, while stepping over Kim who lay stunned on the slick linoleum deck. She dove out the door onto a metal platform housing a set of stairs leading up two floors to the bridge and down to the stern main deck. The stairs alternated from port to starboard down to the stern and they connected the ends of the horseshoe so she could dart to the starboard side of the ship if need be.

The freighter was 20-some years old and looked it. As she ran down the stairs, the railings snapped from her jolting grasp, and old rusted diamond plate steps split under her pounding weight. She flew down the grease soaked steps, jumping over ones that appeared to be rusting through.

Kim fought herself to her senses as Chee rounded the corner.

"I take it you didn't make up. Where is she?"

"She went out the back door," Kim said. "Call the others. Catch the bitch!"

Chee, who worked for the family since he was a small boy, took off in the opposite direction to the internal stairway door, slid down the banister to C deck and opened the door.

"She's trying to escape," he screamed into the passageway and four men piled out of a small conference room where they were playing cards. "You two take the elevator to the main deck. You two go to the stern ladders, hurry. Get her and let me know when you do."

Chee was born out of Chinese law preventing the birth of more than one child per family. His parents wanted to have him but could lose everything if they were caught. Mr. Wong took in the child and raised him in hiding as long as the old man would grow opium for him. Wong ultimately killed his parents and took the land, but Chee only knew that the Wong family had given him a home. He was completely dedicated to the organization and was one of their most trusted soldiers.

Chee flew down the internal stairs to A deck. He could hear his soldiers clamoring down the outside stairs as he stepped into the cool Chesapeake morning. It was clearing and the sun was shinning on the harbor around the ship. Ling passed C deck handily and stumbled on a rusted-through step to reach to B.

She pulled herself to her feet as the men burst onto the stairway platform above her. She scrambled down another set of stairs as they split up, one running down the port stairs and one the starboard. Ling jumped over stairs to the A deck with a thud. All around her was rust and filth coated the main deck steel surface.

The deck coated in a slippery slime made her footing precarious, but for the first time she was in the open. The ship was only 100 yards from the dock. She was still too high off the water and looking for a ladder to the main deck. As she rounded the corner of the superstructure, she spied Chee heading up the stairs. He immediately reached in his coat for his shoulder holster. She spun and headed in the opposite direction, but the two Chinese soldiers bounded down the stairs behind her. She had no concept of the ship's structure, but spotted a door at the stern of the structure to the inside. She didn't want to go back inside, but one of the soldiers had reached the bottom of the ladder and Chee was rounding the corner of steel on the slippery deck.

She pulled open the aluminum door with a porthole in it and ran inside. Ahead she saw some kind of dark dining room and she ran toward it and passed a set of double doors sporting smudged exit signs. She backtracked and opened the door to another set of stairs down to the main deck. She slid down the banister and followed the fluorescent arrows toward the exit. The carpeting was grease soaked from the deck crew coming and going. She turned to the right and headed out the hatch on the port side onto the main deck.

Directly in front of her was the entrance to the gangway. To her right was forward to the holds; to the left was the ladder Chee just ran up after her. She looked out at the cold water leading back to the dock. Could she swim it? There had to be a tug on the other side of the ship. She ran forward as one of the soldiers rounded the superstructure. She heard someone coming down the ladder behind her and decided to run for the railing. Two feet from the rope railing, she dove over it for the sea 20 feet below.

Chee rounded the bottom of the ladder and scrambled for her foot, losing his footing on the slimy deck. He snagged her shoe and she spun, grabbing the railing line and collapsing atop it, falling to the deck on the inside, but Chee was also down on the grimy surface. Ling scrambled to her feet with all her might, screaming, but another soldier ran over Chee and tackled her, taking her to the deck once more. He immediately subdued her. They could pay off the crew, but if an officer discovered her, there would be a major problem. Fortunately this transport contained only four Polish officers.

Chee jumped to his feet disgusted, mad as a hatter and covered in oily slim. He detested the condition of the ship and made every effort to keep his clothes away from contact with any element. He washed his hands constantly after touching anything outside his cabin. The soldier grappled with Ling and pulled her arms to her back. Chee helped him yank her into a standing position, then slapped her so hard the sting bruised the back of his hand. He slapped her again with the same left hand open and felt his palm go red.

"I will treat you as the bitch you are," he said and stomped his feet. "Turn her around!" He put a cable ties around her wrist and pulled them so tight she cried out. "Take her to a hold and chain her there!"

Two soldiers escorted her to the cold and damp hold number four and chained her to the steel bulkhead. They looked her over and commented to each other in Chinese and left her there.

Chance rode back out to highway 95 and got off on Boston Street. As he turned right to New Gate, he didn't know how to feel. He was filled with a myriad of dire emotions he tried to sort out. The area looked as destitute as an industrial wasteland could look. Trash littered the streets of vacant lots covered in dying shrubbery and crumbling 100-year-old warehouses. He wondered why cities flourishing off the income from harbors treat them so badly.

As he turned on Newgate, he couldn't decide whether he was happy that at least he might have let Ling know he was there, or more worried about her, since they knew he wouldn't give up, plus he harassed the bitch on the bridge. He just wished Ling was back in his arms.

He pulled up alongside the ship and jumped off the bike. The Captain hollered from the wing outside the bridge six stories above him.

"We shipping out now, get onboard."

A 20-ton crane swiveled on a large flywheel-like gear and swung its hook over Chance's metal companion. Two longshoremen ran to the bike with fiber straps and looped the frame. Chance made his way up the gangplank as the bike was lowered into a hold. A smiling Filipino boy met Chance at top of gangplank.

"We glad you back," he said. "We shipping out."

"Thank you," Chance said and bowed slightly, hiding his fears and frustration. Soaking wet, he climbed the interior stairs to the bridge.

"Where are we headed?" he asked the Captain.

"Hamburg, Germany, next stop," the Captain said, messing with the gray tele-type machine. "We are empty now and will fill up in Hamburg. We know little about our trip until cargo is loaded. Maybe Christmas in Germany."

"How many days?" Chance asked.

"Depending on storms," the Captain began to explain, "this is bad time to cross Atlantic. Many storms, we have no cargo. Bigger container ships have ballast tanks and wings to prevent rocking. We have nothing."

Chance noted the bump of a tugboat near the stern and returned to his cabin to peel out of his wet clothes and take a hot shower. As he stepped into the small tiled shower stall, he realized the Captain hadn't told him the amount of time it would take to reach Germany. He nearly jumped out of the stall, then decided to go ahead and let the hot water remove the bone-chilling cold. Unfortunately, he was fighting a cold that wouldn't hold an ice cube to the nasty weather in Germany. The shower water was lukewarm. He stood there shivering and terrified for Ling, only a mile away on another ship.

Chang picked up the phone in his lavish home outside Shanghai and dialed Chance, but there was no answer. He hadn't heard from him for over a week. He paced the teak floor of the family home and wondered about what he did to jeopardize the entire family. They were well respected in the farming and distribution business for almost a century. They dealt with every European nation when Shanghai was controlled by the British, French and Germans.

Chang remembered as a child, not being able to enter the city and being treated as a peasant while the whites rode a high and mighty road, lived in luxurious buildings and were treated like gods. He was impatient for a time when China could take it all back. When he was still little, the British introduced opium grown in Afghanistan, Turkey and India to the Chinese mainland as a way to control the enormous population and enhance their own power.

He watched men fade away and lose everything they worked their lives for. He saw beautiful women become slovenly and lose pride for their bodies and culture. Chang promised himself never to be involved with such a devilish substance. He fought long and hard with his family to build strength, power, and self-esteem. He nearly succeeded. The last thing he wanted was for the business to fall into the grasp of the element he hated the most and for his family's reputation to become associated with the opium trade.

He tried the number again. He grappled with the Wong family for several years. They tried to hide their drug business dealings from him when they first approached him to buy the company, but Chang had them checked out. At their next meeting Chang dishonored them in front of his family and their business associates. That started a conflict hurting both families, but he was right.

Ling slid along the icy steel deck. It had no coating except a scratched layer of paint. The temperature of the seawater in the Baltimore Harbor was 38 degrees. That was the only form of heating or cooling in the holds. She stood quickly. The deck was too cold to recuperate on. They wrapped chains around her ankle and then locked it to the forward bulkhead. She wore running shoes and sweats and the sweatshirt Kim returned. She looked around her basketball court sized cell made of thick slabs of hard cold steel. She could hear the water rushing past, and the smell was dank and rotten.

The terror she felt in the bumping truck returned and her feet began to freeze against the cold steel. She tried to move around. It didn't help. The reeking odor was a 20-year melting pot of various cargos, from live sheep, to petroleum products, to lumber, but it all smelled cold. She heard the squeak of water-tight doors as she tried to take a step one direction then another to keep moving her feet around the chilling deck. Her chains clinked against the unforgiving surface. Then the ship found its way out to sea from the Chesapeake Bay and it rocked, throwing her to the steel surface and the chains tying her to the bulkhead snapped taught, against its full length, yanking her back. Her knees slammed against the unforgiving steel shell, and she crumpled on her hands and knees.

"Ah," Kim said, entering the hold through a creaking steel hatch followed by two short stout Chinese men in all black. "As you should be, bowed at my feet. Much more like I would have you." Kim was dressed in black denims and a thick warm jacked with a fur collar.

Ling lifted her head slightly and looked at Kim, searching for answers.

"You might as well know," Kim began, "I'm the boss around here. These men do exactly as I say. My game with you was destroying morale. So it is just as well it worked out this way. If I want you, I will have them tie you to my bed," she said, leaning down close to Ling's face, taking off a glove and sliding her hand inside the neckline of her sweatshirt until her hand cupped one of Ling's boobs. It felt good, the warmth, but Ling tried to bite her forearm. Kim yanked the arm back and backhanded Ling so hard it drew blood from her nose. Her guards who were watching cringed at the sharp crack.

"You will learn," Kim said, "Or you will die." Kim turned to leave.

"Wait," Ling pleaded, "I need something to keep me warm, or I will be dead the next time you come down here." Ling's face was already showing the bruises from Chee's lashings. She sensed that her feet were turning blue.

"Maybe then you will cooperate with my whims," Kim said, spun on her heals, hammering a terrible metal to metal sound against the deck, as she marched to the hatch and disappeared with her guards.

Three days out of the Chesapeake Bay heading north east across the Atlantic, Chance woke up early in the morning and scrambled to the bridge. The ship was virtually empty, to the Captain's chagrin, and it was tossing heavily in the seas. At 5:30 a.m. Chance opened the door to the bridge and peered in. The Captain and one of his Filipino mates were looking over the charts of the eastern seaboard, while the Captain reviewed alternative courses. He looked up at Chance with questioning eyes.

"They tell me one thing and another happens," he said in his broken English.

"What's happening?" Chance asked him.

"We have a storm just here," he said, pointing at an area on the map in the center of the Atlantic level with St. Johns in Newfoundland, Canada. "There is another one north of it, and following us going north is force 7 storm coming from here."

He pointed out an area off the coast of Norfolk, Virginia. "The company told me to head north east, the storm was turning, but it wasn't. Miami tells me storm is heading into our path. I have changed course toward the Azores, maybe south of it we will go. We might spend Christmas in the Canary Islands."

The ship rolled and Chance lunged for the edge of the chart table to secure his footing. He tried to make it past the table to look at the radar screen. The ship slowed to 13 knots. The bridge was blacked-out (no lights) to allow maximum visibility to the outside. It was dark as the hubs of hell outside as Chance endeavored to see anything on the horizon. They were surrounded by an ugly, angry sea.

"We facing 12-foot swells here," the captain said with a humorous grin. "The eye of storm 35-foot seas and 24 foot swells at 450 miles from the center. I trying to avoid."

Chance watched the captain study the seas, the charts and reports for seven days ahead. The ship bounced and vibrated violently trying to find a safe path to the English Channel. He attempted to evaluate when he might try to stand upright.

The Captain explained how the high-pressure areas drove at the lows in generally a counter clockwise direction which picked up the warmth from the Gulf Stream and pushed the heat over Europe. He pointed out to Chance on a chart how warm Europe was compared to the same latitude in Canada due to this massive stream of hot water that rolls up from the tropics and warms almost half of the Atlantic. Without the influence of the Gulf Stream, Europe would be another frozen snow pack, as well as much of Canada.

Chance expected the Atlantic to be an ocean of brisk chills and never ending cold fronts. He was aware of the Gulf Stream, but thought it only reached along a narrow path up the eastern seaboard of the United States, fading out as it reached Canada.

With each swell tossing his cabin furniture across his room, he wondered about Ling, where she was and if she was okay. At meals, Chance's chair slid away from the table as the seas driving from the north slammed against the port side of the ship. Dishes and cups flew from the table crashing against the deck. As days passed, he could only watch the weather, the heavy seas, the charts and pray for Ling's well being, while sharpening his knife.

Ling passed out and collapsed to the floor of the cold ship as it headed into rough seas. She turned pale against the icy deck until the ship entered the Gulf Stream and the hull warmed. She awoke in a warm sweat against the damp deck. A bowl of warm rice lay at her feet with a folded canvas tarp.

As she reached for the rice, the ship was broadsided by a swell, tossing the bowl and its contents across the dirty rusting deck. She reached for the bowl but was only able to capture a pinch of rice. She immediately stuffed the remnants between her lips. She grabbed at the folded canvas tarp and drew it closer to her. She pulled it close and unfolded it and formed a single bed- sized mat. She looked around the large steel area in dismay. She questioned everything about herself, wondering why this was all happening. What did she do to deserve this terrible treatment?

With each dismal thought, there was the hope that Chance was somewhere nearby and coming in her direction. She was sure, in her heart, she would be dead without his efforts to inspire her. Ardently devoted to surviving this experience, she would once again have the opportunity to experience their joy together. She was certain, in a Zen fashion, if ever given the chance, she would treat each moment with him with even more precious respect and admiration.

She still wasn't sure why the kidnapped her, but she was sure, at this point, it wasn't as simple as being thrown into a prostitution ring. She saw something in Kim's dark direct eyes she recognized. Then it dawned on her. It was her brother's competitive cut-throat nature. Suddenly she was sure Kim knew her brother and this had something to do with him. She stomped the steel deck with her left foot and screamed, "Chang, what the hell have you done?"

Chance tossed and turned daily for what seemed to be weeks. Just seven days had passed, and every day was full of anxiety and frustration. He knew they rolled toward Hamburg, Germany, the base of the Rickmer's shipping line. He couldn't sleep in the heavy seas, and naps were impossible in the empty ship until the seas calmed. Suddenly it seemed they had jumped into another ocean. After breakfast, he returned to his room and napped for the first time until the sound of his satellite phone woke him. He sat up abruptly in bed and reached for the phone.

"Yeah," he said in the receiver detaching the battery charger.

"This is Chang. What's happening with my sister?"

"Your sister is on a ship," Chance said. "I'm following it to Hamburg aboard another ship. I got close in Baltimore, but the ship pulled out as I reached the dock. Who is that woman who looks like Ling?"

There was a pause on the phone.

"I am embarrassed to say," Chang said, his voice lowering. "My family is being forced to sell our business to a powerful family in the opium trade. She is the girlfriend of one of the brothers, but I feel she has even higher goals. She has had several of my men killed. She is very dangerous."

"What's she doing on that ship?" Chance said.

"She must be making a substantial delivery, or she wouldn't be along," Chang said and the phone started to break up as the ship rolled. "If we cannot get Ling away from her before they arrive in China, our family will lose everything. If we fail before she reaches the mainland, Kim will kill my sister just to spite me."

"I'm doing everything I can," Chance said. "You better hold it together until I can get Ling."

"I will do it," Chang said and hung up.

An alarm sounded on the ship and Chance ran to the cupboard above his bunk and grabbed his life jacket. Donning the fluorescent vest, he scrambled up the ladder to the bridge and looked around, his adrenalin pumping like a high-pressure fire hose. The steward was on the bridge with a couple of the officers and the Captain.

The Captain had a walkie-talkie in one hand and was giving instructions while standing in front of the crew on deck. He indicated for some of the Filipino crew to go onto the exterior deck around the bridge and man the fire hose. They promptly ran out the back door and pulled the fire hose from its rusting cast iron housing and while the steward unraveled the canvas hose, another member of the crew opened the valve. Three men waited at the railing with the nozzle and attached the heavy brass fitting as the hose reached them. The hose remained calm and lax, as the crew stood around waiting, but nothing happened. Chance went through the hatch to the bridge interior.

"Captain, there is no power," he said.

"We have three salt water pumps," the Captain explained to Chance. "There are two in the engine room and one forward. We are testing the forward pump."

He indicated the two switches on a bank of switches on the port side of the wheel for the pumps in the engine room. The ship was heading 80 degrees and the wind had changed, throwing the swells directly in the path of the ship, which eliminated the rolls but replaced them with swells slamming against the bow, causing the vessel to pitch. As the bow heaved from the sea, the pump was not able to siphon water. When the bow dipped again the fire pump functioned, but then the screw at the stern became shallow in the sea and jerked with the lack of sea water pressure around it, causing the engine to shudder and the RPMs to lunge, which was devastating to the drive line and jolted the ship violently.

The Captain called below to reduce the speed. Still the crew waited with the hose for water pressure. Chance wondered how the ship could survive such brutal treatment without coming apart at the seams. He also knew that somewhere on the Atlantic there was another ship experiencing similar storms and wondered if Ling was safe. Salt water finally filled the hose, but the canvas tube was old and tired. Water sprayed from the cracked edges of the hose and the Captain ordered the crew to replace the hose.

Each day, Chance constantly watched the speed on the radar screens in hopes that the ship was pushing 30 knots to its destination. He was surprised that the ship had a top posted speed of 17.4 knots. Actuality the ship would do more than 19 knots, but his worst fears were realized when he looked at the radar screen informing him that due to the currents and force 7 winds, or because the shallow screw was shaking the ship to pieces, that the speed was reduced to 13 knots. With 450 miles to go to reach the English Channel, 13 knots versus 19 meant a 10-hour difference in arrival time, which could be crucial to Chance's efforts to find Ling.

Rare westerly winds pushing the swells directly at the ship didn't bother Chance. He would have gladly stood on the bow with an oar to boost the speed up to 22.8 miles an hour, if he could.

# -15-

## COULD HAMBURG HOLD A CLUE?

Ling Wu woke up at 4:00 in the morning unable to sleep again. She was drawn and gaunt, tossing from one side to the other in the pitching seas. There was very little cargo left on the ship and with each swell the remaining crates creaked and strained against clattering chains. The sound of each coarse wooden box sliding on the steel deck was as eerie as the blood-curdling scream of a woman scratching and clawing for safety. The ship jolted with each cavitation, pulling at every weld and fastener. Ling was fed one buttery bowl of rice a day, which she had to eat with her hands. Nine days from Baltimore in violent seas just outside the English Channel, she heard the creaking of the hatch leading into her hold from the stern.

A small Filipino man with long hair combed down the center came to her shivering side. "I have something extra for you," he said, but wouldn't look her in the eyes. He carefully placed her bowl of rice on the floor with a cup of hot steaming tea beside it. She reached for it immediately and he held her quivering hands at bay.

"Very hot," he said and pressed her hands back then stood, turned and departed quietly. She lay on tattered canvas with some of it draped over her shivering feet, but she wiggled closer to the tea and reach her hand closer for the warmth. It felt so good she almost cried.

The cup cooled rapidly against the icy steel deck and she lifted it and sipped the amber warmth carefully and then put it under her tarp with her and the bowl of warm rice. She ate the rice slowly, saving some for later and sipped the tea. It was bitter in an odd way but she drank it without hesitation.

She saved a half cup of the rice and a couple of swallows of the tea for later. She placed the two containers on a steel I-beam gusset away from the deck and rats, which she could hear at night scurrying along the bulkheads. As she set the tin cup on the ledge, a wave of something odd engulfed her. She blinked her eyes as if a foggy haze had drifted over them. She hadn't slept and the cold depressed her, but she felt exceedingly tired, suddenly and unnaturally, but it felt good so she succumbed to the cloud encircling her and laid down on the paint splattered, grease-soaked canvas tarp and fell asleep.

Chance woke up and sat straight up in his bunk. He was anxious as hell. He had been at sea for seven days and every time he darted up the stairs to the chart house, the coordinates indicated that they hadn't yet passed the Azores. He was beginning to feel as though they were tied to the outcropping of islands in the middle of the Atlantic and unable to pass. He splashed water in his face, brushed his teeth and combed his hair back and tied it into a ponytail. After drying his face, he pulled on some sweatpants and a sweatshirt and ran up the stairs to the bridge.

The ship miraculously dodged the last storm and the seas calmed. As he entered the inner navigational sanctum, the Polish Captain approached him.

"We making better time," he said, pointing at the GPS screen above the charts on the table. Below the surface of the table was a series of narrow horizontal wooden drawers like drafting table sliders, which contained navigational charts from all over the world and charts of the various ports. Chance looked at the GPS reading 47.45 North and 6.05 East. He studied the chart for the location and noted it was southeast of the English Channel. He was relieved to see the charting on the map and the location considerably east of the Azores. It was nearly Christmas and members of the crew were anxious to see port. Even some of the Filipino members were looking forward to Christmas in Europe.

Some of the Polish officers relished family arriving in Hamburg, and Chance was struck by the thought that he might not spend Christmas with Ling. Sitting in the officers' mess during lunch, the Captain came in with a slip of paper and sat at his end of the table wearing a dark sweater with navy blue leather patches on the shoulders and elbows. The shoulders also held epaulets containing his four gold Captain's strips. He wore denims and running shoes with the uniform top and no hat.

"We not stay long in Hamburg," he announced. "Two and half days max." He also looked dismayed.

His family enjoyed the holidays in Italy, as the Leon steamed closer to the wrong coast. They traveled to visit friends and were trying to drive north, but a storm shut down European travel for three days. The roads were so blocked, people were forced to stay in hotels for a couple of days before moving on. The Captain held little hope of seeing his family, and the demanding efforts for keeping the ship refurbished and moving were so daunting he had little time to leave the ship and travel to Poland, yet he expressed a constant upbeat smile.

The original plan was to be in Hamburg for eight days, but then a telex came in informing him that time in port was limited to five days to maintain the Rickmer's budget, now this. The Captain shook his head, dismayed.

"They tell me that they have crews lined up round the clock to load the ship," he said. "With the holidays it is unlikely, but what can I do?"

"Seeing is believing," Chance said, looking at the Captain who always seemed to joke about everything. Chance attempted to control the turmoil he suffered boiling behind his seemingly calm expression. After lunch, Chance jogged up the internal stairs to the bridge and looked down at the chart again and crossed his fingers. Maybe they would arrive in Hamburg before too long, although he had no notion of what his plan contained once dockside, except to look for the BiBi and attempt to sneak on board.

Chance returned to his cabin and tried to figure out what time it was in China near Shanghai. It had to be near another nine hours ahead. The captain posted signs to alert the crew about every time-zone change, and there had been plenty. The time difference from California was already nine hours ahead. It was surely safe to give Chang a call.

The same deliciously soft voice answered the phone in Shanghai.

"Can I speak to Chang?" Chance asked.

"Of course," she said, her voice drifting like feathers from a pillowcase.

"Chance," Chang said, "Can I help?"

"Do you think the big delivery will take place in Germany?" Chance said.

"I don't know," Chang said, "but it is likely either there or Italy. She will surely have some business in the Reeperbahn area. It's dangerous there, Chance. Many prostitutes, drugs, and strip joints. It was controlled by German gangsters at one time and even the Hells Angels ran some of the girls, but now it's run by the Russian mob. Watch yourself."

"Thanks," Chance said, and shut down the satellite phone. He developed a strange workout to keep his mind from a complete frustration overload. He couldn't stand his lack of control over this situation. He recognized that he had little power over life's card games, and no crap game had the significance of one minute without Ling Wu. His first mission after breakfast each morning was to perform several stretching exercises, followed by 100 sit-ups and some lower back exercises. Then he thought about his mission as he walked up and down the internal stairwell a half-dozen times. From there, he lifted weights, breaking up the weight routines into three categories, chest and triceps, back and biceps and shoulders.

As he took each step up the stairs, he quizzed himself about every diverse aspect of Ling's abduction. He wandered over each piece of evidence and each consideration for his next move. In some cases, he questioned his own motives and future moves to the point where he floundered in one quandary after another. He decided he had to buy into one scheme, perhaps awash with uncertainties, to find the ship and get Ling off it as fast as he could. He could only hope and pray, and he wasn't a religious man. The Leon would catch the Bibi and give him the opportunity to find her. He knew he was being forced to roll life and death dice. It was the extent of his programming distinction at this point. If confronted by the Chinese, he wasn't sure what would come next.

The Bibi entered the Elbe river and took on a pilot for the remaining six-hour cruise down the river for 100 kilometers to the myriad of islands and tributaries making up the massive Hamburg harbor complex. It did not compare to the size of the Rotterdam Harbor, perhaps the largest harbor in the world, but still it was vast and foreboding under cold gray winter skies threatening unceasing rain and snow over the two rivers, Alster and Elbe, forming the Hamburg basin.

Ling awoke with a terrible longing in the back of her throat. She had no notion of the time. She was cold, but she slept the entire night interspersed with dramatic dreams. She hadn't touched her food from the previous morning, although she was starving. She munched down the cold rice and drank the remaining tea just as she heard the hatch creak open and in walked the same Filipino with a smile of pitted, chipped and stained yellow teeth.

He bowed silently and set another bowl of rice down and another hot cup of tea. Ling began to eat the rice, but noticed her appetite waned. She sipped the hot tea, but noticed a distinctive mood change, and wondered if she was loosing her appetite because she was dying. Halfway through the hot cup of tea she felt the urge to just lie back and let whatever it was engulf her again. Something felt good and distracted her from her worries. She ate the rice lazily and lay on the stained oilcloth in a sense of unwanted tranquility.

She tried to shake the lingering effects of the motion of the ship, combined with a strange euphoria and sipped the hot cup of tea some more. Soon her eyes felt heavy and she laid back down against the icy steel deck and fell asleep again. As she slipped away into a colorful dream of her and Chance making love in a field of flowering poppies, the hatch opened again and two of Kim's soldiers ran into the near empty hold. They unlocked Ling's bulkhead chains and lifted her to her frozen feet. She tried to wake up, but something told her not to, and she didn't feel their arms around her.

They wrapped her in a blanket so it was easier to carry her long unconscious form through a number of hatches to a small room near the boilers at the stern, housing an emergency generator. Unlike the rest of the Japanese-built ship, this room housed an American gasoline engine to drive the generator in case there was an electrical power problem somewhere on the ship. The ship contained five diesel generators and only two were online at any given time. This unit would ignite itself within seven seconds of a power failure.

The room was small and self-contained, but warm. They placed her limp form on the diamond-plate, rough steel deck and lashed the chain around a support leg for the fuel tank and locked her down. The unforgiving deck was painted white. All the pipes running to the tanks and carrying wires to the control panels were painted silver, and the engine was painted pea green. An odd telephone booth was bolted to the control panel and housed two phones to the engine room and the bridge. One was battery-powered and the other a direct line in case of emergencies.

Ling rolled in the blanket and opened her eyes slightly. She could sense the relief from the cold but she didn't focus on her whereabouts. She pulled the blanket up tight to her and drifted into another sultry dream as the ship bumped against a dock in the Kohlfleet area of the port. The tugs maneuver the ship to its dock in front of countless buzzing cranes, idling forklifts, and warehouses. It was mid morning but still dark. During the month of December, Hamburg was faced with 13 days of rain, a high of 4 degrees Celsius and one hour of sunlight per day, yet the dock was crowded with contract union stevedores ready to unload the existing cargo and load the ship for its voyage to the orient and beyond.

Another day passed as the Leon steamed along the coast of France, Belgium and the Netherlands and into German waters. The following morning at 4:00 a.m., Chance woke and in the dark checked his watch. Rumor from the crew indicated they would pull into port by 6:00 a.m. and he wanted to be on deck to witness arrival. He dressed and raced up the stairs to the dark bridge. Shades were drawn around the chart table and the ship tossed again.

"A force 8 storm has hit us and we can't get a harbor pilot except by helicopter," the captain said. "I told them they are crazy. With these cranes, no pilot can board like that."

Chance looked at him in the darkness and his shoulders drooped. The bridge was too dark for visibility and Chance moved to the window and stared out as he jolted around in the violent seas. He returned to his cabin and sat in silence, unable to sleep until he heard an out of the ordinary sound against the hull. He darted out of his cabin and back to the bridge. In the tossing brutally cold seas at the mouth of the river, he saw brilliant spotlights aimed at the starboard side of the ship. A small but fast hydroplaning vessel pulled to the starboard side as the two vessels boxed, metal-to-metal in the North Sea. The pilot climbed on board and the craft pulled away immediately and disappeared in the tumultuous seas.

With respect, the Filipino crew members showed the pilot to the bridge, where he gave the Captain instructions. They were being followed by a number of ships also trying to find pilots and escape the revenge of the North Sea and enter the smooth port. They began to motor into the mouth of the Elbe River. In the darkness little was visible, except small lights along the jagged coastline and navigational markers. Chance stood in the shadows, out of the way of the crew. One Filipino stood at the small wheel of the ship. When the pilot called for a heading change, the Captain relayed it to the helmsman, who turned the wheel and studied the compass.

"Two degrees to port," the elderly pilot ordered.

"Two degrees to port," the Captain agreed.

"Two degrees to port, aye," the Filipino helmsman confirmed.

Another Filipino mate manned the charts and made notes as to their headings and locations. Many of the Filipino crew were educated and working their way up the ranks. Chance noted on a couple of occasions some Filipino crewmembers knew more than the Polish officers about one aspect of the ship or another. Even the steward, Clement, graduated from seaman's training and was enduring his first leg of job experience as a steward.

Chance stood in the shadows of the bridge for three hours and twenty minutes until another pilot replaced the current one, where a river from the Baltic Sea intersected with the Elbe. The German pilot with a mass of salt-and-pepper hair wearing a suit and tie and smoking a pipe crawled up the ladder from his vessel onto the side of the greasy ship and came on board. The seas in the river calmed immensely and transporting pilots became a much less treacherous feat. The pilot remained onboard for another two and a half hours, then a Hamburg Harbor pilot replaced him. At each juncture, there was the threat that no pilots were available and Chance cringed at the smallest time delay.

Chance returned to his cabin and tried unsuccessfully to sleep, revisited the bridge and watched intently as the ship motored into Hamburg. Referring to the chart, he became distraught as Tomas, the stout Filipino 3rd officer, pulled the Hamburg Harbor chart out of the drawer. The harbor, a maze of inlets and adjoining rivers and the town, contained a web of canals and lakes. As light replaced the darkness, rain began to fall, switching to snow as the ship slowed to 7 knots.

The chart indicated from the Elbe River to the starboard or right, was first the KIohlfleet inlet leading to a series of container docks. Along the Elbe were a number of dry docks and ships in repair or building progress. One ship was completely covered with scaffolding and netting to keep the warmth in and the rain out. The first inlet was followed by another called Parkhafen, then the Kohlbrand and Suderebe were the third and largest leading to a dozen more hafens or channels. It was followed by a narrow canal called Kohlenschiffhafen, and finally the Leon turned down the following inlet, the Vorhafen, which itself contained six smaller inlets. Beyond were 18 or more port alleys running to any number of docks far and beyond what the chart depicted. Chance looked out the bridge portholes at the snow blowing sideways across the deck and wondered how anything was accomplished without a tent and how he could find the BiBi in this maze.

Once turning down the lane wide enough for two ships to cross paths, they passed inlets Kuhwerhafen and Kaishafen off to the port, followed by Rosshafen. They followed past Oderhafen where the tugs docked. The pilot and the Captain masterfully parallel parked the ship between two other freighters and the Stlanerkai docks in Wilhemsburg.

Chance gazed at the crew of stevedores on the dock, then out at the grizzly harbor. I the cold, he shivered at the thought of another stinking port looking for his girl, this one a daunting maze of inlets and docks spread far and wide.

"I will get you contact with port agent," the Captain said as if he detected Chance's disappointment. Chance just nodded looking out at the colorless surroundings and shrugged his shoulders. He returned to his cabin with the port agent's number and called him for a cab service number. He couldn't ride his motorcycle in zero degrees Celsius in rain and snow, and he would be lucky if he could find his way back to the ship once he left it, but he would try with all his heart.

# -16-

# THE COLD STREETS
# OF HAMBURG

The BiBi swayed gently at the dock under a gray, rainy sky while the holiday stevedores unloaded several crates and forklifts and hustled the cargo from the deck into the nearby, corrugated steel warehouse.

Kim rose in the most lavish cabin on the ship and stretched. She performed several Tai Chi exercises, then showered. Her body was shapely and she ran her hands over her slender form with oil and caressed her nipples. She was horny, and relentless. The man who followed disrupted her mission and put her vast future in jeopardy. As she touched herself, she thought of Ling's smile and wanted her, but the pursuing Anglo biker disturbed her sensual image. She considered turning Ling over to him, but it posed problems. It would jeopardize the conflict in Shanghai, plus she wanted Ling for herself.

She dried herself and laid back on the bed, the oil soaking into her pores. She pressed her delicious breasts together and ran her oiled hands up the ample curves to her nipples. As she touched them, then squeezed each one with her thumbs and forefingers, her mood heightened. She rocked her pelvis until her mound reached for stimulus, then her nipples hardened and she arched her back. Taking in a sharp breath, she imagined her hands running over Ling's tits and down her soft tummy over flesh so gentle it brought tears to her eyes.

Unexpectedly, the vision of the man chasing her in Savannah streamed through her consciousness. She jerked, her body responding to her touch and her mind scrambled. She didn't know whether to scream or cum. Then a sharp knock on her cabin door interrupted her fantasy.

"Kim," Chee shouted, "We must go!"

"Five minutes," Kim said, breathing heavily as reality intruded into her sexual imagination. She spun and sat up with her feet over the side of the bed. She removed her hand from between her legs with a sigh of shame and disappointment. She heard the click of Chee's heels as he marched away.

Five minutes later, Kim stood on the main deck with one of her soldiers respectfully besides her, shielding her from the gray drizzle.

"We will depart in a day and a half," Chee reported. "I have spoken to the Rickmers' agent and he says we are loading a mere 5,000 pounds of cargo, then we must sail to Antwerp, Belgium."

"How long until we arrive in Genoa?" Kim asked.

"Two weeks, but we have our mission today."

Chee knew the Bentley in one of the holds was a direct pat on the back for Kim if handled properly. Her plan was to take it to the Mafia leaders in Italy and make a deal to supply them with opium for the United States. Generally, the mob stayed away from heroin and dealt mostly with cocaine from South America, but she felt confident that with the right infrastructure in place, the Wong family could supply a never-ending quantity of opium to the U.S. through Italy. She wanted a distributor between her and the States and the blessing of the crime lords who knew the business all too well.

She turned to Chee, who was carrying a closely guarded briefcase at his side.

"A day and a half?" she asked. "We need to accomplish another task, and make absolutely sure that no one can get on this ship."

"No one can get close," he said, pointing out several soldiers posted near the gangplank and one in the warehouse. "What are you thinking?"

"Let's get in the cab," Kim said, as a Mercedes pulled up to the ship.

They walked down the gangplank and Chee opened the door for Kim as the rain pelted down around them. One soldier got in the front passenger side and Chee sat beside her in the back. The cab pulled away and around the myriad of tall cranes, forklifts, and stacks of crates and cargo containers waiting to be loaded under the dark gray sky. The smell on the dock was one of oil and machinery.

Chance scrambled off the ship to the waiting Mercedes cab. Every cab in Hamburg was a creamy yellow Mercedes. The reliability of the Mercedes caused them to outlast several other makes.

"Where you going?" the middle-aged cabby asked through a bristling salt and pepper mustache.

"I'm not sure," Chance said. "We need to find a ship called the Bibi."

"Why do you need another ship?" the cabby asked with a curious smile.

"I need to find a girl," Chance said.

"I take you to Reeperbahn for girls," the cabby said, referring to the local red light district.

Chance rubbed his scraggly beard with the palm of one hand and thought about the dirty Reeperbahn district and how it might assist with his plight.

"No, we must find the ship first," he said, pulling a slip of paper out of his vest.

He called the German ship's agent Gunther Souhr, who had access to the location of every ship in the harbor. He gave Chance the location and basic directions. He handed the slip of paper to the cab driver.

"Please hurry," Chance said.

The driver drove out of the gate at the Oderhafen docks and up to the new space age-looking Kohlbrand Bridge winding over a large section of the harbor to the intersection of the Elbe tunnel expressway and across it to Finkenweider Strasse. Rain pattered steadily as he sat behind the driver on the opposite side of the car. With each mile, he became more nervous, more anxious and more fearful.

Chance looked around at the refineries, the stacks of containers and the cement buildings, devoid of any sign of life except the occasional truck lingering along the industrial asphalt roads. No color existed in the area except the blood red rust hue of some containers. A small dusting of snow remained on the ground. No plant life survived the harsh winter, no trees, and if a tree did appear, it was a dark skeleton of its former self. The sky was as gray as the hull of a war ship, as the taxi rounded a bend and another cab approached from the opposite direction.

Chance turned to see another Mercedes, and as it passed, the two drivers recognized each other, slowed and waved. Chance looked past the driver and saw an evil looking Chinese man wearing all black sitting next to him. There was a woman in the back also, but he didn't recognize who it was in the mist and couldn't trust his instincts since Savannah. The car continued, and Chance turned around in his seat to see if it stopped. It didn't, and Chance sighed, knowing he was on the right road to the Bibi and Ling.

His cab rounded the bend to the Dradenauhafen on Amsterdamer Kai and Chance saw the Bibi's cranes above the tin warehouse. There were two tall Buzz cranes alongside the ship.

"Pull up here," Chance said.

"You don't want me to take you to gangplank?" the driver asked.

"I want to surprise someone," Chance said. " Can you wait for me? I'll be 15-20 minutes."

"Ja, I be here," the driver said.

Outside the cab, the weather was raw and icy. Chance tightened his vest over his thick flannel shirt and rounded the corner of the galvanized warehouse as snow flurries blew across the yard. He walked through the warehouse full of crates bound for China and Singapore. He discovered an unused hard hat, picked it up and adjusted the grimy, inside lip to fit his head, then shoved his thick mane of hair under it and pressed the helmet down to partially cover his face.

The rest of the crew were wearing fluorescent overalls and jackets with reflective strips sewn around the arms and legs. He looked around desperately for a loose jacket but in the numbing cold, there were none available. As he was crossing through the warehouse, he spotted a small Chinese soldier dressed in black crouched down next to a bail of 4-by-4s used to support large equipment when lowered onto the hatches of the freighters, so cables could be run underneath for lifting.

Chance turned away from the soldier and jogged back behind the warehouse. He also wasn't wearing work boots, but running shoes. Behind the warehouse, he was caught in the blowing snow. He jogged between container trucks and mammoth forklifts hauling containers around to the ships. He reached the far end of the building closest to the end of the dock and peered around the corner. There were workers everywhere standing next to bins of steel cables and pallets of shipping straps a foot wide.

He had to get to the ship. He knew port security was lax but not Kim's men, and his meager disguise wouldn't cut it. He walked around the front of the building and inside again, but this time at the opposite end from where the Chinese gangster was hiding. He ducked inside and found the changing room for the stevedores. Since it wasn't break time or lunch, no one was inside.

Chance slipped around crates and found the sinks. Digging through the trash, he found a discarded razor, washed he face and shaved, leaving his bushy mustache intact. With his own sharp knife, he cut off his mane of thick hair and threw it in the trash. The floor was grease-stained, the line of sinks covered with grime, and the mirror hazed with fingerprints. He splashed water in his face to ease the sting of the dull razor. He looked in his green eyes and took a deep breath.

"Let's go for it, pal. You know she's there," he said to himself.

He discovered a fluorescent striped parka, donned it, walked straight out of the warehouse across several tracks guiding massive cranes and onto a grubby gangplank made of cast-aluminum steps shaped like scoops working as foot pads at almost any angle. The old, worn steps were welded and re-welded. The snow blew hard against the ship's superstructure and the Chinese tried to wrap themselves with their jackets and cover their faces dripping with snow and freezing rain.

Stevedores walked in all directions, carrying clips for locking containers together and moving 4-by-4s for the next cargo to be lifted onto the ship. The cranes bleeped and rolled, swinging 100-foot booms from the dock to the ship. Three cranes worked at the same time on one ship. Chance made it to the top of the gang plank and stepped onto the deck face-to-face with a Filipino seaman.

"Captain?" Chance asked.

"Deck E," the seaman said and raised his finger and a clipboard as if to ask him something more when Chance took two steps across the narrow passageway through an aluminum doorway to the interior of the ship, as if he knew the drill. He followed the horseshoe floor plan of the ship's superstructure, the same as the Leon. He scrambled up the upper deck dual ladders to the A deck housing the crew's lounge and dining area, the officers' lounge and dinning area, and the main galley with the steward's mess. He punched into the door to the stairway and found it very similar to the Leon.

He heard someone below him say, "Excuse me, sir." He ran up iron stairs to B deck that was the home of the Bosun, the 2nd cook, Handyman and stewards B, C, and D. He busted through the door and followed the deck around opening every steel cabin door and peering inside. Each room was different in many ways and similar in that each cabin had a small rug piled high with filthy shoes. They all reeked with the smell of crude oil, diesel and gasoline fumes, mixed with cheap aftershave. Chance returned to the inner stairway, but heard footsteps inside.

He rushed to the exterior stairs at the end of the passageway and outside ran up another flight to the C deck that housed three cadets, the cook, the head Steward, the third officer, and the 3rd and 4th engineers. He burst in the aluminum porthole door and started checking the doors. As he rounded the corner and passed the stairway door, it exploded open. A Filipino crewman was shoved aside by two Chinese henchmen. Chance turned and slammed the door in their faces, throwing the men back into the stairway.

He ran for the exterior stairs and clamored up to the officers' and Chief Engineer's deck. Bursting inside the door he shouted, "Ling, Ling, where are you, baby?"

He tried the first door to no avail as he heard the men below him struggling up the ladders inside and out. Chance opened the next door, but it led to the officers' laundry room. He slammed the door and grabbed for the next one. As it opened, one of the Chinese came in the stern outside door behind him.

"Halt!" he shouted as Chance opened the door.

Chance yanked on the door and leaped into the room. She was there, he could smell her fragrance. Diving in, he could see women's clothes strewn around the room. It was a small room but she had been here. He stopped dead in his tracks almost hugging her mentally, but she wasn't visible. Where was she?

He jerked opened the cabin door deliberately to face a Chinese man with a limp and a fresh scar on his face. Chance gnashed his teeth; he was livid. The limping man was pointing an automatic pistol directly at Chance's face. Chance raised his hands in mock retreat, stepped towards the gun, and drove the man's wrist against the door jam, yanking the gun from his fingers and breaking the man's thumb. He pulled the man into Ling's room, cold-cocked him with the gun butt, and closed the door. Looking both ways, he had little time to guess which way to run.

"Ling," he shouted, "where are you?" He heard the others coming from the outside, so he stepped into the inside stairwell and slid down the banister to C deck, grabbed the next banister and slid to B deck and finally to A deck, where he burst through the passageway to the dual stairs leading to the main deck. He found his way to the porthole door exit.

He glanced out the hatch as he heard the other Chinese soldiers scrambling down the stairwell. The tall dozen steps to each floor could be jumped and slid through in less than a minute from the bridge. He spotted two longshoremen heading to the gangplank and stepped out onto the main deck, following them down the gangplank. As the Chinese security reached the A deck, he yanked his walkie-talkie and called the guard in the warehouse.

Chance was steaming. He knew Ling was there, somewhere, or with Kim, or was Kim in the taxi he passed? He was sick and tired of this bullshit and pissed at his run of bad hands. When the long-shoremen turned to head away from the docks for their lunch, Chance turned left around the back of a massive crate the size of a motor home. He moved across the back as the chill of the bitter weather caught up with him. He saw the young Chinese guard move into the open and in his direction. Chance knew there were strict laws against weapons in Germany and to brandish or fire one would bring substantial heat on the ship. From his conversation with Chang, he doubted they had much desire for heat. The next weapon of choice would be a quiet blade.

Chance gritted his teeth in rage, spun in the snow and walked around the wooden crate with the Hong Kong destination stamped on it, directly toward the Chinese soldier. The man was in full view standing at the entrance to the building in an opening as large as two 18-wheelers. He looked to be the size of a warehouse rat in the frame, the amber glow of lights behind him contrasting the stark grayness of the outside with flakes of snow blowing across the concrete dock. He looked out of place surrounded by big Anglo men, wearing thick flannel clothes covered with fluorescent red uniforms smeared with grease and grime and wearing orange safety helmets.

An occasional sideways glance told onlookers that they knew his purpose, and they had little respect for his kind. Chance walked straight at the Chinaman, his eyes fixed on the slant of the man's gaze. He was young and his face was suddenly filled with questions and doubt. There was no one around he could rely on, no one to call.

The Chinaman coming at him from the ship was stout and mad as a horse being broken for the first time. One longshoreman saw Chance march toward the small Asian in the doorway and nudged his partner.

Another stevedore, a crane operator, spotted the show down and stopped his crane to see what was going to happen. Chance knew the man was armed to the teeth and he had to get within close quarters to be effective. He reached in his back pocket and pulled his 4-inch locking blade Elisewitz knife and flicked it open with a teeth-jarring snap. The Chinaman looked to the ship for support but couldn't see his partner. As Chance closed the distance he turned and ran to the glee of the men on the docks, who saluted Chance as he continued through the warehouse out the other side and slipped into the waiting taxi.

"Reeperbahn, quick," Chance said, and the car spun in a circle and sped away.

Kim's taxi sped along Finkenwerder Strasse to Waltershofer and caught the autobahn into the Elbe River tunnel to Stresemann and off at Holsten, then back toward the Elbe River and the underground area of Reeperbahn. Over 72 percent of Hamburg was destroyed during WWII, yet the historic presence seemed everywhere as Kim's taxi pushed along streets with businesses dating back to the 1640s.

Kim rolled into Reeperbahn, the adult playground of sex shows, adult video arcades, X-rated sex shops and brothels, and a rich assortment of pubs. Kim turned off Konig Blvd onto David, and passed several young whores working the streets. Some stood in the sidewalks and grabbed at each man who passed; others had one-room bedrooms down long weaving halls on various floors in a single building. They sat on barstools in the doorway, hawking their shapely wares in the narrow halls. The elite had windows on Herbert Strasse, a short block, walled off from the public with gates denying entry to kids below 18 and women.

Kim's cab pulled up to an Irish pub on the corner of Herbert Strasse and she got out with her entourage. She looked at the women on the corner as they approached her security force. Kim was dressed to the nines in tight black pants and a black cashmere sweater, over which was a fine black wool, double-breasted overcoat. Around her neck was a single strand of pearls and she wore black lambskin gloves. Within seconds of her departure from the car, three Russian men came out from the windowed brothel street. They nodded congenially and asked Kim and her group to follow them, leading her down a narrow cobblestone street.

Each stone house contained curtain-less bay windows and pink interiors. Some had candles burning next to chairs. Each girl had on a different outfit, which amounted to very little. Kim eyed each whore seductively while her men watched every move the Russians made. They knew of Kim's preference. Some of the girls were disturbed by a woman's attention, but most flirted with her, some opening their windows slightly and asking to talk to Kim.

Kim walked the length of the street and returned down the other side, checking out each girl and talking to some. One in particular she approached. She was tall and shapely with long dark curly hair and soft make-up unlike most of the over-made-up girls. She was thin and tender looking, and her skin looked angelic through the window. As Kim walked up, she opened her window to the brisk cold.

"Girls aren't allowed in here," she said. "You must be very special."

Kim reached in the window and put her hand on the girl's knee, running her hand over her delicate skin and pushing her legs open.

"I have a certain edge," Kim said as she ran her hand up the girl's inner thigh. "Would you like to make love to me?"

"I would love to," the girl said sliding forward in her chair slightly so that Kim's fingertips could reach her.

Kim touched her through a satin bottom and felt the warmth surround her fingertips. She looked up at the girl and said, "I'll see you shortly. What's your name?"

"Tina," she said and ran her tongue seductively over her lips. "I'll be waiting."

Kim spun to the others. "Let's take care of business. There's fun to be had."

Chee didn't like it. "We have business here," he whispered to Kim glaring.

The Russians led them into one of the stone buildings past some more window girls.

"We'll have Tina come up after we're finished," the lead Russian said to Kim. "You'll have lot's of fun with her."

Slolaf, the blond leader, emigrated from Russia the day the iron curtain set him free. He was 5'11" and stocky, a bully from Leningrad, who knew once the political climate changed, his ability to bully and supply his world with black market products would slip away. He moved to gangster riddled Hamburg to play in a bigger league.

Chance pulled his satellite phone from his inside vest pocket as his cab rumbled along the Konig road toward Reeperbahn. As he looked out at the freezing rain and gray skies, he called his house in San Pedro. "Hello?" Kate said. Her voice was soft and distant, since it was just 3:00 a.m. in California.

"I need some help," Chance said.

"Do you know what time it is?" Kate asked as she came around.

"It's a nine-hour difference," Chance said hurriedly, "but I need the number to Little Joe in Berdoo. It's in my Rolodex."

"Okay, hold on," Kate said, and sat up in Chance's bed. She was wearing thong panties and one of Chance's XL t-shirts that was a perfect nightshirt over her lithe form. She stretched, jogged to his office and flipped through his Rolodex for the number.

"It's 919-822-8181. Anything else?"

"Nope, that's it for now," Chance said. "I'll check in later. I was on the ship, but couldn't find her. I know who's behind this shit and I'm going to kick some ass."

"Be careful," Kate said. "This could get dicey and you could lose her. We're discovering a lot about the opium trade and who is running what. There are some tough organizations getting involved."

"I'll roll the dice," Chance said, wishing he hadn't gone down that path with Kate. But he realized that what she said could be smacking the nail on the head.

"See ya."

He ended the call and dialed Lil' Joe, a member of the Hells Angels for over 30 years. Joe was a tough little bastard with arms as big as tree trunks. He had a mind for business and developed one of the first club product lines. He worked out constantly and got more buffed the older he became. The phone rang several times before Joe picked up.

"Yeah, what the fuck is it?" Joe said.

"Joe, it's Chance."

"You still looking for that broad?" Joe said.

"Yeah," Chance replied getting Joe's inference. "I'm in Hamburg and need a hand. I need an address in Reeperbahn for a Russian gang of drug dealers. I can't explain. I just need an address."

"I'm not sure I can help," Joe said tentatively. "I'll need 15 minutes. Sure you don't need a whore there? I can help you with that."

"Yeah, I know," Chance said, thinking about the offer. "Just the street number this time."

The phone went dead as the cab reached the dingy outskirts of the Reeperbahn. Chance noticed that although it had rained all day and would rain for half the days in December, the water still ran dirty brown in the streets.

The area was beyond seedy and Chance wondered why areas that dealt with sex had to look so bad when they're involved with one of the most beautiful and endearing aspects of life.

The car slowed as the traffic increased to bumper-to-bumper in the town of 1.7 million. The area filled with young people bouncing from bar to seedy bar, while prostitutes plied their trade on every corner. They rolled passed the Doll House, sex shops and men in front of strip joints trying to cajole customers inside.

Chance's phone rang and he checked the signal strength to California. He didn't want to lose this call.

"Yeah," Chance said.

"It's Joe. Here's the address." Joe said and gave Chance a number on Herbert Strasse. "It's upstairs, and you better be careful.

Chance thanked him and hung up. He handed the piece of paper to the cab driver.

"That's where tough guys go," the driver said.

Kim and her two men were led into a large room two stories above the prostitutes, in a building over a hundred years old. The room wasn't special, lined with bricks and mortar. A dark, scratched wooden conference table sat in the middle of the room and several sleek Swedish wooden chairs bordered the thick oak table. On the table were three telephones and in the corner was a small metal stand with a fax machine perched on it. Nearby, a small metal-mesh trashcan overflowed with crumpled paper. One 4-foot fluorescent bulb hung over the conference table; otherwise, the room was shadowed in darkness.

Slolaf and two men offered them chairs and drinks. Kim placed her briefcase on the table, opened it and turned it to face Slolaf.

"Test it," Kim said, removing her overcoat and catching the gaze of every man in the room. She was a knockout in her shape-enhancing outfit. Her men did not sit but moved to the perimeter of the room in the shadows and watched.

By the turn of the century, the habit-forming properties of opium were well known. In an effort to eliminate the addictiveness of morphine, German pharmacists tinkered with its molecular structure. They invented a derivative called diacetylmorphine. The Bayer Company named it heroin and marketed it as less addicting and a less toxic alternative.

Heroin turned out to be 2 to 3 times more potent than morphine. It was, in fact, an already-metabolized version of morphine, so it had a more direct route to the brain than morphine itself. By the late 1920s, heroin was the most widely abused opiate.

The rush is often described as a heightened sexual orgasm and a great relief of tension, which pervades the abdomen. After the rush, the high lasts for four or five hours and is caused by the morphine diffusing from the bloodstream into the brain. It is described as a warm, drowsy, cozy state. Users report a profound sense of satisfaction, as though all needs were fulfilled. There was also a pleasant state of mild dizziness. It was not as impairing as alcohol's effects and included a sense of distancing or apathy toward whatever was going on in the environment

Slolaf indicated for one of his men to analyze it. The man was white as a ghost and gaunt looking. He pulled a Marquis test kit out of his tattered jacket. It contained a couple of swabs and a vial. He dipped the swab tip into the pure white powder and placed the swab in the vial with a moist pad. It turned immediately a brilliant purple, indicating heroin. If it had turned orange to brown the substance was amphetamine, and gray, OxyContin. His mood was nervous and edgy. He pulled out an odd shaped pipe and sprinkled some of the soft white power in it and stepped to the corner of the room, where he lit it and drew on the pipe like it would be his last breath. He winced like he had walked into a freezer and was immersed with cold, then his eyes rolled back and he leaned against the brick wall and began to gradually slip to the floor.

"Why do you bring this to me?" Slolaf asked in a dry business like tone. "You know that I get my opium from Afghanistan, don't you? Most of the organizations on the earth get it from there and Turkey. Why are you coming to me?"

"Poppies can grow anywhere," Kim said, "but distribution is the key. I have set up a distribution network that works flawlessly."

"Seeing is believing," Slolaf said, and looked at his comrade in the corner. "It seems to be very good product."

"You give me a chance to deliver and the content of this case is yours," Kim said. "The street value of it would be substantial."

"I know what it would be," Slolaf said and closed the case. "Thank you. I will think about it." He picked up the phone and spoke Russian in the receiver.

In just a few seconds, there was a tap on the door and Tina walked in.

"Here's a little something for you," Slolaf said and got to his feet. Tina unfolded a thick down-filled quilt, spread it onto the conference table, peeled out of her bikini and crawled up onto the table naked.

"Let me leave you alone," Slolaf said. "Would you allow me to take care of your men?"

Kim nodded, staring at Tina's soft ass and the way her back arched over the soft fluffy cloud like blanket. Her tits hung down and were shaped beautifully, like perfect waves to a surfer. The light above cascaded over her and the rest of the room faded into the background. Kim's eyes feasted on every inch of the girl, but a noise from somewhere far below interrupted the spell.

Chance looked at the girls in the windows, and with each one he was more terrified and concerned about Ling's whereabouts. The gray skies and dark streets added to the filthy look of the cobblestone path. Nothing was clean except the skin of the girls inside. He studied each business, looking for a number, a sign, anything, until he saw a tall lanky girl get up from her seat. She looked at him momentarily, the glint of a grin crossing her mouth. She had a slight resemblance to Ling, except Ling was tighter, in better shape and her tits were larger and firmer.

Chance melted at the thought of Ling as Tina turned to the doorway behind her. Chance spotted a hard-looking man in a black overcoat with black shirt and slacks. A shoulder holster was visible for a second as he turned away. Chance studied the building and finally found the address engraved in a stone next to the door. There was no lettering in color, no light, no nothing.

Enraged at the thought that Ling might be inside, drugged, or forced into prostitution, shot through him like an electrical circuit.

The other girls on the narrow street looked at the big biker. Girls opened their small windows and whispered to him to come to them. They jiggled their breasts and drove Chance over the edge.

He found and stormed the door. The two prostitutes who shared the long window with Tina, two doors down, screamed and Chance pulled his Walther PPK. He burst through the old wooden door and faced a simple iron, narrow stairway. With girls screaming around him he ran for it, jumped on the first rung and started to run up as fast as he could. A Russian guard below him ran under the stairs and pulled his weapon, firing up at the circular stairway.

The bullets glanced off the metal stairs and ricocheted off the adjoining brick wall. All hell broke lose.

Kim ran one hand along the girl's soft back and over her ass. She could smell the nakedness and felt the satin touch like the softness of a rose petal. Tina turned and smiled at her as Kim leaned close to kiss her when two men burst into the room with Chee and his assistant.

"No fun, we must go," Chee snapped, reaching for the briefcase, which Slolaf grabbed.

"A deal is a deal," he said. "You brought trouble. I have no trouble here."

Kim's face turned crimson as she faced another Russian guard who opened another door and they dashed out the back.

Chance flew up the stairs, his lungs crying for oxygen as he struggled to reach the top. The Russian below him fired again and Chance leaned over the edge and double-tapped him between the eyes. The man collapsed like a dishrag.

Chance burst into the conference room, but there was no one there except Tina rolled in her blanket, naked and trembling.

The room was empty. He ran out the back door and down the wooden steps behind the building as fast as he could. He saw a black Mercedes limousine peel out of the alley and down the street, disappearing into the neon filth of the Reeperbahn. He heard the European pulsing wail of sirens and ran down a dirty alley until he reached the street. It was crowded with cabs. He jumped into the first one he could flag down and headed back to his ship.

# -17-

# ESCAPING GERMANY

The Mercedes taxi spun off the main thoroughfare to the Leon, in the dark and bitter cold. Chance looked down toward the tin warehouse and he could see the super structure of the Leon lit and the six cranes beyond. Everything had a thin layer of snow on it. It held the icy greeting of something evil or foreboding. As the cab turned, Chance looked down at the water and a couple of thin, leafless trees attempting to stay alive in the bitterness alongside the oily river. They were bleak omens to a warrior's rough day.

"Slow down," Chance said as they neared the gate.

"Let me out here. Stay out here for 15 minutes. Keep the motor running. If I come back, we'll need to get the hell out of here. If I'm not back in 15, have a happy holiday."

"Sure, sure," the cab driver said and pulled over.

"Do me a favor," Chance, said getting out of the cab and putting his rough deerskin riding gloves back on. "Turn this thing around, so we can move."

"I do it," the cab driver said.

Chance closed the door of the cab and jogged along the slippery frozen street to the chain link fence leading into the dock area. He slowed as he neared the gate guarded by uniformed customs agents. There was a small phone booth on the outside of the gated area and an undersized 500 square foot office. The guard shack was cleverly positioned in the center of the five lanes of traffic entering and leaving the dock. It rested on a concrete island, like a tollbooth prior to a bridge, with large windows on both sides and the front. Above each lane was a fluorescent bank of lights over the vehicles in line, like the roofs over truck fueling stations.

As Chance rounded the edge of a stack of steel containers, he spotted a dark Mercedes limousine backed into the corner. He eyed the area carefully and spotted two young men dressed in long woolen black overcoats heading for a lighted phone booth. Through this gate was his only path to his ship and he couldn't cross it without being seen by either the gang members or the guard. He couldn't return to the ship and he stumbled back around the container. He pulled his vest tight around his chest over the thick flannel and long underwear. It was only a degree or two above freezing and he was desperate. What in the world could he do if he couldn't get back to his ship?

As he pondered his next move, he heard something move on or near the container, like someone tapping on the other side of a wall he leaned against. The sound was hollow and difficult to source. He spun and faced the frozen surface with small patches of snow caught in the slits and curves of the dented, 40-feet long steel box.

He heard another clink and looked up as a man jumped off the top of the container directly on top of Chance. The two men collided and collapsed to the greasy gravel surface adjacent to the asphalt lane. The impact against the dirt knocked the wind out of Chance and the limber bodyguard jumped to his feet and kicked Chance in the gut with a polished steel-toed lace-up boot. Chance rolled and grabbed a handful of gravel. The dirt, snow and grime stuck to him everywhere. He threw the slush at the face of the Russian.

This tall gangster had the unique opportunity to show his boss Slolaf that he was a man and could take care of business. He could destroy the individual, who they suspected killed one of his comrades and show his brothers how tough he was. He escaped Russia and found his way south on a rattling stores truck to Hamburg. He had no trade skills and there was little he could do, but he was big, and his contact for a fresh ID was the Russian mob. He was over 6 feet and weighed 230 pounds, but it wasn't muscle. He was fat but looked big.

His father and mother both worked in a factory assembling car generators, lumbering, boring work with no skills involved. His parents were simple and glad that they had jobs and were not being tortured. War terrified them and they kept their heads low and never missed a day at work. Being from Europe they had the knowledge of the dreadful outcome of several races including Armenians and their own, at the hands of Stalin. Their advice to their son, Krieger, was to go to school until he could get a good factory job and stay out of trouble with the authorities, a simple, but unfulfilling motto.

Krieger, in communist Russia, lived an undemanding life in a snow covered Russian berg, but little samples of the west filtered in. Television carefully monitored, yet pieces of magazines and videos slipped into his humble community through the underground and black market. To youngsters, the sight of something with bright colors and pretty girls dancing gleefully was a gift from heaven and drove them crazy with ambition and desire. Krieger had to get out.

Slolaf, from the Russian mob in Hamburg, looked him up and down, the first day they met. "Can you fight?"

"Yeah, sure," Krieger, said looking at the other gang members in the room. They looked hard and emotionless except for one who grimaced slightly and looked at the musty floor of the back room behind a whorehouse. He was used to bring in supplies and make fake IDs, not fight. Violence scared him.

"Are you sure?" Slolaf asked, looking at Krieger's baby faced features. He was young, mid 20s and still had no beard to speak of. His skin was milky soft with blushing red fatty cheeks. Slolaf had a test, and although he didn't feel like implementing much that morning, he looked at Krieger through his bright, unquestioning eyes and waited for a response.

"Ah, sure," Krieger said and Slolaf hit him in the nose with the power of a jackhammer, breaking the cartilage immediately and plastering his nose to the side of his face. Blood spurted over his clean lips and chin. Krieger stumbled back, losing his balance and falling into several boxes of copier and fax paper. The rest of the Russian crew flinched. Each one of them endured a similar test.

"Well," Slolaf said, "let's fight." He put his leather- gloved hand at his side as Krieger attempted to get to his feet. His whole face hurt. He felt dizzy and stunned and wondered what to do, then charged, tackling Slolaf and knocking the wind out of him. They both went to the floor of the dusty room. Little puffs of filth and grit sprung up around Slolaf's back as he hit the wood floor. Slolaf pulled his knees to his chest as he fell and, although his gut hurt as if he had been punched, he used his strong legs to push Krieger off, then jumped to his feet. Two of his other men ran to his side and attempted to dust him off as he went after Krieger, whose nose still bled profusely down his only shirt. Slolaf reached in his overcoat and withdrew a semi-automatic 45.

Slolaf's men stopped him and his unrelenting anger and aggression. "He's good," one of his men said.

"I should kill him," Slolaf said, salivating and grinding his teeth simultaneously.

"It's your test," another guard said. "He answered it."

"He cannot fight," Slolaf spat, staring relentlessly at Krieger lying in the dust on his back.

"He tried," the guard on the other side said, "isn't that what you want?"

Slolaf wanted an aggressive response. That was his reasoning for the violent test, at least that's what he told his men. Actually, he loved to strike another man. He loved a good fight, and if he had the opportunity to pull his straight edged killing knife, it turned him on. He had little use for women.

Krieger yanked a semi-auto 45 from inside his overcoat as he attempted to dodge the debris Chance threw at him. Chance saw him reach in the overcoat and crawled quickly, like a spider on the ground towards the big man, but his bruised ribs and guts screamed in pain. He had been taught on numerous occasions to be aggressive if a man reaches for a weapon. It was an opportunity to get close before he could take aim. He moved another yard forward and kicked Krieger in the knee with his running shoe. Krieger was like a tall building taking a hit. He buckled and grimaced.

A groan passed his lips under the scared and damaged nose making him look tough. He tried to take aim with the gun but Chance rolled again toward Krieger and kicked again at the knee. Krieger went down. Chance leaped to his feet although he was still rocky from the original 200-pound hit and his legs wobbled. As Krieger fell, he reached out with his gun hand to block his fall.

Chance snatched the weapon by grabbing the barrel and turning it, twisting it in his hand tearing at his fingers. Krieger released the weapon easily, then groaning in pain, blocked his fall, rolled, and grabbed his right knee.

Chance stepped up to his side quickly and smacked him in the temple with the butt of the automatic. Chance stood and stuffed the weapon in his waistband and grabbed Krieger's shiny black boots, pulled him into the alley next to the asphalt street and spun to run back to the cab.

As he approached, the driver spotted him coming covered in gravel and dirt and packing a rather large weapon in his waist. The small man jumped from the driver's seat and ran to the trunk of his Taxi. He opened it and pulled out a rough brush.

"Don't get in," he said and clamored around Chance, quickly dusting him off.

"We've got to get the hell out of here," Chance said.

"I know, I know, but I just had my car cleaned," the driver said, running around Chance and sweeping him madly. When he got to the front, he grabbed the weapon, and Chance caught him as he attempted to pull it from his waistband. Their eyes met as Chance immediately shifted the driver to a different dangerous category. He jumped from a friendly, helpful, and concerned German cabby to one of the enemy in less that a second. Chance spun to release the man's grip and put the weapon to use.

"Please," the driver said, releasing his small grip. "I just put in trunk."

Chance looked at his small hazel eyes with clear whites surrounding the pupils. He had no time for a quiz, but he realized that the man was trying to prevent him from getting into more trouble. He had to make a decision, a judgment call that could risk his life or keep him out of jail. He looked at the little man's face. He was in his 50s and wrinkles had begun to take their toll on his features, but his countenance was basically good and the wrinkles were of smiles, not dour frowns. He pulled the pistol out of his waistband and dropped it into the trunk with a deep thump. The driver tossed his brush inside and closed the trunk. He quickly opened the door for Chance and they got into the warm running Mercedes and sped away.

"What the hell do I do?" Chance said. "I can't get on the ship."

"Where is the ship going next?" the driver asked.

"Somewhere in Belgium," Chance said.

"There are three major ports there," the driver said, "There's Gent, and Brugge. Brugge was the largest city in Europe in the 14th century because of its port connection to England across the English Channel, only 10 miles off the coast. It had the same population of 35,000 as London at the time. Then there's Antwerp, 80 miles down the Shelde River from the North Sea. It's also close to England."

"That's it," Chance said, "Antwerp."

"Take a train," the driver instructed. "When you get to the port, find the office for the ship line and the agent will help you find the ship. You can stay at the Zeemans hotel until it arrives."

A sense of panic enveloped Chance until the driver finished explaining how he could move from port to port following the ship. For a moment he was relieved as the taxi headed toward the main train station in downtown Hamburg. He paid the driver and realized he didn't have much money on him, plus it was almost midnight. The driver wrapped the semi-automatic in a rag and placed it in a colorful Christmas gift bag and handed it to Chance. He walked into the steel and glass depot built in the 1800s as the outpost for the traveling world at the time. It was full of shops and little coffee houses. He found the head and ducked inside. He looked a mess as he peered in the mirror. Chance took off his vest and heavy flannel and pulled off the sweatshirt over his long underwear. Then he peeled off the thin heat shield of thermal underwear.

To the dismay of men coming and going, Chance gave himself a sponge bath and washed his now short hair. He dressed quickly and bought a ticket for Bremen less than two hours away. It was late but he walked out of the station and across the street to a barber shop still open on Christmas Eve.

The barber spun to see this odd looking biker enter his shop. Chance's sleeves and vest were stained with dirt and grime. His running shoes were soiled. He took off his vest again and the flannel. The Barber noted he had washed his hair recently and went to work on it. As he clipped around the edges he also became aware that Chance had recently hacked off a very large chunk of his hair in what must have been an abrupt setting. He snorted at Chance's thick mane and snipped away. He wondered if Chance was a criminal or had a terrible domestic battle, but he decided that it was Christmas Eve and unless this young man turned into a crazed maniac, he wasn't going to alert the police.

Chance looked in the mirror across the room and reminisced about his long hair, but also realized how easy the shorter hair was to deal with. He looked at his rugged features and tried to decide whether he liked the look or not. The barber offered to shave him and Chance agreed but indicated to leave his mustache alone. He couldn't figure out what was happening. For some odd reason, he felt he had some success over the last 24 hours. He knew he ruined relations with the girl and the Russians. He slithered on board her ship, and they knew he would come again. Now he just had to find Ling and punish the bastards who held her. He started to grit his teeth and the muscles in his traps and neck tightened.

"Relax," the old barber said, patting Chance on the shoulder. He had been cutting hair since soldiers came to him for shaves before they boarded trains for the front.

"The sun is out and there is no bombing today," the barber said. "Don't forget your package." Chance looked at him like a teenager looks at his dad when curfew was explained, as if the old man came from another planet. He picked up the small Christmas bag.

Chance said, "Danka." He paid the elderly man and put his vest and flannel back on and went back to the station. He looked damn good except for his soiled clothes. As if lost in a maze, he endeavored to find the correct platform. The people of Hamburg were generally good with English and attempted to assist him, although he thought of his mother's reaction the first time she traveled to Germany.

"I like the area, but don't trust the people," she'd told him. "It's the Nazi past and that harsh language." Chance noted the same about the aggressive language made up of multiple syllabic words that crashed together like swords clashing.

He waited for the train and while he did, counted the marks he had left while figuring the exchange rate. He had enough for the ticket from Bremen to Antwerp, but he was unsure about the access to ATMs. Being alone in a foreign country had its own induced tension when finding his way, working the ATMs and dealing with foreign languages. Then it dawned on him. He had no idea if the Bibi was stopping in Antwerp, and he wouldn't know until he spoke to the port agent. He also missed his motorcycle.

He was drawn back to the present by a train's whistle, wheels screeching against the cast iron tracks as it slowed into the station. He boarded and discovered that he was in a narrow passageway beside a series of cabins. The train was crowded. He noticed all the people around him scurried, carrying colorful bags of brightly wrapped presents. He ducked in a packed cabin and sat next to a very good-looking brunette. He didn't feel he fit for some reason. The people around him were well dressed and had an abundance of packages at their feet and above them in netted shelves.

"Am I in a special car?" Chance said to the girl at his side.

She turned and looked at him, but her gaze did not judge him. "This is a first class car, but generally, unless the registered owner of that seat shows up, you can pay the conductor and stay."

She smiled at Chance as if she wanted him beside her. Their eyes met briefly, and her beautiful gaze caught him. She intrigued him but made him wish Ling was there.

"I'm sorry," Chance said, "But I should move."

He got to his feet and stumbled through the muddle of packages to the passageway. He looked up and down and back at the girl who looked at him with sad eyes. He moved on through the train, trying to find a seat and couldn't. Finally, he came to a car housing a coffee shop. He slid into an empty seat, but again felt out of place. He ordered a cup of coffee and drank it in silence, then moved on through the train looking for a place to sit, wishing he had never left the girl's side.

The sun was long gone and it was after midnight in an area that professed to only have one hour of sunlight each day in December. It dawned on Chance it was Christmas Eve and he was lost and alone looking for the one he loved in a foreign land during the harsh winter season. He was suddenly flooded with the pain like hurt, poor people with the blues, endure during the holidays; like a guy who just lost his girl a week before Christmas. He'd look at each present carried by a harried passenger and remembered picking a present for Ling. Each flashy package broke his heart once more.

The train lumbered from station to station at no particular speed and he watched the Christmas lights flicker in the festive downtown regions and dwindle as he left each glittering berg and rolled into total darkness, stopping at Nordheide, Tostedt, and then Ottersberg before the wheels screeched and crawled into the station at Bremen.

He departed the train, quickly found the ticket counter and asked for a ticket to Antwerp, another port town on the North Sea nearing the English Channel. A crowd got off the train and immediately disappeared as Chance looked at his ticket and the time. He had another hour to wait before a train would take him southwest into Belgium.

The train station was vacant except for debris and the stains of gum on the 100-year-old concrete structure. There were signs of Christmas everywhere and Chance looked upon them with a dismal sense of longing. He wanted her back in his arms and back in the states. He sat on a hard wood and cast iron gothic bench and waited, looking at the pavement scattered with receipts and cigarette butts. It was 2:00 a.m. before he boarded the near empty train for the six-hour journey to another city of 500,000 he had never been in before.

As the electric train clanked and buzzed out of the station, Chance fell asleep and slept hard for almost the entire trip, but when he woke up, his eyes were filled with images of fields covered in snow for as far as he could see. The tall elm trees separating the properties were no longer green but stood with gray trunks and frozen white sprigs and branches. Even the low brick homes and buildings were white with snow, otherwise no color existed.

The sky was full of soft stratus clouds forming a white blanket over the area. As far as he could see was a world of nearly pure white, and he thought of Lings's body and her tender white skin. It was like comparing the warmth of a woman's touch to a sheet of ice. It didn't work. Then the city emerged with a series of neo-gothic spiked walls bored into to allow train tracks laid through them. Construction equipment was everywhere. The stone walls once represented barriers to protect the city. Now, they were in the way of progress.

It was Christmas morning as Chance stepped into the freezing open train station formed of stone, iron and grand glass windows. He was in a new country and found a counter with maps of the city and snagged one. He found an exchange and gave them all the German Marks he had in exchange for Belgium Francs, which in a week at New Years, would be switched again for the new Euro dollar. In many respects the world was changing, in others it stayed exactly the same it had been for centuries.

Chance took the money in his hand and studied the rate of exchange at 40 Belgian francs for a dollar.

As he opened a local map, a gentleman approached. "Are you needing assistance?" he asked.

Surprised, Chance turned to him. He had encountered friendly Germans but none that would approach someone with an open map. "Yes sir," Chance said. "I suppose I just need a cab to the Zeemans Hotel."

"Of course," the gentleman, said removing the meerschaum pipe from his mouth and looking at the map. "The cabs are just out front of the station. You can't miss them. We are here on the map," he said, pointing out the station on the map and circling it with a ballpoint pen. "This is the main street and the port is over here. This portion is along the river and here is where the hotel is. Will that help you?"

"Yes, of course," Chance said, "Thank you very much."

"Merry Christmas," the older chap said and pulled his scarf up tight as he strolled away.

Chance looked at him in a daze and walked into the gray sky outside the gothic train station. The streets were deserted but a few cabs stood waiting in their lane. He stepped up to the first Mercedes and got in the back. "Zeemans Hotel," he said.

"Que faites-vous donc sur la route à Noël?" She said. The driver was a short redheaded French woman.

"I don't speak the Belgium language," Chance said.

"I don't either," Michelina said, "That was French. Why are you traveling on Christmas?"

"I don't have a choice," Chance said as she pulled away from the curb.

# -18-

# CHINESE TEA TORTURE
# AND BELGIUM CHASE

Kim's cab pulled up to the ship and Chee got out quickly and opened
the door. Kim stepped out of the car slowly, her face beet red.
Stridently she walked up the greasy gangplank to the main deck.
Another Chinese guard met them at the entrance to the accommodations and began to blither his report of Chance's stowaway action.

"Are you sure he's still not on the ship?" Kim said in a voice full
of cut glass edges.

"We are sure, Ms. Kim," the young Chinese guard said. "We
watched him leave and Slolaf just called. He wants to talk to you.

"I will call him tomorrow," Kim said briskly. She was brimming
with rage. "I have something to do tonight. Bring the girl to my room.
Bring her tea and leave me alone for the night."

"Shouldn't you call Slolaf?" Chee said. "Business is everything to
the Wong family, not sex."

"No," Kim snapped. "Not tonight!"

Chee bowed graciously and backed away but his eyes were not
self-effacing. He felt the move was wrong. Slolaf had lost a man and
his business could be important to the Wong family.

Kim couldn't get the touch of Ling out of her mind. She wanted it,
wanted her, wanted the business and wanted a deal with Slolaf. Everything
would have been perfect, if it wasn't for the girl she also wanted, and for
the bastard who followed them like a nasty storm that wouldn't let up.

Her tall glossy black heals clipped away at the iron deck as she made
her way to the elevator; one of her humble guards pressed the button.

"Can I get you anything?" the guard asked. If he had killed Chance, he could have reported success, but he didn't dare in a port surrounded by German customs agents. He felt disgusted with his action as if he was a coward and questioned his every memory of the minutes Chance searched the ship.

Kim rode the elevator to E deck and stepped out. She unlocked her spacious cabin and went into her day room and poured herself a drink. She threw her coat on a chair and kicked off her heals. She pulled off her sweater and tossed it onto the chair along with her pants and nylons. She took off her bra and threw it against the chair with the snap of a bullwhip, as if she could do something that would change the events of the day. She heard a tap on the door and grabbed her silk bathrobe. Donning it, she opened the door. Two guards stood with Ling between them. She was lean and gaunt. His hair was dirty and matted and her eyes distant as if she wasn't standing there at all.

"When was the last time she had a cup of tea?" Kim said, demanding a response.

"This morning, Ms. Kim," the young guard said. "She's wants more."

"Yes," Kim said, "we'll give her more."

"Put her in the shower," Kim said and indicated to the other guard. "You, go get her some food and get me some rope. I don't want her to escape tonight. And don't forget to bring me another pot of her special tea."

"Yes, Ms. Kim," the second guard said and ran down the corridor.

The short young guard took Ling into the head and turned on the shower then turned to face her. She was thin and looked tired. Barely able to make it up the stairs, her beauty was still evident as he attempted to pull the sweats she wore for a week, down her long legs. He tugged at the waistband while looking at her sadly. His hands startled her. She hadn't experienced touch or even physical movement for a week and it startled something deep in her consciousness. Her eyes lifted slightly and she saw the shower running. She felt like she was lost in a deep fog, but his touch at her waist brought images back as she heard the water running. She pushed him and he recognized her awareness and backed out the door.

"Make Ms. Kim happy, please," he said pleading.

She didn't respond. He closed the door behind his departure, and she turned toward the small shower and began to lift her top. She thought better of it and just got in the shower with her clothes on. As the warm water ran over her body she let the trousers fall to the tiled deck. She removed her panties, the sweatshirt and the bra and stood on her clothes as she let the water stream over her.

As she looked around she recognized for the first time that she was drugged. Always before, she just felt tired as if they were starving her to death with one handful of rice a day, but that wasn't it. There was something more, much more, but she only ached for her tea. Where was it? She wanted more. She showered for a long time, then heard the door to the head open.

"Ling," Kim said, "I've had it with you and your boyfriend. I would just as soon kill you both. You are either going to work with me or never see him again. Am I clear? We can either have some fun and you can stay warm and comfortable, or I'll throw you back in the hold and you can freeze and starve to death."

Ling's voice was gone. She was in the shower less than a yard from another woman, yet she wasn't. Something deep in her gut yearned for the tea. Yet something deep in her mind questioned it, wondered why she wasn't hungry. "I, I," she muttered, trying to speak and turned toward the showerhead and relished in its warmth.

She heard what Kim said, but couldn't respond. Her mind wasn't capable. All she knew was that she didn't want to go back to the steel torture of the hold. Her back faced the opening in the shower curtain. Kim opened it, soaped a washcloth and scrubbed Ling's back. Her muscles were thinning and the ribs more pronounced. She was still naturally beautiful and her skin and ass were alluring to Kim. She leaned in and kissed Ling on the shoulder.

"I'm sorry about all of this," she said in a softer tone, but there was still demand in her voice. She ran her hand down Ling's form and over her ass.

Ling wasn't sure what was happening to her. In her daze, the shower, the touch and the kiss all felt like she was on a cloud some-where. Compared to the past week, it all felt like she died and drifted to heaven. Ling turned off the shower and Kim handed her a towel. Someone tapped on the door. Kim stepped out of the head, opened it to a guard dressed in black, who bowed slightly, while holding a tray of food and a small steaming teapot.

Ling came out of the shower and the light of the cabin bothered her and Kim recognized it. She turned out the overhead lamps and turned on two amber wall lamps and closed the curtains to the bow of the ship. She sat Ling down at a table and pushed the tray toward her. Kim was a mixture of strained emotions. She was mad, destructive, and yet could not seduce Ling in her condition. Ling saw the tea and reached immediately for it, but Kim pulled it away.

"Eat some food," Kim demanded on deaf ears, "You need the nourishment." As she looked down at the lacquered tray, Ling's robe was open and her bountiful tits hung free of any trappings. Kim's mind was full of lust and she didn't know what direction to go in. She wanted the girl but knew that by force would be ludicrous. If she just drugged her to submission, there would be only a body without response. She decided to try to make a deal.

Ling hadn't spoken yet. She was dazed and aching for the cup of laced tea, but couldn't figure out why or how she was drugged.

"Ling, can you hear me?" Kim asked. Ling ate a couple of bites of broiled fish, two stalks of broccoli, and two spoonfuls of rice. She had no desire to eat, but she knew it was good. She wanted her tea. She looked at Kim and nodded.

"Do you think you can understand me?" Kim said. "I want to talk to you."

"I'm not sure," Ling said. "What am I hooked on?"

"Opium," Kim said.

"Unhuh," Ling said.

"I want to make love to you," Kim said. "I know you want to try a woman. I know it turns you on. If I'm going to have trouble..."

"Just let me have a little tea," Ling said.

Kim recognized that there was some effort on Ling's part and perhaps the best tactic was to succumb to her desire. She poured a small cup of tea from the ceramic pot into a small Chinese ceramic cup and handed it to Ling. She drank it heartily and sat back on the sofa. Kim watched her in amazement, as if she sent the woman suddenly to some far away place. Kim put on some music, and turned as Ling suddenly looked peaceful, got to her feet and disappeared into the bathroom.

Kim didn't know what to make of Ling's movements. At first she thought she had completely knocked her out with one small cup of Opium spiced tea. Ling drifted for a moment then seemed to capture her consciousness. Ten minutes passed and a voice from the head whispered. "Do you have any candles?"

Kim got up and found two candles in small crystal holders and placed them beside the bed and turned off the lights. She was just about to sit down on the edge of the bed when Ling emerged from the bathroom. From her waist up she was naked. Her breast swayed as she entered Kim's bedroom.

She wrapped the maroon silk robe around her narrow waist as low as it would go on her hips so with each naked footstep her hips moved like a love song on delicate feet. She found Kim's make-up and put it lightly on her face and eyes and used red lipstick with black outliner. She found some Channel and delicately dabbed it in places that would grace the room, as if it was surrounded by a field of flowers. The air in the room was warm on her skin and her nipples deliciously danced with each step until she stood in front of Kim. She put her hands behind her back and said, "Please touch them?"

Kim let the tie loose on Ling's robe and it fell open, revealing her nakedness. Kim gently lifted her hands tenderly, as if by magic she could only touch Ling's softness once. She lightly touched the sides of her round sloping tits. She could feel her knees weaken as the sensation of her touch lit a fire in her brain, and she sighed as all the pressures and ambitions of the day vanished with a single caress.

Kim gently cupped Ling's breast and leaned forward and kissed each one just once, then she dropped her hands and pulled her robe from her shoulders and let it drop to the floor. She stepped forward just half a step and put her hands on Ling's waist and pulled her forward until their breasts were touching and she kissed Ling full on the lips. The feeling was a single tidal wave of pure ecstasy. Their lips, as soft as rose petals, consumed one another, as her passionate embrace pressed Ling's natural breasts against Kim's perfectly shaped enhanced boobs.

Kim, over the moon with lust, began to kiss Ling's cheeks and down her neck. She sat on the edge of the bed and nursed on each boob and nipple for long minutes. She was getting so hot that her pelvis rocked yearning to reach Ling's.

Ling lifted Kim's sexy form off the bed and pulled the covers back.

"I want to do you first," she said and guided Kim onto the bed where she tasted her way down the woman's curvy body with her fingers and tongue until she kissed and licked each toe then back up the inside of her legs.

As Kim came in long waves, she lay motionless breathing heavily.

Ling crawled up beside her and held her close as they drifted off to sleep.

The cab driver nodded and pulled into the street usually jammed with traffic.

"How long have you been a cab driver in this town?" Chance asked as the car turned off De Keyserlei and slid down narrow cobblestone streets.

"This is my hobby," Michelina said in a sweet voice. She smiled as she said it. She was only about 5'1" tall and as dainty as her voice. Each word soothed Chance's stress. "I have never been driver anywhere else. I've been on job for three years."

"Must be a good company to work for," Chance said.

"It's wonderful," Michelina said, "I only work here on holidays and weekends. I have a little kitchen and I love to cook. I'm trying to sell bottled gourmet foods, but it is hard. This I do for fun."

"Fun," Chance said. An absence of fun filled his life, and he had to remind himself of the definition.

"What's the matter?" Michelina said, concern wrapped over her delicate features.

"It's too much to explain," Chance said. "I wish you would be available tomorrow."

"I'll be on the job all week," Michelina said. "Actually I'll be driving until just after the first of the new year."

"That will be perfect," Chance said. "Can you pick me up tomorrow morning at 9:00 a.m.?"

"Of course," she said enthusiastically.

"I may need you for several days," Chance said and grimaced over his financial instability.

"Of course," Michelina said her wispy voice soothing him. "You cannot tell me anything about your problems?"

"I must find my ship, first," Chance said. "Then I must find another ship. Just help me if you can. I'll explain as we go."

"Here's my card," she said. "I work to six every day this week. You can always leave a message. If I cannot come, I will see that someone is here to help you."

She rounded the corner on Huikstratt to Falconrui. Two more blocks and they pulled under the parking bar into the lot in front of the Zeeman's Hotel.

"May I call you if I need information about the area?" Chance asked, getting out of the car and pulling some money out of his pocket. She looked him over for the first time.

"Of course," she said and plucked another card out of her sweater pocket and jotted a cell number in the corner. "Here, call me anytime. Do you need some new clothes?" she said, looking his dirty clothes.

"Yes," Chance confirmed, thinking about his soiled attire.

"There is nothing open today," Michelina said, "but tomorrow, everything open again."

"Thank you," Chance said, giving her a sizeable tip and touching her hand. Their eyes met softly and a sense of understanding flowed between them. "I'll talk to you later."

Kim woke the next morning with Ling beside her and she sat for a moment, relishing in their lovemaking and the sensuous body lying beside her. For a moment she wished Ling could always be hers. Everything was so perfect about her body, their touch, and chemistry. She never had a woman stroke her the way Ling did. Then reality lifted its ugly head and she realized the poor girl was drugged and all hell broke loose in Kim's mind. Looking at Ling brought back the problems with Ling's boyfriend, the Russians, and not to mention the conflict back home. Ling was a harbinger of the best and the worst in her life, but she assured herself— toughness would overcome.

She told herself this alluring story over and over, as she stroked Ling's ass, as the morning light crept in the porthole through the dense curtain. She wanted the ship to be done with another port and head toward Genoa, Italy where she would handle one piece of very profitable business for her and the Wong family.

Once again Ling's boyfriend's involvement returned. She shuttered with a growing distaste for the whole problem, and decided to call the Russian first. She kissed Ling on the shoulder, as she lay dormant with her back to Kim. She got out of bed and showered and went to her office in the next room and dialed her Iridium phone.

"Ya," a voice came on the end of the line through the rough connection of the satellite phone.

"Slolaf?" Kim said, "Is that you?"

"Yes," he said, "It's too early. Why you not call last night?"

"I had some other business," Kim said. "You're not the only dealers in town. Besides you stole that briefcase from me."

"Never mind that," Slolaf said. "I'll take care of that. We found your man last night, but he got away. He can't get to his ship. We have it locked down."

"That's good," Kim said. "Maybe he'll just take a plane home."

"He's a fighter," Slolaf said. "He might and might not. His ship is the Leon. That may help you in the future."

Chance was up bright and early in his hotel room pacing the cheap carpeting. The rooms were as simple as the cabins on the ship probably for good reason. As soon as practically possible, he called down to the front desk.

"I need the phone number for the Rickmers shipping line offices in Antwerp," Chance said. "Can you help me?"

"That's not a problem sir," the host said from the plain reception desk. "But they are closed, sir. They won't be open until later this week. You know. Holidays."

Chance wrote the number down carefully, then showered and went to the dining room for breakfast. Scrubbed, he fed himself and made his way to the lobby to meet Michelina. She watched him emerge from the hotel wearing the same clothes he had on the previous day.

"You have come to the right place to be out of clothes," she smiled and said as he got in the cab.

He sat in the front passenger seat with her as she pulled out of the narrow parking lot onto a cobbled street.

"Good," Chance said, "I need to get out of this crap."

She sped along Brouwersvliet Leeuwenrui to the International Boulevard, which was the main street through town and each major block was named after a different country: Itqalielei, Frankrijklei, Britselei and Amerikalei. Chance looked at her lovely features as she darted along the cold streets.

"Aren't these roads slick?" Chance said.

"Yes, but I'm used to them," she said, shifting gears in the E-class Mercedes.

"There are shops everywhere along the Meir. I will drop you there and pick you up at noon."

She pulled up at the major intersection of De Keyserlei leading back to the train station, going east, and into another area for shopping in the opposite direction. Chance reached Kate and she transferred $500 into his account.

"There is a Levis shop, but you will find everything you need. There are shops everywhere in this town."

Chance hustled down the center of the wide walking street brightly decorated for the holidays. It was teaming with people dressed extremely warm for the bitter cold. He wandered into a department store called Inno. He bought some new Levis in the franchised store. He wandered down Wapper Street and glanced in the home of the famous painter Peter Paul Rubens (1577- 1640). He was startled to become suddenly aware of the man who developed and reveled in the rubenesque woman. His art was predominately religious as was required during an era of religious control, although he was allowed to paint portraits.

Loaded with plastic bags full of clothes and wearing some of the items, he met Michelina in front of the Hilton next to the Cathedral of Our Lady, the largest cathedral of its kind in the lowlands or Europe. The wind whistled along the cobblestone plaza in front of the magnificent church, never architecturally finished.

Two things struck Chance as he wandered through the ornate building full of individual areas of worship. Each one was decorated with rich metal ornamentation and ornate wood, marble and ivory carvings, in addition to massive panels of art by Ruben and other artists. He could sense the real fear people in the 13th to 18th centuries had as they even approached the steps to such an edifice of power. He was also completely in awe of the craftsmanship of the artists who devoted their lives and talents to the church.

Almost holding his breath, he left the church, wishing Ling was at his side to enjoy such spectacular art, which she studied in college. He met Michelina in front of the Hilton and invited her to lunch.

"I will only come if you will tell me?" she muttered, her eyes looking into his for acceptance.

"Yes," Chance said lowering his eyes, "I can tell you facts, but I can never portray the hurt I feel."

As they wandered down De Keyseriei toward the grand railroad station Chance began to spill his guts about two lives in dangerous upheaval. They turned under bright green awnings of Fouget's restaurant for lunch.

"I have some news for you, Chance," Michelina said. "You're ship will be in port tomorrow."

Chance snapped and hugged her. "How did you find out?" he said.

"I'm a cab driver," she said with a mischievous smile, "I have connections."

Ling woke up after Kim left and rolled over. Cold in the room, she pulled the curtain aside and looked outside. It was gray and the wind whistled, blowing the snow sideways along the icy face of the ship. Someone brought a tray of food in with scrambled eggs and onions, some meat and toast. Besides the plate, there was a steaming pot of tea and a small diminutive Chinese ceramic cup.

She rolled over and faced the smells of the food. She laid back and began to think. Her mind was still clouded and she wanted the tea. It made her a mummy to the external aspects of life. She escaped the pain and cold of the steel hold. She was no longer hungry or frightened but she didn't know whether it was the drug making her feel the way she did. She got out of bed and into the shower, where she cleaned herself thoroughly again. She dried and avoided the tea. For a few minutes, she needed to grasp a minor sense of reality.

Kim started to open up to her and Ling realized that in order to be treated with some respect she needed to give Kim what she wanted, which was not altogether appalling. She let the hot water flush her senses and allow her some motivation and reality, but the smell of the tea pulled her like an anchor pulls the voyage of a ship to a halt. She sipped the tea, then in an impulse of survival poured the remaining tea down the toilet and set the pot back on the tray.

She ate a few bites of food and crawled back in bed. As she lay in the wide bed, she felt the vibration of the ship increase, then the honk of a tug and she looked out the bedroom porthole. A tug was along side; the ship was pulling away from the docks. They were leaving Hamburg.

Ling's mind crawled along the edge of being drugged into silent submission. She knew she needed to find a way out, or a manner of survival that would take her back to Chance. She remembered her mother telling stories of women who were captured and tortured until they became sexual concubines. She remembered her mother telling her about mothers and their sons. She said that if an infant acted up the mother would play with his genitals to calm him. Sensing that there might be a formula for her own good by helping Kim, she drifted off into an opium caress. As she slipped away, she knew the drug would be a formidable foe.

Chance led Michelina to a table in the smoky interior and they sat. It felt so good for Chance to be in the presence of a woman, even while spilling his guts about the task at hand and his blues for the woman he loved. Michelina took one of Chance's hands in hers and massaged it.

"I wish I could help," she said. "You are such a warm man."

"There is one thing you could check for me, the whereabouts of the Bibi."

"I will look into that tonight," Michelina said. "Anything else?"

"I need you tomorrow at the same time," Chance said. "We need to get to the Rickmers' office or find my ship."

# -19-

# HOLIDAY CHASE

Ling awoke to the clinking of a stainless steel tray carefully delivered to Kim's room in the early afternoon. She floated down from a series of sensual and alluring dreams, and she tried to rinse her drug soaked mind and make sense. She looked over her shoulder in a cloud as Chee laid the tray down and looked at her knowingly. He couldn't decide whether the sexual release was good for Kim or added to her hunger for power. He was acutely aware of Kim's back street past. He wasn't opposed to working for Kim, but he had his own set of fuming ambitions. He put the tray down and backed quietly out the door, locking it behind him.

The Bibi steamed out of Elbe River over night, under the guidance of harbor pilots, and the crew on the bridge set the course for west along the coast of Belgium and into the English Channel. As the freighter encountered the bristling North Sea the winds and swells increased, her tray rattled with the impulse from the 15,000 horsepower engine somewhere far below Ling's forced accommodations.

Ling turned and her body ached as if she fell down a set of stairs. She immediately reached for the pot of tea and poured it into a small ceramic cup with a delicate illustration of a fiery dragon circling the pale white-fired glaze. As she reached for it automatically, she stopped herself. Through the mud attacking her central nervous system she was keenly aware she had to control this substance or be destroyed. She had to fight herself through a withdrawal without Kim being aware. She gazed at the steaming cup of Chinese green tea mixed with opium.

She had only one cup in the morning and poured out the pot. She ached for this cup but was unsure of the quantity of drug per cup.

Could she wean herself off the drug? She decided to sip one cup again and pour the pot out. She lifted the dainty cup to her lips and sipped it, letting the steaming liquid drift down her throat. She tried to stay alert to its effects. She sipped some more and could feel her body cheer for release from all that was reality. It was as if a blanket of pain and anguish was wrapped around her. It tied tight a knot with ropes of physical addiction straining against the release in need of more drugs. As she nipped at the warm liquid, the blanket of pain was lifted and replaced by a sensation so wonderful it compelled her into a state of inability, and her desire to fight back disappeared.

She tried to hang onto some fleeting sense of motivation as the drug consumed her. As reality escaped her consciousness to be replaced with euphoria so great it competed with orgasms, she pushed herself to her feet and dumped the pot of steaming tea in the ceramic toilet bolted to the tiled deck. Behind it, a Rub Goldberg set of chromed pipes weaved in and out of the bulkhead. Momentarily, she was entranced with the glittering array of chromed brass, like a dancing family of chromium snakes slithering against the crystal white wall. She forced reality through the strange images and flushed the toilet, watching the swirling liquid disappear into the sea. Dazed and distraught, she closed the lid. It would have to do for now.

Chance jumped to his feet in his hotel room. He felt a sense of guilt, like spikes to his heart. His logic told him Ling was in pain as he laid comfortably in a soft bed with clean sheets. He enjoyed the company of another woman and was afforded the opportunity to shop and purchase clean clothes. It wasn't right. He was a puzzle without all the pieces and while he slept, for all he knew, the best piece was on the edge of a fire and being singed. He had to do something constructive. He wanted only one woman at his side and she was trapped on some piece of shit ship. He threw his bag of old soiled clothes against the wall of his room and stormed to the shower

He called the cab company and asked for Michelina to meet him at the Zeeman's Hotel Lobby. He ran down the stairs and ignored breakfast and dashed out into the freezing cold. Michelina was sitting in her purring silver four-door Mercedes in the parking lot.

"What's the matter?" she asked as he got in the back.

"I'm sorry," Chance said abruptly, "I'm out of line. I need to focus all my attention on finding my girl. You've been a great help, but I don't dare relax. I need her like I need my left arm, and I'm left handed. I'm going to find her, get her back and take care of the bastards who have her."

"You're not going to like the news," Michelina said. "The Bibi is not coming to Antwerp. It's sailing directly to Genoa, Italy. Your ship will be in this morning. I thought we would be going there, but it's too early. You can do nothing but go to breakfast."

Chance's shoulders fell as if they were the walls of a 17th Century building being bombed during WWII. He couldn't believe what she was saying.

"Are you sure?" Chance said, his green eyes flickering.

"That's what the agent told my friend," she said with a small pout. "I am truly sorry, Chance."

"Well, hell," Chance spoke up. "You might as well leave me here. I'm going to make a phone call or two. Pick me up in a couple of hours and I'll get back on that fuckin' ship."

He scrambled out of the car and handed her a Belgium Francs note. Distraught, he jogged back into the soft lemon-aid colored lobby with a 12-foot Christmas tree looking as if it grew to maturity in Siberia. It was thin and lifeless with sporadic limbs that held less than a dozen dull ornaments. He went to the bar, which was open 24 hours a day and ordered a double Jack Daniels on the rocks and slugged it down. As much as he was trying to find some sort of release from all the strain, he was emotionally beat up and drained.

He strolled to the restaurant and ate scrambled egg whites, wheat toast, returned quickly to his room and packed. He picked up the bag of clothes crumpled against the wall. He put the new clothes into another shopping bag, along with the pistol, and set them next to the bed. He picked up the phone and dialed Chang's number in China.

The phone rang a distant ring like it was being filtered through a pillow. The same sultry soft voice answered, but he could swear there was some tension in the small diminutive sounds. "Can I speak to Chang?" Chance said.

"Of course," the unknown girl responded, her voice rising considerably as if she had been suddenly told good news. She recognized his voice. "Are you all right?"

"Yes," Chance said, "I'm fine, and I know a great deal, but I'm having trouble reaching Ling."

"Can you?" the voice said and the two words hit Chance in the chest as if he stepped into oncoming traffic and was flattened by a trash truck. Chance gasped and paused. She could feel his apprehension rush to the surface. In two words the entire struggle burst to the exterior like an atomic powered submarine breaking the surface of the Pacific.

"Yes," Chance said with some trepidation, "I believe I can, but I may need help. Who are you? You have always greeted me with such a wonderful voice. It calms the waters in just a few words. Although this time you sent a tidal wave through the phone lines. I need to muster my confidence to ride."

"I am Chang's fiancé. My name is Wing," she said with fear creeping into the words.

"Is everything all right?" Chance reacted to her statement.

"With us, fine," She said, "With the family, not so good. Let me get Chang."

"Chance," Chang said alertly on the phone as if he expected some tremendous news. "What is going on?"

"Not much, I'm afraid and ashamed to report," Chance said. "I've gotten close and disturbed that woman, her team, and a Russian gang, but I haven't reached Ling yet. I hope my blunders aren't putting Ling's life in jeopardy. That's why I called."

"They are pressuring me about my family's land. They must keep Ling alive, or they have no pull with me," Chang said. "We must both be stronger than we've ever been in our lives or everything will be gone."

"Ling's ship is heading directly to Genoa, Italy. I'm stuck in Antwerp for a couple of days, I would bet. If I can't get to her in Genoa, the next stop may be Singapore. Then it can't be long before I'm in China."

"You must save her before you arrive in Hong Kong," Chang's voice was dour and demanding. "You must or there will be nothing left. The Wong family threatens us daily."

Chance hung up and stared at the phone. Dazed, he got to his feet and picked up the shopping bags and went to the lobby, thinking every step of the way.

Chang hung up the phone and turned to Wing, who sat looking at him like a sad ceramic Chinese doll. She had been a strong spiritual light for Chang and was now dimming under the strain the family endured.

"You cannot hold out?" Wing said, "Unless…" she bowed her head and could not utter what went through her mind.

Michelina pulled to a stop in the freezing temps outside the hotel and Chance was waiting. "How are you now?" she said as Chance opened the back door and got out.

"I don't know," Chance said, his forehead curled into the wrinkles of deep thought and questions. "I don't know if I should fly to Genoa. I need to talk to the Captain. I want to know how I can get on the Bibi."

"Unlike this port, Genoa is very guarded. It has several gates and airplanes watch the ships coming and going. Where are you going next?"

"I'm not sure," Chance said as she turned off the highway onto a series of streets leading to individual docks. Unlike some harbors, each dock and warehouse in Antwerp was well marked all the way from the freeway. "Your agent told me the Leon would be docked at 334. I will take you there. Will I hear from you again?"

"Yes, of course," Chance said. "We'll be here for a couple of days at the minimum. It feels good to know you're close."

They slid down snow-covered streets between containers, old buildings and over railway tracks, past large stacks of I-beams and massive wooden crates. As they passed each one, covered in a coat of snow, Chance asked himself what was in each one and who knew or kept track of each piece of cargo.

The Leon was moored to the slick, sludge covered concrete dock containing a series of iron cranes on tracks running parallel to the edge of the dock. A large corrugated warehouse stood adjacent to the ship with the numbers 334 painted precisely on the side of the building. Michelina pulled up beside the ship next to the gangplank and stopped.

"Chance, you are a good man," Michelina said, turning to him. "I know you will find her, just think and listen. A way will come." She touched his gloved hand gently. "I will be thinking also."

"Thank you," Chance said and climbed out of the small Mercedes. "I'll call you later."

He took long steps up the oily gangplank, dodging the slick grease coated steel cable that lifted and lowered the plank. He made his way up the five levels to his cabin and opened it. Nothing had changed. He threw the bags in the room and went to the bridge to find the Captain. The young Captain sat at the teletype communication machine reading and typing responses with one finger.

"Excuse me, Captain," Chance said, "I'm back."

"Glad to see you," the young Captain said. "The customs agents will be here shortly. You'll need to come in my cabin with your passport."

"Sure, sure," Chance said, "How do you know what's in the crates you load?"

"I show you," Andreus said, getting up from the teletype machine. He pulled a notebook from a shelf behind the communication table. "Here is the list of material that will be loaded here and in Genoa. As you can see, very little is defined. In many cases it just says machinery. We do not know."

The Captain giggled and his even teeth shown bright. He was constantly in a good mood, which drove Chance nuts. "I remember one time loading a merry-go-round on board. It had a colorful tent, and horses on sticks, and it was called machinery. This I don't believe." He burst into laughter.

Chance stood in front of the Captain with his shoulder bars and four gold stripes. He wanted to slap the shorter man, and shake his teeth loose. He wanted answers and action.

"When are we leaving? Can I fly to Genoa? What's our next port after Genoa? I need to know."

Suddenly the Captain's face was washed of all its humor. He looked out the windows facing the bow and thought for a second.

"We are to be back at sea in three days. Yes, you can fly to Genoa, no problem, but it is difficult to get into the port, because we will not be tied up at the cruise ship docks. After we load 13,000 tons of material here, we will load another 2,000 in Genoa, after some costly cargo shifting. Then we travel to the Suez Canal. It will take three and a half days. If we arrive early, from three to six in the morning, then we go through the canal that day. If not, we anchor for a day, then it will take us 13 days to arrive in Singapore. Then two days to Jakarta, then Vietnam, then Hong Kong and Shanghai and another port in China."

Chance had tremendous respect for the man, but his frustration level was an emotional tidal wave. "Thank you, Captain." Chance said. "Sorry to interrupt."

"This is no problem," the Captain said.

Chance started to walk away, "One more question, Captain," Chance said. "How's my motorcycle?" "We take very good care," the Captain said looking at Chance his face brightening. "It will be ready to ride in Genoa."

Chance returned to his cabin immediately and called Chang. Wing answered the phone. "Hello."

"Keep the faith, Wing," Chance. "Let me speak to Chang."

Again he sensed the anguish in Chang's words. "We need to work together. You're in the export business, correct? Can you contact Rickmers shipping and make arrangements to have a crate loaded on the Bibi in Genoa. I need to get on that ship."

"I can do that," Chang said.

# -20-

# FLOATING IN THE MEDITERRANEAN

The tramp Bibi motored for two days rolling in the tumultuous seas along the coast of France, Portugal and neared the coast of Spain. It was scheduled to change course from 180 degrees due south to an eastern bearing into the Mediterranean. Ling forced herself into a push/pull attempt at self-drug rehabilitation, while taking on the role of Kim's mistress.

Kim got up in the morning, showered and dressed after fondling Ling's body.

"I want to please you tonight," Kim whispered. "You make me so happy. I can't tell you."

Ling rolled away from her Korean mistress each morning and faced the bulkhead covered with Formica, wallpaper-styled, panels. The bedroom was carpeted and the furniture teak, containing a wall of teak closets. The bed was permanently mounted to prevent the rocking seas and incessant ship's vibration from constantly shifting the queen-sized mattress. Kim spoke to her, assuming Ling was still in opium-induced semi-consciousness.

"I can't wait for tonight. I will be back after lunch for some afternoon delight," Kim said, looking at the form of Ling's lovely body.

She stroked it as if Ling was a pet, touching her how and wherever she wanted. Kim leaned forward freshly showered with touches of perfume wafting around her body. She pressed her naked warmth to Ling and held her close. Her large tits grazed Ling's back as she ran her hand down over Ling's tits and along her flat stomach, then over her ass and between her legs.

"I will fuck you tonight, bitch. My little slave."

Kim shuddered with delight and jumped to her feet. She pulled on a fresh set of black t-back laced panties and a matching bra. She slipped on a pair of skin-tight black pants over hose, and donned a soft black Cashmere sweater holding tight to her store-bought, voluptuous boobs. She slipped on a set of black rubber-soled shoes with slight heels built in and grabbed her jacket and went to breakfast with her crew and the Polish officers.

During the day, she spent sometime in the communications room calling China and her connection in Genoa. She followed crew members and Chee into the hold to inspect the lashing of the carefully built carriage holding the maroon and crème Bentley securely in place.

"Is everything set in Genoa?" Chee asked, looking in Kim's beautiful eyes. Her demeanor had softened since she could control Ling and have her way with her. She enjoyed every minute and her cocky behavior belied her confidence.

"I spoke to them this morning and we have no worries," Kim said. "I have made peace with the Russians. We're in business."

Chance slid out of his bunk, showered and shaved immediately. He noticed, since he chopped his long biker-looking hair and shaved, except for the full mustache, the crew's respect for him increased. But his anguish heightened daily as he watched the process of unloading all the containers off the Leon's main deck, including two cement pumper trucks and a number of pieces of heavy machinery. He bumped into the Cargo Superintendent, Captain Dierk Meier at breakfast.

"What's the deal with the cargo?" Chance asked, his frustration growing. "When are we going to leave?"

"I cannot control the stevedores," Dierk said. "They have put on extra shifts, but with each day we get closer to New Year's Eve, more men take holidays off. This holiday is killing us. Then the men who are forced to work those days make much extra money, so they work slower to get as much time in as possible."

"But why are they unloading the cargo that took days to load in Hamburg?"

"I know you want to ship out," Dierk said, "but you must realize that shifting cargo is something you will have to tolerate until you reach China. It is costly, but we have no choice. We need to take the cargo off the holds in order to open them and put more cargo inside."

"Jesus," Chance said.

"You should go out on the eve of the holiday," Dierk said. "You need to relax."

"Where should I go? I want to go to Genoa."

Dierk shook his head and walked away, he had a bundle on his plate without Chance's anxiety. Chance grabbed a cup of coffee after dinner and stepped up to the bridge. He looked out at the snow blowing across the bow of the ship, as if someone on the other dock shot a snow-blower at them. Four degrees Celsius outside; the crane on the icy tracks below crept up the dock and positioned itself, so it could hoist ten stands of pipe from the barge tied to the port side of the ship and lift them slowly into the hold, where another crew of stevedores waited to guide and position them.

The men in the holds laid down strips of wood in-between each row of pipe. They were loading a thousand stands of pipe, 50-feet long each, by hefting 10 stands aboard with each plodding maneuver. The process was ridiculously slow. He returned to his cabin, but couldn't help himself and continued to watch, then like clockwork the crews completely shut down and went on breaks or an hour for lunch, then back to work. It was a maddening experience, but he knew historically, management took advantage of the workingman or there wouldn't be unions. Still, he was exceedingly frustrated.

He couldn't sleep at night in his bitter cold room. He couldn't concentrate, except to run his conversation with Chang around in his mind. What could he do except to get to Genoa and somehow try to find Ling. He was sure security would be tightened since his last foray onto the Bibi. He wondered if there was a way for him to slow the Bibi down, so he would have time to reach his girl. He paced the bridge, and the ribbed rubber matting protecting shoes from the steel deck beneath.

The Captain came onto the deck dressed in black slacks, dress shirt and a black tie. He was young looking and needed a haircut badly.

"I have church entertainment coming on board tonight for Filipino crew," he said.

"Where's the Bibi?" Chance questioned, ignoring the Captain's comment.

"I do not know," the Captain said. "You have a problem with our sister ship?"

"Uh, no and yes," Chance stumbled. "I'm curious about a passenger."

"I can check," the Captain said. His dark eyes flashed with an inherent desire to assist. "I could find out."

"I may take you up on that," Chance said. "I spoke to Dierk about the cargo. It's slow. Is there anything we can do?"

"No," the Captain's smile waned, "once in port I have no control. When at sea, I have lots of control, but not in harbor." He shrugged his shoulders and turned to the tele-type machine and began to type with a single digit.

Chance shifted to the cupboard under the starboard window where the coffee pot was housed and made a cup of instant coffee. He sipped the dark liquid doctored with cream and sugar and looked out at the ship below through the broad expanse of windows. The sun faded in the west over the cranes, derricks and masts protruding from the immense harbor. The silhouettes against the sky looked ominous and the angry shapes of metal took on a war-like appearance.

Chance looked out and pondered the 30 years of war movies he'd seen, made in cold harsh gray settings like the one he was standing in. They held some influence on his perception of the industrial port looking like a dump, while it supported the 500,000 thousand residents of Antwerp. Ports all up and down the coast provide for the industries of Belgium and England. Chance just shook his head and strolled reluctantly down one set of stairs to his cabin.

He paced across the indoor-outdoor carpeting of his day room and racked his brain for answers. The more he marched, the more frustrated he became. He tried to read and tried to call Chang, but there was no answer. He looked out at the snow and the whitecaps on the water as the sun vanished and he passed on going to dinner.

He read an old newspaper discarded on the bridge and was further disillusioned by the terrorist movements in the world. There seemed to be upheaval everywhere on earth, as if human beings were resorting to violent 11th century levels. He didn't pretend to understand all the religious strife or their beliefs, but he sensed the world should all abide by the code of the west, or a single simple set of respectful rules. The world news just enhanced his level of aggravation. He wadded up the paper and shit-canned it.

It was after 2200 when he heard a slight rhythmic beat emanating from four decks below in the Filipino crews' lounge. The sweet melody of a woman's voice filtered between the steel bulkheads, the elevator shaft and the stairwell. It reminded him of Ling's soft humming tones as she moved around his house. He sat back in an arm chair, paid attention to each note as he closed his eyes and imagined Ling moving around her booth in downtown Long Beach, singing and humming as she set up her colorful plant display with care and artistic creativity. He thought of her as she placed each carefully decorated, ceramic bamboo plant and pot on a carefully arranged shelf, as she admired a pot she fired or an illustration she drew. Every move was an R-and-B classic song in motion.

Chance heard something skitter in the hall as if someone dropped a coin. He could still hear the group play a holiday melody down stairs as he stuck his head into the hall. He saw the leg and foot of a man enter one of the passenger's cabins near the rear of the super-structure. The horseshoe shape of each passageway deck afforded crew and passengers a way out. The two ends opened onto exterior levels with stairs leading down to the main deck. The woman who had that cabin was a matronly, schoolteacher type, and he had no interest in who she invited to her cabin, but Chance could see the stern door leading to outside. It was left ajar.

He suddenly remembered speaking to Dierk about the crew's entertainment. Dierk told him a colorful gypsy scenario. He described the young, good-looking daughter of the ring leader dancing seduc-tively in front of the crew while his two teenage sons scoured the crew's quarters, stealing anything not tied down.

Chance remembered his reaction to the seemingly far-fetched anec-dote. He quietly moved quickly between the stern cabin and the bare alu-minum door. The man stepped out into the slick polished passageway and looked past Chance at the exit contemplatively. He was the same height as Chance and wearing a knit cap over dark disheveled hair.

Chance couldn't tell the weight or muscle strength of the nervous man because of the depth of his clothing. His attire was heavy with a thick, black, hip-length hiking jacket over several shirts, a sweater and a scarf. His pants were thick black denims with long gangster pockets and he carried a colorful purse under his thick bicep. His lace-up work-styled boots shuffled down the hall as he looked the other way and took off running.

Chance bolted after him in the narrow hall and caught him at the inside edge of the corner, driving the thief against the forward bulkhead. As the man slammed into the steel wall, Chance kicked him in the knee to prevent further escape attempts. He struck the young man in the neck with his right hand held in an open web. The man, with three days dark beard growth and thick black eyebrows dancing around his face, while looking for an immediate escape, gasped for breath, his throat restricted. Chance struck him with his other hand bunched into a tight fist and flattened the man's nose showering his face with blood.

Just then another steel door opened to the stairway and the Captain stepped into the corridor. "Hey," he shouted as Chance launched two more pummeling blows, one to the man's jaw. The Captain heard the crack.

"Stop, stop," the Captain shouted.

Chance stepped back, panting profusely. His adrenaline launched through the roof. If the Captain hadn't showed up, he would have killed the man.

"I caught him coming out of Margaret's cabin with her purse," Chance said, breathing heavily, as fast as his chest would allow. He took another deep breath and sighed.

"I will call the authorities," the Captain said, and the two of them dragged the man into the Captain's day room. "You will be happy to know we are departing tomorrow on New Year's Eve, 1500 hours."

Chance took a deep breath and sighed once more. Sweat beaded on his brow. "That's the best news I've had today," he said.

The Captain handcuffed the thief and called the police. He called a couple of crewmen who came to his room and watched the prisoner. Chance returned to his cabin. He called Michelina on the satellite phone.

"Hello," Michelina said.

"Hey you," Chance said, "We're pulling out tomorrow."

"When? I would like to see you before you go."

Ling awoke and edged to her feet after Kim left. She showered and put on fresh make-up and dressed in the single cloth gown Kim left, which included no underwear, but a light Pareau of silk material.

She felt naked as she wrapped herself and tied a knot over her boobs. She straightened up the room. Chee brought her meals and three pots of tea a day. She struggled to throw the tea away. Each day, she weaned herself off another portion, but it was tough. The drug was stronger than life itself. It was only survival and her love for Chance forcing her to fight it. Otherwise, she would have drifted somewhere soft and ultimately comfortable and awaited death gladly.

At noon, Chee brought her tray of food, which she tried to pick at. Ling made the bed but laid on her side as he entered the room. He was a suspicious sort and studied the room carefully as he set the tray on the coffee table and departed. He didn't feel right about the cleanliness of Ling or the tidy two-room cabin. He never tried the drug he dealt. He witnessed its effects on homes and businesses. He considered himself a professional.

The English brought opium from Turkey to China to control the Chinese. It had a devastating effect on the lives of many. Homes were destroyed as the inhabitants lived life on the drug and became helpless skeletons devoted to just one thing—opium. They quit work and gradually sold or gave everything they had away to stay high. Some became permanent residents of opium dens, smoking the harmful herb until they could breathe no more. Ling seemed to be leaving the drug-soaked lifestyle behind. Chee's face gnarled as he shut the door and went out.

At lunch with Chee and her other men, Kim thought about Ling and the touch of her body, Kim's addiction. Kim's loins ached with desire and the knowledge that a beautiful, soft, seductive woman waited in her room half naked—her slave. She ate quickly and gave Chee a list of mundane things to do to keep him busy for an hour or two. A steward pulled out her chair as she indicated the desire to leave.

"I will meet with you later," Kim said, rising.

Chee watched her move, and witnessed the joy in her steps. She was softening. He recognized her ambitious, cunning movements slowing. She was satisfied. He hoped her killer instinct would not slip far away. Genoa was fast approaching and they would be dealing with the Mafia. He needed her leadership level to be on high alert or he would take it from her.

Kim walked up the inside stairwell to E deck for the exercise. With each floor, her heart raced some more. She was panting by the time she reached the last level before the bridge. Her hands tingled as they left the banister and her crotch was wet.

Ling ate a few bites of rice, some small pieces of chicken and an orange. She didn't want to give Kim any more evidence of her appetite returning. She set her tray aside on the desk and cleaned the day room. After she ate, she put on some music and freshened her make-up. The day room was sparsely furnished with a long, built-in couch, a small teak wood coffee table and two white muslin-covered armchairs. It held a small teak desk built into the bulkhead with cupboards surrounding it. The entire room was paneled with rich warm teak wood. The desk resided against the Starboard bulkhead and the couch against the port wall separating the living room from the bedroom.

Two large portholes looked out over the bow of the ship, the cranes and cargo beneath them. For navigational purposes at night, the bow facing rectangular windows were covered with thick curtains. Ling pulled them aside and attached them out of the way with broad ties connected to hooks on the bulkhead. As they neared the Mediterranean, the weather improved substantially and the sun shined on the swells. They swayed south toward the equator and then east into the Med.

Ling sat on the edge of the couch as Kim entered the room. She was dazzled by the tidiness of the room and the bed that was carefully made. Music danced off the bulkheads. Ling sat with her hands folded in her lap on the edge of the long narrow couch, her head slightly bent. The frock she wore was a light pink with multi-colored opaque flowers, nearly transparent. It was tied around her in a seductive fashion, enhancing her every curve and pressing her breasts to her chest, flattening their gentle fullness.

"This is very nice," Kim said as she entered the small foyer and hung her overcoat on one of the hooks in the small room where she also kicked off her shoes. The decks of the ship were grimy from the multitudes of cargo maneuvering and shoes tracked the oily substance throughout the ship. Kim stepped into the day room barefoot except for black hose and looked at Ling, whose hair was freshly shampooed and pulled back behind her head. Her neck and shoulders were completely exposed.

"I don't know what to say," Kim said as she wandered closer. She stepped up to Ling and stood above her as she ran her fingers over

Ling's bare shoulder and up the side of her soft neck to the pure silk surface of her cheeks. Ling slid slightly foreword and placed her knees on the carpeting and looked up at Kim's seductive features and large sweater-covered tits above her. She ran her hands up the back of Kim's calves and over her legs and ass then to the front and unsnapped her waist band button, then unzipped the fly of her expensive black pants. She pulled the pants down along with her hose and helped her out of them. Then kneeling in front of her crotch, pulled her panties off.

As Kim stepped out of the pants, she spread her legs slightly and Ling carefully folded her clothes neatly on the couch. She moved just a couple of inches closer to Kim's thighs while removing her Sarong and vigilantly folded the soft material and laid it next to Kim's clothes on the couch. Kim looked down at Ling's nude form as she moved on her knees with tiny steps until her tits brushed Kim's leg. Ling ran her hands around Kim's thigh and hugged the woman's smooth leg to her body, taking in her fragrance.

Kim was stunned as she watched Ling's young sexy form wrap herself about her leg, her soft nipples brushing her skin. Kim had never encountered such overwhelmingly entrancing lovemaking. Even with paid women, the sense was never so tender and devoted to pure pleasure.

Ling dedicated herself to each touch, kissing down her soft thigh, slowly rounding her leg until she kissed the tender area behind the knee and licked it gently. As she kissed the back of her calf, she slowly drifted lower until she licked the woman's ankle and Kim gazed down to see Ling bowing at her feet kissing her toes. She didn't think she could stand another minute as Ling's tongue flicked between each toe gently and kissed the top of her foot, before moving to her other quivering foot and began with a tender massage of the muscles on the top of her foot to her Achilles tendon at the back of her ankle.

Again, she kissed each toe and teased the valleys between them then and made love slowly to her calf and thigh, kissing and licking the back of the delicate area behind her knee. Kim responded shuttering uncontrollably. Ling slid her moist tongue around the back of Kim's trembling thigh to the front to where her legs met and she kissed her perfectly shaved mound once and looked up at Kim who stood shaking like a building experiencing a heavenly earthquake.

"Can I kiss you now?" Ling said obediently asking permission to please her mistress.

"Uh, huh," Kim said, her mouth dry with desire. Ling's form below Kim was sexual artistry before her eyes with the slope of her back narrowing to her waist then blossoming to her faultless ass. Then she felt Ling's tongue.

Kim collapsed like a dish rag thrown into the chair.

"I can't speak," she whispered. "Get up and go lay in the bed."

Without a word, Ling got to her feet and went into the bedroom, pulled back the covers neatly and laid down on her back. Kim came in and stood over her while removing her sweater and bra.

"God, I want you," she said and crawled into the bed.

They came in waves of pleasure, then rolled to face one another, kissed and held each other deeply, their breasts pressed together.

"Are you fighting the drugs?" Kim said, kissing Ling's cheek.

"I must," Ling said, "or I wouldn't be able to make love at all."

"What do you mean?" Kim asked.

"It is an orgasm for hours," Ling said, "That takes all your desire for life away. There is no need for life as we know it, when you're high."

"Just don't change," Kim said, "And don't run away."

Chance slept fitfully, but his fight with the thief helped. It took his mind briefly away from his search for the woman he loved. He awoke with his usual adrenaline rush and headed for the shower. He didn't eat breakfast with the crew, but ran to the gangplank at 9:00. Michelina was waiting on the snow-covered concrete dock in her silver Mercedes taxi.

"Hello," she said as he got into the cab, "How are you."

"I'm better," Chance said, folding himself into the front seat beside her.

She had a blossoming flower-like exuberance. Although it was 0 degrees Celsius in the early morning, they were surrounded by color-less gray hues of lifelessness. She was like a bloom of brightly-colored flowers dead center of a desert. Her auburn hair glowed, her green eyes sparkled and her lips were a kissable radiance.

"How much time do you have?" she asked, a small smirk crossing her pretty lips.

"I have until three this afternoon," Chance said.

"Are you hungry?"

"I didn't have breakfast."

"I want to take you to a lovely café attached to the Hilton on the Square next to the Cathedral," she said. "Their food is divine." She slipped her hand onto Chance's thigh. "I'm so thankful that we have this time together."

Her fine features were joyful, even in the dark car interior, surrounded by ancient gray block buildings and dark cobblestone streets. They turned down Sint-Jocobs Markt and buzzed along the shops and small streets until they reached the Hilton on the corner of the large square. Small mountain kids dressed in their Ecuadorian handmade attire laid out a quick display of knitted items along side the stone walls of the Cathedral of Our Lady.

Chance imagined the same display of goods took place 700 years ago. The wind whipped along the narrow street facing the church. The children huddled around their wares in the cold, and Chance wished he could afford to buy all their garments and send them home and out of the icy wind.

Chance's mind sputtered with irregular thoughts. He pulled on his mustache as he watched Michelina's beauty and warmth fill the car. He needed the touch of a woman. He grappled with the notion of being in the throws of a romantic adventure with this peach of a woman, against his mission in life, his devotion to Ling and the notion that her accommodations could be filled with pain, while he danced on pressed sheets in a Hilton Hotel.

Michelina parked the car and they walked to the vast spinning doorway into the interior of the Hilton. They crossed the luxurious lobby of marble floors and pricey jewelry. One particular display caught his attention. It was an antique ring. The band, simple and round gold, surrounded a heart of small diamonds and a glimmering fiery opal. He wanted to buy it and give it to Ling. He dreamed of holding her soft hand and slipping it onto her naked finger.

Chance helped Michelina out of her heavily padded jacket, while he ran the image of the ring over in his mind. She took off her scarf and gloves, handed them to the woman at coat check and slipped her a Belgium Franc.

The coffee house doubled as a glassed in atrium overlooking the cobblestone square and the myriad of brightly decorated shops.

"I would like to buy you brunch if you like," Michelina said. They sat at a small square table covered with two tablecloths. The table was dressed with ornate silver and crystal.

"I will have none of that," Chance said. "You have bent over backwards for me. This is my treat."

He leaned to kiss her on the cheek and she turned and met his lips with hers.

# -21-

# Morphine and the Italian Coast

The Mediterranean was as smooth as a cup of warm unstirred tea as the BiBi roamed across nautical miles toward Genoa. Ling could see the WWII concrete breakwater through the forward portholes as they neared the outskirts of the Italian coast. She watched out the bow windows as the pilot boat bounced in the ship's wake and splashed in the green foaming sea alongside until the pilot climbed aboard.

The Bibi, with its bright forest green hull and white cranes slowed as the pilot instructed. For what seemed like the first time, the sun shown on the decks and the ship was any hue other than a gray steel cage to Ling. She was amazed at the sights, even of the colors of the ship's decks and the emerald green sea of the Mediterranean.

Two more days passed as she fought her addiction to the opium-laced green tea. It was the first morning she awoke with some sense of pure reality. Her mind seemed to be once more owned by herself and not the drug. She had developed a portioning system and it appeared to keep her stable, without extreme highs and lows. She continued to taper off the drug as her will allowed. She was stunned by the vision of the beautiful harbor, the multitude of enormous cruise ships, and the ancient city sprawled against the Italian hillside.

Kim awoke early, patted Ling on the ass and kissed her a couple of times, then jumped out of bed. She was in a hurry to be on the bridge as the Bibi entered port. Distinctly aware of Chee's watchful eye, she was also concerned about the man who was chasing Ling, but she knew he was trapped in Antwerp, as the Bibi steamed into the

Atlantic. For the moment relief filled her senses, but he would come, she was sure of it. She wanted to have her Italian business finished and unhampered by the big biker.

As she showered, she wished Ling was under the warm water with her, washing her with those so-soft and teasing hands. She knew then she wanted to make love to Ling in the shower in the near future. She hurriedly washed her tall Asian figure and shaved herself everywhere. She climbed out of the shower, and for the first time since nearing Europe, she was able to reach for her towel without being snagged by bitter cold. It was such a relief not to be constantly running from the bleak chill.

She delicately applied a light touch of eye make-up and lipstick to her smooth features. Neither Ling nor Kim had much use for foundation make-up. Their skin was alabaster tenderness, satin to the touch and without blemishes.

She dressed in her usual uniform of all black and ran up the stairwell to the bridge. The Captain, a 6-foot German with a direct English accent, stood next to the Pilot who was clad in a seaman's coat over a dark sweater. He wore Kaki pants, a shade lighter than the Captain's tan uniform containing black and gold emblems.

One Filipino crew member studied the charts and occasionally watched one of two radar screens, one on the port and the other on the starboard end of the wheel house console, which contained a small wooden wheel. On each side of it was a myriad of indicator lights and switches. On the port or left side were the switches for water pumps to the fire hoses and a breakdown of the ship and fire indicator lights. All the exterior light switches were listed.

In front of the wheel were the controls for the automatic pilot and a compass. There were as many as six compass readings on the bridge. The GPS and both radars displayed compass readings, in addition to an exterior compass on both wings of the bridge, one in front of the ship's wheel and another centered under the glass sliding windows at the very front of the bridge. On the starboard side of the ship's wheel, the panel contained the engine controls, from automatic to manual alerts to the engine room.

Another Filipino man stood watch with the wheel and followed the pilot's orders explicitly. The pilot strolled back and forth along the bridge watching the lighthouse, the jetties and buoy/indicators and hollering bearing changes as he scrutinized everything that moved. At each end of the broad ship's bridge were two sliding aluminum doors on tracks. The pilot hauled each wide door open and wandered out onto the wings for a better perspective at the bow and the channel into the Harbor. Genoa had been a seaport since the 11th century. It was the largest Italian seaport and the second largest port in the Mediterranean.

Kim made herself a cup of instant coffee and grabbed a couple of cookies from a tin next to the pot. It was customary for one of the crew to offer the pilot food or drink while he was on board. Most turned it down. Navigating a ship was treacherous, since it's difficult to correct a problem or stop a 10,000 metric ton vessel once it's set on a course. Kim immediately noticed as she stood in the background, that this would not be a long slow voyage up a river before the ship made dock.

She looked at the medieval city strewn along beautiful forest covered hills. As the Bibi turned gently into the harbor and motored parallel to the concrete jetty, it passed the busy section of the town. She waited for an important call, but only after the delivery was made and the product inspected. First, the ship had to moor and be carefully unloaded. She could sense her palms sweating as she held the cup of coffee.

"Ten to port," the pilot barked, marching from one end of the bridge to the other.

"Ten to port," the young man at the wheel confirmed turning the wheel. He watched carefully the large illuminated dial above the window at the bridge. The indicators above the bridge gave the RPMs of the stern screw, the wind velocity outside, the list of the ship, the angle of the rudder to starboard or port and wind direction.

"Mid-ships," the pilot snapped.

"Mid-ship, sir," the Filipino kit shouted in return.

"Dead slow," the pilot said.

"Dead slow," the Captain said turning a large black pointed plastic knob that set off a set of bells in the engine room. The Chief Engineer in the rumbling engine room actually controlled the speed of the ship and made the appropriate adjustment. Dead slow was approximately five knots.

Kim watched as the ship turned west along the inside of the breakwater adjacent to the docks. They motored along at less than 7 mph, leaving the town behind and entering the grim industrial side of

Genoa. They passed one historic lighthouse called the Lanterna, the symbol of the town. It had been welcoming seagoing merchants for 700 years, but it too was surrounded by industrial rubble.

Finally, they were directed toward a dock perpendicular from the mainland pointing directly to the sea, from which the ship came. The pilot parallel parked the vessel through careful instructions, which were carried out with exacting detail by the crew. Once the lines were tied to the dock and the moment the ship was secure, the Captain called for shutting down the engine. He bowed and shook hands with the pilot, who had him sign a receipt and departed post haste.

Without further adieu, the bridge was abandoned, but Kim stayed and watched the stevedores below on the chilly docks go into action. A crane on railroad-type rollers was pulled into place and several containers were lifted off the deck of the ship so that the massive wheel driven doors of the holds could be operated and folded away from the mouth of each steel hold.

Kim knew she could have no control over offloading her very special cargo. From this point on, it was merely a wooden crate lifted off the ship carefully with 4-inch wide shipping straps and placed on an assigned flatbed truck and delivered to a specific destination.

She didn't want to have any connection to the delicately built carton or the car. It drew attention, as it was a stylish 1948 Bentley coupe, in fully restored condition. Cars were often brought to Genoa, but big cars were very rare on the cramped narrow cobblestone streets of the ancient city. She watched from the bridge as the classic was carefully lifted above the hold, swung over the edge of the hull of the ship, and watchfully lowered to an ordinary flatbed hauling truck. The agent from Rickmers exchanged a few words with the driver and he pulled away.

The day was clear as she looked out at the harbor, which was a mixture of rotting buildings and rows of containers. She sighed with relief as she watched the carefully-built crate surrounded by filthy concrete, rusting containers, a 50-gallon drum bonfire with dirty stevedores standing around warming their hands, and chunks of machinery with exposed threads wrapped with soft cloths and duck tape. It was an odd sight for a few tentative minutes, to witness a jewel of a $200,000 restored luxury car being pulled from the rusting hold of a junkyard ship onto the dour industrial docks of Genoa like a large polished diamond found in a pile of crushed beer cans. In a few minutes it was gone, like the vibrant luster of a blossoming flower in a weed patch.

Kim strode down the stairway to the E deck and the communication room to wait for a call. She was tall and statuesque for an Asian woman. She wore little jewelry but her appearance was impeccable, an odd contrast to much of the ship's exterior and many interior compartments. The Radio Room was a perfect example. It was once the center for communications equipment in the '70s when the ship was built. With satellite communications, fax machines and telex, much of the old transmitters and receivers were arcane and rusting.

The room was finished in a dull white, perhaps painted only once two decades ago. A long deep desk housed much of the scattered equipment. There was one faded computer with a 5-inch floppy disc drive, a Telex fax machine, and scattered fax copies scattered all over the counter, some of which were being organized into several open three ring binders. A xeroxed map of the world was taped to the bulkhead. The tape yellowed and peeled away from the painted surface, leaving a stain. A dark black and white faded copy of the ship's Lloyds Registration was framed in a cheap wooden border and screwed to the bulkhead. Under the desk were coils of used coaxial cables and equipment no longer in use, including a Kelvin Hughes Off Course alarm, which was replaced by the new GPS satellite systems.

The furniture was used, cracked and stained. In the back of the room, a pile of used wooden shelves were torn from the walls and discarded.

The major communication device was a T764 ITT Marine radio transmitter and receiver. The majority of the communication was handled through the Telex machines on the bridge, which were digital satellite communications. The Captain could e-mail, fax or send documents via the Telex. If the satellites were down, he could tune into various frequencies when close enough to inland receivers. In the center of the cluttered office was a satellite telephone, which made all the rest of the massive equipment appear obsolete.

Kim paced the deck patiently waiting for news, when the phone rang and she picked it up. "Kim?" the voice was garbled but familiar.

"Yes," she said, "this is Kim."

"We received money from Slolaf." It was the Wong family accountant. "Good work." He was a tiny man who was cautious, careful, and very protective of the family, old school Chinese. A humble man, he lived with his family near a rice paddy on the outskirts of Hong Kong.

"That's very good news. Have you heard from the Italians?" Kim asked.

"Yes," he said, "they would like to call you directly. Would that be all right with you?"

"Of course," Kim said. "How's the family?"

"What you are doing is wonderful as long as there is limited risk," he said, lowering his voice. "I am concerned about this war with the Wu family. I don't like it, but it is not for me to comment. We are doing so well with your help. We have no use for needless conflict with families who know only fighting."

"Tell the Italian family to call me here," Kim said. "Thank you."

She hung up and her joy was tainted. The American hadn't ruined her deal with the Russians, that was good, but he would still come. She also knew Ling was a fighter and her brother a master. She sensed her time to make a major score and leave for the United States was running out. The last thing she wanted was to get caught in the middle of this tumultuous battle.

As she thought long and hard about her plans, the phone began to ring.

"Hello?" she said.

"Kim-a," the Italian voice said.

"Yes, this is Kim," she replied.

"The package arrive. We-a, like show you town," the voice continued over the garbled equipment.

"We pick-a you-a up at luncha tomorrow," he said.

"I'm at Ponti Libia," Kim said, giving him the dock location. Each dock was named after a country.

"We-a know," the voice sounded as if Kim should have known that they would be on top of her location. "See you-a, noon tomorrow."

She hung up and returned to the lounge where Chee waited with the three other guards. She strolled into the room and closed the door to the lounge then slid the sliding doors to the mess hall closed and turned toward Chee.

"I have some news. First, the Russian paid, "she said and the group muttered to themselves happily. "Second, our package here was delivered and confirmed. I have a meeting here in town tomorrow. I will take Chee with me. I want you to watch this ship, one of you outside my cabin and the other watching that gangway. This is Italy. They know weapons and murder. If that sonuvabitch comes near this ship, kill him."

They nodded like warriors waiting for a long overdue battle.

"Do you expect him?" Chee asked.

"Not today," Kim said, thinking. "It would all depend on when he left Antwerp. I'll see you at the gangplank at noon tomorrow."

Kim turned and opened the door to the passageway and left. She caught the A deck elevator. As it rose slowly past the B deck, she smiled. Two missions completed out of three wasn't bad. The last one concerned her more than the first two combined.

Chance waved to Michelina as he strode up the creaking and grease-soaked gangplank. His mind whirled with thoughts that shot in several directions as he took two steps at a time up the internal stairway to E deck and the Captain's cabin. If the door was open, it was the Captain's signal to welcome visitors. Civilians and officers walked in, crew stopped at the door and knocked.

Chance bolted in the door and turned into the Captain's day room. Dierk, the nimble bespectaled German superintendent with a salt and pepper crew cut sat across paperwork- strewn polished wooden coffee table from the Captain. They both turned and looked at the big man. They were still surprised to see him clean-shaven and his hair cut short. His mustache was still bushy, his thick sandy hair wind blown and his rugged features still transmitted his anxious air.

The Captain raised both of his hands in mock surrender. "1600 the pilot comes," he said in his usual confident broken English. "Cargo is loaded and the Chief Officer is supervising lashing now."

Dierk smiled. "So far we took on 13,000 metric tons of cargo. Another 2,000 tons in Genoa after they shift much," he said and rolled his eyes. He was the man responsible and standing squarely between the stevedores and the Rickmers agents or sales people.

Chance looked at both men. Inside he was screaming to kick this canoe in the ass and do a wheelstand out of the harbor. He wondered what made them click? Dierk was once a ship's captain himself, but didn't like the extended times at sea. He chose to work for Rickmers, jumping from port to port in Europe, and then returning to Germany for weeks of relaxation before another round. He would not take the ship to Genoa, but unwind for a couple of days, then fly there.

"Have you been to Genoa?" he said to Chance.

"No," Chance said, still lost in thoughts of vanishing time, catching the Bibi, or his short poignant moments with Michelina.

"Beware of the pick pockets. They are everywhere. They come from Morocco. I was walking along the seaside restaurants not long ago and three handsome young men passed me. One of them brushed me and excused himself. I nodded and kept walking then noticed that my pen and glass case were missing. I went after them and took both back. I found out later that they kill people without thought and I was lucky. They use knives. Don't put anything in your available pockets and be careful."

Chance nodded. "Thanks," he said, thinking about Dierk's gypsy musician story as he returned to his cabin and changed clothes. He strode to the bridge as the pilot came aboard and stood in the background as the tugs arrived.

"We must leave within a half hour of the pilot's arrival," the Captain said, "or they charge us double for the pilot and the tugs."

Lights came on around the brisk harbor as the ship motored north through the man made canal to the second set of locks. The ship had 32 meters of draft, which forced them to take the deeper locks into the Schelde River, then north again into the Black Sea.

There were two small 250-foot tankers in the lock, which made the pilot nervous.

"I don't like passing like this," he said as he instructed the Filipino at the wheel to steer the ship very slowly, less than three knots into the starboard side of the lock. "All stop," he told the Captain and he adjusted the speed of his vessel with a switch on the bridge counsel alerting the engine room. Crew on the main deck made arrangements to jump to the concrete canal wall and pull the massive ship's line to the appropriate cleats.

The Pilot shouted directions at the bridge crew as he paced back and forth to make sure the ship would fit in the lock between the small tankers and the concrete walls of the lock. At one point, he slowly, at less than a knot, brought the ship up against the starboard side of the lock, then had the Captain move the ship forward gradually. The Filipino men on the dock walked slowly with the lines as the Captain gave them instructions with a handheld radio.

From the bridge, the Captain walked out onto the exterior wings of the vessel into the freezing cold to maintain an alert vigil as the ship inched forward into position alongside the tankers. Members of the tanker crew came out onto their chilly decks to check the ship sharing the narrow space. Once the lock was closed, it was filled with water until it was level with the Schelde River. Then they were released.

Chance tried to stand still in the background, out of the way of the Captain as the ship sat dead still in the lock with crew members on the adjacent dock at both the bow and stern. Dismayed, he watched them drag the heavy mooring lines to the cleats along the edge of the concrete dock, and it broke Chance's heart to see them lift lines, nearly 4 inches in diameter, and place them securely over the massive steel cleats. At this moment in his life, his heart beat for one woman and his love for her was his driving force.

Kim opened the expanding gate to the elevator, then the steel door to deck E and stepped onto the polished linoleum deck. Her cabin was just around the corner and unexpectedly she heard a voice, a groan, she did not know what. It was animal-like and sent a terrified chill up her spine. She grabbed her room key and her hand shook as she inserted into the stainless dead bolt lock on the door.

The sound filling her senses was something dreadful, unnerving and she couldn't make her motions reach inside fast enough. She stepped into the small foyer where she hung her coat and looked in the bedroom, it was a mess. The bathroom smelled of the pungent aroma of puke as she passed it and stepped into the day room. Ling lay on the carpeted deck between the coffee table and the couch. She was rolled into a quivering, moaning ball. Her legs kicking, her skin was covered in sweat and goose bumps.

What the creators of opium-related drugs discovered was the active ingredient in all opiates - morphine - had a chemical structure similar to endorphins, a class of chemicals present in the brain. Endorphins are feel-good chemicals naturally manufactured in the brain when the body experiences pain or stress. They are called the natural opiates of the body. Endorphins flood the space between nerve cells and usually inhibit neurons from firing, thus creating an analgesic effect. On a lower level, they can excite neurons as well. When endorphins do their work, the organism feels good, high, or euphoric, and feels relief from pain. After a constant supply of the opiate, the brain shows adaptation, or a change in its circuitry. When opium is taken away, long inhibited neurons start pumping out neurotransmitters. The imbalance of chemicals in the brain interacts with the nervous system to produce opiate withdrawal symptoms, which include nausea, muscle spasms, cramps, anxiety, fever, and diarrhea.

Kim picked up her phone and called down to the lounge. The Steward picked up the phone,

Officer's lounge?" he said in a Filipino dialect.

"Let me speak to Chee," Kim said.

"Yes ma'am," he said and there was some hesitation as she watched Ling squirm on the deck.

"Kim?" Chee said.

"Bring me some tea, and make it strong," Kim said and hung up.

Kim grabbed a towel and ran to Ling's side. "What the hell are you doing?" she said, wiping Ling's pale sweat-soaked brow. She was shaking uncontrollably.

Ling tried to look at Kim, turning her fever-ridden face up slightly. Her lips were hysterically pursed. Dark circles surrounded her eyes. She shook violently.

"I don't want you to go through this," Kim said. "We can get you help in China."

Ling's eyes were clamped shut as her body jerked uncontrollably. Kim stared at the woman who was bringing her so much pleasure. A gratification she didn't want to release, not yet. She lusted after her constantly. Her tongue, her touch and the feel her body gave Kim was her drug of choice. She wasn't about to let it go.

There was a knock on the door.

"Come in," Kim screamed.

Chee came in with a small tray with a pot of tea nestled in the center. He saw immediately what was happening.

"She's been dumping the tea?" he asked.

"You're right, but only to control the drug, not to escape," Kim said and looked at him hard her dark eyes flickering in the warm light of the room. "Don't get any ideas."

Chee shook his head and set the tray on the coffee table and poured a small cup and handed it to Kim.

"You know when her skin's like that, that's where the adage, 'cold turkey' comes from. Her twitching legs mean she's trying to 'kick the habit'."

He giggled in a low voice as Kim fed a small portion of tea to Ling, who took it willingly.

"Are you falling in love?" Chee asked, looking into Kim's dark eyes directly.

"She's the best love slave I've ever had," Kim said, looking back at him hard. "That's all!"

# -22-

## Sex and Lots of Drugs

Chance awoke with tightness in his guts. He sat bolt upright and looked out of the porthole into the bristling English Channel. He went through the same maneuver every morning for the last two days. The MV Leon loaded with 17,000 metric tons of cargo motored through the gray channel and into the rough Atlantic. It was still dark as he reviewed the condition of the sea. The ship vibrated against the force of the sea and the 15,000 horsepower diesel engine screamed against the bulkheads below the main deck. From time to time the passageways were full of the scent of fuel. It was a toxic heavy smell inducing a lightness in the head and turmoil in the guts.

The ship pushed along at 16.4 knots, which was never fast enough for Chance. He began a workout routine and did sit-ups until his guts would bust just to transfer some energy in some direction away from his thoughts of Ling and the people who captured her. He had four days left to steam into the Mediterranean and try to find her in Italy. He was determined to do something before they arrived in China. The Captain reminded Chance of the organized crime effects on the port, and Chance became more determined to take the ship by storm.

Chance burst out of his bunk and ran the stairs in the interior of the superstructure. There were 12 steps to each level, and there were five levels. He took them one step at a time one lap, and two steps at a time the next, running the stairs for 30 minutes. He quickly discovered the air in the well was poor, filtering up from the engine room. He had to breathe deliberately through each level or he became weary in one lap. Dripping with sweat, he stormed back into his cabin and showered for breakfast at 0730.

The Steward, a well-educated Filipino named Clement, announced the menu each morning, which generally consisted of eggs and bacon, sausage, or pork. Once a week, pancakes were the morning fare, but no maple syrup existed on the ship. Chance generally ate corn flakes with fruit and yogurt. He rarely spoke to the other three passengers, but ate quickly, was courteous, and took a mug of tea back to his cabin after excusing himself.

Just after he caught the thief in the passageway, Marilyn, the schoolteacher passenger, made a big deal out of the conflict to her companion passenger and tried to pull Chance into the discussion. Chance nodded politely and excused himself and departed from the dining room. With tea in hand, he climbed the stairs once more to the bridge and checked in with the Captain.

The second day in Genoa, a black Mercedes sedan pulled up to the ship sharply at noon. Kim and Chee were whisked away. Kim spent the afternoon with Dominic Cavaleria, a tall Italian who treated her like a queen. He was handsome and tanned, 40-years-old with thick wavy dark hair and a light touch of salt and pepper in his sideburns. He was dressed impeccably in black slacks, a crisp crème dress shirt and a black double-breasted sport coat with gold family crest buttons. His gold jewelry was light and tasteful. His face was round and full, his shoulders wide and his nose large and outstanding.

"Come-a," he said getting out of the back of the sedan and welcoming Kim with open arms. "Please-a. We go to lunch and I show you town."

He had the demeanor of a man surrounded with riches and self-confidence. He didn't seem to have a care in the world. The car was solid black, with leather interior inside and burl wood trimmings. His initials were imprinted in the dash in gold.

"You are very beautiful," he said, extending a hand adorned with a family ring to Kim. She responded and he took her hand and lifted it, so that he could kiss it while maintaining a direct gaze into her dark eyes.

As she looked at him, she was surprised that he had no trace of her expected hard mafia demeanor in his eyes. He was the consummate host.

"Do you want to discuss business?" Kim asked from her seat in the plush Mercedes.

"No, no," Domenic said, tapping his driver on the shoulder. "Giuseppe, let's take a ride through town." He turned to Kim. "I'm astounded," and he shook Chee's hand with a friendly squeeze. "She's amazing." He was referring to Kim. "So beautiful, we will talk business tonight. Everything is fine, let's have some fun. I want to show you our beautiful city."

The black sedan skirted into town through the junkyard looking dock areas stacked high with shipping containers and crates. There seemed to be no organization to the freight as the car weaved around one stack of steel shipping boxes and between another stack of awkwardly placed 40-foot containers. There were several security gates leading in and out of the industrial area manned by heavily armed guards. Domenic's driver slowed at each gate, was recognized and the guards gladly waved them through as if they were family. Kim assumed they were.

In the middle ages, the bay became the heart of the Maritime Republic, whose colonies spread from West to Far East, from the Pillars of Hercules to the Black Sea. Everyone in the world, from Byzanthium to Burges, knew Genoese merchants.

They buzzed out of the harbor into the Ferrari Square housing a great blossom of a fountain. Kim found herself looking in various directions through the labyrinth of dark alleys and small sun touched squares, where poor old houses stood for hundreds of years next to luxurious palaces.

"These cobblestone alleys are called 'caruggi'," Domenic said, pointing down a narrow corridor. "Everywhere there are pieces of art on the frescoed vaults of Baroque churches, on the old sculpted slate doorways, even in some ancient shops."

Kim watched fascinated as fish vendors hawked in front of elegant pastry shops. She was amazed at the mixture of people from ancient noble Genoese families mixed with Arabian, Chinese, and South Americans, the late generation immigrants. The car stopped in front of a warm looking, stylish pastry shop across a stone plaza from a Romanesque church.

"This is a fine place for a snack," Domenic said as his driver opened the door for Kim. Chee got out and followed them inside. Domenic was well-known and respected or feared by the owner. He ordered cappuccinos, sandwiches, and pastries for the group.

"How long will you be here?" he asked

"Just three days," Kim replied.

"We have just today and tomorrow left?" A forlorn look shadowed the face of the bright cheerful host.

"Yes," Kim said, "I'm afraid so."

"I wish I had known," Domenic said with dismay, "but I will see from this moment on that you see and feel the city of Genoa."

He never gave Chee any indication that he wasn't invited, but his focus stayed firmly on Kim's attention as the driver picked them up.

"Is there anything you would like-a to see in particular?" Domenic asked and Kim thought for a second looking out on the Via S. Lorenzo and across the street to Piazza G. Matteotti.

Her mind whirled with thoughts of Ling, her business with Domenic, and the notion that somewhere out at sea another ship was coming. The business was her first priority and her relationship with the Cavaliera family. She smiled broadly and pushed out her chest in Domenic's direction slightly.

"You are my host," she said, smiling with her red lips perfectly glossed.

Domenic did not miss a beat, her shapely globes pressing hard against her black Cashmere sweater, the ivory white flesh, or her tall slender, succulent neckline. He read her look with precise indifference. He previously tried to check out her past and desires for the future. He wished he knew more, but the Wong family was guarded. He also had business on his mind. His crew took the Bentley apart and scored the drugs. The quality was suburb and the quantity was exactly what he requested. There was nothing to discuss. They had conferred on the price in advance. The money was waiting for just the right moment.

Domenic took Kim's hand. "I know you have a lot on your mind," he said. His English was terrific although he couldn't help but put an 'a' at the end of many words, although he struggled not to. "I need-a to know only one thing, that you are a quality person to deal with. I sense that you are, but don't know yet. You are headed back to your homeland, and if you remain-a on that ship, you can't get there fast, so you should relax. It is a very humble but sophisticated way to travel."

"I will let you be the guide," Kim said, "and you are right. Thank you." Domenic knew little about Kim, and had no notion of her competition with Chee, the troubles brewing in China, the kidnapped woman onboard the ship and the man chasing her.

Another day passed and Chance made his way to the bridge as the ship meandered in force six winds towards the Straights of Gibraltar. This was one of those historic landmarks still desperately involved in a political battle even recently. Gibraltar is on the coast of Spain but controlled by the British for over a century. It is a tiny peninsula. Some time ago, the British decided they needed it to ensure safe passage of his majesty's ships and would not relinquish it to Spain. As punishment, the Spanish would not give the inhabitants water, forcing them to create a concrete wall along one bank to prevent erosion of the small parcel of land and a way to collect a meager amount of rainwater.

The day was overcast. A dense fog clung to both coasts as they passed Gibraltar on the port and Tangier, Morocco, on the starboard and into the Mediterranean for the final leg of the journey to Italy. Within half-an-hour, the ship was transfixed from a choppy ocean climate to a warming lake-smooth atmosphere. Chance was surprised and befuddled by the extreme climate change.

He worked out taking laps up and down the stairwell. He trained in the Filipino martial arts, going through a series of moves over and over. With each workout, he improved his technique, but as he lost focus with his heightened anxiety, he stumbled and performed poorly. He knelt down on the carpeting and scrambled through several abdominal exercises, lower back sets and pushups. The air was still cool in his cabin as he began to sweat. He drank bottled water and picked up his international cell phone. He needed information.

He dialed Chang and waited as it rang. The soft voice answered. "Hello?" Wing said.

"Wing," Chance said, "It's Chance, is Chang there?"

"Yes Chance," Chang said, "I was hoping you would call. Let me get him. Please hold on."

"Chance," Chang said.

"I'm a couple of days from Genoa," Chance said, "Can you find out if the Bibi is still in port? She's on that ship. The harbor may be guarded but I'll shoot my way onboard if I have to."

"Be careful, Chance," Chang said, "but hurry. I need my sister. I will call you back with ship information."

Chance hung up the phone and called Brad at the dojo in California. The gym wasn't open; the time difference between Spain and California was eight hours earlier. The phone just rang and went to message. He hung up the phone and returned to the bridge.

Kim returned to the ship in the afternoon to change and prepare for dinner. The guards stood fast at the gangplank and near her cabin. They were extremely alert and pensive as she approached. There was no sign of the Anglo man. Two container ships sailed into port but there was no sign of another general cargo ship.

She went to her cabin and found Ling curled up in the bed asleep. Since her failed effort to wean herself off the drug, she had become more despondent and Chee liked it that way. Kim slapped her peach shaped ass lightly and Ling rolled over.

"Are you feeling better?" Kim asked.

"Yes," Ling said. She was brutally aware of the pain she endured trying to fight the drugs off altogether. The opium tea Chee brought was much stronger and she slept for an entire euphoric day after the withdrawal attack.

"Please," she said, "don't let him kill me with the drugs."

"Would you like to take a shower?" Kim said, beginning to peel out of her clothes. She was hot looking and Ling enjoyed watching her slip out of her contoured slacks and skin-tight sweater. Her bra bubbled over with her massive tits and Ling reached up and touched the nipples tenderly escaping the lace edge. Kim reached behind her to unhook the snaps and Ling stopped her.

"Yes," Ling said, "but wait just a minute. Please sit."

Ling crawled out of bed nude and went into the bathroom. She freshened herself and brushed her hair, then turned on the shower and returned with a towel tied around her waist. She walked like someone on a cloud and drifted back into the bedroom where Kim sat on the edge of a small teak stool. She massaged Kim's neck and shoulders, then unleashed her bra and slid the straps carefully over her shoulders and off her slender arms. She ran her hands around Kim's tits and massaged them carefully where the straps and line of the bra held them captive.

"Are you going to wash your hair?" Ling said.

"No," Kim said beginning to relax. "Not tonight."

Ling undid her ponytail and turned her long hair into a bun and tied it on top of her head. Then she pulled her to her feet and knelt between her legs and leaned forward and kissed her mound as she pulled down her hose, then grabbed the silk black thong panties and pulled them down around her ankles. She took her by the hand and walked her into the small steamy bathroom and pulled the shower curtain aside. The air outside was cool and the warm, shower spray felt wonderful running down her body. Kim was getting turned on with the visions of the night and Ling kneeling at her feet, while making love to her.

Kim pulled Ling to her and kissed her hard on the lips, as the water ran down between their bodies and the sense was incredible. Kim could feel her knees beginning to weaken. Ling kissed down the side of her neck and across her tits until she sucked each nipple. As long as she satisfied this woman, maybe they would allow her to live. She grabbed the soap and stood back from Kim for a brief minute and lathered her body, playing with her soft bouncy tits and soaped her pussy spreading her legs slightly, then played with her ass. Kim went crazy with ecstasy watching her.

As Ling finished lathering her torso she pulled herself up to Kim again and used her body as a titillating wash cloth gliding her form all over her female warden, while running her soapy hands where her chest, hips and legs wouldn't reach. She rubbed her tits and torso all over Kim's then spun her to glide her soapy tits down her back. Slowly Ling slid down her body over her ass while massaging her pussy with her soapy hands and then down her legs holding one leg then another between her tits, as she knelt on the floor of the shower stall.

With Kim's pleasing back toward her she rinsed Kim from head to toe then pushed Kim so she bent forward and held the wall of the shower stall with her hands as if she was being searched by the police. Ling rinsed each shapely leg and her small feet. With Kim bent and her legs spread, Ling played with her ass then leaned forward as the water ran down her back and along the crack of her ass.

Kim began to pant immediately as Ling followed the warm water with her tongue. Kim's legs tingled and twitched as she neared an orgasm. She screamed as the rush of pleasure exploded within her. She shuddered and fell against the wall clutching at it as her legs turned to rubber.

Ling ran her hands up and down the woman's legs and over her ass until Kim didn't know if she had just cum or was about to. There was a terrible knock on the cabin door.

"Kim, Kim!" The voice was anxious. "The car is waiting."

Kim leaned out of the bathroom door and hollered, "I'll be ten minutes. I'll meet you on the main deck."

As she turned back, Ling wrapped her in a towel. "You did it again, Ling," Kim said and kissed her. Kim reached between Ling's legs and touched her lightly. "I wish I could stay," she said and pulled her hand away disappointed.

Domenic waited at the dock besides the Mercedes. Domenic kissed Kim's hand as she stepped off the gangplank.

"You are more beautiful every time I see you," he said. "You are glowing."

"I'm sorry," Kim said, "I just got out of the shower."

The car sped away through town and up Assrotti to the scenic ring road, Circonvallezione a Monte, the main road leading through the ritsy suburb on the mountainside. The driver pulled into a circular Palace Driveway. They stopped at the front door and Domenic stepped out of the car.

"Tomorrow I will take you to the top of the mountain on the Zecca-Righi funicular so you can see our vast bay."

A woman came to the door and held it open. She had a polished silver tray in her hand holding drinks.

"This is a nice Champagne," Domenic said as they climbed the 17th century steps. "But if you would like something different, anything can be arranged."

"This is fine," she said, plucking a narrow stemmed crystal off the tray. "Thank you," she said to the girl holding the tray, who bowed slightly and moved away.

"Please," Domenic said leading Kim and Chee into a vast study with ceilings 20 feet high. Ornate art filled the walls and a small fire burned in the metaphorical fireplace. The room smelled of fresh flowers and fine woods.

Domenic was the head of the Cavalerie family in northern Italy and although he was pleased with the shipment and the price, he would never let his supplier know. Domenic raised his glass in a toast.

"Here's to your health, our trade, and our families," he said and raised his glass graciously. He wore a black evening blazer, freshly dressed and shaved, the warm aroma of his cologne drifted around him seductively.

"We do not generally deal in this substance," he said, making sure not to mention the product due to the high-tech surveillance devices known to the police. "I was forced into it by the competition. We hope our involvement will cease soon, but just this once. Before any further business is conducted, we will discuss our financial arrangement."

Giuseppe opened the tall double brass-handled carved wooden doors and came in carrying a very sleek, black leather-covered brief-case with ornately cast gold accents.

"I'm sure you will find the payment in order."

The round, mid-thirties driver and guard placed the thin case on the baroque coffee table in front of Kim. Chee opened it. It was lined with bundles of 100-dollar bills.

The long heroin product journey to America's streets began by planting the opium poppy seeds. The flower's botanical name was papaver somniferum. Sumerians called it Hul Gil, the 'flower of joy.' The flower grown mainly by impoverished farmers throughout small plots in remote regions of the world, flourished in dry, warm climates, but the vast majority of opium poppies were grown in a narrow, 4,500-mile stretch of mountains extending across southern Asia from Turkey through Pakistan and Laos. The Wong family controlled connections in Laos, which was close to their distribution facilities in Hong Kong.

About three months after the poppy seeds are planted, brightly colored flowers bloom at the tips of greenish, tubular stems. As the petals fall away, they expose an egg-shaped seedpod. Inside the pod grew the opaque, milky sap, opium in its crudest form.

The sap was extracted by slitting the pod vertically in parallel strokes with a special curved knife. As the sap oozed out, it turned darker and thicker, forming a brownish-black gum. A farmer collected the gum with a scraping knife, bundled it into bricks, cakes or balls, and wrapped them in a simple material such as plastic or leaves.

The Wong family prepared packages for transport to their morphine refinery. Most traffickers handled morphine refining close to the poppy fields, since compact morphine bricks are much easier to smuggle than bundles of pungent, jelly-like opium.

At the refinery west of Hong Kong, which consisted of a series of rickety laboratories equipped with crudely heated oil drums and shrouded under rusting corrugated tin roofs, the opium was mixed with lime in boiling water. The organic waste sank to the bottom. On the surface a white band of morphine floated. Drawn off, reheated with ammonia, filtered and boiled again, it was reduced to a brown paste. Finally the hardworking farmers poured it into molds and dried the morphine base in the hot humid sun, which has the consistency of dense modeling clay.

Morphine base, smoke-able in a pipe, was introduced by the Dutch in the 17th century. It was also ready for further processing into heroin. The first to process heroin was C.R.Wright, an English researcher who unwittingly synthesized heroin (diacetylmorphine) in 1874 when he boiled morphine and a common chemical, acetic anhydride, over a stove for several hours. The modern technique entailed a complicated series of steps.

When the Wong heroin emerged from laboratories in places such as Bangkok or Hong Kong, it entered a multi-layered chain of distribution. Top brokers usually deal in bulk shipments of 20 to 100 kilos. A broker in New York might divide a bulk shipment into wholesale lots of 1 to 10 kilos for sale to underlings. A kilo of Southeast Asian heroin in 1997 costs $100,000 to $120,000. By the time heroin is peddled on city streets in small "bags" for $5 to $100, its value ballooned more than ten-fold since its arrival in the United States. Not many years ago, virtually all the heroin sold on America's streets was so heavily diluted it was rarely more than 10 percent pure.

Purity rose sharply in the mid-'90s routinely reaching 50 to 60 percent, as dealers tried to expand their market beyond those addicts who injected heroin into their veins with hypodermic needles. Higher purity meant a user could inhale it. They smoked it, and users got high without the threat of AIDS. Greater purity reflected high level of worldwide production. Recently the illicit output of raw opium amounted to a record 4,300 tons, an increase of almost 1000 tons since 1992. By an age-old rule of thumb, every 10 tons of raw opium amounted to one ton of heroin. In other words, the worldwide opium output in 1996 translated to 430 tons of heroin. About half of that was destined for the United States.

Kim pushed the briefcase to Chee. "If you don't mind," she said genially.

"The briefcase is a small present to you," Domenic said, indicating the gift was for Kim. "The case is made of fine teak wood and covered in lambskin. The details were cast in 14 carrot gold by the finest Asian jeweler in Genoa."

The beauty and the weight of each ornate dragon guarding the case stunned Kim. The finest detail was used in the shaping of each scale on the skin of the dragons right up to the rubies in their eyes. The covered handle had two traditional dragonheads and the tongues of each fiery mouth licked the studs in the case to form the links and pivots. She quietly admired the details as Chee carefully counted the money. Domenic casually sipped his champagne and told Kim the history of his home, originally a palace. He wanted to make absolutely sure they were not pressured to count the bundles of cash hurriedly.

As Chee nodded and confirmed all the cash for the drugs was properly accounted for in the custom briefcase he nodded to Kim, closed and locked the leather case and stood, extending his hand to Domenic.

"Thank you for your honor," Chee said and bowed. "Would you have your driver return me to the ship?"

"Of course," Domenic said, indicating to the fashionable maid to fetch Giuseppe. Chee slipped out the door with the driver and would call back to the palace once he was on the ship safely. Chee and Kim agreed, if everything was handled properly, she would stay for dinner and Chee might meet with them later and maybe not.

After drinks, she was invited into the dining room for an elaborate dinner. As the young sexy maid lead them into the lavish hall for dinner, Domenic slid up besides Kim and touched her waist gently and whispered in her ear.

"Tonight is yours to do with as you please," he said. His eyebrows lifted slightly, brightening his warm blue-eyed gaze. "We have everything at our fingertips here."

Kim turned to him and looked at his fine Italian features. She was sure by the confident gaze he was a wonderful lover. Her mind took her to the shower and Ling. She wished the girl could be at her side, yet the thought of her brought along the stalking notion of her man who could arrive in the port at any time. A sudden nervousness swept over her face and Domenic read the anxious fine-boned features in her face.

"Is everything all right?" said he asked.

"Yes, yes," Kim said. "In most respects wonderful."

"Is there anything I can do?"

Kim looked at him quietly, assessing the offer. He might be able to help, but she did not want to bring her problems to his door, not now. She would have to deal with this on her own.

"It's nothing," Kim said, and took his strong arm pulling it against her breast. "Let me think about your offer while we eat."

# -23-

# OUTSIDE GENOA, ITALY

Chance's iridium satellite phone rested on a padded chair under his massive forward porthole. He waited for it to ring, but nothing happened. Because of the antenna placement and his electrical hook-up, the phone was locked in one position.

It was midnight on the night before the Leon might pull into the port at Genoa, Italy. The Captain received incessant telex communications, demanding that he arrive sooner, since the weekend was approaching.

Every minute under the union apron of the stevedore-controlled ports was costly and Dierk did his damnedest to see that the cargo could be shifted and loaded as efficiently and quickly as possible. It was a delicate dance between Rickmers, the agents, the customers, and the unions to make sure everyone was taken care of. It was a game that didn't always play out as intended.

Chance couldn't sleep. He tried to read a book at midnight, and after one o'clock got up and sauntered to the bridge. The course from Gibraltar on the Spanish coast to Genoa was basically a straight shot to the crotch of the Italian coast. It was dark on the bridge except where the illuminated chart table was surrounded with thick lavender curtains. Above the chart table were a couple of old steel desk lights with rheostats to allow the watch to adjust the light level up or down. At times, it was so dark even with the lights turned off above the varnished chart table, the sea was not visible below. Some 32 feet of window, like the windshield of a ship, ran across the bridge. On this coal dark night, the crew could not see the sea rustling about below as the cold steel hull banged along at 16.4 knots.

Chance stepped back behind the chart table and looked at the screen on the MX200, a Magnavox GPS navigator. It displayed the course, the speed, and the position of the ship. Chance looked at the reading and then at the map. He carefully traced his way along the map until he found the position of the ship and put his calloused finger on the spot.

Two massive navigational charts rested on the vast table. One illustrated the immediate area of travel and the other showed a large chunk of the Mediterranean and the coast of Italy above the islands of French-controlled Corsica and Italian-controlled Sardinia. Chance played with the coastal display chart. With a set of calipers, he tried to figure out how long it would take them to reach Genoa.

Tomas, the Filipino third officer looked over Chance's arm as he moved the navigational device along their course. Chance thought he could simply measure between time indicators depicting the distance they traveled in an hour and multiply that by the distance to reach the coast. Tomas shook his head.

"No, sir," he said in his broken English. "I show you."

He indicated the change in speed and pointed out the markers on the chart were for every half hour, then took the measurement again. According to his calculations, they would not see the coast until almost dark, at 1800.

Chance stood up straight and looked across the counter housing the watch list, the ships log and the GPS Log. Several copies of Admiralty publications on safety and pilot services were stacked at the end of the chart table, aft of the bridge area. There was a dark steel door just behind the counter to the interior stairwell leading to the decks below.

Chance turned his muscular back to the chart table and stared at the wall. He wore black sweat pants, a dark sweatshirt and black socks and tennis shoes. The bulkhead was covered with instruments like barometers, the fire alarm panel and a series of operational alarms. There was a Seiko QC-6M2 chronometer and another panel of controls indicating the temperatures in the holds. He wanted to punch the steel wall in frustration, but he would have broken his hand and damaged a crucial mechanism necessary for running the ship.

Chance turned back toward the chart table and Tomas, a middle-aged Filipino man who handled training on ships for 10 years. He was a member of the Filipino Seaman's Union and as such, he worked 8 hours a day and was afforded overtime for his watches on the bridge. During the day, he did what the other deck hands were requested to do. He scraped and repainted deck appliances, chains, and lifeboats.

Chance looked at the short, stocky man with a leadership air about him and smiled slightly. He discovered that very few Filipino crewmembers could speak much English, the common language, since none of them could speak Polish. Also, none of the officers attempted to speak Filipino, a class thing. Other than Chance and the Captain's regular dialog, the ship was made up of three separate countries of folks living together under the same tin roof. He could never explain to Tomas what he was going through, and even if he tried, depending on Tomas' nature, the story could be construed as banal and meaningless.

Chance said goodnight to Tomas and headed down the stairwell to the E deck and beyond. He knew he couldn't sleep and decided to head toward the chow hall and the steward's galley, where he could pour himself a steaming cup of hot water with a Lipton tea bag and enjoy the warmth on the generally cold ship. He couldn't figure out why the air conditioning seemed to run constantly except that the thermostat was in the center of the engine room, and it was always hot there.

With a mug of tea in hand, he wandered through the low rent uninhabited lounge and looked at the photos of half-naked Japanese calendar girls posted on the bulkheads. None of them looked remotely like Ling, but just the fleeting resemblance heightened his frustration and he began the trek back up the stairs to his cabin. He had to get some sleep; tomorrow was the day.

Kim thoroughly enjoyed dinner of fantastic veal, a pasta to die for and wines so superb her toes tingled. After the semi-dull repetitive fare of the ship, this meal was incredibly scrumptious. The two of them sat at a Baroque table capable of sitting 25 people. It was long and adorned with ornate silver candelabras and matching chandeliers.

The room was vast and ornate. A flamboyant fireplace contained several sculpted faces, lion faces cast into the corner forms of the highly elaborate finery. Lavish details laced the room and were painted a soft ivory white while framed panels were painted a cream yellow, so light, if it wasn't for the white surrounding it, she couldn't detect the soft buttery hue. A large marble pedestal resided in each corner including a flowing flower arrangement sweeping over the polished edges.

Domenic sat bolt upright as he ate and never discussed business, only Kim and her trip. He never mentioned the evening to come. As they finished their main course, the maid entered the room carrying a portable phone on a tray.

"Sir, she said, leaning toward Domenic. "I have a call for you."

Domenic picked up the phone as if he knew who it would surely be.

"Yes?" he said.

"It is Chee," he said. "Thank you for your hospitality. I am back at the ship and the cargo is safe. Can I speak to Kim?"

"Thank you," Domenic said comfortably. "Of course you can."

He handed the phone to Kim, who put her linen napkin in her lap sat up straight and took the light receiver.

"Yes, Chee," she said.

"Everything is fine. Would you like me to return?" he said.

"Yes," Kim said. "I would like you to ask Ling to put on some nice clothes and come along."

There was a long silence on the other end of the line.

"That's not possible," Chee said, a bead of sweat building on his brow. It was too dangerous to take their captive ashore. She could get away, create problems with Domenic or any number of events could happen that could destroy the goals of their mission.

"What?" Kim said, raising her voice.

"You heard me," Chee said. "With all due respect to the Wong family, we've been fortunate enough to be successful this trip. The only problems we've had have been with that woman and her man. She's addicted to drugs. She tried to escape. Listen to me."

Kim recognized she stepped over the line. She wanted to demand Ling's presence, but she was also facing a man who could mean considerable business for the Wong family.

"I understand," Kim said and hung up the phone. She sat down somewhat shaken.

Domenic looked at her and recognized signs of discomfort. Kim was obviously a woman with considerable power and ambition. He knew of her past, which could lead to unceasing aspirations for power.

"Do you like your entertainment boisterous, or hushed?" he asked, his blue eye searching her soft round features for truthfulness beyond words.

"Let's start with noisy," Kim said and her face brightened as if she might be taken away from her thoughts. She was consumed with the notion of Ling and their lovemaking and she wanted an atmosphere full of warmth and lust wrapped around her like a new car interior, full of comfort and softness.

Domenic made a motion to his maid and she darted from the room. He poured Kim a small glass of port wine in a beautifully etched flute.

"Come," he said, leading her toward the massive living room with a view of the ancient harbor as the sun began to fade in the west. "This is my favorite room in this part of the house."

Kim looked out the leaded glass windows over the sprawling European city with nearly a thousand years of history and a grand placement on a shimmering coast line. She could see the region where the ship was docked and watched as the richness of the colors of the sky painted the cumulus clouds with deep pinks and orange hues as the buildings in the city took on additional color. Everything around her bathed in sunset colors emulated a passion for life and washed away the dread emotions of everyday existence.

As Domenic looked at her standing in the frame of the tall glass paned window, he thought she was even more beautiful than he imagined. Kim was statuesque for an Asian woman, which made her more alluring. Her hair was long and straight, but pulled into a delicate satin ponytail. It revealed a milky white fine soft neck begging to be kissed. Her features were not Chinese, but more Anglo. He knew immediately that she could not be a member of the Wong family by the shape of her face. She either had Caucasian blood flowing through her or she was perhaps Korean.

Below the window frame in the circular driveway came the Mercedes. Giuseppe stepped out of the car and waved at them through the window above him.

"Would you like to go to one of the most beautiful areas of Genoa and to the best discothèque?"

Kim, dazzled by the beauty of the sunset and the city beneath them, smiled.

"Yes," she said, turning toward him. "That would hit the spot."

"We will see the sun's final rays dance on the beach," Domenic said.

He was the archetypal aristocrat and a faultless host. They freshened up and the big thick driver drove them back into the city down the sprawling majestic Boulevard Via Corica to Corso Italia on the beach and pulled up to the front door of a brightly lit new building strung harshly with neon. Speakers on the outside of the structure blared with the interior rock and roll. A stream of jet setters strolled in and out of the swinging glass door emblazoned with the letters DC. Two tuxedoed men burst out and ran to the car opening the doors.

"Dom Cavaleria, welcome," the handsome young Italian shouted, standing almost at attention.

Domenic smiled broadly and climbed out of the car. The other male host opened Kim's door as she slithered out of the Mercedes into the waning sunlight. She was striking in her slinky black dress with one strand of perfect pearls around her neck.

"May I introduce you to my son," Domenic said graciously, putting their hands together. "Kim, this is my son, Domenic Jr."

Kim looked up at the young man who was 6 foot 3 inches and slender with wavy jet-black hair like his father's.

"You are as handsome as your father," Kim said, allowing his warm grasp to squeeze her hand gently.

"Please, come in," Domenic Jr. said. His partner at the car jogged to the broad doors of the disco and thrust them open. The happy sounds of jamming music hit Kim with their vibrations, coupled with the soft smells of garlic and oil on pasta. "You are just in time to watch the sunset from the balcony."

Domenic Jr. led the way up the wide sweeping balcony stairwell bordered with polished oak banisters and stainless steel pedestals supporting them. The stairway led to a landing overlooking the bandstand and the hardwood and marble dance floor. It glittered with sparkling lights and young couples dancing to hip new American music.

Domenic Jr. rushed to the front of the group and opened another door leading into a private area with a broad 30-foot white leather couch and its own bar. The couch allowed Kim to gaze down over the street below and the pebble beach on the other side, and rich drifting sunlight on the Ligurian Sea. A waitress from the bar below hustled up the stairs and asked Kim what she would like to drink. Kim ordered a Singapore Sling while Domenic spoke privately to his guest.

The bartender/waitress stepped carefully behind the bar and mixed the drinks without making any sounds to disturb the Cavaleria conversation. Domenic senior watched Kim intently.

"You have taken it upon-a yourself to help the Wong family grow." It was the first time he made reference to business.

"They have been kind to me and can no longer succeed in business within the confines of Mainland China," Kim said. "If we don't reach out amid the political changes in China, we could be out of business." She lost her cunning, cutthroat edge under his warm gaze.

"But its one of the biggest countries on the planet," Domenic Jr. said.

"Yes, I know," Kim said candidly, "but the people don't have a lot of money. The people of China make less money than countries a fraction of its size."

The young slender waitress smiled; she had long sparkling waves of amber hair flowing over slim shoulders like chocolate syrup over a mound of vanilla ice cream. She was delicious looking in her slight mini-skirt and tempting skin-tight top over well-rounded breasts. Kim visually devoured the girl and Domenic noted her attraction.

"I respect your efforts," Domenic said, "but there is considerable risk."

"I am doing all I can to prevent any mishap," Kim said. "That's why I'm working with you." Her eyes danced along the waitress' ass as she departed.

Domenic noticed Kim's features and the substantial size of her chest mesmerized his son. He was pleased with her deal but didn't see her as a long-range business associate, more the type who wanted to make a few big hits and had other ambitions. He read her like a two-bit garage-sale western paperback.

"I have some other business to attend to," Domenic Senior said and got to his feet. "We want to show you more of the city tomorrow. Will that work for you?"

"Yes, of course," Kim said. Suddenly she wished her tongue held itself in check.

"Do you mind if I leave you in the most capable hands of my son?" Domenic asked.

Kim looked at Junior and smiled. He was handsome beyond words. He had his father's features except he was two decades his junior. He obviously trained and took good care of himself.

"That would be just fine," she said.

Domenic bowed gently. "Son, you take care of Miss Kim," he said, "I'll talk to you in the morning."

His son jumped to his feet and they hugged. Domenic patted his son on the back.

"The club looks fantastic, and," he said raising his eyebrows in a gleeful manner, "it's actually making money."

"I couldn't have done it without you, Dad," his son said respectfully.

"My son doesn't like our business," Domenic whispered to Kim, smiled and turned toward the door.

Giuseppe quietly opened the door and held it for Domenic, then nodded to junior and followed his father out the dark doors. The disco was a deep navy blue against chrome and stainless steel. Junior built his penthouse to be the bridge on his ship and his couch faced out over the brightly lit streets, the streaming cars and sparkling taillights filling the foreground as the sea splashed against the beach in the background, reflecting the neon of the club and the lights of the street and shops.

The succulent waitress brought Kim another Singapore Sling and Domenic Jr. a glass of wine.

"Do you like our town?" she asked.

"Very much so," Kim said. "It's delightful."

"Do you know where you would like to go tomorrow?" Dom said.

"I'm not sure when the ship is leaving," Kim said and slid a little closer to Dom. "I'm not sure when I'll get up in the morning."

"What if you spend the night with me?" Dom said, lifting his arm and she slid under it, nestling up to his costly fragrance. She eyed his clean-shaven face and his dark waves and reached up and touched them.

"I think that could be arranged," Kim said. "You have lovely hair."

She slipped her hand down over his chest brushing it slightly and rested it on his thigh near his crotch. He tensed then happily relaxed.

Domenic winked at the bartender, who prepared a special tray with champagne glasses, a bottle of Dom and some light squares of sandwiches created below in the kitchen and sent up via a dumb waiter. His bar in his adjacent living quarters was sumptuous and also navy blue with chrome and stainless railings. Stainless rails over the bar held glasses lit by matched and sunken lights illuminating her working area, sinks and coolers for beer and wine. Sections of the bar top railings were laced in nylon line like the wheels on sailing yachts for effect.

The waitress brought the stainless tray and set it off to the side of the snuggling couple on a glass and chromed coffee table. Without a word, she set it down.

Domenic whispered in Kim's ear, "She, too, could stay."

"I would like that," Kim said, turning to the girl and running her hand up her nylon-encased leg under her skirt and over her ass. "Maybe another time."

Kim was getting wet at the thought of undressing the girl, peeling her out of her mini-skirt and tight top, but turned to Dom and kissed him on the cheek and said, "Very nice of you to offer."

She slid her hand up his thigh softly and touched him.

"You should take off your jacket."

The waitress watched them carefully as she departed and locked the door behind her.

He sat forward on the milky white leather couch and pulled off his jacket. Kim helped. She took another swallow of her cocktail and realized that she was getting a bit tipsy and horny. She looked at Dom with a playful smile and touched one of his cheeks.

"Can we fool around here, or will you be interrupted?" she mumbled.

"We can do anything we like," Dom said and pulled her toward him, kissing her soft lips deeply. Their tongues explored each other, seeking and finding a lover's connection. As Kim kissed the handsome man and ran her fingers through his hair, her other hand swept down over his muscular chest searching for a button. She found one and unleashed it and touched his dark mat of black chest hair. She was a pro at one time and knew how to move on a man and enjoyed it.

She yanked on his shirt and pulled the tails free, then undid his belt, unzipped his pants and as he arched, pulled the black slacks to his knees.

"I've got to have some of that," she said. "It's been a long time."

She stood up and enjoyed what she saw. She pulled her form fitting dress up over her head and tossed it on the couch. She stood in front of him wearing a matching bra and panties and no stockings. She slowly reached behind her thrusting her gorgeous tits out at him and released them, tossing the bra aside. Removing her panties, she left the high heels in place and spread her legs.

Completely nude in front of the bank of picture windows over-looking the brightly lit street 20 feet away, she slipped her hands under the perfect curve of each luscious boob and squeezed them gently. Tenderly, she ran her hands up to her nipples and touched them as if they were something extremely precious. They came alive and hardened with each caress, then one of her hands slipped unhurriedly down her stomach and between her legs.

Domenic went out of his mind with lust. She was one of those women who looked as good, if not better, when she undressed.

"Come to me, baby," he pleaded and she delighted to adhere to his wish. She straddled his waist, so he could slide easily inside her.

Using her trimmed leg muscles, she leaned forward and bounced on him while she put one hand on either side of his head on the back of the leather couch. He leaned forward and felt her boobs slide like satin pillows against his warm cheeks. Her body like a well-formed marble volcano pulsed against him. Abruptly, all her senses and the world around her came to life as she neared an eruption. Everything felt stupendous, tantalizing and entrancing. She exploded with her first orgasm.

He rolled her to her side and she laid on the soft couch, her head against the padded arm, and he moved into her again. She could cum a number of times, but suspected he neared explosion.

"Don't stop," she said as she felt her loins beginning to tingle once more. She cried out as her fingernails dug into his hard triceps and she exploded with him in a long rumbling orgasm. They spun off the couch and collapsed on the floor in each other's arms. They had all night in front of them. The lights of the street and the speeding traffic rushed past as the Mediterranean splashed against the shore.

After Chee's return up the greasy gangplank to the ship, he ate a dinner of rice and tough beef with a stale apple for desert. With each bite, his resentment grew. He leaned over his plate and rested his arms on either side as if someone was going to steal it away. His face was round and clean. He tried to grow a mustache but it never filled in. A few whiskers resided on his chin, so he let them grow and they formed a long evil growth of but a few hairs sprouting out of the bottom of his puffy chin. A few more slithered down each side of his mouth enhancing his evil appearance. He wasn't handsome in any sense of the word. He shoveled the food to his mouth abruptly as he jealously raged.

Kim snatched his opportunity for power in the Wong family. If it hadn't been for his treatment in the early days, he would have launched his own drug smuggling business. At least he would like to think so. He pushed his plate away and went to the lounge and poured himself a glass of cheap vodka. No ice cubes or mixers were available in the meager excuse for a lounge bar. If he wanted service besides pouring from the bottle left on the counter, he would be forced to call the scraggly steward. He knew Kim was being treated like a queen and it grated on him like an unrelenting rash.

"Excuse me, sir." The steward stood carefully at the door. "The tray is ready. I thought you might want to take it, since you are on the ship."

His eyes didn't say anything but remained stoic. But he was sure the crew suspected Chee of trouble. A scary bastard, there were rumors of the hidden passenger, but the knowing Filipinos were paid handsomely for their silence.

Chee nodded to the young Filipino and turned back to his vodka. He finished the glass and poured another shot and drank it quickly. Lost in his hateful emotions, he put the tumbler on the bar top and turned to the steward's galley, a narrow room with one porthole over the stainless steel sink and counter looking out over A deck to the sea on the port side. It had steel shelves for plates, cups, and glasses. The deck was tiled in mosaic style similar to those used in the main kitchen. He had a refrigerator for chilled items used on the table and leftovers. The tray sat on the counter with its usual fare of rice, some meat and vegetables and an orange. A pot of tea steamed in the corner of the tray.

Chee pulled out a vial of processed opium and sprinkled a healthy amount into the ceramic pot. Technically, it would have been considered heroin, but they liked to refer to their base plant. Ling's appetite returned when she fought the drug, but it waned when the drug snagged control of her nervous system. That brought a slight smirk to Chee's swollen face as he thought about her and raised the tray for his trip up four decks to Kim's cabin.

That also grated on Chee's nerves. He knew, but didn't understand, why their prisoner was allowed to stay in the best quarters on the ship. He ground his teeth as he fought the cage door open to the elevator and rode the vibrating and clanking steel box up to the deck housing the owner's and captain's cabins. He shoved the door open and walked down the passageway to the owner's cabin. Balancing the tray on the heavy-seas railing, bolted to the bulkheads down most passageways, he pulled the key from his pocket and opened the door without knocking.

The cabin was neat, but Ling's energy level was depleted, and she was incapable of any more picking up for her master. The drug, her imprisonment, the fear of her future sapped her abilities once again. She sat alone in the day room and stared out the forward portholes at the harbor and the buildings peppering the hillside beyond as the sunset. She could see laundry hanging outside several windows in the tall 300-year-old apartment houses.

Chee leaned over and placed the tray on the coffee table in front of her and turned to look at her face. She was still beautiful even in a state of addiction, but her hollow gaze told the story.

Her hair had a natural wave and was pulled to the back of her head in a haphazard fashion. She wore only sweatpants and a gray sweatshirt and had a dazed look on her face.

She looked at him in an unknowing fashion, as if she was served by any number of waiters, and said, "Thank you. Is Kim coming?" Her voice was drawn as if being played through a slow tape player.

Just the thought that his prisoner would say thank you and refer to Kim sent his ire through the roof, and the fact that Kim almost took her ashore to enjoy her success embroiled him. He lashed out and slapped Ling across the face, bloodying her nose. She spun with the blow and fell out of the chair on her hands and knees. In his angry intoxicated mood, he pulled down the sweats exposing her naked ass.

"I am not your servant, bitch," he shouted, "I will show you who you are. If it was up to me, all my men would take you whenever they wanted."

He unzipped his fly, pulled his pants down, and dropped to his knees.

# -24-

# MEDITERRANEAN MADNESS, SEX AND FRUSTRATION

Chance woke with a start at 0630 in the morning. Without so much as taking a leak or brushing his hair, he ran to the bridge to see where their position was concerning arrival in Genoa, Italy. He looked at the map in dismay.

The Captain approached.

"Good morning," he said. "We have slowed. A problem with the lashing in hold number 4. The pipes in that hold are moving around."

Chance ignored his dilemma and stared at the chart.

"How long will it take us to dock in Genoa?" he barked, trying to figure it out by looking at the course markings on the chart and the latest indication of where they were in the hours leading up to daylight.

The Captain, who had trained cadets and taught astronomy, was always anxious to give a lesson. He picked up the protractor and measured the distance.

"It may be as early as 1700 or as late as 1900, depending on our speed and the time it takes to repair the lashing."

The Captain looked up at Chance and saw the strain in his features.

"If we have damage in hold number 4 and take on water," he continued, "the ship will recover. If we had damage to holds 3 and 4 and could not pump the water out fast enough, we would sink. There are lots of options. We would also consider manipulating our ballast. That has its own dangers. If a container ship was taking on water and released its ballast, it would roll over."

The Captain smiled as if he had told Chance something incredibly funny. The image of a ship hauling 8,000 containers and rolling over on the high seas blew over Chance's head.

Chance looked at the man dead pan. "Thank you," he said and moved away from the chart table, a taught iron-bar of angry frustration on two feet.

He stared out at the Mediterranean. Looking in all directions he could see nothing, no coast, no ships, just open ocean. Yet, the ship motored along in dead calm seas as if they sailed on a small lake.

Something in his guts told him that he was running late, late for Ling, and late in life. He was troubled for Chang, for his family, Wing, and he wanted Ling back, before he lost her. It scared him, the thought that she might be killed before he reached her, before he could hold her.

Kim awoke in Domenic's bed. The covers were scattered, the empty bottle of Dom lay on its side on the floor, and the tray still held a couple of small sandwiches. Their champagne flutes still rested beside the bed. Domenic stirred beside her. His bedroom was spacious and another floor above his dining room.

Domenic rolled and leaned over the side of the bed and pressed something. Shades over another set of windows rolled silently open, affording them a morning view of the quiet beach and the Mediterranean. It was an awe-inspiring sight. Domenic leaned over her and pulled the dark hair out of her face. He kissed her cheek.

"Excuse me," he said. "That was a night I will always remember." He climbed out of bed and disappeared into the bath.

Kim sat up in the bed and looked out the window at the small waves splashing at the beach. She was living her dream, dancing on a cloud fueled by opium. She sipped a taste of flat champagne, and believed for long moments that her plan just might work.

Domenic returned from the bath, showered and shaved, in a soft cream- colored terry robe with the DC initials embroidered on the breast. He carried another matching robe.

"The bath awaits you, my dear," he said, extending his arms holding the robe.

Kim got to her feet. "I put two aspirin beside the sink, if you would like. The bath is running and I have ordered breakfast and something more casual for you to wear."

He slipped the robe over her shoulder and kissed her neck."

"Thank you," Kim said, blushing slightly and smelling his clean fresh cologne.

"Call me," Domenic said, "if you need anything."

Kim walked into the steamy bathroom, the shining, navy blue, marble floor cold against her small feet. She gasped at the sight of the magnificent matching marble Jacuzzi tub, next to a large glass-encased shower with two stainless steel heads. The bathroom was as large as her entire area on the ship. He filled the tub, put in just the right amount of Jean Nate fragrant bubble bath, and kicked on the jets.

She hung her robe on the chromed hook behind the door and her tits jiggled as she tiptoed across the floor and stepped into the bath. It felt magnificently decadent as she slipped into the perfectly heated water.

There was a gentle tap on the door.

"Yes," Kim said, "Come in," expecting Domenic.

The door slid open and the little bartender/waitress stood in the doorway caressing a tray holding a long fluted crystal glass fill with a mimosa of champagne and fresh squeezed orange juice. A flower also rested on the silver tray and glistened in the light filtering in from the windows beyond.

"May I come in-a?" she asked with that Italian addition to English. It sounded so romantic, elegant and sometimes just cute.

"Yes, of course," Kim said.

"My name is Toni," the lovely girl said, setting the tray down on a marble pedestal beside the bath.

"Are you going to wash my back?" Kim asked as she looked into the girl's bright brown eyes. Then she noticed that all the girl was wearing was another bathrobe. Her face was round with pudgy cheeks and a gleeful upturned smile.

"I will wash you everywhere," she said, and peeled out of the robe and let it drop to the floor. She was 5'6" tall and thin like a model. Her breasts were small, but her waist narrow and her hips perfectly formed to carry a knockout ass and long legs.

She giggled and stepped into the large Jacuzzi and slid up right beside Kim. She started running her hands up and down Kim's body with the soapy water and Kim rocked back delighting in her touch. Toni soaped up a cloth and began under Kim's chin and worked her way down cleansing her every inch to her toes.

"Breakfast is ready," she said as she finished and stepped out of the tub.

Kim didn't know what to do. She tingled and wanted more, but pulled herself back to reality and stood while Toni took a small chromed flexible nozzle and rinsed the suds off Kim's tall body and wiped her down with her hands. Occasionally, she let her soft wet hand slide up her inner thigh, teasing Kim. She shuddered with each caress.

"You like that, don't you?"

"You're damn right," Kim said as Toni began to dry her from head to toe. When finished, Toni stood toe to toe with Kim, bent slightly and licked each nipple.

"So do I," she said and kissed Kim once quickly before snatching Kim's fluffy robe off the hook behind the door and watching haughtily every slender curve and sway of Kim's breasts as she stepped into the robe. Toni pulled on her own robe and opened the door for Kim.

They walked down the stairs hand-in-hand to a beautiful dining room table behind the leather couch looking out to sea. As Toni pulled the seat out for Kim to sit, she whispered, "I wish we had more time."

Kim looked up to her and their eyes met. She smiled but thought of Ling back on the ship. Domenic came out of his private office dressed for the day. He had on tan slacks, a powder blue button-down collar dress shirt, and a navy blue blazer.

"Your ship won't be leaving until 1600, according to the agent," Dom said, reaching for his chair. "If you're late, they will hold the ship."

Their breakfast consisted of Eggs Benedict, fresh fruit, and pastries so delicate, they seemed to melt in Kim's mouth.

"I have picked some clothes I hope-a will fit you," Domenic said. "They are light for a drive and walking. It will be sunny today but cool."

She dressed in comfortable slacks, a beautiful lace bra fit her perfectly, and a cashmere sweater. He gave her a soft brown leather jacket and they walked out to his Ferrari. As she slipped into the seat, she felt as if she had stepped into another world. She knew none of it was real for her, or was it? Sure, she was a high-class whore, but when the trick was done, she returned to her humble digs. She had nice clothes, and the Wong family paid her well, but not this well.

Chance grabbed a piece of toast and a cup of tea for breakfast. He was tempted to go to the hold and inspect the chief officer's progress with the troubled lashing of hundreds of stands of pipe. He returned to his cabin and put on long underwear and a sweatshirt over his thermal and a t-shirt, then grabbed his old flannel and his vest. He stuffed a scarf in the neckline and grabbed his gloves.

He took the elevator down to main deck and got out. The brisk temps grabbed him as he entered the passageway to the outside. Strips of indoor/outdoor, oil-absorbent, green mat ran down the center of the passageway. As he neared the exit, the grassy jade shade of the matting turned dark then completely black as he reached the hatch door. Outside, the shear cold of the Mediterranean struck home. He clutched the vest close to his chest and tried to work his way through the equipment toward the bow.

The deck had an air of leftover syrup on a plate after the pancakes were gone. It was sticky and greasy. The condition of the ship hit home as he walked toward the bow; railings rusted to the point of rotting and could not be repaired.

General cargo ships had the mystique of being large lumbering vessels with hardworking crew braving the elements to deliver mysterious shipments to far away places. From the looks of the modern make-up of current ships, the romantic image was gone, changing to fleets of tin cans, quickly built and packed with luggage, then sent from port to port as quickly as possible, until the salty brine corroded them.

According to the Captain, the romance and freedom of shipping slipped away. More ships were being built everyday and sent to sea almost on automatic.

"There has been talk of running these ships on autopilot in the near future," the Captain told Chance. "They would have no crews."

Chance passed a bent and rusted-through steel box beside one of the holds. It contained corroded chains and quick locks of different sizes and shapes. They linked the corners of containers together.

He picked one up. It was heavy, cast steel with a locking lever sticking out the side. He tried to move the lever and couldn't. He wondered how many were in place between containers and not locked into place. Chance looked up above him to see containers stacked on top of the holds, along with massive boiler-like drums, and trucks. The containers were lashed with shackles and chains to the decks and holds. It struck him that all this business had to do with people, but due to the costly stevedores' unions and the price of low-paid Filipino crewmembers, that management was trying to eliminate people from the equation. Chance shook his head, knowing it was all about money. He moved forward along the starboard side and tugged on his vest again. He leaned toward the center of the ship, against the bitter cold and away from the sea lapping against the side of the ship, as if it was the bearer of the freezing weather. To an extent, the assumption was correct.

As he moved along the deck, he spotted rusting equipment everywhere, as if he had stepped off the ship into a junkyard of rusting chains, quick-locks, shackles, and lines. He stepped over one tool after another. When he reached the area between holds 3 and 4, he stood at the base of the Stuelcken jumbo derrick crane capable of lifting 200 tons, whereas the other cranes, of which there were five, were only capable of lifting 20 tons a piece. Chance spotted a hold hatch, but moved on, stumbling over cargo lashed down in web like directions to insure cargo safety. The base of the crane held hatches into areas for stocking equipment, straps, container hooks, and such. As much as he loved to work on greasy motorcycles, he avoided touching anything on the ship. As soon as he came in contact with any surface, the filth transferred to him.

As he moved along the deck, he noticed how abused the ship had become. Every ladder leading up the side of the crane was bent and twisted, or so rusted it would be risky to climb. The damage was caused when errant containers or cumbersome cargo crashed into some element of the ship on its way to its resting place. He noticed as he looked at new trucks tied to hatches, how they suffered a similar fate. Running boards were crushed and new taillights smashed. He wondered how a customer would feel when his new truck arrived, as if it had already been in a traffic accident?

Chance stepped over bowstring-tight chain links, as he reached a freezing ladder leading to the bow level where the massive anchor winches were located and the large dock lines, the chalks and bollards for mooring. Below the ladder on the starboard side was another ship's storage space and the hatch was left open. It contained the paint locker, the stores of 5-gallon cans of paint, strewn with streaks of paint from black to mustard, to a red-lead colored rusty crimson, white and a grassy green, the logo colors of the Rickmer's line. He climbed the stars to the bow and saw the two anchor chains dipping into the hull to reach the anchors. Each chain was secured with a latch the size of four car bumpers and four bands of smaller, more manageable chains laced back and forth and through one link over a foot long.

Chance looked at the chain and felt the tinsel strength of each link wrapped around him, tying him to a situation he wished would end. One more four-rung ladder lead him to a small platform above the Panama chock. It was less than two feet wide and only about eight feet across with a simple railing. It was the most forward point on the ship overlooking the bow, as it cut through the Mediterranean Sea. Chance stood on the diamond-plate platform and looked out at the sea. It was an open majestic plain of deep azure blue, a vast torment to any man's soul.

The bright red Ferrari with tan leather interior attracted considerable attention in a city full of tiny gray and black cars and thousands of scooters zipping in all directions. Many waved, and several honked, knowing the owner as he cruised across the winding city through a medieval tunnel.

"Look," Domenic said, pointing across the street to a small building adjacent to a wide staircase leading to a large victory arch. The building was narrow and two story with a smaller than normal front door and windows holding tilted shutters.

"Columbus was born here and that's a house he lived in at one time."

Kim stared at the building built out of simple stones and coated with plaster. It was unpretentious and small by today's standards. The traffic was intense and there seemed to be foot traffic and shoppers everywhere on the streets and in the narrow shop-strewn alleys.

Domenic pulled his car in front of a sprawling newsstand and shut the engine off. One of the owners of the shop ran out from behind the mobile news rack.

"Dom, Dom!" he shouted, embracing Domenic. "You have come to visit, thank you."

Domenic handed him the keys to the car.

"We'll be back in two hours," Domenic said, as he opened Kim's door.

As she stepped out, the young man in his early thirties spun and gasped openly.

"She is magnificent!"

"Kim," Domenic said as gracious a host as his father, "this is Ricardo. He is a friend since childhood."

Ricardo was a handsome young man in a round way. He was stout, his hair dense and wavy, and his eyebrows thick and wide. He smiled and his teeth were bright and even. He had a thick bushy mustache. He kissed Kim's hand from almost the same height.

"Come-a," Domenic said, "We go up the mountain."

He pulled her across the street and she felt like this was all a picturesque movie set and they were the stars. She danced on a coke-lined cloud. She never before experienced such overt social opulence. Domenic bought the inexpensive funicular railway ticket.

"You will never see anything like this in the world," Domenic said, helping her step up into the car built in the '20s. "Everywhere you will see flights of steps and those uphill paths, even buildings with the main door on the roof. These paths once were the lanes leading men and mules loaded with goods from the port to the inland plains."

The train climbed through a picturesque valley along blossoming cherry trees. Kim felt a sense of freshness so close to the city and she could hear frogs croaking in the clear water streams below. At the top of the hill, the train stopped where there were 17th century town walls overlooking the Polcevera Valley and the picturesque Mediterranean coast.

They watched the town below and the ships coming and going. Domenic stepped up beside Kim and put his arm around her narrow waist, as she looked at the harbor and glimpsed another cargo ship entering the port and another one off in the distance. She tensed as if she stepped on a nail.

"I'm sorry," Domenic said, recognizing the standoffish trend. "Am I being too familiar?"

Kim's mind raced with the strange recognition that her life was not a movie, and she had real-life conflicts ahead of her.

"No, no, I'm sorry," she said, turning and grabbing Domenic. "I wish I could just stay here with you and leave my life behind."

She pulled him toward her and wrapped her arms around his waist and hugged him. For the first time, he saw a child-like tenderness in her. She wasn't an all hard-driving, cynical executive. She sensed the same in herself and it scared her. Could she be something other than a cutthroat dealer, or an ex-prostitute? She longed to see Ling, but her captive represented too much turmoil. Ling felt pure, but she knew all lives held their quagmires.

"I'm having a wonderful time," she said and let go of him.

He leaned and kissed her tenderly on the lips and she collapsed in his arms once again.

Lunch came and Chance was already showered and dressed for the port. He returned to the bridge and stumbled into the Captain mumbling, with his face buried in his hands sitting in front of dual Teletype machines. He desperately needed a haircut. Wisps of his hair stuck out in all directions.

"What's up?" Chance said.

"I don't believe it," the Captain said, raising his hands in a frustrated gesture, his eyes bright with dismay. "Jakarta sent a message. They want to know when we will arrive. I don't know what we are loading here or in Singapore. It could take two days just to get through the Suez Canal. It will take another 14 days to reach Singapore after the Suez, and I don't know how many days we will be here shifting cargo."

He shook his head. The notion was incredulous to him.

"They would be better off to contact the people who know what we are carrying in Hamburg." He laughed with sardonic glee.

Chance looked at him and smiled, but the numbers the Captain mentioned startled him. If he wasn't successful in Genoa, if the ship wasn't there, it could be another three weeks before they reached Singapore. He backed up and leaned against the corner of the wooden chart table dumbfounded.

"What's the matter?" the Captain asked, standing up from the rolling chair.

"Nothing," Chance said. "I just need to take care of something soon."

"We will be in Genoa by 1600," the Captain said, hoping to boost Chance's melancholy. "That's only three and a half hours."

The days ahead terrified Chance. It dawned on him that he hadn't heard from Chang and walked briskly back to his cabin.

The phone rang on the other end in China.

"Yes?" the soft voice said.

"Wing," he said, "this is Chance, is Chang in?"

"No," she said in her usual butterfly soft voice, "He told me to tell you that the Bibi is still in port. Are you close?"

"Yes," Chance said, "We'll be pulling in at four o'clock as far as I know."

"Good luck, Chance," she said.

"How's everything there?" Chance asked.

"We are managing, I think," Wing said, but there was a distant tone in her voice. "Please call, if you can reach Ling. Chang will want to know."

He thought it was odd that she didn't want to know Ling's condition.

"I will," he said. "Good by."

Anxious and relieved to hear the BiBi was still in port, Chance hung up and returned to the bridge.

Domenic bought Kim a pastry and a cappuccino, and they sat in the cool sunlight as they watched the harbor panoramic below them. They took the Funicular railway back down the hill and retrieved Domenic's Ferrari. He opened the door for Kim and squeezed her hand as she sat in the cushy soft leather seat.

"I want to take you somewhere wonderful for lunch," Domenic said, his hand on hers and feeling it first as if he was making love to each digit, then he squeezed it lightly. "Then I will take you to the most romantic palace in Genoa."

He drove to Voltri, a restaurant in the historic center and pulled to a stop in front of the establishment. Again, a man bolted out through thick oak doors and took the car to a safe place.

They sipped wonderful wines and shared Focaccia bread seasoned with sage, and a wonderful Torta Pasqualina, a puff pastry with artichokes, eggs, curd and ribbon-like noodles topped with Pesto sauce, made with cheese, garlic and Genoese basil. They finished the tantalizing meal with espresso and Pandolce, a cake studded with raisins, pine nuts and candied fruits.

It was nearly three o'clock as they climbed into the Ferrari again and sped in the direction of two romantic villas.

"Lunch was absolutely wonderful," Kim said, squeezing Domenic's thigh just below his crotch playfully. "I wish we had more time."

Domenic turned to her as his cell phone began to jingle in his Navy blue blazer pocket. He pulled the unit out and flipped open the case.

"Yes?" he said. Kim couldn't hear the voice or what he was being told. He listened intently and glanced at his watch.

"I understand," he said and hung up.

As he slipped his phone back into his jacket pocket, he pulled into the gates of the Marques Ignaszio Pallavicini Villa.

As they rolled over the cobblestone street into the park passed the Museo Civico Di Archeologia Liqure (Archaeological Museum), Domenic said, "This fairyland park was built at the beginning of the 19th century. That road over there climbs to the hill passing exotic and medieval buildings, grottoes and lakes, but we cannot go on." He muttered it sadly. "You have been summoned back to your ship. I must hurry."

Kim recognized the change is his demeanor.

"I thought they would hold the ship," Kim said.

"Something about another ship coming," Domenic said, his face transformed from his loveable playboy manner, to deep concern. "I dislike the business my father is in and try to avoid it at all costs. I'm saddened by this event. I was enjoying your company."

Kim couldn't speak. She was warned, Chance would keep coming. She was also stunned Domenic had this information and the timeliness of it bothered her.

"Who knew?" she asked.

"I don't know," Domenic replied, shifting gears and revving the 16-cylinder engine as it scuffed along the winding road like a missile with wheels. "My father received a call. That's all I know or want to know."

From a lover, he shifted to a man on a mission, darting in and out of cars. He pulled on a navy blue ball cap and his hair swept back, curling over the edges of the cap. He opened his glove box and yanked out a navy blue scarf and handed it to Kim as he shifted again and the roar of the engine forced her back in the contoured seat designed for racing. She ducked, unfolded the scarf, and noticed that it, too, was monogrammed with the family initials. She engulfed her whipping hair and tied the soft scarf under her chin as the car spun effortlessly along the narrow historic streets at 80 mph.

Domenic slowed as he entered the harbor and waved as they shot through one of the security gates. Sliding between stacks of containers, he wrestled his way through the harbor maze as if he performed similar driving drills on a regular basis. Suddenly she sensed he knew this harbor like the back of his hand. He pulled the bill of his hat down as he careened around a boiler set on crates.

"Ponti Libia, correct?" he asked, Kim holding fast as he maneuvered between lumbering trucks and stacked crates.

"Yes," she said as he screamed onto a dock and she could see the forest green hull directly in front of her. He jammed on the brakes adjacent to several longshoremen and the light exotic car slid to a stop. She looked at the dock as he ran to her side of the car.

The area was cleared except for dockworkers standing at the mooring lines. The ship was loaded and there wasn't another item, crate, container, nothing on the dock. The boxes of quick locks were gone, along with longshoremen gear, broken pallets, strips of wood used to create space under I-beams and tools. Even the crane on tracks motored clear of the ship.

Domenic opened her door one final time and she graciously stepped out of the car. She pulled off the scarf and attempted to return it to him.

"It's a gift, as these are," he said, handing her a small velvet box. "Do not open it now; hold me. Then you must go."

Without a word, she burst into his arms and they kissed deeply as the ship's horn blasted in the background. When she broke from his warm embrace, something warm embraced her. Their arms struggled to release their grasp and she ran to the gangplank as a tugboat pulled along side the BiBi's starboard side. Torn between the evils of her mission and Domenic's embrace, wealth, and the riches of this land, she lost herself in an adult Disneyland.

At 1345 the ship pulled away from the pier. Kim ran to the external wing of the bridge waving at Domenic as it motored to port and the channel slipping the ship out to sea. An intense lover of all women, Domenic was taken by the sultry Asian woman who showed her heart to him. He knew it was unlikely he would ever see her again. His car glistened in the center of the rough asphalt dock stained with years of grease and paint. The passenger side door stood open.

The Bibi steamed out of the harbor and to the southeast toward the Straight of Messina between the tip of Italy and the island of Sicily.

Chance stood on the deck as the Leon neared Genoa. It was 1600 as they slowed to receive the pilot for entrance into the port. A tugboat steamed up along side and took a line from the stern to act as brakes in case the ship headed into harms way. Just a slight tap against an unforgiving dock with a loaded down hull could cause major damage to the ship's structure.

The Leon steered into the port from the west. A constant stream of ships departed and entered the largest Italian harbor.

It was another half hour before the Leon nudged against the dock in Genoa. Chance was dressed and ready to go. His first mission was to get his motorcycle, if possible, and scour the port. He had to find her this time, take her back with him to the Leon and safety.

Stevedores stood on the docks and waited for the small mooring lines to be tossed to them. Each thin line was tied to one heavy line 4 inches in diameter. The men on the docks wearing fluorescent overalls hauled away to pull the heavy lines to shore and wrap the laced eye over a massive steel bollard on the concrete dock.

Another half hour passed as the lines were carefully placed then winched tight to moor the vessel perfectly for crane access. The dock was cleaner than Chance remembered docks in the past ports, but trucks pulled close, quickly carrying crates and equipment to load on board. A tremendous amount of shifting would take place first just to gain access to the holds. Chance stood on the bridge until the pilot and the Captain departed. He looked out over the bridge wing and watched a couple of cars pull up, one containing Deirk, the cargo superintendent, who flew from Antwerp to meet the ship.

As the gangplank lowered, Chance already called a taxi in lieu of waiting for containers to be lifted off the ship in order to reach his motorcycle's hold. He ran down the scooped aluminum steps leading off the ship, while grabbing grease-smeared cannabis railings and posts.

"Dierk!" Chance shouted, reaching the bottom of the steps. "Can you tell me where the Bibi is?"

Dierk turned to a salt and peppered haired Italian man at his side. He was Francesco Colella, the line manager for the agent Paolo Scerni.

"Do you know about the Bibi?" Dierk asked.

The handsome gentleman in a sailing jacket, slacks and polished soft leather shoes turned to him with an astonished air and raised his hands. He worked in the port of Genoa all his life and retired 12 years prior, but could not stay home and returned to the ships.

"This-a is Pointi Libia," he said with a look of dismay. "The last ship here was the Bibi. It has been gone-a less than one hour."

Chance ran his fingers through his hair, clutching each fiber as if he was strangling a thousand people. He could not believe his ears. Dumbfounded, he turned and ran to the end of the dock and stared out to sea as the sunset sprayed the coast with golden-amber rays. His mind whirled with disappointment, hate, dismay, and questions.

What would he do next? He watched a ship on the horizon begin to dip from sight and wondered whether that was the Bibi heading for the Suez Canal.

# -25-

# Singapore Airlines, A New Direction for Chance

Chance returned to where Dierk, the Rickmers cargo superintendent, and the agent, Francesco, stood on the dusty dock, but they had already boarded the ship. The cab driver sat in his small compact and looked at him curiously.

"Wait here," Chance said. "I'll be back in five minutes."

He followed, rushing up the creaking gangplank onto the main deck across the grease-soaked steel surface into the interior stairwell, where he jogged up five flights of stairs. Panting, he burst into the passage way as they departed the elevator.

"Dierk," Chance said, still breathing heavily, his emotions on the brink of bursting through his chest. "Do you have information on the agent in Singapore?"

"Yes, of course," bi-speckled Dierk looked at him curiously. "I always carry his card." He dug out the card and handed it to Chance.

"Can I have this?"

"Of course," Dierk said as Chance walked briskly past him to his cabin. He dialed Chang and stood next to the porthole at the end of the antenna leash.

"Yes," Wing's soft voice came on the line.

"Wing," Chance said, "Is Chang there?"

"I don't know," Wing said, her voice lost its original softness. "What happened?"

"I got to Genoa and the Bibi was gone," Chance said. "I don't know what to do?"

"Let me see if Chang is here," Wing said. Her voice again shifted from its gleeful, caring sensation. Perhaps the pressure rocked her world.

"Chance," Chang said, "I'm sorry to hear you couldn't reach my sister. I've got to have her back."

"Listen," Chance said, "I'm not in your shoes, but how is Wing doing? Have you two been together for a long time?"

"Not so well," Chang said. "Tough to say, now."

"Okay," Chance said. "I must get on that ship in Singapore. I'm playing in the wrong game here. I need to improve the odds. Can you help me?"

"Of course," Chang said. "What is it that you will need?"

"I need absolute trust and secrecy from you," Chance said. "I'm going to fly to Singapore from here. I need to figure a way to be loaded on the Bibi. Can you help arrange this?"

"I think so," Chang said, but his original confident air was gone. "I will do all I can. We must hurry."

"That's not good enough," Chance said. "We must get aboard that ship. Besides, you are footing the bill. I have the shipping agent's contact info, and I'm going to fly there immediately. I will have a couple of weeks to find someone I can trust and get on a declaration for China."

"You do not understand," Chang said. "Life is rough here and getting more hazardous all the time."

"I'm flying to Singapore today, if at all possible," Chance said. "I will call from a hotel there. Get me a secure number or cell phone where we can talk freely."

Chance hung up. He wished he had more insight into their relationship and the struggle going on there, but his mission remained the same, get Ling off that ship.

He started to pack his belongings, throwing his clothes in a bag. He picked up his book of notes and ran across the IMBI phone number and decided to give it a call. Sometimes Brad trained guys early in the morning. The phone rang and rang.

"IMBI," the voice was panting.

"Is this Brad?" Chance said.

"Yes, this Chance?" Brad said.

"Yeah, I need your help," Chance said. "Can we talk?"

"I'm sparring and about to train a class," Brad said, also a long-shoreman. "What do you need? Whatever it is, we'll put it together."

"I'll run it down quickly, then get back to you," Chance said. "I missed her ship again. I'm going to fly to Singapore, but I need to be loaded on the Bibi with the cargo, like in a crate. Let me know how we can do this. I'll call you from Singapore."

"We'll get on it from here," Brad said and hung up.

Chance disconnected the phone, grabbed the portable antennas and packed them. He had to leave behind the fixed mast antenna to the bridge. He looked at the connection and thought about Ling riding out the rest of the voyage in that cabin with him. A smile crossed his lips for a split second.

He gathered his gear and stacked it on the long day room sofa. He went to the Captain's office and walked in on a meeting with Dierk and the agent, Francesco.

"Sorry to interrupt," Chance said.

"It's okay," the Captain said. "Customs official will be here at any minute. Please bring your passport."

"I'm leaving the ship and flying to Singapore," Chance said. "I thought that was cool."

"It is," the Captain nodded, "but you must sign in with customs to get ashore."

"But you are not going to enjoy our lovely city," the agent said and stood up to shake Chance's hand. Chance realized that his haircut and clean-shaven face gained more respect.

"I'm sorry," Chance said. He wanted to say something polite, but his mood didn't call for it.

"Keep everything valuable out of ordinary pockets," Dierk muttered, looking over his shoulder. "I've been robbed here before by pick-pocketing immigrants. Nice young men who will slit your throat for nothing."

Chance nodded, thinking that he would love for some unsuspecting pickpocket to try to reach in his coat. His adrenaline pressure would instantly allow him to break every bone in the man's body.

"Thank you," Chance said, and turned to leave the Captain's day room.

Chance grimaced, returned to his cabin and dug out his passport from his gear. He paced the inside of his room like a bull waiting in a

pen to be unleashed on some unsuspecting rider in a national championship. Over 2,000 pounds of pure screaming muscle waited to flex with bullwhip speed. His cabin phone rang and Chance grabbed the receiver.
"Yeah?"
"Captain here," he said. "Please bring your passport."
Two officers sat on a couch in the Captain's day room, laying out papers and looking at a stack of crew passports.
"Hello," the narrower of the two said, sitting in his gray uniform with red lappets and silver embroidery. He looked at Chance's passport, stamped it and motioned for him to leave.
"Have a good time," the wider of the two said, looking around the room as if he expected a small bag of gold for his services. He didn't fit his uniform at all. His long wavy locks needed a haircut badly, and he gained a tremendous amount of weight since the last time he had his uniform fitted.
Chance didn't understand. It was as if he was on another planet. The two officers had the demeanor of two men expecting a bribe. Chance didn't give a shit; he was just glad to get the hell out of there. He jammed back to his cabin, stuffed all his shit in his bedroll and tank bag, headed for the docks, and hailed a cab.
"Airport please," Chance said, slipping into the back seat of the Mercedes after the young driver placed his rough luggage in the trunk.

Ling awoke two days out from Genoa in a euphoric cloud. The weather changed again for warmer climes as they motored toward the coast of Egypt. She sensed a touch, but her mind moved in slow motion, then she realized someone was kissing her. A soft caress touched her ass. She rolled over on her back being lead by Kim's soft hands.
"It's my turn to please you," Kim said and lifted another pillow so Ling could slide her back up toward the headboard. She pulled her legs up and in a drowsy drugged state looked down her long legs as Kim kissed between her thighs.
Ling was again lost in the evil drug. Everyday, she felt a distance developing between life and the cloud she lived in. She knew it was wrong and something told her if she didn't let it flow, she would be dead or in the freezing hold dying.

She missed the love she had with Chance, and the reality of building something together. She wondered if he gave up and went home.

She looked down at Kim's beautiful naked form and her soft lips kissing her most tender parts.

The slithering delight and sensitive tenderness of the caress drove Ling crazy. It was the only sensation that competed with the lustful nature of the drug's rush. She arched her back and dreamed that this feeling would never stop. It was downright unfair. She cried out as the wave increased in intensity then she collapsed off the pedestal and pulled Kim to her.

Chance caught a Singapore Airlines flight to Singapore. Indonesia had a lawless air about it, except for Singapore. The city of four million sat on a small island 26 miles long and 14 miles wide. The reputation of the independent city was one of extreme regulation to the point of regulating spitting on the sidewalk, which cost a citizen a $200 fine.

Chance had only one notion as he sat on the plane in Levis, brown cowboy boots and a green sweatshirt. He felt a sense of motion. This time, he would wait for the BiBi to arrive and take control of this situation. His mind whirled with what to do and how to do it. He had notions of a large sprawling harbor city full of small boats and cute people. The stewardesses on the flight were gorgeous women in their early twenties with radiant smiles and soft comforting demeanors.

The first Singaporean girl flew in 1972 and their nation's airlines spread their wings across Asia and onto Europe, Australia, North America and Africa. They developed a reputation for a top-level of in-flight service. Each beautiful stewardess was a charming ambassador for Singapore, reflecting their warm and caring nature and an unwavering commitment to the pursuit of excellence.

As Chance read through the city's literature, looking for any information, which might help him, he discovered he wouldn't have a problem getting around town, since the city was blessed with over 15,000 taxis and 2,800 buses running 24 hours a day. He also discovered the port was the busiest port in the world with ships entering and leaving every four minutes.

As the jet entered the space above the island captured and terrorized by the Japanese during WWII for three years, until the war ended, Chance looked out the window and saw what appeared to be a fleet of ships coming and going from the harbor resting on the main artery between the Orient, the Pacific, and Europe. Whole islands off the coast of Singapore were devoted to oil refineries.

Chance was beginning to feel secure in his new mission. He could find a shipping company to build his crate. On the other hand, he was alone in a city very close to the equator and completely out of touch from anyone. He kept reading madly and discovered two airports. One was the original Singapore Airport. It was used exclusively for island-to-island and Malaysian travel, whereas the newer Changi Airport nearby was the international airport. Plans were underway for another airport due to open in a few years. Chance still held images of sampans and grass shacks as the airliner touched down near the state-of-the-art terminal.

Thumbing through a book about the city, he rolled through the list of hotels, including the tallest hotel in the world, the Westin Stamford and a number of other high-class joints until he stumbled across a hotel built in the original Singapore Post office, the Fullerton, and decided it would work. One of the stewardesses made a call for him and confirmed a room was available.

The majority of the passengers on the packed plane were Chinese. Some 75 percent of the people in Singapore were Chinese, 14 percent Malay and 7 percent Indian. With the threat of communist take-over in Hong Kong, many of the wealthiest people began to invest in Singapore and moved their headquarters to the island.

Chance was impressed as soon as he stepped off the jet into a terminal lined with slate floors, floral arrangements and three-story fountains. He moved to the turnstile to pick up his luggage, which he checked onboard due to the weapons he carried. He waited patiently, while asked by a porter if he needed assistance. The lovely stewardess from the flight stepped to his side, "The help from porters is free." The generally accepted language in Singapore was English, which relieved Chance.

He grabbed his bags and headed through customs, praying he wouldn't be searched and then walked casually out to the taxi stand. A small Malaysian man came to his service, put his bags in the trunk and opened the door. Chance was already impressed with the country and he hadn't left the airport. The grounds were perfectly landscaped with lush green vegetation, blossoming bougainvillea vines, and wild palm trees. Chance was immediately caught by the hot steamy humidity, until he sat down in the small air-conditioned compact cab covered with a peel-and-stick, silk-screened advertisements for Carlsbad Beer. Even the centerline hubcaps read the name of the beer. All three cab companies were controlled by the government.

As they pulled out of the sleek, pristine building and passed the Changi Airport Control Tower rising above the landscaped grounds, Chance began to relax. He immediately recognized and sensed he was entering a place where he could find cooperation.

"The Fullerton Hotel," Chance said, looking over the back of the driver's seat to the control panel the cabbie faced. It seemed incredible, the myriad of gauges and communication devices.

"Are you from Singapore?" Chance asked, testing the water for information.

"Yes sir," the young man said, wearing driving leather gloves with holes punched in the fingers. "All cab drivers are born here. They all know the area and can help you in many ways."

"What is all this crap on the dash?" Chance said disparagingly, but not meaning it.

The driver lifted his sunglasses to turn back and look at Chance as they entered the well-kept East Coast Parkway freeway system leading into the city.

"This is satellite navigation communication system," he said, pointing to a shoebox-sized screen facing him from a mounting post on the center consol. "This meter shows you how much I charge. This is my stereo. This is voice communications." He held up a mike on a curly-Q cord.

"This is my credit card dispenser. We take all credit cards, but there is extra fee. This is a processor," he said, pointing at another unit with a digital readout mounted to the dashboard and accepted some sort of credit card. "It is used for frequent traveler systems."

Chance rolled his eyes as he added the air freshener glued to one of the air vents, a satellite phone rack mounted along the curve of the dash, the box of Kleenex stuffed between the seats. Finally, the driver had a toy bicyclist screwed to the vent close to him. The wheel spun as his fan briskly blew threw the spoked wheels, and the rider peddled like mad. Chance sat back and shook his head.

As they drove along the beautiful lush green corridor, he started jotting notes on a piece of scrap paper with a pen the smiling stewardess gave him. Each time he looked at her, the warmth of Ling poured over him. At the top of the list, he wrote 17 days. According to his captain, the ship would take 3.5 days to reach the Suez Canal. One or two days to pass the canal, depending on arrival time and traffic, and it would take an additional 13 days to travel through the Red Sea, across the Indian Ocean, around the tip of India through the Sea of Bengal and into the Andaman Sea to finally turn into the Malacca Straights to reach the tip of Malaysia and Singapore.

He had a deadline looming. His attitude was one of never-say-die and can-do cliché's, but they were part of Chance's never-a-dull-moment life, and since he met Ling, there was never a dull second.

"You must go to Chinatown," the driver said, pulling off the highway onto Fullerton Road rounding the magnificent colonial edifice, which was the post office during the 1800s and was not destroyed during the Japanese occupation. It was four concrete stories high and looked every inch a government building, from the iron gates, as it sat overlooking the Singapore River. Relieved to see something from the past, Chance spotted several small wooden boats with canvas tops and tires tied to the sides motoring up and down the river.

"I'll go," Chance said, getting out of the car.

"You will never want to come back," the driver said and sped away.

Chance looked after the flashy Carlton Beer taxi and wondered what he meant. A porter ran to Chance's side and grabbed the luggage.

"Checking in, sir?" he said in his tan uniform buttoned tightly around his neck in the simmering heat and humidity.

"Yes, I am," Chance said.

"Thank you sir," he said, "Welcome to Singapore."

Chance looked up the street bordering the river. There were two magnificent high-rise buildings, and then a series of plastered, narrow, almost French buildings, two stories high all painted various brilliant colors. Most had outdoor seating on the river with umbrellas over each table.

Chance followed the porter inside and was stunned. The hotel was vast and the floors were covered in a beautiful black and tan colored graphically designed marble arrangement. A tall broad fountain stood in the center of the room and clear water fell for three stories over an arch of dark glass to a pond in the floor below. He entering the massive room and was mesmerized by the shear vastness of the area. He never stayed in a hotel of this stature in his entire life and wasn't sure he should. He checked in and was struck by the elegance of his room's interior and view of the city's lush green landscape, high-rise buildings and the sea. He called Chang immediately.

"Hello," Wing said.

"Wing," Chance said, "It's Chance. How are you?"

"I'm better," Wing said sweetly. There was a return of her former grace, but Chance continued to feel the pressure. "Where are you?"

"I picked the hotel built out of an old post office, because I was trying not to spend much money," Chance said.

"It is very expensive, but that is fine," Wing said, "We need you to be comfortable."

"Is Chang in?" Chance said.

"I will tell Chang you called," Wing said without responding to his last question. She hung up abruptly.

Chance hung up the phone and honored the design of the phone and interior accouterments of his room. He quickly unpacked. The sun set and his stomach growled. He knew there was nothing he could do but to familiarize himself with the town. The first thing on his list was to call the agent in the morning and find a shipper. He also knew that his attire would need to change quickly in the Singapore humidity.

Below in the lobby, the concierge smiled broadly when Chance asked for a place to buy clothes.

"The Suntec Center is the largest high-rise shopping mall in the world, and it's only a short distance away."

Chance started out the door then decided to return to his room. He waited by the phone for Chang to return his call, but it didn't come. The sun slipped over the horizon, and he couldn't call shippers and proceed with his plan. He paced the room. Then decided what the hell, he would get some clothes for the tropics. He took a cab to the Suntec center and fought a vast hurried crowd trying desperately to make their purchases before the stores closed.

He bought three loose fitting light Hawaiian type shirts and a couple of pairs of Dockers and some shorts. Each floor of the five buildings was alive with tourists, Europeans, but predominately Chinese, and English was spoken regularly.

Chance noticed something strange in the third shop he approached. He recognized one of the customers from the Dockers franchise. The customer was a young, harsh-looking man. Most people meandering in and out of the malls seemed busy, if not pleased. They chatted and were coupled to cell phones constantly. This young man was dour and seemed disinterested in the clothing line. He wasn't wearing anything particularly out of the ordinary, but through Chance's training with his buddy, Mark, who was a bodyguard and security specialist, he had learned a couple of things that now returned to the center of his memory field. This young man was wearing baggy, loose fitting clothes, a T-shirt and worst of all a parka like affair.

Only business people forced to wear suit jackets had anything on resembling a coat. To Mark's security-minded thinking, anyone wearing a jacket in 85 degree temps at 70 percent humidity was carrying a gun.

Chance noted the man's position and tried to place himself so that he could check the small man out thoroughly, so he wouldn't miss him again, if in fact, he was being followed. The young man's hair was closely cropped and parted, nothing out of the ordinary. His face was round, but athletic. His jaw muscles twitched. Either he was grinding his teeth or chewing gum. He didn't wear glasses, but there was a small ¼-inch scar above the right side of his mouth like a childhood cut. His nose was small and thin and his eyebrows narrow. His eyes were dark and darting. There was a nervous air about the man.

Chance paid for his shorts and a pair of Teva boating sandals and headed back to the hotel. It was getting late and he wanted to get as much sleep as possible. Besides, he hated shopping and this was the second time in years he shopped for anything other than a sweatshirt at a motorcycle run or a Harley shop.

Chance had no experience at dealing with someone following him or worse. He wasn't a spy and had no experience dealing with them, either. Hell, he had no familiarity with most of the crises filling his current life. He was shooting in the dark without even a candle. He took the elevator to the Suntec Lobby and stepped out into the warm evening.

He knew he wasn't far from the hotel and decided to walk down Temase Boulevard past the Pan Pacific Hotel to Raffles Link along the Marina Mandarin Hotel and the Marina Square Shopping Mall. He decided if he was being followed, he'd try to confirm.

As he walked along on the well-lit sidewalk boarded by pristine landscaping, he tried to find something he could use for reflection to see behind him. His lack of knowledge in the area of surveillance didn't help, and he was burning up in the thick leather cowboy boots and Levis. He reached the corner of Raffles Avenue and Esplanade Drive and looked both ways as if to pass. He could see nothing except yards of traffic. He grabbed the first cab he could find and returned to the Fullerton and the solace of his room.

He ordered a Jack on the rocks and a Sushi appetizer platter from room service and took a quick shower. He put on a pair of workout shorts, a t-shirt and opened the door for room service. When the young man placed his tray on the table, Chance signed the check and handed him five Singapore dollars. The young man brightened and said, "Thank you."

"Do me a favor," Chance said. "I'm waiting to surprise a friend. He's wearing light all-black jogging pants and a parka. Would you let me know if you see him?"

"Yes sir," he said gleefully, "of course."

Chance laid down on the big sprawling king-sized bed and sipped the drink. The coolness of the glass felt good in the air-conditioned room. He pulled out the slip of paper he had notes on and review it with tentative eyes. He had no notion of the import business, but he would learn quickly.

The slick phone on his night began to ring.

"Yeah?" Chance said in his usual abrasive tone.

"Mr. Chance?" the bellman said and Chance could feel his successful grin over the line. "I have found him. He just came in the hotel."

"Don't say anything to him," Chance said. "It's a surprise."

"Yes sir," the bellman said and hung up.

Chance sat up and swung his legs over the side of the bed. He downed the amber liquid in his glass and leaned against his knees, sensing that he might have more than one challenge ahead of him.

# -26-

## Singapore Shops, Kim negotiates

Kim dressed and walked briskly to breakfast to meet Chee and her two security guards. As she entered the room, she immediately sensed a cold atmosphere. Usually, one of her guards jumped to his feet and held a chair for her. No one moved. She knew of Chee's ambition and dealt with it, but the others were always loyal.

She pulled out her chair and stood in front of it with her fists bunched on the white linen tablecloth. She was dressed in a simple suit of dark pants and Chinese preacher-like shirt that buttoned up the front to a collar and embraced her slender neck. The neatly trimmed sleeves came to mid forearm. She had on little make-up and her straight black hair was pulled into a ponytail. She was simple, statuesque and well kept.

"What's the problem?" she asked before sitting. She towered above them.

"We have heard that the American was coming again," Chee answered for the crew. "I heard this morning that he is in Singapore. We are tired of this. We are close to home. We've done our job."

"Shut up!" Kim snapped. "You have no notion of what is going on at home. You're job is not complete until I say it is."

The little man on her right suddenly remembered her anger. He worked for the Wong family since he was a teenager. He watched the family grow and falter, then grow again under Kim's leadership, which many times took a turn for the violent. Yew looked up at her as she turned on him and he reached inside his jacket for his silenced, stainless, Walther automatic. She slapped him, disarmed him, and held it firmly in her hand while spinning silencer out of the barrel before he could react. He was stunned and stepped back.

She had always been fair with him and that's why Yew was willing to take this voyage, but he was tiring of it. As he watched her release the cylinder from the barrel of the gun and toss it against the steel bulkhead, he recognized the old Kim and was afraid.

"We don't need silencers on the ship," Kim said, pushing her chair farther back with her leg. The dining room was narrow and long, and she stood at the head of the linen-covered table. She backed against the teak divan housing the silver for special occassions.

"Now, let's review," she muttered, wiping down the weapon in a sexual fashion which was her style. She had a way of turning emotions and twisting them, mixing sex and fear. She stroked the barrel of the gun sensuously.

"We succeeded in Russia, and in Italy," she continued. "This woman could mean that our ability for distribution is greatly enhanced, but we must take her to China. If I want to play with her along the way, that's my choice. Maybe I should share her with you."

She knew that Chee was behind this unrest, and she would have to deal with him directly.

"The man who is following is her lover. He will falter, or if we scare him, he will flee. We can handle one man."

Kim ejected the magazine from the gun as if inspecting it.

Chee sat across the table from Yew and beyond her reach. He rapidly reached for his shoulder holster, like a slick martial arts move. Kim knew that her joy with Ling made her appear weak, but she needed her men. She twisted with the weapon in one hand and the magazine in the other and pointed the Walther at Chee's face.

Chee's hand was fully wrapped around the grip of his 9mm Browning inside his jacket. His finger was firmly on the trigger. The gun was cocked and the safety off. The blued butt of the weapon was less than an inch from the edge of his lapel. It would take him but a split second to yank the weapon into the open. Her weapon appeared unloaded, the magazine removed.

Kim's finger pressed on the trigger of Yew's weapon, but the magazine was gone. Was there a round in the chamber? That was the question. The wrong answer could mean his life. A bead of sweat burst onto his brow. The ship rattled all around them as if none of this existed. The pistons still pumped in the cylinders, the generators still produced electricity for the lights, but these four people knew nothing of the world around them. The tension in the room was palpable.

"It is your choice," Kim said. "I'm beginning to wish you would pull your weapon and I would be rid of one vote against me."

"I am not afraid," Chee said, and his hand budged. Kim fired and the air of the private dinning room reverberated with the shot and the smell of gunpowder. The bullet took off most of Chee's left ear and ricocheted off the steel bulkhead, crossed the room and splattered against an iron beam. The sound filled the small room with a terrible blast, as if a bomb went off in a box. Chee jerked and reached for his bleeding ear with his left hand and yanked the automatic with his right.

Yew and his partner spun in their chairs, knocking them off balance as they dove for the deck. Kim watched Chee intently as she brought the magazine back to her weapon, inserted it, and released the slide to chamber another round. Chee took aim while slightly off balance. For a split second, he had the upper-hand and moved to take advantage of his position.

But Kim dropped to one knee behind the table, in one sensual fluid motion, and they both fired. The range was close. Kim had allowed Chee one more chance to be vigilant and loyal. She needed all her men to understand the goals and support the efforts to the end, but Chee would not abide.

In a final evasive move taught to her by many martial arts experts, she spun her head to the side, listing it like a ship struck by a tsunami. It saved her life as her bullet split Chee's skull, slamming bits and pieces of his life against the steel bulkhead behind them. Yew and his brother were trained killers, but this was at such close range, so intimate, so explosive, and in tight iron quarters. They prayed that the standoff would end peacefully.

"Get up," Kim ordered abruptly. "Toss his body over the side of the ship and clean up this mess. Am I understood? If the crew asks, and they will, it was an accident."

She spun, picking up a napkin from the table and wiping the gun down before dropping it on the table cloth. She bolted from the dining room, stormed to the elevator, took it to the E deck and jogged up the final steps to the bridge. She was flustered as she walked across the deck to the wing door and thrust it open.

She stepped out into the sunlight and felt the blast of wind and the sea spray against the soft surface of her face. She stared out at the ocean as she felt her knees buckle. She grabbed the thick railing over-looking the bow of the ship and held herself from falling.

Her hair blew in the wind and her eyes watered. The first mate came out of the bridge to her side. He was a short Polish man with a thick, dark mustache. He had a tough time with the English language as he looked up at her. His eyes were always red as if he could never overcome a cold or a hangover.

"Would you like coffee?" he asked.

"Yes," Kim said without looking at him. Her mind was bursting with questions, but no answers. She had to make a decision.

Chance awoke with a jolt. He immediately felt the pressure of the job ahead and the insecurity of being in an unfamiliar country. As he reached for his old Harley-Davidson watch, he thought about his motorcycle on the Leon, and then he remembered that someone might be following him. He showered, dressed and slipped out the side entrance from the hotel and grabbed the first cab to roll past. It was already sweltering, humid and hot outside, an oppressive moisture-laden heat demanding he stay very calm throughout the day or be drenched in sweat. The day was beautiful, as clear as a polished brass ship's bell, and already the streets bustled with people.

"Take me to Chinatown," Chance said.

"Are you new to our town?" the driver queried. He was obviously Chinese with thick glasses and the dress of a teacher. He looked middle aged, with receding hair, dark slacks, dress shoes needing a good polish, and a powder blue dress shirt, slight ruffled.

"Yes," Chance said, "I arrived yesterday."

"You must go to Chinatown at night," the driver said. "The lights are nice. It's not so hot."

Chance listened and opened the map of Singapore he copped from his room. "Can you show me where we are on the map?" Chance said.

At the next stoplight, the driver pointed out the Fullerton on the map and Chance circled the area. They drove up Boat Quay to South Bridge and turned left only a few blocks to Cross Street.

"You will find anything you need," the driver said, pointing down the colorfully decorated South Bridge Road. Bright red Chinese lanterns hung from every light post, and paper dragons were strewn across the street. Lampposts were adorned with art. The Chinese New Year was celebrated from 26 January to the 26th of February.

"Just see the side streets of Mosque, Pagoda, Temple and more," his driver advised.

"Thank you," Chance said, stepping out of the cab into the stifling heat. He pulled his dark shades down over his eyes and stepped into the busy street.

He didn't noticed any signs of being followed, but he kept a watchful eye. At one of the first booths, he found a small folding make-up mirror and bought it from the vendor for $3.00. It wasn't anything special, but the short Chinese woman took the time to carefully wrap it neatly and place it in a small silk sack before Chance could tell her it wasn't necessary. The elderly woman with cracked brown teeth and thin mussed gray hair bowed slightly and thanked Chance deeply for the purchase. He graciously accepted the gift of her nature, said thank you and moved on.

Each narrow street was lined with booths selling Chinese New Year trinkets and ornaments. He stopped dead in his tracks at the first booth selling bamboo plants. He swallowed hard as he watched a good-looking young Asian woman place the ceramic pots in a colorful display. She took serious care and exuded a heightened level of artistic creativity with each plant, similar to Ling's caring nature, and he could hardly watch, though the shape of her small feet, her slender legs, and her air of quality and comfort mesmerized him.

He dragged himself away from the scene as the gentleman who was with the young woman approached Chance.

"I have beautiful pots, don't you think? Good price."

"Thank you," Chance said, "She is beautiful."

He walked away, helplessly adrift with thoughts of Ling. He looked from booth to booth. Some sold Chinese trinkets from jade and fake stone carvings to handmade wooden toys. He lost his focus, and direction. Everything he picked up was made in China. He stopped at a stand selling drinks and ordered a cup of tea and a handful of almond cookies. He was starving.

A man with round features and narrow eyes looked at him sternly. "You are American?" he asked.

"Yes," Chance replied.

"Don't be concerned about the water here. It is the highest quality. If you get sick, the city will pay your doctor bills. That is their guarantee."

"Thank you," Chance said, his concern for drinking water quality abated.

He wandered on. He knew he would need to make a trustworthy contact in Singapore. He couldn't handle the entire operation on his own. He continued to browse among the trinkets, costume jewelry and souvenirs. On Temple Street, he discovered a row of food vendors and bought a bowl of fried rice.

In the afternoon, he picked up another cab and asked about more shopping. The driver took him to Orchard Road and dropped him off on the corner of Scotts Road. He wandered up the broad boulevard, his eyes searching for anything unique.

The street was a maze of one shopping high-rise after another with names such as the Paragon, the Promenade, and Lucky Plaza. The Singapore Marriot stood on the corner and the Hilton just up the street. He was in the wrong section of town, although it was a bustling community of thousands of people wandering the streets and shops such as Hugo Boss, Rolex, and Hang Ten, Louis Vuitton, Robinsons, and Marks & Spencer.

Chance tried a couple of malls for inspiration, then the smaller independent stores, but there was nothing he could find, which hadn't already been shipped to Singapore from China or Europe. He needed something indigenous to the area he could ship to China or the US, something preferably soft, so he could be a part of the cargo without major discomfort.

He needed to pack it in a crate of his making or have someone build the crate, and then he needed it delivered to the Bibi. He found another cab. Nearly melting, he dropped into the back seat. He was relieved as the working air conditioning cooled the air around him.

"Take me somewhere else," Chance said. "I need to find something that's made here, maybe an art gallery or something."

"We have many art galleries," the driver said, "but it is very expensive."

"How about Little India?" Chance said.

"That is a very good choice," the Indian driver said and sped to the Rochor Canal.

"Go there," he said pointing, "all the way to Lavendar Street. You will find much."

Chance began walking up and down the old historic streets. They were unique, plaster buildings, bunched close together. The paint chipped and faded, canvas awnings torn and shredded, the area stuck out in contrast to the rest of the slick city.

Indians resided in Chulia Street near Chinatown for decades. Most of them resettled to the present Little India due to the introduction of cattle rearing on the fertile land of Rochor River. Immigrants of Madras, Calcutta, and Malaya joined them soon after. Little India was the center of the local Indian community. Chance thought about what the cab driver said before he sped away.

"You should come here in the mornings so you can enjoy the spicy aromas, the colorful traditions, the strains of sitar music and bright garlands," he'd told Chance. "Don't miss the vibrant Indian-inspired murals painted by Singaporean youths next to Sir Verramakaliamman Temple."

The notion of shipping local artwork intrigued Chance, but the day waned. Frustrated while searching the closing shops, he flagged down another cab and escaped the heat.

"The Fullerton Hotel," he said, and thought to himself, he would return in the morning.

The cab pulled up to the front of the hotel and Chance got out. As the porter held the door open, he realized that he wasn't being as attentive regarding the man who may have been following him. He had no indication during the day that anyone was on his tail. He used his new little mirror to watch his back from time to time. He moved through the crowds in erratic fashions to reveal a follower or loose him. As the heat consumed him and no sign of a spy came to light, Chance became more focused on his mission and lost touch with the man in black.

"Ling," Kim said, opening her cabin door. A trickle of sweat ran down the side of her lovely forehead. She looked strained and drawn. The violence and its accompanying rush of adrenaline drained her energy. She wanted to crawl in bed and hold Ling, but she couldn't. Yew and Sun, her two remaining guards, followed her inside. Ling had tidied and cleaned Kim's room, made the bed, and had fallen asleep in the day room armchair behind a fresh cup of tea. She was dressed only in a light batik sarong and she was a beautiful picture curled in the chair, the light material barely covering her ass. Her unhampered breasts pressed against the light, translucent fabric.

"Wake her up," Kim said dryly. "Collect her things and move her to the pilot's cabin at the end of the passageway."

Her authoritarian voice signaled the Kim of old to her men. They shook Ling violently and when they couldn't overcome her drug-induced stupor, they pulled her bodily down the hall and threw her on the small bed in the tiny room for harbor pilots. They returned dutifully and collected Ling's things and anything Kim set aside for her, and took them back down the hall. They tossed the stuff on the deck, shut and locked the door.

"I will not see her again until we reach Hong Kong," Kim said to her men. "It is imperative that we are successful with all of our missions for the Wong family."

The men nodded respectfully and backed out of the room, convinced their leader had once again taken the iron reins in her hands and held them tight.

Kim shut the door and collapsed on the sofa. A tear started down the side of her cheek. She thought for sure only one thing had meaning for her in life and it was money, but suddenly, she realized there was more.

# -27-

## THE PACKAGE,
## TIME RAN OUT
## FOR CHANCE

Chance returned to the hotel and was relieved to walk in the grand, ornately framed glass door. The heat sapped his will to continue to walk. His Hawaiian shirt clung to his sweat-soaked back and underarms. Although each step was labored, he continued walking to the elevator and took it to his floor. There were no phone messages and he dropped on the bed like a sack of stale potatoes.

He drank what seemed like a gallon of bottled water and began to cool down. He called the IMBI in San Pedro.

"IMBI," a young voice said over the phone.

"Is Brad in?" Chance asked.

"Yes, sir," the voice returned. "Please hold."

"Brad here," he said in his usual upbeat voice.

"It's Chance," he said quickly. "Do you have a minute?"

"Sure," Brad said. "I've been checkin' around and have compiled some info. Do you know the agent?"

"Yeah," Chance said. "Tell me how this is done, risks and pitfalls."

"Here's the bit," Brad began. "All you really need to know is the number for the agent. He's the sales guy. He wants to load the ship full of moneymaking cargo. Regarding crates, that's up to you. He may be able to offer a lead, but generally, the customer handles the packaging and delivery to the port. Sometimes the agent will help with clearing the cargo through customs. Any inspection is handled before the container is sealed. Sometimes there is a random check at the port, but generally, they go by the declaration the driver has in his possession. Let's see, is there anything else?"

"What about the manifest?" Chance asked about another term he had heard bandied around the ship.

"That comes after all the cargo has been determined for a particular ship," Brad said. "It's the list of what's on board. Have you called the agent to see if you can load something?"

"What do you mean?" Chance asked.

"Do they have space for your cargo?" Brad questioned.

"Goddamnit," Chance said, "I don't know, but I'm going to find out in five minutes. Thanks, brother."

"Call me if you need anything else," Brad said. "Oh, and get your ass back to the gym."

Chance set the designer phone down and pondered what Brad said as he opened his notebook and dug for the agent's number.

"Rickmers." A soft English/Asian voice melted the phone and Chance thought of Wing. "May I help you?"

"I need to speak to Lin Hock," Chance said anxiously. "Is he in?"

"No, sir," she said in a voice that would make most men happy just to stay on the line with her. "You can reach him on his cell phone."

"Thanks," Chance said and hung up. He immediately dialed the agent's cell number.

"Rickmers," the words came across cleanly without a bluring accent. "May I help you?"

"I hope so," Chance said, trying to conceal the desperation in his voice. "I want to ship a crate to the US on the Bibi. Is that possible?"

"How big is it?" Lin said, startled that someone would ask for a particular ship. "And I need to know how many and how much it weighs."

Chance was dumfounded. He had no notion of the size or the weight. He felt like an idiot trying to clear his scrambled thoughts. "It will be three meters square and five to seven hundred pounds. There will be only one crate."

"I'm sure we will have space for that box," Lin said, and Chance was relieved. "I will need the declaration in a week and the box at the port no later that the 20th. Will that work for you, sir?"

Chance's throat went completely dry as he reached for his last bottle of water. It only had a few drops left in the bottom. He let the droplet bounce to the back of his nervous arid throat.

"I'm sure it will be fine," Chance said, wondering if he could pull it off. "What will be the cost?" Chance didn't really care, but he thought he'd better inquire.

"I will have that figured as soon as I get to the office, sir," Lin said, driving along in a new E-class Mercedes. "It won't be over $1,500 for that distance."

"Let me know," Chance said and gave Lin his satellite phone number and hung up. His nerves bounced on a trampoline of fear.

The soft alarm awakened Chance at 8:00 a.m. Everything about the Fullerton had grace and style. Chance was unaccustomed to his surroundings, including the twinkling sound of the alarm. It was the 7th of February on a sunny Thursday. He had 14 days left by his fleeting cargo ship estimation. Ships' schedules were altered constantly due to a myriad of influences ranging from weather to dock preparedness, so betting on an arrival time held uncertain odds for Chance, and he was very aware of the consequences if he couldn't board that ship in Singapore. The following port was purportedly the Muslim port of Jakarta, an unhealthy location. Then Vietnam near Hanoi and finally Hong Kong, and it would be too late.

Chance splashed water in his face and looked into his own deep green eyes in the lavishly framed mirror for help. He had to keep moving. He showered and jammed to the lobby for coffee and a croissant, which he took to go, but as he turned to leave, he felt eyes upon him.

Under normal circumstances, he would have assumed his fly was open but not here. He spun and reviewed the people in the breakfast area eating. He saw nothing but one table containing a steaming cup of coffee and a half eaten breakfast of eggs, sausage and toast, but no customer. He scanned the room carefully then walked briskly to the taxi stand and jumped in the first available cab. He didn't want to think anyone knew where he was or why.

"Little India, please," he said, turning to look at the taxi stand behind him as they pulled away, no one except a fat tourists and well-groomed Chinese business people.

The traffic was consistently packed like sardines, and small cars buzzed like bees along the narrow streets. The middle-aged cab driver peeled along North Bridge Road to Rochor, left to Sungei, and dropped him on the corner of Serangoon. Chance experienced exactly what the cabbie described the previous day. Colorful artwork and proud young artists' faces bordered the street, but he was intrigued by a couple of stalls selling small leather goods, such as wallets and coin purses. He watch the people move around their booths. He needed a single man who knew his craft.

By noon, he was tired and hot. Couples or entire families manned most of the leather trade booths. Most did not make their leather goods, but imported them from India and displayed them for sale. The sky was clear and the sun at its near-equator hottest. Chance melted as he wandered up Dickson Road and down Upper Weld Road. He inspected the booths and shops on Chander, Klang, and Belilious Avenue.

He stopped for bottled water and a bowl of Nasi Gorrine, a spicy fried rice dish that made the back of his neck warm and sweaty. He tried to be cognizant of the fact that someone might be following, but the heat melted his attention to that effort as he drug his feet down Veerasamy onto Jalan and then Hindoo, which was a dead end.

The streets in Little India had a haunting, mystical aroma about them. The people were darker and occasionally evil looking. The buildings from the 1800s were in disrepair and the area didn't feel as safe as other pristine areas, which was evidenced by the lack of tourists. Still, the vendors were out in strength, trying to make a humble living. It was early afternoon, as Chance began to search his heated brain cavity for alternatives.

Hindoo Road was a narrow a cul' de sac of shops and booths. The deeper Chance strolled into the district, the more imposing it became. Big dark men with dark eyes huddled together in the shadow of a canopy. Few women were visible in the cluttered street. A stripped 20-year-old Jeep hung from one teetering jack as Chance discovered a small building with a table out front holding a number of wallets and purses. A thin, elderly man sat back from the table in the shade at a bench scattered with tools and leather pieces. His leather had a unique design configuration. He maintained the Indian style with his own touch, and since he was the one performing the leather tooling, it had a special, more unique and refined air.

"Excuse me, sir," Chance said. "How much are your wallets and these coin purses?"

"Do you buy one or many?" the man asked as he stood up from his worktable. He was in his mid sixties and haggard looking. His skin was nearly coal black, yet lighter in wrinkled areas. His dark eyes sunk deep into his narrow features.

"I might buy many," Chance said, "and ship them to the United States."

The man's eyes brightened and he began to spew prices. Chance had little interest in the price. "Your name?" he asked, finishing his litany of costs.

"Chance Hogan," he said, calculating in his mind some idea of how many he would need and their approximate weight. "What's yours?"

"Omar Melaka, thank you," came the reply.

"Do you have an inventory of your products, Omar? I need many."

The man looked at him with the look of someone who didn't understand, then realized what Chance was asking and beamed.

"Yes, I have inventory," he said. "You come back tomorrow. I take you to place. I work by myself and cannot leave."

Chance looked at his watch, not for the time, but the date. He looked up at the sun beaming above, pulled his bandanna, and wiped his brow. He remembered his joke about wasting time. He thought to himself, I'm burnin' daylight.

Ling woke up to a tap on her door, and then it opened. Yew stood in the doorway with a plate of food and pot of tea. He set it on the small desk built against the wall, bowed slightly, looked at her inquis-itively, and backed out of the room without a word. She realized that she hadn't seen Chee or Kim since they moved her into this small con-fined cabin. She was relieved Chee hadn't shown his frightening face.

Yew was a small Chinese man with long hair pulled into a pony-tail. He had experienced the rage of Chang Wu when they first tried to do business with the Wu family. He would not touch Ling for fear Chang's anger would be thrust on him. He also witnessed Chance's size and determination and wanted nothing to do with that man, either. He would fight for the Wong family, but he did not want to die unnec-essarily. He would avoid such problems at all costs and wished they could return the girl and eliminate the threat.

Ling sat up in the small narrow bed and looked out the small single porthole. In the mist, she could see the coast. It was the coast of Egypt as the ship neared the Suez Canal. She wanted to reach for the tea, forget the food, and drift off into her euphoric state once more. She ached for the drug, but something else bothered her deeply. A fear swept over her. She knew being Kim's slave was her saving grace until they tossed in this closet of a cabin. The kidnapping dynamic changed. Desperation swept over her. Her education was all lost. Her hopes and dreams for her and Chance were gone, if she continued to be addicted to this drug. She started to cry and as the tears washed over her face, she tried to understand what was happening to her.

The next morning, Chance scrambled out of the cab early next to the shop on Hindoo Road before it opened. He walked around the corner for coffee and a pastry, returned, and knocked on Omar's shop door hanging roughly on its 100-year-old hinges. The street was deserted except for a couple of skinny dogs sniffing around for scraps of food. The older gentleman opened his door and stepped into the sun. He must have been waiting inside.

"Morning," he said.

"Good morning, sir," Chance said.

"Follow me," he said, and closed his door and walked deeper into the dead end street.

Four doors down, they stopped in front of a set of tall double wooden doors. Omar unclipped a massive array of keys from his belt and opened the doors wide. They creaked and wobbled until they were thrust broadly against the building. The smell of dank leather filled the alley and Chance was smitten with a small warehouse packed with boxes of leather products. They were stacked in no specific order and broken into no definite sequence, their contents spilling onto the ground. Omar stood proudly beside the open doors.

"We have any quantity you need," Omar said, standing an inch taller.

The boxes were crumbling and each one was stamped with "Made in India." It was obviously a vast array of cheap leather goods sold in most of the shops throughout Little India.

"I don't want the stuff you can buy at any store," Chance said. "I want your workmanship."

One of the dogs trotted up a tattered cardboard box, sniffed, and began to lift a hind leg. Omar's facial features dropped at Chance's comment and he was about to debate when he saw the dog.

"You," he snapped, and turned to chase the dog away, but stumbled and fell at Chance's feet. Chance stepped back and looked toward the street. A Chinese man with his back toward Chance ran around the corner onto the main drag.

Chance bent down beside Omar. Blood formed a puddle around his mouth. A small hole was visible at the lower back of his skull. It was also oozing.

Chance checked his pulse at the base of his neck. Omar was dead and Chance, well aware the bullet was intended for him, backed away from the man and walked briskly toward the first side path to another street. He hailed a cab and peeled away from Little India. He didn't understand, knew he was even in Singapore?

He returned to the hotel, went directly to his room and sat on the edge of his bed looking out at the vast city. He wasn't sure what to do next. He picked up the phone and stared at it, confused. He dialed his trusted friend, Mark, in Los Angeles.

"Yep," Mark said, answering the phone.

"Hey, I need some advice," Chance said. "Someone is trying to kill me."

"So what's new," Mark said sarcastically, his usual nature. "I'll bet it's a girl again."

"Okay, okay," Chance said. "I'm guilty on all accounts, but the fact remains that I'm being stalked."

"Do you know who's behind it?" Mark asked.

"No," Chance replied.

"That's part of your problem. If you don't know their motivation, you don't know how anxious they are, or what their program is."

"Listen," Chance, muttered, loosing his patience. "It's not bullshit. They want me out of the picture before the ship arrives on the 21st. There is a goddamn deadline. I will bet it is the Chinese kid who followed me to the hotel."

"Okay," Mark said, "here's the drill. Stay around a lot of people when you're on the move, so he can't go public and take a shot without being seen. Find a restaurant, or a place where you can sit with your back to a secure wall. Make it a place where there is only one entrance, so he'll be forced to come in the door. Do you have a gun?"

"Yes, a Walther," Chance said.

"You may be in a situation where you will be forced to draw down on him," Mark said. "If I was there, we could take him out together, but if you can shoot that pea-shooter, get down behind your table, take aim, and hope he pulls his gun first. At least it will look like self defense."

"Fuck!" Chance said. "It's like the fuckin' OK Corral."

"You never know what might happen," Mark chided him. "He might shit himself and run."

"Then he'll be back," Chance said, resolving himself to his job.

# -28-

## SINGAPORE UNCERTAINTY

It was still early, just after 10:00 a.m., when Chance dug out his stainless Walther PPK and checked the magazine. It was a small, accurate weapon with a six-round 9mm magazine. Chance carried a small leather sack of spare ammunition, enough to reload the magazine twice. That better be enough, because that's all he had. He didn't know if the shooter would return, or if the man thought he hit Chance and was successful?

Chance sat bolt upright. The gunman would need his hit confirmed to collect his wages.

He looked at the stainless PPK, a startling reminder of the day's bad events and premonitions. He splashed water in his face and wondered what the hell was next. He showered, dressed, and hit the deck running. He took the elevator to the spacious lobby and walked to the entrance, thinking with every step that whoever was following now knew what he knew. Chance would be much more cautious this time.

Chance stepped into the afternoon sunlight and felt the blanket of humidity engulf him. Instead of snatching a taxi, he crossed the roadway and stepped quickly onto the wide, busy Singapore river walk and headed down toward a colorful row of restaurants. He needed to eat and rethink his plans.

Surrounded by noon-day shoppers and tourists, he walked slowly, looking out at the narrow canal and the wooden relic water taxis buzzing from small pedestrian pier to quay. He passed two high-rise buildings before he entered a lane of restaurants. Small, two-story buildings were on his left and outdoor seating resided on his right bordering the river. People were everywhere, but his confidence waned. He tried to look around, but couldn't. He just kept walking and staying close to the throngs of small people. He stuck out like a sore thumb.

The first building housed an Irish pub filled with Europeans but it wouldn't suit his purposes. He was also concerned with the morning's close encounter, and he certainly could not afford to shoot a citizen of Singapore. If he was trapped in a restaurant, he couldn't run. He would be caught immediately and incarcerated for life. If they throw people in jail for spitting on the sidewalk, what was the punishment for killing an innocent citizen, certain life imprisonment?

Chance inspected the European crowd and an Indian restaurant next door, with picture menu marques on the sidewalk to entice customers. He glanced at the menu, while checking the interior of the restaurant and watching his back. It was dark and sliding glass doors led to the inside. The doorway was not narrow enough. He moved to the next restaurant, a Chinese eatery, with another easel-board out front boasting the fare. A lithe Chinese woman came to his side.

"Can I get you a table, sir?" she asked in a voice as soft as the caress of a silk handkerchief. Chance looked into her bright eyes. A small boy ran to her side and tugged on her silk Cheap-wa dress. Chance could not endanger her or her son.

"I'm just looking, thank you," he said and moved on.

Next came a building with another table out front and menus spread on the white linen. It was a Thai food offering and Chance loved Thai coconut soup. He looked up from the table to a narrow entranceway leading into the restaurant. It was shadowed with Bamboo plants on either side and dense shrubbery framing the door.

"You do not want to sit beside the river?" a tall Indian fellow asked.

"No, it's too hot," Chance replied. "Do you have air-conditioning?"

"Yes sir, of course. Come."

The man directed Chance through the narrow passageway into the small interior of the restaurant. It was clean and comfortable with undersized tables and no other windows or doorways, except hallway to the kitchen.

Chance felt like a rat in a trap as he picked a table with direct views of the front door. The restaurant interior was deserted due to the lovely scenery out front. Only two employees moved back and forth from the kitchen, carrying orders to the riverside tables. Chance was caught by the delicious curry smells and the fragrant nature of the Thai cuisine. He pulled up a chair and sat.

"Would you like something to drink, sir?" the tall man inquired.

"Bring me a Thai iced tea and some chicken sate to begin with," Chance said, setting the menu down without looking at it.

The waiter disappeared into the back, and Chance reached into the big safari pocket in the front of his khaki shorts, pulled out the Walther PPK, and cocked it under the table. He pulled another chair close to his right side, folded a napkin and set it on the chair with the small automatic on top of it. He hid it with another napkin.

The waiter brought a tall tapered soda fountain-type glass filled with dark tea and heavy cream poured over the top. It slowly drifted into the tea, forming a beautiful mixture of the white cream and amber tea. The waiter set down an ornate plate housing six strips of chicken on long wooden skewers with vinegar, cucumber and pepper sauce in one small dish, and the famous Thai peanut sauce in the other.

Chance looked around the room and pondered his situation. It was crazy. The hitter would know that he knew. If he was smart, he would leave Chance alone for a couple of days until Chance weakened or wandered, and then he could strike easily. He would have to know that to come into this restaurant would be a trap.

On the other hand, Chance looked at the tea and the sates long-ingly and grimaced. If he began to cut the sautéed meat and dip it in the delicious sauce, his hands would be encumbered and his life at risk. He had to wait. He stirred the tea with his left hand, leaving the right hand free, sipped the fabulous cool liquid and set the glass back down. He waited five minutes, his eyes darting to every employee who entered the small dining room.

He tried to relax and ordered coconut soup for lunch because he could eat it with one hand while the other stayed poised close to his weapon. The waiter brought a dented aluminum donut-shaped bowl with a burner in the center and set it on his table and dished his bowl full of the milky liquid with chunks of simmering chicken. With one sip, Chance was mesmerized by the flavor of lemon grass and spices. It was far and away the most incredible soup he had ever tasted. He dipped into it heartily when the door from the kitchen opened slightly and then burst open.

Chance had the spoon nearly to his mouth when he sensed something wasn't right. Something was not working as planned. He noted a rhythm from the restaurant staff wandering back and forth, to and from the galley. He became quickly accustomed to the way they carried trays on their shoulders and nodded to him as they passed.

Swinging kitchen doors always appeared to be such a nuisance, always a risk of crashing into another waiter, and spilling a tray. He broke Mark's rule. The Kitchen door was behind him at the other end of the room. It swung rhythmically, but not now. This time the motion was direct, a slam bang. Chance started to turn from his position watching the front door. The first silenced bullet poked a neat round hole in his aluminum decanter of soup and it pissed soup onto the table as if a small faucet had been deliberately opened.

Chance had no time to reach for his gun. Mark taught him that the first move was to move the target out of the line of the weapon. He twisted away from the bowl and dove to the floor, looking back at the door. The same man stood behind the counter, holding a silenced automatic. Chance took the chair housing his pistol to the unforgiving concrete floor. A waitress entered from the riverside, spotted the intruder and screamed, distracting him.

He had no target. He turned the gun on the screaming woman as Chance recoiled with his PPK and took a distracting shot, missing his target. About to shoot the waitress, the hitter startled by the un-silenced crack of the 9 mm bullet slamming inches from his head into the plaster wall. He backed through the swinging kitchen door and ran.

Chance jumped to his feet and sprinted across the small dining room through the swinging kitchen door. The galley was small and compact, tiled in old broken ceramic squares and slick as snot coated with the steam and sizzling oils. Chance bolted through and stopped at the back door, kicking it open. Two bullets smacked the center of the door and Chance assessed the trajectory of the fire, knelt and pushed the door open a crack. The shooter was uncomfortably crouched behind two trash containers immersed in the stench and flies from food refuse.

Chance fired at the lip of one open trash containers, two inches down from the top. The shooter abruptly stood and for a split second, Chance realized he faced exactly what Mark had warned him about. It was not much different from a shoot out in the old west. Two men faced each other with weapons drawn, life hanging in the balance. Chance tried to collect his scattered thoughts and aimed as the man with the scar on his lip fired. So did Chance.

Chance knelt as the bullet sliced through his thigh, spinning him into the interior of the kitchen, and sliding on the slippery deck. He winced in pain, but quickly discovered he wasn't badly hit. He turned and scrambled for his dropped weapon and gingerly opened the kitchen door again. The shooter lay on his back in the alley behind the restaurant. Flies already buzzed around the pool of blood spreading around the man's head. Chance's shot hit him in the mouth, next to the scar.

In quick moments, the restaurant was awash with police, ambulances and curious public. Chance was gone. It was self-defense, but he couldn't take the time to deal with the questioning and what about his weapon?

Ling awoke the next morning to the tap on the door. It opened slowly and Yew delivered her food and placed it with the pot of drug-soaked tea on the desk. He looked at Ling's tired eyes, nodded, and backed out the door. She arose, washed her face and stared deep into her pools of amber, coupled with pallid features and noticed the red rings in the soft flesh around her eyes.

Alone for a couple of days, she assumed it was going to be the drill. Terrified that she might die of the drug effects or placed unceremoniously into a Chinese prostitution ring, reality seemed to wash over her. She wished Chance could somehow contact her.

She looked out her porthole. She had no notion of where they were, but they were swaying in some vast, calm, desert region. She guessed that it had to be the Suez Canal. She could see Egyptian monuments from the ship, surrounded by poorly kept tenement houses with laundry hanging from the windows, next to luxury hotels facing a beach. Boats of all sizes and shapes seemed to surround the ship.

Swept with a fleeting level of control, she began to once again use the tea sparingly. She read some and moved around the tiny cabin as a feeble attempt at some form of exercise. As the stark influences of the tea warmed her soul and the maw of the drug engulfed her, she lost her ability to sense reality once more, lay back down on the bed and drifted away.

Chance made his way to the Singapore Seaman's Hospital and passed out. As he awoke, his injured leg throbbed. His mind was filled with a drug-induced fog. He looked around the room. It was empty. He searched for some control, bells or whistles to beckon assistance. He could see the doorway and the polished hospital floors beyond, but no one was there. He strained his head to see if there was a call button behind him on the wall. There was and he stretched to reach over his head for it and pressed the button. A small beep followed, and he felt some comfort knowing someone would come.

Five minutes later a small, diminutive female nurse entered his room.

"Ah, you're awake," she said. She was Chinese, less than 5 feet tall and as pretty as a picture. "Would you like something to eat?"

"How long have I been here?" Chance asked through his drug haze.

"You were brought in yesterday," she said, "and operated on last night."

"What time is it?" Chance looked around the room and spotted a large clock on the wall with an enormous second hand that jarred with each second motion. It said 1:30. "I need to get out of here, now."

"You can't," she said as her eyes brightened. "You will be fine, but you must stay until tomorrow."

"Bullshit," Chance bellowed and the sound seemed to rock the walls. "Let me speak to your supervisor!"

"Sir," she tried to calm him, "please relax. It is only for your own good."

"I don't care if it's for the good of God," Chance shouted. "I'm out of here!" He struggled against the straps holding him in place when an Indian woman, who stood almost 6 feet tall and had very dark skin, in contrast with the pristine white medical gown, entered the room abruptly. Her hair was shoulder length and her eyes black, but bright like pearls.

"Sir," she said, "calm yourself." She indicated something to the nurse who hurriedly left the room. "We have operated on you and removed a bullet. It tore through a muscle on your thigh and you are very lucky."

"Listen," Chance interrupted, "I don't want to be a pain in the ass but I need to leave."

The little nurse returned and walked past the doctor to the other side of Chance's bed.

"I understand," the female doctor said, staying very calm, "but you have had surgery and you would not want to damage the tendons of one of the largest muscles in your body. Damage could hamper your ability to walk forever. You can be released tomorrow morning after the surgeon exams you. I would suggest that you stay very still until then. You need to heal as fast as possible to be released."

Just then Chance felt the prick of a needle entering his leg, and the little nurse quickly backed away. Chance knew that the shot was more drugs to calm or knock him out. He could feel himself fading almost immediately.

"You need to rest, Mr. Hogan. The doctor will check you in the morning."

Ling awoke the next morning to the same tap on the door and she rolled over as the door creaked open. Once again, Yew set her tray on the desk, except this time he left a magazine for her to read. Without a smile but a knowing gaze, he backed out of the doorway. It had been several days since she had seen Kim or Chee and understood for her own sanity, it was the best, although she still had no concept of what the future might bring her.

The opiate tea filled her with lethargy and released her from her longing for the future and Chance. She noted to her disdain, that as soon as she attempted to control the drug's effects a painful reality flooded back which led her to the tea once again.

She looked out as the ship passed the town of Suez and the final lap of the Suez Canal leading into the Gulf of Suez, then to the Red Sea.

The pot of tea reached out to her as a jester of evil taunting her to find release from evil dreams of an imprisoned life, and she danced on the stoical cloud of opium.

Chance awoke sharp at 7:00 a.m. and rang for a nurse. The same small petite Chinese woman appeared apprehensively at his door.

"Mr. Hogan," she said, anticipating his questions, "I will have the doctor see you first. He should be here by eight o'clock. Would you like some breakfast? You should eat."

"Yes, yes," Chance said. "I'll take the chow, but get me out of here as soon as possible."

Chance hated hospitals almost as much as he disliked cops and police stations. It gave him the creeps. She brought a tray of tasteless hospital food, but he wolfed it down and counted the minutes until the doctor arrived.

Another aspect of human behavior that dismayed him was the failure of doctors to keep prompt appointments. It was almost 9:00 before Chance heard voices in the hallway. The Indian doctor wandered in his room in no particular hurry with a small round Chinese man in tow and the little bright-eyed nurse. The nurse was the only one who indicated any concern for the time, her facial features and darting eyes indicated her empathy. Chance was crawling out of his skin with angst.

"Mr. Chance," the doctor said and his round features brightened. He was an older gentleman with puffy looks of a professional with too much good food on his hands. "I hear you are anxious to leave. Are you concerned about the police?"

"That's not the reason," Chance said, "I'm on a mission, so to speak, and I'm running out of time."

The doctor did like so many doctors do and ignored his concerns while unwrapping the bandage.

"The police may have questions for you," he said. "Guns are not allowed." He pinched and pressed the flesh and made Chance wince. He said something in Chinese to the lovely nurse, and the girl began to dress the wound with fresh salve and wraps.

"I can release you," the doctor said with a wry smile, "but you must return to your hotel and go to bed. You cannot walk on this leg today. Maybe tomorrow."

Chance rolled his eyes and nodded. "Thank you, doctor," he said extending his hand. "Was I damaged much?"

"You were very lucky," the doctor said, handing him a limp palm. "We will give you antibiotics to prevent infection. Keep it very clean."

Chance thanked the nurse as she unstrapped his leg from the bed so he could sit up and throw his legs over the side of the bed. He immediately felt a throbbing in his thigh.

"How about some pain pills?" Chance said to the Indian doctor.

"We would prefer that you stayed off the leg," he said, "but I sense that won't be the case, so we will take care of it."

Before Chance could feel the thick sunlight against his face, he had to pick up the prescriptions and sign papers in the lobby. It was almost noon on the Monday the 11th. He took one of the pain pills before he left the lobby, using the drinking fountain to wash it down. He hobbled to the curb, hailed a cab and returned to the Fullerton.

He could barely walk and a porter helped him out of the cab, up the steps through the revolving door and into the lobby. He limped to the desk and returned with a wheel chair. Several of the employees stared at Chance. The rumor of the rare shootout spread fast. Suddenly, he was lionized as a receptionist ran to his side and offered to bring him a drink.

"I have phone messages for you, Mr. Hogan," she said, handing him a small sheaf of paper. When he asked for a Jack on the rocks, she was surprised then giggled with the other girls who recognized it as a purely American macho drink. With several employees following, the porter pushed him to an elevator and then to his room.

The porter set the drink beside his bed as Chance stumbled to the couch and sat down.

"Will there be anything else?" the porter asked.

"Yes," Chance said. "See that I have a goddamn wake-up call for 6:30, will you?"

"Yes, sir." The porter stood erect and spun toward the door. "Right away, sir."

"That's six-thirty this evening," Chance said.

"Yes, sir," the porter confirmed, closing the door behind him.

Chance struggled to get up off the soft couch and walk around. The pain diminished with the effects of the drug and the whiskey, but it was difficult to walk without stumbling. The more he walked, the madder he got. He flipped through the messages, but most were local numbers for the press. He couldn't have anything to do with them. Then he saw one from Chang with a new number. He called it immediately.

"Yes?" Chang answered.

"Chang," Chance said, "I'm glad you called."

"Are you all right?"

"Yeah, I'm okay. Someone tried to kill me. Someone knew I was staying here."

"This is a cell phone number," Chang said. "I will only call you when I'm alone."

"Are you alone now?" Chance asked.

"Yes, my family is coming apart." Chang said. "I will kill all of the Wong family soon, if need be. I am desperate. If I do, they will surely kill my sister."

"Try to hold off," Chance said, and realized he had made a similar request in the past. "I will call you in a couple of days with a report. I can't guarantee anything, but I'm trying like hell. I love your sister. I'll die trying to get to her."

"Can I help?"

"Not now. Just don't tell anyone anything. Don't even tell anyone I called."

As Chance hung up, the phone rang again.

"Yeah," Chance said.

"Yeah?" Mark said. "Lovely to hear your voice, too. I have asked that your name be taken off the registered list and replaced with mine. You checked out, got that? I gave them my credit card number. You are now Mark Lonsdale, understand? Whoever is trying to kill you will continue. If you're still there, they'll know you're alive. You only need a couple of days, right?"

"Little more than that," Chance said, "but that will help, I hope. They tried again. This time I got the bastard, like you said. Thanks."

"Yeah sure," Mark said sarcastically and hung up.

Chance tried to walk some more as he sipped his drink and headed toward the bed. He laid down and was out like a light.

At 6:30 sharp, the phone jingled Chance awoke and a mechanical voice welcomed him to the waking world. He looked out the shear curtains and saw the waning sunlight grace the city with warm, colorful tones. He struggled to his feet, his leg stung and was stiff as he moved around the room. It was tender, as he struggled into the shower and scrubbed himself down, shaved and dressed.

He took a pain pill and headed downstairs. With sideways glances from the staff, he walked lopsidedly to the massive rotating door as a porter darted to his side holding a beautifully polished wooden cane.

"Here, sir," he said, bowing slightly. "You may need this."

"Just as long as it has a dagger in it," Chance said. "Thanks."

He stepped into the first cab and said to the driver, "Chinatown."

"Yes, sir," the driver said, and looked at Chance in the review mirror. His eyes brightened and he sped away. He fought through the traffic that was equally heavy on the streets of Singapore at night and turned left on Cross Street, dropping Chance off on Eu Tong Sen Street.

Chance stepped out of the cab and straightened deliberately. His leg was stiff but the rest and the pain pill helped. He knew if he was brisk, he had a couple of hours to walk and search. He was beginning to think about building a crate and stuffing it with newspapers, but that wouldn't work. He needed a product to create a declaration for customs officials to hopefully approve. He turned in on Temple Street and was taken back by the lights and the crowds.

Chinatown was in the midst of its New Year celebration and a multitude of red paper lanterns lining the streets were brightly lit. Streams of tiny bulbs were wrapped around overhead colorful banners criss-crossing the streets. He could hear fireworks snapping in the distance. The streets were packed with people, shopping, eating and wandering.

Chance made his way down one street and up another, looking at shops full of Chinese ceramics, Chinese teas, herbs, CDs, and he was caught again by the multitude of small bamboo plants in ceramic pots. With each lane, his leg ached more, and occasionally a pedestrian, a teenager, or old woman bumped into his thigh as he made his way through the throng of people. Each touch was extremely painful and he lurched to move away from the excruciating sensation. He looked down at his pant leg to see a blood stain seeping through the Khaki material. He knew his time was limited as he turned and almost fell down on Banda Street.

To catch himself, he grabbed a stainless steel rod from a clothing rack and lurched sideways stumbling and throwing several batik sarongs to the pavement. A young man came to his rescue, helping him back to his feet.

"Please sit down, sir," the young man said. He was a good-looking kid with long black hair pulled into a ponytail.

"Thanks," Chance said, feeling the muscle screaming for release. He sat and the young man brought him a cup of hot tea.

"Drink and relax," he said, looking at Chance's leg.

Chance nodded, his attention diverted from his surroundings by the throbbing in his thigh muscle. He sipped the tea and the warm liquid tasted good and cleansed his thoughts of the hurt momentarily.

"I heard something in the streets about a shooting?" The young man said.

"I wouldn't know," Chance said, beginning to check out his surroundings. "Do you make this stuff?"

"I make the fabric," the handsome Chinese kid said, "I have girls who hem it into skirts and sarongs, even scarves."

Chance mentally reviewed the size of the booth and determined that if he bought everything the kid had, he might have enough to fill a crate.

"Can I buy everything in this booth?" Chance asked and the kid's eyes brightened.

"I don't know why not," he said. "Is your name Chance? It has become almost legend."

"Yes, that's my name," Chance said grimacing. "You?"

"My name is Qu Yuan," he said, offering his hand.

Chance shook his hand and looked him square in his dark eyes. He was 5-foot-5 inches tall or thereabouts, a slender form wearing a white t-shirt and dark shorts and sandals. His feet looked calloused as if he was a surfer. He wore no jewelry except a leather thong around his neck with a jade coy fish hanging from it.

"Do you surf?" Chance asked.

"Not often," Qu said, "I go to Hawaii twice a year to sell my material and garments. I do then."

Chance's eyes brightened. "So you can sell me everything here?"

"Of course I can," Qu said. "I thought you were kidding."

"I've got to get back to the hotel, and this is a busy night for your retail sales," Chance said. "Can I see you tomorrow morning?"

"I will be at my warehouse late tonight. I live there," Qu said, watching women wandering in and out of his makeshift booth. "Here's my card. Yes of course, I will be there in the morning. You need to rest that leg as much as possible."

"But I must…" Chance wanted to explain, but throngs of people swarmed his booth and it was not a good time to try to explain. "I'll see you tomorrow."

Qu said something to a woman in Chinese, and she ran to the intersecting street and flagged down a cab. Chance hobbled to it and nodded gratefully, stumbled into the taxi and left. He looked at the card in his hand and held it up to the driver.

"Can you read this?"

"Yes, of course," the driver said. "It's not far."

"Thank God. Just take me to the Fullerton, now."

# -29-

## CHANCE SEARCHING
## FOR A WAY

Tuesday, the 12th of February during the rainy season in Malaysia at 11:00 a.m., Chance stepped carefully out of the cab under clear skies near a strip of old-time buildings. Singapore held such a stark contrast from old to new. From street to street, the new, slick, high-rise buildings overshadowed the fleeting remnants of the past. Chance was just happy to find the building he was searching for. His time running out, his wound didn't help him with his plight.

His leg stiff and sore, an infection added to the pain and a fever ensued. He drank bottled water and ate the antibiotics in an effort to subdue the aggravation. He stepped onto the sidewalk under Palm trees, and Qu waited for him.

"This way," he said. "How are you feeling?"

"Rough round the edges," Chance said, and with his cane in hand, followed Qu to a small narrow building with 100-year-old wooden doors much like Omar's. Chance flinched as Qu opened the doors and he looked up and down the street for any strange behavior. His leg throbbed as an aching reminder. Qu's garage was packed with shelves of garments.

He bent over a large plywood table where he painted the fabric with a bamboo brush of paraffin. Behind it were steaming vats to dye the cotton material in. The garage looked like a shop with tools and chemicals on shelves. It smelled of dyes and sizzling paraffin. He had a vast array of bamboo brushes used to smear the paraffin designs on the cotton material before it was dyed. Qu always dyed material, beginning with the lightest die and using the paraffin and working his designs between dyes and rinsing.

Chance looked at the array of material and wondered how many to buy. He spotted a wall of tools including wood saws and hammers, and was relieved to think that perhaps he could build his crate here. Qu wandered around the shop, tidying up for Chance's sake. Chance wasn't concerned about the condition of the shop, but his mind fluttered with a number of questions.

"How do you ship to Hawaii?"

"I use UPS," Qu said, sweeping around one of the vats. The concrete was stained with a myriad of colors from the process over the years.

Chance's hopes were high as he asked the question and absorbed the response. He shuffled the cane against the concrete floor with nervous energy.

"I've had large orders and was forced to ship a crate load on a cargo ship," Qu said, "It's much trouble and once the crate broke and they lost much of my shipment."

Chance's eyes brightened as Qu brought him a chair to sit in. "So you have dealt with making crates and customs?"

"Yes, a couple of times," Qu said, "but I don't recommend it."

"I'm going to be on a ship with containers," Chance said. He was still trying to figure out how much to buy and how much to tell Qu. "I have a girlfriend who is opening a store for girls near a beach and this stuff would be perfect for her to sell."

"Why was someone shooting at you?" Qu asked, looking at Chance from across the room.

Chance stopped in his tracks. He wanted to be honest with Qu, but was concerned. He didn't know him well enough.

"Let's go to lunch," Chance said. "I need your help with a couple of things, including how to order."

"Sure," Qu said, "but you didn't answer my question."

"I'll get there," Chance said, "I like to play cards with a guy a few times before I tell him much about myself. It helps me understand whether he's on the up and up or not."

"I'm not sure I understand," Qu said.

"You will," Chance said, as he pulled himself out of his chair. They moved slowly down Cross Street walked a couple of blocks to a grand old open-air eating center built completely out of cast and wrought Iron. It was ornate like steel French lace with a tin roof. Inside, it contained a hub of isles leading out from the center. Each row was a bank of a particular style of eating booths from Indian, to Chinese, to Thai.

"Do you have a choice?" Qu asked Chance, spreading his arms to display the vast array of food.

"I like my food spicy," Chance said. "Other than that, you take me to the best."

Qu entered the row with the Chinese dishes and ordered Chance a Kung Pau combination. They sat in the center of the row at a table with two jugs of bottled water and waited for their food.

"My problem is that I need the crate ready at the Pasir Panjang Wharf by the 20th," Chance said. "Can you handle that? I will need help with the crate."

"Are you in the drug business?" Qu said.

"No, absolutely not," Chance said.

"Nothing illegal?" Qu said.

"Nope, nothing," Chance said, "not a goddamn thing, but there is danger involved as you guessed."

"I must know," Qu said, his dark eyes sparkling with intrigue.

"I must know if you can do it," Chance said. "Do you have the inventory? Can we make the crate in time? Do you know the customs ropes? And I need a truck to haul the crate to the wharf."

Qu stood up from the table, retrieved the food, and sat back down. An elderly woman approached while they ate. She was old and haggard looking. Her hair was gray and she bent over severely. Chance grimaced. Watching her walk made his leg throb. She pulled a sarong out of her purse and laid it across the table.

"You like?" she asked.

Qu stopped eating and got to his feet. He touched her kindly on the shoulder and looked at the hem work along the bottom of the simple fabric and the way she had made a tie out of the same fabric at the waist.

"This is very nice, Mrs. Kuan," Qu said. "How are you doing with the order?"

"I am fine," she said in a gruff voice, trying to look at his kind face. She looked at him with deep caring eyes. "If you like, I make some?"

"Yes, of course," he said. "I'll double my order if you can have them ready tomorrow."

Her light gray eyes brightened and glee spread across her face. "You very kind, Qu," she said. "I go work now." She moved on across the center and disappeared.

"Are you married?" Chance asked.

"I am in love," he said and his head dropped slightly. "I met a girl in Hawaii and she moved back here with me, then one day, told me that she didn't like Singapore and wanted to go back to Hawaii. I've never been the same. I work with many lovely women, but she broke my heart."

"I'm sorry," Chance said, "My problem is also about a girl. You will be helping me get her back."

Qu looked at him deeply. "I will?" he asked. "We can we do it, will it be a lot of work?"

"Let's work out an inventory," Chance said excitedly. "I'll go back to the hotel and get a deposit for you."

"I will need all my girls to help package all the garments, then helpers for the crate," Qu said, gobbling down the last of his plate of Chinese food. They discussed the inventory on the walk back to his shop and agreed on a price.

"I will work on the packaging and gathering all the products today and tomorrow," Qu said. "You need to stay off that leg as much as possible."

They walked to the curb and Qu flagged down a cab.

"What time would you like me at the shop tomorrow?"

"We have our work cut out," Qu said. "Rest until noon, then come find me."

Chance shook his hand. Qu's grip was sincere and strong. Chance hobbled to the cab and sped back to the hotel.

Ling read the copy of Time magazine in her steel cabin, slowly making it last as long as she could. She was terrified of the drug withdrawal symptoms and would have given anything to avoid them. She continued to drink the tea very carefully, trying to wean herself off of it very slowly.

It was like the snake that tempted Adam and Eve. In one moment, she felt secure and strong; in the other, weak as a kitten hungry for her milk. With each tray of food and pot of tea, she tried to be as resilient as she could. Alone each day, she could see her ability for vigor grow.

She had no use for the drug. It was once the tool to become Kim's slave, but that effort was no longer needed. She needed to think clearly, to understand her predicament and perhaps escape, but as she looked out the porthole at the hull of the ship slipping along in the Red Sea, she knew that there was no escape. She knew the reason for her capture had something to do with her family in China, but she didn't know the reasoning.

It had to do with drugs, but she knew her brother would oppose any involvement in drugs. Perhaps that was it?

Chance returned to the hotel and was greeted by the respectful porter. Still hobbling, he made his way to the elevator on foot and returned to his room. He dialed Chang's new number immediately.

"Chance," Chang said, "Is that you?"

"Yes," Chance said, "Are you okay?"

"No," Chang said, "but I'm praying that you are successful and we can end this thing."

"I'm closer, but I will need some more money," Chance said, "I have a kid who is going to…" Chance stopped himself short. "I better not say. I just need a couple of grand."

"Check the balance on the credit card," Chang said, "It would be impossible for me to send money. All eyes are watching everything I do. If I send a check, it would be traced and whoever you were dealing with would be at risk."

"Just keep this goddamn card alive," Chance said, "or I'm dead in the water."

Chance hung up and realized that if someone called on the card, they could trace his transactions. A nervous chill ran up his spine. His cash was short and he couldn't cover the sarongs with it. He went down to the ATM in the lobby and withdrew $500.

He grabbed a cab and drove across town to the Conrad tower and removed another $500, and kept rolling until he had $3000 and returned to the hotel. The three grand in Singapore dollars represented $1,666 in US.

The only time Ling saw or heard from someone was at meal times for a few seconds. Her desperation was heightened as every meal passed, and she attempted to speak to Yew without response. He was fearful of her and respectful, but unable to express himself or afraid to do so. She stood at the porthole and looked out at the tongue of the crane mounting point beneath her position on the super-structure. It was securely strapped to its landing as the ship motored through the dense Red Sea at 17 knots.

Her hand shook on the steel porthole ledge and her nerves were shattering. She could reach for the cup of tea and all her growing anxiety would be gone, replaced by orgasmic revelations. All problems would be erased. She stepped around the bed, both hands quivering, while reaching for the pot. She lifted the wicker handle to the white ceramic base fired with blue dragons dancing around the exterior. The clay lid rattled with her nerves and the sound was jarring to her heightened senses, enhancing her need for the drug.

She poured the steaming liquid into a small matching cup and set the pot down with a bang. She snatched the cup knocking the pot over, spilling her escape from her imprisoned reality.

Angrily, she grabbed the pot once more and poured again, shaking violently, her eyes red with desire to escape her pain. She drank the amber liquid down quickly, ignoring the hot fluid and threw the cup against the wall shattering it along with her desire for strength. Once again, she was lost.

Each morning, Chance's leg improved. The redness of the infection subsided and Chance was able to improve his gait. He took the cane along as a support in case it flared up again; besides, it was adorned with a saber on the inside coupled to the brass band that twisted into the base of the wooden cane. The steel blade added a nice heft to the polished staff in the event he had to use it as a club.

He had no indication that he was followed, but he knew that it was just a matter of time before someone else would be sent, and he was running out of time on more than one account.

Chance entered Qu's shop before noon. The wooden doors were open and several young Chinese women scurried about. They set up a table with a plastic bag sealing apparatus on top of it and each garment was potted in a clear plastic liner with a label indicating what the garment was, size and Qu's company logo, which was a simple line drawing of the jade coy fish along with the particulars on his company. Another woman stuffed the garments in mid-sized boxes.

Qu stepped through a doorway in the back that lead from a small patio.

"Chance," he said and his face brightened. "Come here."

Chance stepped forward to squeeze between the women and the packaging platform. At the sound of Qu's voice, they turned to look at the American standing at the opening of the doorway. Some blushed and looked away, others check him out from his sandals to his thick wavy hair, still others returned to work.

"Wait," Qu said, "I must introduce you." He stepped through the throng of boxes, the vats, shelves and crates of plastic liners. "I want you to meet my staff," he said, and with each introduction, he touched each girl in a caring nature. In turn, they reached for him and offered a hand or bow to Chance. Each offering moved him and especially by the way Qu honored each woman. He knew that it wasn't commonplace to treat women with such regard.

He followed Qu into a small patio where several other women ironed and folded garments and then organized them. There was a large table surrounded by plastic chairs, and after Qu introduced the women in the patio, he indicated it was time for lunch and they converged on the table while two more women brought steaming rice dishes from another building into the cool shade of the patio surrounded by palms and lush greens, shrouding it from the sun. Chance followed Qu inside the building to a small office upstairs.

His office furniture was all made from wicker. It was neat and a painting of his coy fish logo adorned the wall above his desk. One window in the second story room looked out at the high-rise buildings beyond. Chance pulled a Fullerton Hotel envelope and offered it to Qu. He opened it, and his eyes brightened.

"Cash," he said.

"Yes," Chance said.

"This is very good," Qu said, "I can offer you additional discount."

"That's not necessary," Chance said. "Listen, I want to tell you more about what's going on. I will continue to pay you cash everyday until we are finished."

Chance was about to spill his guts to the young entrepreneur when they heard the clip of shoes against the steps coming up the stairs.

"Qu!" the cute young thin Chinese woman shouted breathlessly reaching the top of the stairs.

Chance was filled with panic, terrified that someone had followed him to Qu's shop. He couldn't stand it if someone might hurt the diminutive women who worked so hard and were devoted to the project. He stood and pushed away from his chair reaching for his cane, grabbing at the handle. Qu was startled by Chance's reaction as the woman in the batik skirt burst into his room.

"Qu," she said, "We are short by five garments." The panic in her voice was profound.

Chance almost collapsed in the chair, shaking his head, then beginning to laugh in fearful release. Qu looked at him strangely. As he tried to say something, Chance raised his hand in objection.

"That's quite all right," he said, trying to remember the girl's name. "I will take what you have."

The petite girl smiled broadly, then departed back down the stairs.

"I have more in my retail inventory," Qu said, laughing. "You were going to tell me something?"

"I told you that this effort had to do with a woman I love," Chance said. "There is more and I can't explain fully, but she is in great danger aboard a particular ship. I need to get on that ship. I'm going to be one of the garment orders in that crate."

Qu looked at him in dismay. He thought for a minute about the article in the newspaper about the man who was attacked in the restaurant and his mind filled with questions.

"I have so many questions," he said without an inquisitor's tone in his voice.

"I can't tell you much more," Chance said. "She is a prisoner on that ship, and I must get aboard before she leaves here. They have guards on the ship. I can't just stroll aboard. They are waiting for me. It is dangerous for you to be working with me; that's why I'm bringing you cash. We must finish the crate, load it partially with your garments, and leave space for me. I need to be able to crawl into it before it is loaded on the ship, and I must be able to get out of it once the ship is underway. I will accomplish this to find the woman I love, or die trying. Is that understood?"

Qu was dumbfounded. His head filled with deep emotions mixed with fear and the threat of being exposed or linked. He remembered his Hawaiian love and his deep regret at losing her. He wished for a second that he could have her back in such a way, that she had not left him, but was taken and he could rescue her. In a sense, he was jealous of Chance. Inside, he hoped his efforts would help the man whose face was awash with concern.

"I will do all I can," Qu said.

Chance sighed with relief and released the fear consuming him for the last several days.

"We will finish the packaging today, and tomorrow we will build the crate," Qu said. "Let me think about the crate and customs. Let's eat something.

Chance returned to the hotel and checked his messages. Still, reporters wanted to speak to him and he ignored the requests, but there was another from the agent Lin Hock. Chance dialed the number immediately.

"Rickmers," Lin said professionally.

"Mr. Hock," Chance said, "did you need to speak to me?"

"Yes sir," he said. "The Bibi will be in port on the 19th instead of the 21st. We have a dock waiting for her. Do you still want to do business?"

Chance thought, hell, no; just gimme my girl back. He wished there was another answer, but there was only one.

"Of course," he said, "We will have the garments crated tomorrow."

"Good," Lin said, "then I will hear from you by the 15th."

"Yes, sir," Chance said, and hung up. His heart was in this throat. The deadline was moved up two days. His plan had to work or all was lost.

# -30-

## CAN CHANCE MAKE IT IN TIME?

An annoying dream consumed Chance's sleep as he tossed and turned. It was a long frustrating excursion into his rattled subconscious. For reasons unknown to him, he could not reach the ship. No matter what he did or got away with. The ship was an evasive force preventing his every attempt to board. He awoke in a sweat and swung his legs over the side of the bed, already on a harsh mental edge.

A sharp tinge of pain still held onto the muscle fibers in his leg. He needed to hurry, but he gently pulled himself to his feet and limped to the head, showered and started to move and flex his muscles. Before he left the room, he called Mark Lonsdale for advice.

"Mark," Chance said, "I'm getting this crate together. I may be stuck in it for a couple of days. Got any advice?"

"Oh sure," Mark said, "You're going to bolt yourself in a coffin and you want my advice? Take a lot of protein bars, and water supply, eight ounces for everyday and something to piss in. If you monitor your liquid intake, you will sweat it out, and avoid urination. Hopefully, you will have enough room to stretch and do some form of exercise or you're fucked. Confined, your muscles will atrophy immediately. And make sure you have ventilation."

"Okay, goddamnit," Chance said, "I can figure out that for myself."

"Then don't call me, you crazy bastard," Mark said. "Have you been into one of these holds? Do you know how they stack crates? Better have more than one way to get out. Take a weapon and some long cable ties."

"What are the cable ties for?" Chance asked, tapping the bed side-stand with his fingernails, in a racing rhythm, drumming a hurried cadence.

"You don't want to be forced to kill every sonuvabitch who gets in your way, do you?" Mark said and hung up.

Chance added Mark's items to his list and ran for the shower. Constantly looking over his shoulder, he grabbed the first cab he could snatch and headed across town. They stopped at a hardware store, and Chance picked up some tools and cable ties and bought two 5-inch folding knives. He asked the skinny driver to stop at two ATMs, withdrew money and added it to the additional cash he'd withdrawn the night before. They stopped at a health food store where Chance bought a dozen protein bars.

Concerned about buying too much, Chance still purchased six small plastic jugs of water. They pulled up across from the Concourse high-rise complex and he scrambled out of the cab with his cane and his box of goods. It was a sultry hot day, but a nervous chill ran down Chance's spine, as if he was standing in Wallingford, Connecticut, during a winter snowstorm. He moved quickly down the narrow street to Qu's creative workshop. From a distance of half a block, he could see closed doors as he neared. They were locked.

For some unknown reason, his leg secmed to throb, an alert to Chance like a foghorn on the bridge of a ship. He moved quickly along the edge of the street and suddenly looked behind him, expecting to find another hit man standing in the center of the street taking aim. There was no cluster of giggling, lovely women scampering around Qu's place. He knocked on the door— no response. His mind whirled with evil options.

He wondered if someone had gotten to Qu, or worse, killed him, and his body was in his business somewhere buried amongst his creations. Could he have turned on Chance, suspected something and called the cops? A cloud dampened the sun's warmth, and suddenly the moist air turned gray. Chance moved against the wall adjacent to Qu's doors.

He didn't know what to think, as a small truck turned onto the slim street. An industrial step van, common to the area, slowed. Then it sped directly at Chance and the sun's reflection against the windshield prevented him from seeing who held the wheel. He brought the cane up across his chest and prepared to pull the sword from its lacquered wooden sheath when the truck slid to a stop in the dirty leaf-strewn street.

Qu jumped out of the cab and two small Chinese women crawled out of the other side and struggled down the step to the street.

"Chance," Qu said, "as usual, you are early."

Chance breathlessly nodded.

"Are you all right?" Qu said, coming to Chance's side.

"Yes," Chance said, bringing himself around. "Just coming around this morning."

"We have all the material for the crate," Qu said, scampering around to the back of the truck to help two more women out of the truck. He took a number of his girls on his mission, to find all the supplies he would need.

Chance helped him and the women unload the truck into his patio, where they set up a pair of sawhorses and began to cut chunks of 1-inch plywood, creating two square crate ends, and four rectangular walls. It was a simple structure with four 4-by-4s cut to support the inside corners. They made the box ends 4 by 4 feet, and the sides 4 by 6 feet tall. Qu nailed the tunnel together. He nailed one end into place and the other end was attached with hinges, and they worked on a hasp on the inside, so Chance could open the end, he hoped. They drilled a few 1-inch holes in the plywood for air and visibility. Then the ladies went to work lining the crate with paper and started loading the boxes of sarongs, skirts and scarves.

Chance handed Qu a box of tools, cable ties, protein bars and jugs of water.

"Put this near the bottom," Chance said. "It's my tool kit."

"Before you get into the crate, take a couple of boxes out and empty the contents into the crate," Qu explained. "Then you will have some softness to sleep on."

The sun drifted toward the west and the light waned in the lush patio as they completed the lid and screwed the hinges to the ends of the 4-by-4s at the top of the crate. Chance looked over as Qu attached a packing slip and painted the description and destination on all four sides of the crate. For the first time, Chance looked at it and saw a crate like so many currently on the Leon. He grabbed a battery-operated handheld drill and drilled several more holes in each side for air circulation. He thought about his motorcycle and hoped that it was safe on the Leon. Then it dawned on him that he hadn't given Qu another payment and grabbed at his back pocket for the envelope, afraid that it was in a cardboard box in the crate. It wasn't, but folded neatly in his hip pocket. He handed it to Qu.

"We are going to need to haul this to the docks now and handle the paperwork."

Chance thought about the date, and then something hit him like a brass hammer to his naked thumb. He thought about Ling and the lovely women around him who had worked so hard to see this project finished. It was Valentines Day. Chance excused himself and limped out to the street and turned right to a market, where he bought a dozen flowers and returned and gave one to each lady to their surprise.

"That was very nice. I will call my customs agent tomorrow morning," Qu said, "You need to see the shipping agent. If all goes well, we meet here tomorrow at noon, and I'll have my buddy from the market come over with his fork lift and load the crate in the back of my truck. Then we go to the wharf with the crate and meet with the agent."

"Aren't we cutting it short?" Chance said.

"We have no choice," Qu said, reaching for Chance's hand. "We'll make it."

Chance prayed he was right as he limped to the main drag and caught a cab.

Jarred by the angry bell and ship's horn sounding the general alarm as the Bibi entered the Gulf of Aden dangerously near the coast of Somalia, Ling rolled in her tiny bed with its 3-inch thick mattress. Pirate activities were notorious along the narrow straight leading into the Indian Ocean. She rolled over in her bunk and reached for the pot of tea.

She fell prey to the drug again. She had nothing to drink but the tea, no one to speak to, and just one small bowl of rice with bits of meat thrown in.

Her mind was left to wander on its own treacherously clouded path into the history of Chinese women who would do anything to be taken in by Anglo men before WWII. Women were of little use to the Chinese race being attacked by Japan and during awful treatment by Chiang Kai-shek's Kuomintang. Women found slave labor in homes, bought a husband, or became whores. She sensed that her fate amounted to something similar and her will was leaving her to rot in the haze of drugs sweeping her away from the impending doom, loss, and pain. Weight melted from her beautiful shapely form with the will to live, in each sequestered day in solitary confinement.

The ship shimmied along a bright sunlit, calm sea as it passed from one war-torn region to the next. Her heart screamed with the pain so many people felt throughout history, as one nation struggled to broaden its corruption against another, until war, famine or revolution stirred the peoples' emotional mixing bowl, only to have another crooked government take the place of the last. It was no wonder opium in various forms spread throughout the world.

On the morning of the 15th, Chance awoke nervous and concerned about the approaching weekend. Would the holiday hinder his preparations? He called Lin Hock from the Rickmers' office just after breakfast and made an appointment to see him.

"I will be in the neighborhood," Lin said. "I will call you soon and we can discuss the arrangements."

This singular agent dealt with hundreds of tons of cargo material constantly, and Chance's order was small potatoes. In Chance's whirling mind, his cargo was life and death, the most important package of his life. Chance paced his lavish hotel room over and over, plotting, running through all the elements of his actions, looking for additional problems above what was already present. At 10:00 a.m., the phone rang and Chance jumped.

"Yeah?" Chance said.

"Mr. Hogan," Lin said, "I am in the lobby. Let's have tea."

"I'll be right down," Chance said and hung up the phone. As he hobbled hurriedly toward the elevator, he realized he had never met this man in person. A vision of the hitter crossed his battered mind as he entered the elevator. Well aware of his dire mission, he kept moving. To hell with more security.

Lin stood in the lobby in sharply pressed dark slacks, polished loafers and a crisp linen shirt. He wore a Rolex watch on one hand and a small gold bracelet on the other. Tall for Chinese, he was a good-looking young man; standing in the center of the lobby, talking on his cell phone, a briefcase in one hand, while a pager rested neatly on his fine leather belt.

Chance strolled briskly out of the elevator, a man on a mission, and immediately recognized the salesman's attire. "You must be Lin," he said, extending his hand.

"Yes sir," Lin said, sizing Chance up in his loose fitting Hawaiian shirt, shorts and sandals. He had tourist written all over him, and it was just as well. "The tea and pastries are wonderful here," Lin said, leading Chance to a small table in the luxurious café, surrounded with rice paper pen and ink framed art and tall bamboo plants. Lin sat and a lovely, slight, Asian waitress was immediately in attendance. Lin ordered for both of them with Chance's nod.

Chance didn't want to order anything, drink anything, or do anything except business, but he couldn't exude the slightest notion of anxiety. His guts turned into knots.

"I hope the ship's schedule didn't harm your plans?" Lin said.

"No, not at all," Chance said, "What is the price?"

"I will need the exact weight," Lin said, "but my estimate shows twelve hundred approximately."

"Are there any other charges?" Chance asked. He didn't want any last minute glitches.

"Do you need help with the declaration and customs?" Lin said and sipped his tea.

"No," Chance said, "I think I'm cool. Here's a deposit. He pushed an envelope across the table with $500 in it."

Lin opened the envelope and raised his eyebrows. "I don't usually receive cash."

"We haven't done business before, it's a small order, and we don't have a lot of time," Chance said. I didn't want anything to get bogged down with checks forced to clear banks. Can I bring you the rest with the crate this afternoon? I would like to meet you at the wharf."

As Lin counted the cash, he noticed a Polaroid picture in the envelope of the crate with some of the ladies standing around showing stacks of sarongs and bolts of batik material they loaded.

"There is the weight, size, and no, it has nothing to do with drugs." Chance said as Lin looked at the photograph.

"This should be fine," Lin said. " I appreciate the photo. I would hate to risk everything in the lousy drug trade. I've been in shipping too long. We will touch base this afternoon? I'm in and out of the port all day."

"That will be fine," Chance said, testing his own memory for more questions. "Oh, what about the weekend? Will we have any problem if it rolls into the holiday?"

"Only with stevedores loading the ships," Lin said, rolling his eyes. "They have it all sewn up. We are at their mercy, but that's my problem, not yours. The harbor is always open to deliver a crate."

"I'm relieved," Chance said. "Must be hard to keep track of everything coming and going."

"Yes," Lin said, stirring sugar into his tea. "Last week, a ship came into port and had to shift cargo to offload. When they put the cargo aboard again, they took two containers they weren't supposed to and left two." Lin snickered at the dilemma. "I'm still trying to solve that one. My customer is upset."

Suddenly a lump formed in Chance's throat, and his tea wouldn't pass it. He gagged, coughed and grabbed a napkin. "Please make sure this package is on the Bibi."

"There shouldn't be any problem," Lin said, smiling his best salesmen's grin.

Chance returned to his room more nervous than when he left.

Qu enjoyed morning tea with several of his women who spoke highly of Chance and the fortuitous deal they made. Qu didn't explain the order fully to his girls, but told them romance was involved, which induced them to put more effort into the shipment. They were tremendously pleased for Qu and themselves, because they made almost a half-year's wages on one crate load of garments. They were extremely pleased.

Qu called his customs connection, who arrived early and filled out the paperwork, checked the crate and gave him a signed declaration. Another hurdle overcome and he called his buddy who owned a rusting but operational forklift. Within a half hour, Qu heard the rumble of the gasoline motor-driven fork lift and saw the smoke from its corroded exhaust over the roof of the shop at the corner before it jiggled onto his rough back street.

It rattled, coughed, and oil dripped from the forklift driveline, from too many salty-wharf jobs during the '70s and '80s, until now. The driver and proud owner, Jalan Toa, a local Indian, made a living driving it and trying to keep it operational. It rattled up beside Qu's gate. He was thin and dark with a plume of unkempt hair that seemed to be cut with a bowl and electrical sheers. He wore an old stained Dallas Cowboys t-shirt, tattered denims and sandals. His face was long and held the elements of seriousness and concern, but his bright white teeth constantly gave away his cheerful existence.

"Hello," Jalan said, wiping his eyes of sweat and the burning fumes from the creaking engine. "Let's hurry, Baby hasn't been running so well."

Qu opened his gate and Jalan drove his burping forklift inside, slipped the forks underneath the box easily, where Qu installed 4-by-4 wooden spacers, and backed out with the crate in tow. He rolled, shook, and wobbled down the narrow back street to the corner and swung the teetering crate into traffic for one block to the fish market, where he used the scale to weigh it. He set it on the scale, noted the weight, gave the operator of the scale a pack of Marlboro cigarettes, lifted the crate, and backed away.

The kids standing around the sloppy wet fish stand, coated in briny scalesand fish guts, waved and coughed at the exhaust intrusion. Jalan smiled at his success at keeping his rattling rig moving through another chore.

On the way back to Qu's, it sputtered and died. A bead of sweat formed on Jalan's brow as he reached for the ignition key. The entire key-switch tumbler turned as he twisted the worn and bent brass key. He reached under the dash to hold the switch taught, so he could turn the key and simultaneously pumped the fuel peddle. It gasped, blew a billow of blue smoke out of the exhaust and rumbled to life once more.

Jalan wiped his brow and put the lift in gear, wobbling to Qu's street then up the narrow tree shrouded lane. But just as he reached Qu's truck, the forklift died again. Once more he reached for the key and held the ignition body, but it would not fire. He tried again and again without success. The battery strained against the electrical revolutions and cried its dismay, straining to turn the engine over again.

"Why don't you check the plugs?" Qu said.

"I need new ones," Jalan said, "but before I replace the plugs, I need new valves."

"Can you fix it?" Qu said. "We were hoping to take the crate to the harbor today."

"Of course," Jalan said, and Qu knew by the look in his eyes that he had offended Jalan. He watched as his glimmering teeth faded behind dark shaved lips. He knew Jalan was once a noted Bumboat mechanic on the Singapore River. Bumboats were long wooden craft, currently used as water taxis, but once played a pivotal roll in the shipping trade before modern vessels. The hardy wooden crafts, with lucky bright eyes painted on wood-slat bows, hauled cargo from ship to ship.

"How can I help you?" Qu asked, hoping to encourage the smile to return.

"I need early payment or a loan, and my tools," Jalan said, looking at a removed sparkplug with alarm. It was an oily mess.

"What needs to be done?" Qu asked. "I'm sure I can assist and my customer is very anxious. Maybe he can help."

"I need to remove the head, have it machined and the valves ground," Jalan said. "I need three hundred dollars."

His look was one of a man destroyed. He had no inclination how to find that kind of money. He would only make five bucks from Qu for his task.

"Let's go get your tools," Qu said as he looked at the crate dangling in the air less than two feet from the bed height of his truck. He had all his paperwork, and he was ready to go. If he could find enough people, they could perhaps lift the crate into the truck, but the bed was high. It would be awkward. It would also destroy his friend's state of mind.

They met on the bumboats as teenagers. Jalan was the mechanic and Qu a pilot. It was a fun job for a couple of Singaporean kids. The two men climbed in Qu's truck and it came to life. As they pulled away, they left the old forklift sitting in the middle of the street with Chance's wooden shipping box in its grasp. It was an odd landmark, like a rusting ship adrift in a lake of asphalt.

Chance crawled out of the taxi and stood at the end of Qu's street alarmed. His crate dangled from the tongs of a worn-out fork lift. There was no truck, no people, nothing. Once more a lump formed in his throat, and his mind filled with evil revelations. He wasn't sure what to make of it, but with cane in hand, he limped toward the wooden box floating in the air, supported only by the steel tongs.

Hot as usual, the air was sticky with humidity. The sun was brilliant and Chance was ready to peel out. He wandered up to the shop doors and knocked. Some time passed before a young Chinese woman came to the door. She smiled at the sight of Chance.

"Mr. Chance," she said gleefully, "how are you?"

"I'm fine," Chance said, "thank you. Do you know where Qu is?"

"He left with friend in truck," she said in broken English.

Chance was aware that she didn't know much more and he decided to take a walk to the corner for a drink and something to munch on.

"Thank you," he said, and bowed slightly, looking at her fine features and thinking of Ling. She even smiled, and caring eyes calmed his spirit and he wanted to reach down and take her in his arms, but he couldn't.

He smiled. "I'll be right back," he said, and turned to drag his swollen leg up the small street to the corner, and a block to the market for some chicken sate from the Thai food joint and a soda. He couldn't deny he was a nervous wreck and would prefer a double-shot of Jack Daniels but that would do little to finish the job, and he had to keep up his focused appearance and keep moving.

He returned to Erksine Road where Qu's shop was hidden. The forklift still stood near the center of the narrow street. He stood against the wall, assuming there had been a problem with the lift. His Coke was warm, but he wanted the caffeine fix, while he munched on skewers of chicken with warm peanut sauce. Halfway through his second skewer, Qu's truck bounced onto the street and screeched to a halt in front of the lift.

"Chance, this is Jalan," Qu said. "This is his fork lift. It needs headwork. Can you loan him some money?"

"Can we get another lift?" Chance asked, and Jalan's face fell.

"Not in the neighborhood," Qu said. "I'll bet we can rent one, but I'm not sure how and what it would cost. I can call."

There was a part of Qu who wanted to assist his longtime friend, but he knew time was critical and if anything went wrong… He didn't want to think about it.

"Why don't you have one of your girls chase down a heavy equipment rental company right now," Chance said. "Then let's discuss what needs to be done here and how long it will take."

Jalan's face brightened some. "I need a top end," he said.

"Yeah, I heard that," Chance said, his impatience peaking. "How long will it take, two hours or two days?"

"I have a friend who can machine the heads and do the valves as soon as we have it torn down," Jalan said.

"Do you have all the parts, gaskets and tools?" Chance asked. He didn't know Jalan's history with engines.

"Yes, I believe so," Jalan said.

"So?" Chance said, "how long? How much?"

"It will be $300," Jalan muttered, "if we can get the parts to him in the next couple of hours, we'll have them back first thing in the morning."

"I know how machine shops work," Chance said, "they get the job in and they sit on it for a week. Does this guy know if it isn't ready at eight o'clock in the morning I will kill him?"

Jalan's face dropped like watermelon on the concrete. He looked at Chance directly in his flickering green eyes and saw that the man was dead serious. The young thin Indian took a deep breath and swallowed hard.

"We can do it," he said, "I'm sure."

"You have exhaust gaskets, head gaskets, carburetor and intake gaskets?" Chance continued to question. "Do you have a torque wrench? Is the exhaust system going to crumble into a pile of rust when we remove it? Is the battery dead now?"

"Ah," Jalan said, recognizing that Chance had some experience of his own. "Yes, I think I have everything. We just got back from the parts store."

"Do you have another crappy t-shirt?" Chance said with the same directness as he asked the other questions and Jalan was dumbfounded.

"I have," Qu said, coming up behind Chance. "We called about a forklift. It could be delivered here with a heavy equipment operator and a crane to remove it from the truck tomorrow afternoon. You would have to go down to their shop and put a deposit on it. We both would have to sign and the cost would be more than this and we would only need it for five minutes. We would be forced to pay for a day."

"Get me that t-shirt," Chance said, and he turned to Jalan and handed him three one hundred dollar bills. "Let's get to work."

Jalan crawled under the fork lift and unbolted the exhaust system. As Chance suspected, it was rusted beyond repair. To use it with a new engine would burn it up in short order. Chance removed the carburetor and the intake manifold. Qu grabbed some cardboard boxes and started to sort the parts. He had one of his girls begin a list of parts and materials they would need. Chance turned to the battery and pulled the cables. The cables were rotted from battery acid, bent, and in terrible shape. He mentioned it to the girl, who wrote frantically. Chance reached into the cab and discovered the damaged ignition switch and called for a new one to be purchased.

"Qu," Chance said under his breath, "would some of the girls mind getting their hands dirty?"

"No," Qu said. "They would love to help."

"Let's tear the sheet metal off this bastard and set up a paint booth," Chance said. "How late is the auto parts place open?"

"It's open until six," Jalan said from under the lift.

"Where are we going to get new exhaust?" Chance asked, taking the head bolt off the flathead engine. Jalan got out from under the lift and began to remove the valves. They were in sad shape. Chance handed him another hundred-dollar bill.

"Okay," Jalan said, "I have everything off the engine. I need to get to the machinist."

"Here," Chance said, "pick up this list at the auto parts and take what's left of the exhaust and see if you can find some pieces that will work. Get some heat paint and get your ass back here so we can prep this thing for the parts coming tomorrow morning."

Chance was excited and nervous at the same time. Qu brought out some various types of sandpaper and the girls began to clean and sand the sheet metal and parts that needed cleaning and painting. Chance eyed his watch constantly. By 3:00 in the afternoon, Jalan had returned and they pushed the forklift to the side of the street, while it was torn to shreds. Chance wrote a couple of extra items on the list, which gave him a lot of old time pleasure. He loved working on motorcycles. There was nothing in the world like taking an old Harley-Davidson apart, refinishing the parts, fixing the broken brackets and linkage and returning the motorcycle to life.

Chance replaced the forklift ignition switch with a solid-state marine unit and the starter switch built in. He replaced the battery, the cables and rerouted many of the errant wires. Qu had some fun with the battered sheet metal with a batik pattern and the girls' help. It was like a family operation. Two of the girls huddled around the seat, cleaning and putting a new leopard seat cover over the seat back and the pad.

At the first sign of a drifting sun, Chance stopped working. "Qu, would you call the machinist and make sure he had enough valves and parts to make it all work for delivery first thing in morning?"

"Sure," Qu said and hurried in the house. They cleaned and spray-painted the intake and exhaust manifold, and Jalan fashioned a makeshift exhaust system out of parts for some cars from behind the auto parts store. The new muffler pointed off in an odd direction, but it would work once they manufactured a new bracket. By sundown, most of what could be done prior to receiving the parts was completed.

Qu's main assistant grabbed a couple of girls and they began preparing an evening meal.

Jalan went to the market and returned with a six-pack of Tsingtao beer.

"We need to change the oil in the morning," Chance said, "before we fire this sucker. Did you get new plugs?"

A new morning list was scribbled on a spare chunk of cardboard. Chance was covered from his toes to his mussed hair with grease, chips of rust, paint and sweat. He didn't want to budge from the site until he was absolutely sure everything had been considered, but the sky darkened, and he knew there was nothing left to be accomplished. As a family, the whole crew sat around the table in the patio under a number of bright red Chinese New Year lamps. They enjoyed a feast of shrimp fried rice, Mongolian beef and fried won ton.

Chance stood up during the meal and toasted the group.

"Jalan, you will have a rebuilt forklift tomorrow. That sonuvabitch better run, 'cause everyone worked their asses off for you. Thank you," Chance said to the group, to applause and giggles from the girls.

After dinner, he excused himself, although Qu offered him a place to crash for the night. He changed shirts again, said goodbye and limped to South Bridge Road, where he caught a cab at once and returned to the Fullerton. The neighborhood celebrated the passing of the year of the Snake and was welcoming in the year of the Horse. People crowded the streets as the cab buzzed toward his hotel.

He scrambled into the lavish hotel through the revolving doors, realizing he hadn't thought about being followed all afternoon, and hadn't experienced the spirit he felt while working with his hands for months. Plus, he hadn't seen a woman smile like he saw during the day for some time. His passion for Ling welled up in him and was spilling into his throat. The bright young faces at the table made him wonder if he could ever replace her and the answer was emphatically no.

# -31-

## PACKED AND READY

Chance stirred little during his first solid night's sleep. He awoke feeling strong, yet his palms were still stained with the evidence of grime. The job wasn't done. He showered, grabbed his cane and hobbled to the taxi stand.

"Erskine Street on the corner of Maxwell near Chinatown," Chance said, plopping into the seat holding a cup of coffee and a biscuit.

"Yes sir," the cabbie said, pulling out of the Fullerton and heading over to Battery Road that became Chulia Street then North Canal Road before he turned on South Bridge into Chinatown. He pulled up to the corner, Chance paid him, gathered his gear and hopped out. He looked up the street at 8:30 and Qu's staff all bustled around it like bees to a hive, surrounding the forklift. They had returned with the machined components.

The girls painted the wheels and were detailing the exterior. Jalan made a clamp and a bracket for his bizarre muffler jetting above the engine compartment at an odd angle. The head was back on the motor and the exhaust system in place. Chance took off his Hawaiian shirt and replaced it with a Harley t-shirt, then reinstalled the distributor with new points and condenser, and Jalan finished installing the carburetor and hooking up the fuel system with new lines and clamps. All the fluids had been changed, and by 11:30 it was ready to test.

The entire Qu family stood back as Jalan gleefully primed the carburetor and jumped into the pilot's seat. The new key fit easily and turned effortlessly. The new battery turned over the tighter engine without hesitation, and then it fired to life, blowing a few puffs of blue smoke. The engine ran better than it had run in 15 years. Jalan's face was brilliant with pleasure and confidence. He let the engine warm carefully and put the lift in gear, moved it a couple of feet and lowered the crate into the back of Qu's truck and set it carefully in the bed. He backed the lift up and lowered the tongs to the applause of the entire team. He shut it off, jumped to the sidewalk and stood with everyone admiring their mechanical accomplishments.

Qu looked over at Chance and read his expression. "I'll be right back with the declaration," Qu said.

"Bring your cell phone," Chance said. "I will call the agent."

They buzzed along Keppel Rd converted into Telok Blangah Road then Pasir Panjang Road as it entered the wharf area. The port, the busiest container port in the world for three years running, moved over 15 million containers a year into and out of the Pacific Ocean. Chance could feel his hands become clammy as they turned right at gate 3 and pulled up to the concrete islands with small booths for customs agents. An officer came out of the booth and up to Qu's truck.

"You're paper work please," he said in an apathetic voice. He was a short stocky Malaysian man with thick wavy hair and a navy blue uniform like a cop.

He reviewed the declaration and went to the back of the truck to look at the box that had been previously inspected. Other container trucks were lining up behind Qu's small stake bed from the intersection and the agent was under constant pressure to keep the trucks moving. Besides, it was good for business and Singaporeans were very aware of their success as a people.

"I can open the box for you," Qu offered.

"No need," the officer said, and took the declaration inside his booth and returned with it signed again and stamped by the port authority. Chance sighed in relief as they continued into the port. They had to stop at another gate and show their paperwork again.

"We need to get to berth PT6," Chance said to one of the officers, who grinned and told him to turn right at the intersection and follow it, noting the changing numbers on the warehouses. Chance thanked him as they pulled away.

"You have one more problem to think about," Qu said as they turned and passed PT3, heading for PT4.

"What's that?" Chance asked.

"It's not easy to get into this port," Qu said. "You need to get back here to get in the box before it's loaded."

"Can we come up with another excuse to meet the agent?" Chance asked.

"I'm not sure," Qu said. "I'm sure you can come down and watch the crate being loaded, but that won't work."

"Maybe I need to get a job as a truck driver," Chance said. "Something will work, goddamnit, or I'll die trying."

Qu glanced at Chance and noted the determination in his eyes. He had no doubt that what Chance had distinctly uttered was fact.

Ling didn't know it, but she was floating through the center of the Sea of Bengal past Sri Lanka from the Arabian Sea. Soon the Bibi would enter the Straits of Malacca. She had no human contact for days except for food and tea delivery and it had taken its toll. She lost all control and desperation drove her back to the drug. She hadn't eaten more than one or two spoonfuls of rice with bits of meat in days. Her face was drawn and pale and her eyes puffy behind the constant doses of hot, drug-laced tea.

Kim received the report that their man in Singapore failed his mission and suffered the ultimate price. From the Wong base in China, they recruited another soldier and he was on a plane to Singapore. She knew Chance would attempt to board the ship and efforts were going to be made to bribe the guards at the port to keep a special eye out for a big sandy-haired biker who might try to slip into the port. But she couldn't begin the bribe process until she arrived. It frightened her. She might be too late.

Kim questioned the captain relentlessly about the length of their stay. She only had two more ports to endure in Jakarta and Vietnam before she would sail into Hong Kong and all of her efforts would be complete. Within a couple of weeks, she would have succeeded at her final mission. She could prance the streets of Hong Kong as the queen of an ever-burgeoning drug trade and their distribution arrangements would be complete. Unfortunately, her dream was no more solid fact than the steam rising above a pot of opium-spiced tea. She was well aware another fight brewed in Singapore.

Like her guards, she wished for some small miracle so the girl could be released, but it certainly would not happen from the bridge of the Bibi in the middle of the Indian Ocean. She had to be guarded and patient for a while longer.

Chance and Qu pulled his bouncing miniature stake bed truck up to a sign painted with large white letters PT6, and into the tin warehouse. Lin's small silver Mercedes cooled quietly beside the building. He stepped out of the car as they pulled up.

"Are you sure this box isn't full of drugs?" he asked as Chance unfolded himself from the small cab. Lin was very cool and professional looking, whereas both Qu and Chance were a mess of grime and over spray.

"We'd make a lot more money if it was," Chance said.

Qu giggled at the thought and walked around to the back of the truck. Lin motioned for a stevedore driving a forklift to remove the crate from the bed of the truck and place it inside the door to the warehouse. The building was steel and tin and as long as a football field. On the other side of the building, it was painted PW6 to indicated the wharf area where the ship needed to be moored.

Inside the building were hundreds of such crates not tremendously different from the one they built by hand. Chance looked around the building in fright. What if they moved his crate? Each crate was marked with the weight, size, contents and destination. Chance also noted some other black stencils on the crates.

"What are these?" he asked Qu and Lin.

"Ah," Lin said, "I'll take care of that as if it matters. He rounded his shiny compact luxury sedan and popped the trunk. He pulled out several stencils and a can of black spray paint. "Is it fragile?" he asked.

Qu and Chance looked at each other and nodded. Lin sprayed a stencil that looked like the silhouette of a margarita glass on the top corners of the wooden sides. Chance continued to review his surroundings. Outside the building was a massive parking lot where brand new E-class Mercedes were carefully parked. They still had sheets of white protective adhesive paper stuck to the sheet metal to prevent errant scratches, although the cars were covered in a rainy slime. In another section, asphalt grounds were stacked with tons of various sized I-beams rusting in the sun. Next to them were bales of lead bars. Everywhere Chance looked were piles, drums, or crates of some cargo waiting for transport to its next destination.

Lin sprayed arrows on the wooden sides indicating the direction of transport and a pattern of raindrops to indicate that this cargo was to be kept out of the rain.

"A lot of good any of this will do," Qu muttered under his breath. "I've seen the way they deal with this stuff." It was the first time Chance saw Qu act in any way other than purely upbeat. He remembered Qu had a bad experience and the memory wasn't a pleasant one. "I lost a good contract over the bad handling of one important box," Qu said.

"We'll watch this one," Lin said.

Chance rolled his eyes while looking at Qu and walked away. He had experienced the stevedore rumble at several ports and knew the care they took with the cargo was less than nominal. Usually it was downright destructive and not always their fault. Time was of the essence, little or nothing else mattered; besides, the agents rarely came to supervise or even monitor loading. They left it to the cargo superintendents. Chance handed Lin an envelope with the cash to cover the shipment and shook his hand. The job was done.

"Are there anymore changes in the Bibi's arrival?" Chance said.

"No, It's due to arrive on the 19th about 1500," Lin said confidently.

"Do me one favor," Chance moved close to Lin and stared him directly in the eyes. "I want you to call me if there are any changes to the schedule here in Singapore. Anything."

Lin placed the paper work in his briefcase, along with the envelope full of cash when he looked up and met Chance's gaze. He knew that the man was serious as a heart attack. He didn't understand why, but he knew.

"Yes sir," Lin said, and slipped into his Mercedes.

Qu and Chance waved him off and looked in the warehouse. The doors remained open. No guards paced the exterior, and the stevedores only motored past on their way to deliver or unload cargo.

"I need to get in here tomorrow night," Chance said.

"Perhaps," Qu said, fidgeting with his keys and looking at the asphalt and the chain link fence separating the port from the passing street, "I could find a spot with my truck close enough to the fence so you could jump over."

"That might need to be the plan," Chance said, looking at another area that once was a gate, but the fence was locked. "On the other hand, maybe the bumboat captain can deliver me to the docks?"

"That could be tough," Qu said, getting into his truck. "It's almost impossible to climb out of a small boat and climb up the side of a wharf 15 feet above you, especially at low tide."

"There's got to be a way," Chance said as they cruised around the port before heading back to the gate.

"I can't thank you enough," Chance said as Qu pulled his ragged little stake bed truck under the massive pillars in front of the majestic Fullerton. "You can't imagine how much this means to me. I will try to deal with the next obstacle on my own."

"Look," Qu said, "I wish I could bring my girl back. I wish there was anything I could do to change her mind. I would love to think I could go after her, so if there is anything I can do, don't hesitate. You have my cell number. Call me if you need anything."

"I will," Chance said and shook his hand like a brother, "and no matter what the conclusion is, I will call you with the final results."

Chance stepped out of the truck and Qu sped away. Chance looked after him and thought for a second about the man, his grace and caring. He wondered why all people couldn't have that level of heart. He turned and walked with a diminishing limp toward the rotating automatic hotel door. As he stepped into it, he saw his favorite attentive porter stepping into the door at the same time.

As the young man in the oversized uniform recognized Chance, he started shaking violently, hollering, trying to capture Chance's attention and keep it. He was over anxious and Chance waved and paid little attention. The little Indian man continued around the revolving door and back into the lobby to the chagrin of several customers outside waiting with their luggage.

"Mr. Lonsdale, I mean...," he said trying to keep his voice low. "Another man, he looking for you. The girls at reception tell me and point him out. Not a nice guy, he pushed one of my fellow workers around."

"Is he still on the premises?" Chance said.

"He left in a cab," the porter panted with each word, his hand on his knees, "about a half hour ago."

Chance pulled him aside behind a marble wall leading into the dining room.

"Listen carefully," Chance said staring him in the eyes, "if he returns in the next 45 minutes, call my room immediately. If not, have a cab waiting for me at the back entrance at that time. I will check out and leave." Chance looked at the kid with concern. His face was a map of his feelings and this hitter would kill him for information without hesitation. "Do not try to protect me, and don't do anything foolish. I will be gone in 45 minutes. I don't want anyone to hurt you. Understand?"

"Yes sir," he said and stood tall, understanding the gravity of what Chance said. "Thank you."

Chance went directly to his room and called Qu's cell phone. "Do you mind if I bunk with you tonight? They apparently sent someone else looking for me."

"Of course," Qu said. "Would you like me to come back for you."

"No," Chance said, "I need to make sure I'm not followed to your place. I'll see you in about an hour, give or take 15 minutes."

Chance double-locked his door and quickly showered. He cleaned and packed all his stuff in his bedroll, leaving behind anything he could spare. He called down to the front desk and checked out, glancing around the lavish room once more. He never before had the cash to stay in such a luxurious room.

He hoped for a second he would have the opportunity in the future to spend time with Ling in a joint like the Fullerton. He darted out of the room and down the back stairs to the rear entrance. Right on time, a cab stood idling at the door. The young Indian porter held the door for Chance. "It's been my pleasure sir," he said.

Chance wished he had something to give the kid instead of a substantial tip. He patted him on the shoulder as he looked in the cab to check for surprises. He threw his bedroll inside and climbed in.

"Thank you," he said to the porter. "I won't forget you."

The young man smiled and bowed reverently as the cab pulled away.

"Where to, sir?" the cabbie asked. He was a Malaysian man and Chance was relieved. He didn't want any surprises at the moment.

"Chinatown," Chance said and slipped as deep as possible in the rear seat. There wasn't much room for a big man in the back of most of the cabs, and the driver leaned over and pulled the passenger seat forward as much as possible.

"Thank you," Chance said, noting that in general, the people of Singapore were generous and helpful. He would miss the atmosphere, but not the humidity.

With cane in hand, he got out of the cab and found a small Chinese restaurant with the correct security systems in place. He walked immediately in and sat down. He ordered a bowl of fried rice and a cup of tea. He waited to see if he was followed. He waited for 20 minutes before he lost himself in the crowds and moved through several shops, stopping and starting until he was sure no one was behind him. Only then would he go down Erskine Street to Qu's place.

He slipped into the patio and knocked on the back door as the sun settled into the west, and he noted how the perfect sunset shed rich crimson hues into the patio. He was tiring of his plight, nervous and anxious to see it end.

"Come in," Qu said, opening the door. He grabbed Chance's bedroll and set it on a small table. He was alone in his house/office. They walked up a very narrow stairway to a small sitting room over looking the patio with a large picture window. The room was painted white with wicker furniture and grass mats over a polished hardwood floor.

He poured a colorful drink from a glass pitcher into a wide tumbler. "Here's something you need," Qu said. "This was invented here in Singapore in 1910. It's a Singapore Sling and will relax you."

"We need a plan," Chance said, swirling the glass in his hand.

"We have one," Qu said, sipping his own drink. "I will take you to the harbor at the slowest time of the night, about 4:00 a.m., so you will be able to sleep in comfort tonight. I will pull into the area of docks that the government built for Evergreen Shipping. Unfortunately, they charged the company too much to dock, so they took their business somewhere else and the docks and expensive cranes sit unattended. It is very close to Pasir Wharfs, and you can walk over from there."

"Are you sure?" Chance asked, enjoying the strong drink.

"Yes, I checked it out before I came home," Qu said. "Fishermen were on the spits this afternoon, fishing just a few yards from PT6."

Chance was once more impressed with his efforts. He sat back in the chair and took another slug of the exotic drink. A comforting dessert, he felt himself fading.

At 3:00 a.m., Chance felt someone nudging him and he sat up straight in Qu's guest bedroom.

"It's time," Qu said, bleary-eyed himself. "I'll make some tea."

Chance stumbled to his feet with fleeting notions of the night before. Qu pointed to the head and Chance took a shower and shaved as if he was going to meet Ling for breakfast. He tingled with anxiousness. When he got out, Qu made a couple of egg sandwiches and a pot of tea. They drank the tea and grabbed the sandwiches to go. As Chance made his way to Qu's truck, he thought that it sure would be nice when he could sit and have a decent breakfast again. He slid in the passenger side of the truck as Qu started it. They hardly said a word as they jiggled and jerked through town toward the harbor.

"Chance," Qu said suddenly, "do me a favor?"

"Anything," Chance said as the truck buzzed along the rarely empty streets.

"I would love to speak with your girl someday," Qu said. "I realize that it's an odd request, but she must be a special woman, and I hope to have the same in my life someday."

"I'm sure you will," Chance said. "Regarding your question, I will see to it."

They saw the gates of the harbor coming up on the left. Overhead, the city was building an above-ground transportation system and the enormous concrete pillars were being built in various stages. As they buzzed along the road, the pillars grew until they were full-sized and formed large sprawling concrete Ts hanging over the street below.

"There's gate 3," Qu said, still driving along at 40 mph. Another half mile and he started to slow. Driving on the left was still foreign to Chance and he watched closely as Qu turned into an area of over-grown weeds around abandoned fences. He passed the forsaken gate and traveled along recently constructed warehouses that were also deserted. Past them were a series of piers home to tracks and cranes, but he turned left and bumped up onto a grassy area separating the Pasir Panjang Wharves from the new construction. The fence between the two yards behind a warehouse was in disrepair.

Qu backed the truck up to the 6-foot fence. Chance shook his hand.

"Thank you," he said in a low voice.

"Good luck," Qu said, "and give her my very best."

"I will," Chance said, and jumped out of the truck. He tossed his bedroll over the fence and crawled up on the bed of the truck, jumped the fence and knelt down as Qu pulled away. He moved to the edge of the warehouse and peered around.

Qu was right; the PT6 building was only across the storage yard of shipping materials that could be left in the open. Chance ran from clusters of crates to heavy machinery, behind a row of Mercedes, in the heavy morning air. It wasn't light yet, but not dark either, as he reached the corrugated tin building. The door was open and he peaked inside. No one was inside. He stepped in, but his crate was no longer there. He froze, then heard voices and ducked behind a crate with his bedroll and cane in hand.

"Never a dull moment," he murmured under his breath.

# -32-

# THE PACKAGE IS
# SHIPPED

The Captain of the Bibi slept in on the morning of the 19th of February. He knew what he would face entering the congested port of Singapore and it would be a long, daunting ordeal. Captain Miskulin was Croatian and in his 60s. He witnessed better days and the shipping industry dragged him down. The paperwork alone was overwhelming. He spent over 40 percent of his time over the last two months answering over 2,000 telex messages from various departments within the Rickmers' Hamburg, Germany corporate offices.

He was captain of a 20-year-old ship on its last rusting steel legs. The crew numbers were too small to maintain the corroding hull and mechanical repairs, plus the company wouldn't afford him a repair budget, yet they expected the motoring cargo hold to take on twice the capable load, stay way ahead of schedule in each port, and minimize expenses.

He rolled over on his thin cabin bed and reached for a pack of cigarettes. The corporation monitored him like a pre-school scrutinizes a psychotic three-year-old. He took up drinking Chivas Regal on a regular basis, between dealing with the unions, stevedores, pilots, the crew, and the officers, all of which were union backed. When in ports, he had to deal with the agents, the cargo superintendents, immigration, customs, security, plus he had several ornery Chinese passengers. He was certain they were gangsters, so he gave them a wide berth on the ship and waited for the passage to end.

Slightly over six feet tall with a thick mane of gray hair, he peered over thick glasses. From all of his 40 years on ships, with low hatches and doorways, he constantly hunched over and walked like he was ducking one steel obstacle after another. He downed a couple of stiff drinks the night before, as he tried his damnedest to sort through the stacks of papers and forms piling up on his desk.

He ran an entire floating business with little or no assistance at all. His crew included five Polish officers and 20 Filipino seamen. Some of them were also considered officers and filled the bill as 2nd and 3rd officers on the bridge plus worked the grimy decks with the other seamen while in port. Filipino officers were not afforded the privilege of meals with the Polish officers. The Polish officers generally treated them as second-class citizens, since communication was tough.

None of the Poles, including the captain, spoke Filipino, and none of the crew spoke Polish. The common language was a rough attempt at English. They all spoke a little of it, so the officers communicated with themselves and the crew did the same.

The officers in most cases could hardly be called such. There was an electrician, the chief mechanic, the chief officer who was basically the chief boson's mate, a second engineer and a fitter who was basically a handyman. The Captain had to navigate the ship, handle all executive functions and perform the accountant and bookkeeper duties on his own. The only function he ducked was the loading and off-loading of the cargo, unless there was a problem.

He had no XO, like naval captains or even an assistant, a secretary, a bookkeeper, or a comptroller. He was even responsible for ordering all the food stores, the booze and cigarettes used to bribe the immigration and customs officials at the various ports.

The sun was exceedingly bright by noon when he went to the officers' mess for lunch with the other officers. The Filipinos had their own mess and lounge area that looked like an old fraternity party pad. The carpeting was soaked with grime, torn and stained. A beat up set of drums stood in the corner. The upholstery on the bench couch was slit and shredded. A stereo and television system was tucked in a corner with a Karaoke box, all strapped down for heavy seas.

The Captain sat across from the tall gangly chief engineer in the officers' dining area and attempted to explain the lack of budget to him regarding spare parts he needed to keep the ship running. He ate his Filipino spiced lunch while the passengers ate at the far end of the table. The passengers, two sullen-looking Chinese men and one hot looking mistress who ran them like a stolid captain runs a crew, ate lunch in silence. She had another man with her who disappeared awhile back, but the Captain wasn't asking any questions.

Since he was entering port, he returned to his cabin and took off his light clothing and donned a summer khaki uniform with four stripes on his black epaulets over his shoulders. He returned to the bridge, where the young Filipino 2nd officer attempted to reach the pilot station via radio. After several efforts, the station responded with the coordinates of the meeting place and time, 1400.

The Captain looked at the radar screen with dismay and concern. He sat dead in the water, surrounded by 40 or more ships, all waiting for instructions from agents and pilots. Some would be forced to anchor outside the harbor inlets. In addition, Singapore was located on the main channel running from the west to east from Europe through the Suez Canal to the Pacific. The ship traffic was considerable, but the seas were calm and the skies clear. The required speed was less than 20 mph, but it took a ship miles to change course or to stop, which made any lumbering vessel treacherous.

While entering a busy port such as Singapore, the Captain had three crewmen on the bridge to monitor the radars and one at the helm to take instruction from the harbor pilot, who was supposed to come alongside at 1400. As the Bibi neared the Singapore Strait leading from west to east, the Captain studied the radar closely, watching for cross traffic while monitoring all the ships entering and leaving the harbor. The harbor was so damn busy, a ship entered or departed every three minutes. In addition, he had 63 offshore islands to contend with as a navigational chore.

At exactly 1345, he entered the main channel to cross to the pilot buoy, which he did successfully and entered the pilot pickup area at precisely 1400, but there was no pilot. So he motored closer to the harbor at 3 knots or dead slow while requesting information on the whereabouts of the pilot.

An hour later, the pilot arrived in a fast-moving harbor cruiser and dashed to the elevator wearing white cloves to protect himself from the grease and grime common on most general cargo ships. He was a short Chinese man with a square jaw unlike most Chinese. His hair was Italian wavy and trimmed neatly with some strands of gray. He appeared to be in his mid 40s. He scrambled up the steel interior ladders onto the bridge, his face firm with dour concern.

The Captain met him at the chart table.

"Captain here," he said, extending his rough Polish hand, "Welcome aboard."

Ni Zun dismissed the handshake and walked briskly to the windows overlooking the bow.

"Do you have an operational bow thruster?" he asked abruptly as if they were running out of time.

"Yes, of course," the Captain, said responding quickly but disgusted by his stoic behavior.

"All stop," the pilot announced, and the Captain, pressed by harbor protocol to pass the instructional baton to the crewmember at the helm, forwarded the order.

"All stop."

"Slow astern," the pilot said, walking the length of the bridge as if he was pacing the deck, and then indicating for the Captain to follow him to the chart table.

"Slow astern," the Captain repeated, following the pilot.

"You are too close to this shallow area," Ni Zun said in a condescending tone while pointing at the chart, "You should never enter this area. We will need to back down to this point, where we can use the bow thruster to turn the ship between those two buoys and head into port."

"But sir," the Captain stated, "I could not wait for you in the busy channel."

"You are not supposed to enter the channel," Ni said, looking over the top of his bifocals at the Captain, "unless the pilot is there to meet you."

"If the pilot was on time," the Captain began to fume, "I would have been in exactly the right spot."

Ni looked at the Captain, prepared to contradict him, but realized that he was in a delicate position and didn't care to jeopardize the situation with a time-consuming argument.

"Captain," Ni said quietly, "I retire after this shift. This is the last ship I moor. I do not want any mistakes." He walked back to the bridge and looked out at the harbor he had commanded for over 30 years. "All stop," he said.

"All stop," said the Captain wryly, but with a modicum of respect. He was looking forward to being in Ni's position in six months. He could relate.

"All stop, aye," the sailor at the helm announced as he executed his order.

"Hard to starboard." Ni raised his voice to make each command perfectly understood. "Captain, can we assist with the bow thruster?" The Captain took care with the controls and the ship began to turn to the right.

The Bibi aligned with the buoys and headed on the correct bearing within 10 minutes. In a half hour, they passed 30 ships waiting for pilots, at anchor or leaving the port. It was a Los Angeles freeway interchange for ships and small craft. They passed two islands off the coast of Singapore, beginning with Pulau and Bukono, which were used solely for oil refineries. As the sun settled in the afternoon, the ship pulled alongside the Pasir PanJang wharfs, next to the abandoned Evergreen container piers.

"Captain!" The pilot suddenly seemed dismayed, his face scrunched into a questioning frown. "I have discovered that you have almost 9.9 meters of draft. Is that correct?

"Yes sir, it is," the Captain confirmed.

"There seems to be a problem," Ni said, looking at the map of the wharfs. "The agent has you at 9 meters draft and mooring at a 9.5 meter dock. Except you are 9.9 meters, which would cause you to run aground. I cannot allow that."

The Captain looked at Ni's smallness and listened to his words, as if the little man was slapping him in the face with the form. His large nose, splattered with a drunkard's red veins, seemed to throb. He sent the draft data to the agent no less than four times. That indicated the agent's mistake or another Asian ploy to dupe a company out of additional fees.

This would cause extra stevedore costs. It would cost to have another pilot come onboard and for additional tug service. He could feel his neck redden and his collar become tight. He called the first officer and in Polish, asked him to man the anchor detail. He telexed the agent immediately.

Two years ago, he was on a similar ship in Singapore, the city of strict penalties for spitting on the sidewalk. The chief engineer at the time was bribed by the fuel barge people to undercut the fuel consumption. When the fuel was tested, they discovered that 16 percent of 10,000 tons of fuel was seawater. Such deals were regular occurrences in Singapore. He was forced to have his fuel tank drained in Japan and refilled.

The pilot came to the chart table and indicated to him a spot on the chart less than a quarter mile from the docks where he could anchor. With binoculars, the Captain could see the stevedores sitting on crates, in the back of pickups and on the dock waiting to work.

There were 10 new crewmembers with their suitcases standing on the dock at the door to a tin warehouse, waiting to pick up their new ship. It was hot and even the evening humidity was stifling. He anchored, let the retired pilot depart the ship and the tug steamed off to assist another vessel. He shook his head and pulled at his bulbous nose in consternation.

Telexes spit out of the computer in reams, but the sunset was spectacular. He took a quick second to look at the strato cumulus clouds turning evil colors of crimson and gold as if a powerful spirit had engulfed the sun and dragged it, kicking and screaming, to the sea.

It was 1745, and before he could leave the bridge to chow on another cold dinner, he received the telex pointing out that the ship at the dock would be moved back to allow him to enter at 2200. That meant that the engine room personnel would have to shut the driveline down, then fire it back up again. He would have to pay the deck crew overtime to man the anchor detail again, and the stevedores would lose a half-day's work in their haste to load the ship and send it on its way. Rickmers was required to pay the idle longshoremen for their wasted time. Besides, most of the cargo strapped above the holds would need shifting to allow for new cargo, which was costly and time-consuming.

At dinnertime, Yew knocked on Ling's door and let himself in. As he picked up the lunch tray, he noticed the food had not been touched. It was the third time he had entered her room to find her asleep in the same position. He set the tray down and approached her still form on the bed. Terror ripped through his body as he got close to her. He realized that he hadn't talked to her and no one had. He noticed that her food consumption diminished severely until she hardly ate at all, but no one seemed to care. He touched her shoulder.

She rolled to face him, her face gaunt and lifeless. Her eyes weren't open. She was not dead, but seemingly on the edge of life. He held her lovely face in his hands and saw that her eyes fluttered slightly, but her lids seemed stuck in place. He got up from the bed and dampened a washcloth and returned to the bed and wiped her eyes and face.

Her lips were dry, cracked and withdrawn. Her teeth looked stained from the tea. She opened her eyes as if her translucent lids were sheets of heavy lead. She looked and reached, simultaneously touching his shoulder, and a glimmer of hope flickered and waned.

"Chance?" she muttered through dry lips then dropped her hand to her side, limp. She knew the thin shoulders did not belong to Chance.

"You must eat something," Yew pleaded.

"What for?" she said harshly and rolled away from Yew and faced the bulkhead.

He got to his feet and backed toward the door. He didn't want anything to do with the girl. Violence surrounded her in so many respects. He was scared that if sometime in the future she was free and could recognize him it would bring him great harm. He backed out the door and locked it. If she died, it could be worse for the Wong family, much worse. He didn't know what to do.

Yew returned to the galley with the lunch tray, then to the dining room to have dinner. He looked at Kim, who also seemed drawn but impatient. She was tiring of the voyage and the pressure. Ever since her violent exchange with Chee, she had been distant and removed. At dinner, since the Polish officers sat within earshot, they did not speak even in Chinese. That was the way Chee initially wanted it and Kim mocked his concerns earlier when she smiled and danced along the deck. Now she favored the rule.

She really had nothing more to say and felt betrayed by her guards. She would never open up to them again, she promised herself. They would never know another thing about her.

Yew wanted to tell her of Ling's condition, but was cognizant of the rule and decided that he would try to speak to Kim after dinner. The sunset filtered in the portholes behind them and the rich colors danced along the white linen tablecloths. Kim looked out and saw the dull concrete wharfs and corrugated steel warehouses teaming with dock workers and material to be shipped.

She felt certain that this was the last dock where they would have to deal with the American. Another hit man had been sent to town and she needed to make sure her men were on the alert and bribe the customs agents at the gate.

As the Polish officers ate quickly and left, Kim turned toward her crew. "I want you in my room in ten minutes," she said, looking at her white gold enhanced Omega watch.

Without looking at them directly or confirming that they even understood, she got to her feet and departed. She took the elevator to her cabin on E deck and unlocked her room. As she did, she turned and looked down the passageway in the direction of Ling's cell.

She missed the woman. She missed her touch, the fantastic sex, her lips, everything. She kicked herself for never getting to know Ling. The questions kept coming and something raged in her chest and her throat closed.

She opened her refrigerator quickly and grabbed her bottled water and poured herself a small glass. She sipped the cool liquid, but the pain did not subside. Her feeling was real, yet psychological. She saw Ling's hurt features as plain as day. Stabbing guilt struck at her. She looked around the room as if there was a door to escape her culpability and sense of loss. There was no getaway. She pinched herself on the forearm until she drew blood and the sensation subsided some as the pain bit her arm. She strode to her liquor cabinet and began to pour herself a stiff drink, as Yew tapped on her door.

"Come in," Kim snapped. "Where's Sun?" she demanded.

"He's right here," Yew said, feeling her wrath and bowing slightly. He didn't want to be shot, so he didn't want to be in this room with her, especially if she was going to drink.

"Sit down," Kim snapped, and the two guards sat close together on the long narrow couch as near to the door as possible.

"I'll make this quick," she said, then gulped at the drink and set it on the coffee table. "Neither one of you is to go to town. I want to keep a very close eye on this ship. I don't want any mistakes. You both know how he looks and his size. There will be no excuse for allowing him to sneak aboard. The one who fails will face the same punishment as Chee. Am I clear?"

They both nodded.

"Then get out of here," Kim said. "I don't want to see the gang plank ever unattended. Understand?"

"Yes ma'am," Yew said and bowed, backing toward the door. He wanted to tell her about Ling but couldn't muster the courage. She was in a foul enough mood; he would have no part in adding to her angst.

The stressed wooden container had been moved harshly three times. Each time, the slick but jarring tongs abruptly snatched the heavy box from the concrete surface of the warehouse, and then hauled it around without suspension and dropped it again on hard concrete. Between two moves, Chance found it, opened the end, stuffed in his gear and climbed inside, and then closed the end cap and screwed himself inside securely.

Chance awoke to the exhaust note of a forklift and the jarring effects of the tongs scratching the base of his crate once more. He was being lifted. He could feel and hear every screw and nail in the crate creak, as the wooden box hoisted and moved closer to the corrugated steel door. Chance looked around in his dark tomb that smelled of dank wood.

Without warning, a streak of light entered the 4-by-4-by-6 space and Chance followed its source to the lid of the box above him.

Each time, the structural integrity of the nailed and screwed container was tested, stretched and damaged. The carefully built plywood floor was nailed to the corner posts, but the nails yanked at their bindings and Chance panicked. He looked at his watch in the sliver of light. It was almost noon and he was already sweating like a stuck pig.

He wished he could have played a hand with the devil and gotten his ass on the ship sooner.

At 2145, the Captain reluctantly returned to the bridge and waited for another speeding harbor craft to deliver one more agent and for another tug to pull alongside.

The crew climbed to their positions adjacent to the massive anchor windlass, where they dropped two shackles of chain to the bottom as the Captain backed down the anchor to set it firmly in the sandy bottom.

This time, the pilot was much younger and very tall for a Chinese-looking man. He had thin hair and the air of someone who was always ready to make a deal. It made the Captain wonder about the situation at the dock. Since he anchored offshore, a very large car-carrying ship tied to the Pasir Panjang dock where he was supposed to be moored. They moved the next ship alongside the dock forward 100 meters so that the Bibi could be parallel parked between the two. It looked like someone had cut a deal.

The chief engineer and his crew warmed up the 15,000 horsepower supercharged diesel while the chief officer's crew raised the anchor. The third officer manned the pilot boarding ladder, while another crewmember and the 2nd officer manned the bridge.

"Dead slow ahead," the pilot ordered.

"Dead slow ahead," the Captain passed the order to the 2nd officer at the engine room controls.

"Dead slow ahead, aye," replied the 2nd officer and the process began with a daunting slowness as the ship with cargo weighing 31,000 metric tons was coerced into place alongside the heavy concrete docks. The procedure, which seemed to take forever, took nearly an hour to move the ship 200 yards to the docks.

The minute the gangplank was lowered, a steady flow of ant-like beings flooded the ship and poured onto the adjacent dock in trucks and forklifts, under beaming nightlights. Stevedores scrambled aboard along with new Filipino crewmembers, customs agents, immigration agents, and one European, the cargo superintendent.

The progression of off-loading the ship, shifting cargo and loading materials bound for the South and East China seas and the Sea of Japan was underway.

# -33-

## THE WOODEN COFFIN

The crate sat bent and damaged on the dock, like a wooden coffin that fell off a horse-drawn carriage in the 1800s. Slightly crumpled alongside several other crates, the blistering sun beat down upon them, backed by 90 percent humidity. Sweating stevedores sauntered around the dock as the ship's crane operators busied themselves unloading trucks and steel containers in order to reach the holds. The crew joked among themselves about the Rickmer Company. It wasn't a shipping organization but a "shifting one."

Unfortunately, the ship was charged for every shifting maneuver involving indigenous longshoremen, almost twice the cost of loading it originally. Plus, costly shifting created damage hazards to cargo, adding further to the cost.

Chance tried to shift his position without making a sound. He pondered how American prisoners of war must have felt when forced by Japanese captors into tiny sweat boxes under blistering sun and drenching humidity. Soaked in sweat by noon, he fought to stay calm. He could not see a thing outside, but could only imagine what was happening around him by the angry mechanical sounds. He didn't dare move to have access to the holes they drilled and risk making a sound, as he listened to the Chinese dialog and broken English between the teams on the docks.

Trucks rumbled, brakes squealed, fork lifts clanked and banged into containers and various crates. He was terrified but determined. The top of the box could come loose and he would be discovered. As the sun roamed through the equatorial sky, the beams of light slithering in the holes and between the lid and the walls pressed him. As the heat warmed the crate, the nails creaked and pulled from their bearings.

He tried to dig himself deeper into the box, but it was very difficult in the tight space and would take dismantling the cardboard boxes and burying himself in the garments. He considered the tactic every time he heard someone nearby. He was equally frightened for fear of making a noticeable sound. If anyone heard something move in a box, it would be shredded instantly, turned over to customs and the stowaway handed over to immigration.

The work on the docks began sharp at 0600 and continued consistently, except for a lunch break. He could tell the sun was setting in the afternoon through the cracks in the roof of his box and the temperature reduction. He was almost relieved as nightfall came, but the work continued until after midnight, and as quickly as teams arrived the previous morning, they dispersed and quiet befell the harbor like a warm, thick blanket. The noise from the forklifts, the electrical whirring of the cranes, and the clashing of gears from the diesel trucks died. Only the squeaking sound of an occasional hungry dock rat interrupted his attempt to sleep.

He unexpectedly awoke consumed with fear. He hadn't coped with the inability to escape the crate once delivered aboard the ship. The thought made him shudder with fear. Another point raced through his taut mind. He considered eliminating any crewmember who stood in his way from reaching Ling, but his thoughts steered him toward another frantic notion. There were only three enemy staff on the ship. The remaining crew were innocent bystanders facing a prospective stowaway. Suddenly, he had dealt himself an awkward hand. He thought about approaching the ship's captain with Ling and the story once he found her. That would be a given, but what was the captain going to do once he was detected as a stowaway? His mind paced around the crate like a gambler playing his last chips.

Ling lay very still as the sunlight beamed in her porthole reflecting off the bay outside. The door opened and Yew stepped in over the bulkhead and set the polished tray down. For the last two days, he tried to force-feed her some mouthfuls of rice and make her drink water. She looked drawn and haggard. Her dark eyes were bright red from the lack of nutrition, and her face distant as a lingering storm cloud and just as ominous.

When she could muster the energy, she spit the rice in his face and eagerly reached for the drugged tea. Burning her fingers on the hot ceramic pot, she poured the steamy liquid quickly and gulped at it. Her lips were cracked and blistered, but she didn't care as long at the cunning nature of the opiate reached her blood stream.

Her mind was lost in an addictive fog. She gave into a blanket of tranquil surrender and life faded from her once lovely form. She was sure the worst lay ahead, and she had nothing left but to drift away before torture consumed her. She couldn't see a future anymore, or Chance, or her family. It was all gone and so was she.

As soon as the gangplank was lowered to the concrete deck and customs and immigration officials did their duties, Kim left the ship and stormed passed several crates stacked in front of the warehouse in preparation for loading. She caught a cab into town and met with the friend of the Wong family, Yuro Duo. He hadn't found the American, but discovered by torturing the Indian porter at the Fullerton, his recent departure, but the porter didn't know where he had gone. Frustrated, she picked up a box of Marlboros and a case of whiskey. She sent the hired hit man to an office supply joint with specific instructions to make up a flyer looking for this Anglo man with his description, like a wanted poster.

They met later and he delivered the fliers. The hit man was a small, rough-looking Chinese gentleman with a pudgy face full of nasty scars. His mug was a roadmap of torture. He was evil looking from the scar that split one eyebrow to the obvious knife attack that sliced open his left cheek. He was ugly and intimidating, but she wasn't scared. Pissed off about the whole interruption, she felt emotionally tormented by the process. She would have killed this little man in an instant if she felt he failed. He sensed her dry compelling nature and acted with respect, not to raise her ire.

She climbed in his rental with the flyers, and they drove quickly to the head office of customs to meet with the manager, with her case of cigarettes and whiskey. She made a point to dress in a low cut seductive outfit that hugged her curves with pure black, as if it had been painted on. Her hair was pulled tightly against her head into a ponytail and her lips were painted bright red, although she avoided the appearance of wealth by removing any gold jewelry before entering the building on Pasir Pajang Road. She slipped on a simple jade bracelet and matching earrings, but no gold.

If she was a man, she would have never met the commandant of the commission, but her looks and sad face convinced the officer at the desk that she held urgent news for the commander. She was whisked into his military looking office complete with country and regional flags. Pang Chun was a small, crisply uniformed man in his late 30s with a thin mustache and an angry air about him. He was a man of forms. If the declarations were filled out appropriately and stamped properly, his ass was covered. He kept to the rules, packed the filing cabinets in an orderly fashion and enjoyed his free time on the fringes of Singapore's society elite. This was a unique and rare shapely interruption.

"Ms. Wong," Officer Pang said, "Please, sit down. How can I help you?" His dark flitting eyes full of skepticism brushed over her like a man inspecting a new car. His imagination began to wander.

"I am on a ship, the Bibi, sir," Kim said, bowing her head respectfully and speaking humbly, as if she would be slapped if she missed a beat. "We have heard a man is trying to sneak aboard our ship and would like your guards to be extra careful at the gates." She bowed again and handed him a sheaf of fliers.

Pang looked at her more inquisitively with each moment. Her cleavage was wonderfully opulent. He lived in a world of gifts and bribes, and suddenly realized that if he played his cards right, this could be a special opportunity. He set the fliers down without looking at them, as if they meant little or nothing to a man of such stature.

"I have strange people coming around the harbor all the time. We run one of the busiest ports in the world, Ms. Wong. We have little time for special considerations for one ship." He stroked the pointed end of his carefully trimmed mustache at the corner of his thin mouth.

Kim thought about the small .25 caliber Browning semi-automatic in her handbag. She would just as soon kill this sonuvabitch as look at him.

"I'm very sorry to bother you with this, sir," Kim said and began to get up. "I brought gifts for your crew," she said, bowing and opening the door for Yuro to bring in the case of whiskey and Marlboros.

Pang looked at the small man behind the cardboard boxes, who bowed carefully and disappeared quickly out the door. Pang thought he saw scars and a nasty looking demeanor, but dismissed the notion as the man left quickly. Another scheme developed in his mind.

"Thank you, but I'm very busy," he said, "but if you have the time to escort me, maybe we could discuss it further. I must attend a very important luncheon."

"Gladly," Kim said, acting like his servant.

Pang's face became bright with enthusiasm. He was not a ladies' man and rarely had the opportunity to use his office for this level of pleasure. The head of the police had such opportunities constantly. Other officials enjoyed similar sensual benefits on a constant basis and this would be a chance for Pang to show them all his prowess.

He turned and reached for the fliers, but then decided it was best to milk the situation as far as he could. His lack of panache was evident to Kim. He marched out of his office, Kim following humbly, which had the desired effect Pang wanted on his employees. They all bowed as he approached, but looked at the woman with intriguing gazes. He was fooling only himself.

His car was brought around to the front of the building and he held the door for Kim to get in.

"You will enjoy this," he said, motioning for his driver to take them to the luncheon at the Raffle's Hotel.

Kim glanced at her hit man, raising an eyebrow to indicate for him to follow. As the car pulled away, Pang gazed at the warm robust size of her boobs, and Kim realized she had to do something to encourage the wound-tight official to call back to the office and instruct his staff to distribute her fliers. She cringed at the thought but placed her hand on his thigh near his crotch and squeezed.

"It is very nice of you to invite me on such short notice," she said, batting her eyes at Pang gently. "We could have some fun, but I am concerned about the ship and our cargo."

Pang immediately responded to her touch and wanted to reach for her soft hand. He lifted his hand and put it on her thigh and she spread her legs slightly, which sent a shiver up his spine.

"I will call immediately and have the fliers delivered to the gates."

"That would be most helpful," Kim said, moving her hand up slightly. "It would mean so much to me."

Pang snapped his cell phone open and suddenly wished he had no luncheon to attend.

The next morning at 0600, the docks sprang to life once again. Chance awoke with a start, cramps, muscle aches, a mouth that felt hangover dry, and the unrelenting desire to pee. He struggled to move slowly to reach his empty water bottle to take a piss in it when he heard longshoremen approaching. They passed into the warehouse, but as he picked up the plastic jug, he heard an approaching fork lift and could smell the pungent diesel exhausts. He was about to unzip his fly when the steel tongs jostled the wooden box and he fell on his side as the crate was lifted then spun and delivered to the dock immediately adjacent to the ship. He could hear the morning voices of stevedores surround the box and cables being dragged along the concrete and then shoved under it. For the first time, they were wrapped along the underside and fastened to something above the crate, the crane hook.

Chance tried shifting to a more comfortable position as the cables slapped the sides of the crate and the crane jerked him off the pavement. He was airborne, dangling from one of the ship's 20-ton crane cables. The box was light compared to some of the objects. They loaded heavy items, including whole trucks weighing several tons. The crate cried with every movement. The plywood walls cracked and creaked and bent to the will of the cables. He was swinging like a kid with a rock in a slingshot. Then the steel cable started lowering his coffin toward the stern hold.

Hold number five on the second level was the determined destination and the case banged into the steel bulkhead separating the deck from the iron container, slamming Chance against the quivering wooden cage wall. The morning sunlight blazed in the splitting roof of the box and a couple of holes.

Chance looked up at his plywood hiding place roof, which was ajar. He cringed. He heard stevedores shouting and one stepped onto the rectangular plywood roof above him. Chance could see the man's boot heal as he undid the strap to the crane hook and jumped free of the crate. Chance felt the cables and straps fall free, then slide under the crate, up the other side and disappear over the side of the ship.

Chance was stunned. He no longer needed to pee. He felt for sure he was busted. He could see that the top of the crate was off center by an inch or more. If anyone looked over the edge he was cooked. He scrambled in the box beneath him to find his box of tools and weapons as he heard another crate crash into the hold beside him. In another minute, another crate landed on top of his, sealing him inside, but not entirely. He huddled in the corner of the box the farthest he could be from the opening, with a knife at the ready and shuttered as one crate after another was dropped around him.

The number five was a portion of the smallest hold on the ship. All holds had two levels. One was on the very bottom deck above fuel tanks for the vessel. Steel sheets, 1-inch thick were welded to the struts forming the structure of the hull. Cargo could be stacked as high as 24 feet to the next level, which was made up of massive doors of steel. They slid and tilted open to allow loading and off loading. The second level was 15 feet high, and then enormous doors on tracks wheeled out of the way for loading, and then closed over the loaded material to allow more cargo and containers to be stacked in the open air on top.

Hold five was the stern-most hold and the narrowest, but still capable of holding 3000 metric tons of cargo. All day, Chance remained in the corner, waiting for the shoe to fall. As the sun began to sink, the evening crew came on duty, and he could hear stevedores moving around the hold, jamming wood between crates to prevent shifting in high seas. He slammed himself against the wall of the wooden box and wondered what would happen if they discovered the top of the crate ajar. He was sure stevedores would move the crate above him and open his wooden box for a souvenir, or at least their curiosity would get the better of them and they would pull the lid aside to check the contents.

Kim attended the luncheon with Pang Chun, the head official of the Singapore Customs Bureau, to his immense delight. He fondled her ass on a regular basis in the Grand Ballroom of the exquisite Raffles Hotel adjacent to the city hall on Stamford Boulevard. The lavish creamy white hall was packed with the elite band of civil servants. In conjunction with the Chinese New Year, for the first time Pang enjoyed a celebration with a hot female escort. He wasn't a popular official with his hard-nosed attitude and lack of social graces, but this was different.

When the car pulled up at the hotel and the porter, a large light skinned middle-aged Indian man, opened the door, his eyes brightened as he saw her shapely legs swivel and reach the soft gravel in the driveway. His hair was full and fringed with gray. His tan face framed a well-manicured full beard. He wore a turban of sorts with gold fringe.

The perfect uniformed host bowed slightly. "Madam," he said, bowing deeply as he opened the door.

Kim nodded as she eyed the elaborate uniform and the broad entrance framed with impressive columns, all painted a rich ivory white. As she entered the ornate front door, she turned to Pang who was 4 inches shorter.

"I would like to use the ladies' room and make sure I look my best."

"Of course," Pang said, a smirk gleaming from beneath his mustache. He pointed the way and took her by the arm in the direction.

In the elaborate black and white marble bath, she pulled her gold jewelry out of her purse and donned it, touched up her makeup and took off her panties, wadded them and put them back in her black purse. Her dress was slick, contoured and slit up the side. It was all black as usual and simple with just the right amount of succulent cleavage visible.

With her mission accomplished, she had at least two days in port to shop or have some fun. Her mood had been anxious, and she would prefer to keep moving. On the other hand, she was beginning to hate the ship, her guards and her forced inability to see Ling. As she left the restroom, she sensed her evil desires rear their ugly heads again. Ling somehow chased them away and something warm emerged, unexpectedly, when Ling entered her life. She lost her cunning, nasty ways from her days trying to scramble from one rung to the other in the prostitution game, then the drug trade.

Kim left the bathroom wearing a fine gold necklace that held a very carefully engraved jade coy fish, and she slipped on several gold rings graced with multi-carrot diamonds. Pang raised his eyebrows as she approached, strutting in her royal way. She took Pang's arm and he led her into a dining room where kings and the president of the United States sat from time to time.

Many streets, buildings and areas were named after Sir Stamford Raffles. He was a 19th century British civil servant who was responsible for the founding of Singapore in 1819. Raffles scoured the Straits of Malacca searching for a small trading post to counter the

Dutch influence in the area. Singapore was perfect, since as a fishing village, it housed the crossroads of the east and west.

Pang offered her a perfectly hand-tooled and finished wooden chair, carefully upholstered with velvet material befitting the quality of the hotel. As she sat and felt the cool air-conditioned air between her legs, her mind raced with devious thoughts. At first she considered making a fool of the man, but his port position was key to her effort. He held it for over a decade and in all probability would continue for years to come. This was the type of situation Kim excelled at. She could very feasibly have a lasting customs connection in Singapore. She snuggled against him and looked her submissive finest.

While they sat together and he placed his napkin in his lap she reached across and took his hand and aimed it at the slit in her dress. She had no hose on and his small palm slipped over the top of her soft thigh and reached her carefully shaved mound. His eyes brightened and he looked into hers for the first time. His face was aglow and flushed. She turned and kissed him on the cheek while lowering her own napkin to conceal his hand.

At that moment, a colleague tapped Pang on the shoulder, but he couldn't move for a long moment, mesmerized by her beauty, the softness of her thigh and the brazen sexual behavior. As he pulled his eyes away, he wasn't sure if he was in lust or drugged.

# -34-

## The Dark Hold

Chance felt his back would break as he awoke to the jarring of the ship in the stiff, thick heat and humidity. He had been sequestered in the box for over two days and wanted out. He was determined not to try to escape the confines of his hideaway prison until the ship set sail. If they caught up with him in port, he would be banished from the ship and perhaps thrown in prison. Besides, there was a hit man waiting somewhere.

At least at sea, he had from Singapore to Hong Kong to reach Ling. The lid was still ajar as darkness befell the harbor. The shift changed at midnight and the harbor shut down until six in the morning. A sense of deep fear overwhelmed Chance as he sat and waited. This was his last effort. He felt small and unsuccessful. His drive and desire were all he had left, coupled with his images of Ling's smiling face and her love for him. He had nothing left in the world but his willingness to reach her and finally his motorcycle, at sea somewhere on the Leon. He was still terrified that he would be discovered in the partially open box.

As silence engulfed the harbor, Chance huddled, scrunched over on the crushed cardboard boxes beneath him and tried to straighten the lid to cover as much of the opening as possible. Several nails were still holding on by the short hairs and wouldn't budge without a hammer, which he didn't have. He sat back down, slightly relieved. No one would be tinkering with the boxes in the dark. At least, he hoped not. He heard of the gangs who ravaged ships and the thought made him shudder. He didn't need another foe.

As the morning sun filtered over the horizon, he wondered how long he would have to wait. He was running short of water and protein bars. His back was killing him, his piss bottle was full, and at night the steel hold was bitterly cold. He bundled himself in the colorful sarongs and held on.

Kim returned to the ship in the morning, her outfit disheveled and her make-up smeared. Forever, as long as Pang had a sex drive, she had a smooth connection with the customs agency in Singapore. He actually was an enthusiastic lover and not bad in the sack. Besides, if he got in the way, she knew where he lived and how to gain access to the sanitary interior of his high-rise apartment to kill him. As she stepped onto the greasy gangplank and struggled up the quivering steps, trying not to touch the ropes or railings, she considered her mission complete, but where was the white guy?

She wanted to see the Captain immediately and procure an underway report. Her desire was to see the pilot onboard and the ship pulling out straight away. She looked to the port side of the ship and noticed all the crates stacked on the dock were loaded. It looked as if the crew was sealing up the holds to load the containers back over the five cargo hatches.

As she stepped off the gangplank onto the grimy deck, she noticed her guard was missing. She marched across the deck to the hatch leading into the interior of the ship. Sun was slumped in a chair sleeping while ducking the night's chill in the inner portion of the ship. She fumbled with her purse madly, pulling the small Browning pistol and cocking it.

A small wry sort, but damn good at martial arts, and mean as cat-shit in a fight, Sun could fight. His short hair was tough and straight like a bristle brush, and he wore his everyday uniform of a black turtleneck sweater and a black sport coat. His hideout from the cold was just off the exterior passage in the ship's interior superstructure. Just inside a quick turn to the left, he leaned against a steel bulkhead in a crew's laundry. It was one of the dirtiest spaces on the ship, piled high with grease-soaked overalls, helmets, gloves and socks.

The machines were covered with greasy fingerprints. Footprints marred the deck with grimy smudges. The bulkheads were tattered and smudged. He positioned himself so he could see the gangplank without being seen, yet out of the way of the crew members who drifted inside.

She extended her arm and the tiny weapon fitting neatly in her palm came dangerously close to Sun's forehead. Even in a semi-con-science state the cold steel of a weapon sends a threatening signal; his senses fired to life and his right wrist twisted pushing the cold weapon clear of his skull with the outside of his palm, and then his wrist shifted again so his fingers encompassed and snapped the weapon from her grasp. He was on his feet instantly, the gun now in his hand and his other hand reaching for her throat. He sprung into action like a tightly wound spring.

Unfazed, Kim stood straight up a few inches taller than Sun.

"How dare you sleep on your watch!" she snapped.

Aware that it was his mistress, he snapped to attention, putting both of his hands at his side and bowed deeply. He cradled the weapon in crossed palms and offered it back to her.

"I'm sorry, Ms. Kim," he said respectfully. "I have been asleep but a moment."

She snapped the pistol out of his outstretched palm and put the safety back on with a snap.

"Get Yew up and have him search the ship," she ordered, and turned and walked away.

The stevedores swarmed the cargo vessel along with agents and cargo superintendents. Sun rang Yew's room. Yew was due to change watch with him after breakfast. Sun extended the message from Kim and his apology for what occurred.

Kim took the elevator to Edeck. As she stepped off, she thought of Ling and wished she could see her. She took the stairs to the bridge and tried the door. If the door was locked, it meant generally that there was no sign of leaving the port. If it was unlocked, the second officer or the third might be plotting their course or calls were being made for tugboat and pilot arrangements.

The door was unlocked and the Captain was at the Telex machine bent over trying to read the various messages on the black screen in small difficult-to-read yellow type. He was hunched over and obviously uncomfortable.

"Captain," Kim said. "Are we leaving today?"

The Captain looked at her in consternation. He didn't want to be disturbed. The Rickmers Company breathed down his neck forcing more cargo fit than was humanly possible and the old ship to move faster than it was capable of going.

"Yes, yes," he spat, avoiding her good looks with his eyes. "If I can complete my reports and they will finish loading, we will leave by noon."

He turned back to the machine and continued to type with one finger.

Yew searched the ship thoroughly before breakfast but avoided the holds where the stevedores worked. He was sure a stranger among them, especially a white man, would be detected, questioned and asked to leave or reported. He searched the engine room to the dismay of the crew and the superstructure to the deck above the bridge. Then he went to the galley and picked up the tray for Ling and returned to her room. She was in the same condition as he'd left her.

Her lips were cracked and dry. A faint order of perspiration surrounded her, as she hadn't showered in a week. Her bed was dirty and he made a mental note to have the steward clean her room. Yew brought a small jug of bottled water and poured a few caps-full down her dry throat. She coughed and sputtered. He did it again and tried to get her to eat one spoon-full of rice. She wouldn't.

As he stepped away from her, he was sure she would die soon. There was nothing he could do. She no longer responded except while struggling to reach for the opium-based tea. He knew if he took it away from her, the withdrawal symptoms would immediately kill her. She didn't have the strength to overcome the control of the drug. Yet with it consuming her blood stream, she failed to eat or drink the nutrients she needed to stay alive.

Chance awoke to raucous clamoring of the stevedores tearing at the ship like a drunk rips a beer can after guzzling it. He felt like he was a ball bearing in the bottom of the can. He had too much time to think. His mouth pasty, he took a swallow of water from what little remained in the bottom of his plastic container. He tried to open his eyes to the sliver of sunlight cutting its way into the interior of the box. He could hardly move. A chunk of machinery weighing 38 tons was lowered using two 20-ton cranes into his hold. The entire ship shook violently, and when it collided with the deck above number five hold, he felt like the ball at the bottom of a can of spray paint as it was being shaken for the first time.

Ships had a mystique of being grand vessels cutting romantic swaths across broad expanses of powerful oceans, yet more and more, Chance saw them as semi-trucks on the water, beat-on, pushed around, and packed in a mad hurry to save a buck here and there.

Jostled and welded on until the rust and the roughshod handling took the craft to the bottom. They were but tools for import and export.

Lengths of pipe were being shifted and the noise was horrendous. Then a crew of stevedores scrambled into the holds clamoring over one case after another with a Skil saw, hammers and lashing equipment. They cut lengths of 4 by 4s to jam between crates and strapped cargo down with chains and cast hooks snapped into lopes fastened to the decks. The noise was incredibly brutal and threatening as they neared his crate.

Suddenly, Indian and Malaysian stevedores stood around his crate, banging and shoving strips of wood between his crate and the one next to it. Chance huddled in the corner as one of the men pried at the top of the box with a hammer trying to align the lid, then drove long nails through the lip of the crate into the 4-by-4 beneath. Nails split the wood, missed the thick beam and entered the interior, as if cannibals were shooting steel darts at Chance through the box.

Then it dawned on Chance that if they put chain lashing over the end of the box he couldn't get out. The box was surrounded with other crates. His secret door could be useless. His only escape was the top and they were nailing it shut. Another scenario slid into his consciousness. He could starve to death in this sonuvabitch. He pushed himself into a corner with his back against one wall and feet against another and shoved hard so that as the stevedore above drove nails they missed the beam, but what about the chains? He listened intently.

Suddenly the men disappeared and he heard a terrible creaking sound as the iron lid of the Mac Gregor folding hatch began to close. A wicked vibration began to shake the ship. The 15,000 horsepower diesel engine fired to life. He heard another engine running close by, followed by the air horn of an approaching tug. He couldn't believe his ears; the ship was actually preparing to leave. A sigh of relief swallowed him. He knew the crew would continue to check the lashings as the ship motored out of the harbor, and they would monitor the cargo while under way, but for a split second he relished the thought that he was now on the ship with Ling and she was no farther away than the superstructure of the ship, maybe 200 feet.

He would find her, unless he was lashed in the wooden box to die. He laid down against crumpled Sarongs and pressed his leg upward against the lid and shoved. He dug in the darkness for the box of tools Qu prepared for him. To his amazement, it contained a mag light and a wedge-like device used for prying nails. It was a flat bar of sprung steel. He wanted out bad, but knew that he had to wait until nightfall when 90 percent of the crew would be asleep.

With the assistance of a tug, the Bibi pulled away from the Pasir pier and was set free to motor out of the harbor and into the West Raffles Passage, heading east and then south along the island of Sumatra, and then toward Jakarta.

Unlike the crew quarters or the cabins on the ship, the hold contained absolutely no insulation. The vibration was ear-numbing, enhanced with the creaking of the crates and the rattling of steel pipes against steel pipes by the thousands. Directly below him in the hold under the 1-inch thick deck plates were sheets of steel mixed with rolls of tin weighing more than 7 tons apiece. Each chain and strap strained, screeched and groaned as the ship moved with the sea. Chance could feel every revolution of the supercharged diesel engine as it neared 100 revolutions per minute at cruising speed.

It wasn't long before he heard crew members come down the steel ladders into the holds. They turned fluorescent lights on and crawled around and over the crates checking and adjusting the lashings. Chance could sense their closeness and huddled deep in the corner of his box. He could hear a crewmember dragging a chain across the top of the crate next to his. His nerves were jangled enough when he heard the shackles being tightened. Suddenly a gloved hand was inside his box and trying to adjust the lid. It wouldn't budge from the last effort to nail it down. Then he heard the chain and felt chunks of wood being driven between his box and the one behind him. Terrified, he pushed his face up against the rough plywood to see if the chain was being strapped over his crate. It was.

He looked around for anything he could use to wedge the chain away from his crate. He could only use the flat bar Qu left for him. If he stuck it up through the crack and was seen, he would be discovered. On the other hand, he could starve to death in a coffin he helped make. He peered up through the crack and could see the chain lying there then he heard the crew member tightening the links with a yard long cast steel chain bender that makes each chain tight as a bowstring. He could feel the box press toward the deck as the links tightened, then the crew moved onto other project.

Chance flopped in the corner disappointed and disillusioned. He felt as if he was in a building during the aftershocks of an earthquake, with quaking walls all around him, threatening death. He wasn't sure what to do next.

Kim ate in silence with the officers of the ship and her guards. Before their meal, Sun assured Kim the ship had been thoroughly searched and there were no intruders on board. As the ship rumbled out of the harbor, Kim strolled around the bridge area and wondered what happened to the Anglo? What had he done; where had he gone? She was sure he wouldn't give up. She struggled with the notion that he might try again in Jakarta. His time was running out. She called Yew.

"Bring Sun up to the bridge."

"Yes, Ms. Kim," Yew said, as Sun stood slightly behind him, his eyes still shaken from the morning confrontation.

"Follow me," she said, and led them to the open deck behind the bridge where her voice would disappear from prying ears in the wind. "I want you to search the ship once more. I want to be completely assured that there is no one on this ship who shouldn't be here."

"Yes ma'am," Yew said, and he and Sun bowed as they stepped onto the exterior ladders at the rear of the superstructure and descended toward the deck five stories below.

They decided to search the main deck first and all the storage compartments for lashings. They both went below first, armed themselves and grabbed two pairs of black gloves. The main deck was the dirtiest area on the ship and prone to collecting any debris from the loading process. Sheets of steel planks were separated with scrap wood, which ended up splintered and cast about. The grime was a result of the heavy grease used to soak the cables operating all the cranes. Each time a crane maneuvered, the cables spun in and out, throwing a light mist of grease in their path.

Under each crane were compartments used to store lashings, chain, and quick locks for containers. Yew crept down the port side of the ship to each crane hold and searched it, while Sun searched the opposite side of the ship, crouched in a martial arts readiness stance. They kept their guns hidden because the Captain and $2^{nd}$ officer watched from the bridge.

Kim returned to her cabin to await their reports. As she stepped off the clunking elevator, she turned toward Ling's cabin. She wanted Ling in the worst way. There was a constant tightness in her chest since she sent her away. For a while, she believed knowing Ling was near would cause her pain to fade like the wind to a fog, but it didn't work. She tried touching herself at night, but it only caused the warm memories of Ling's love to come flooding back.

She turned and walked the length of the passageway until she was outside Ling's door. A lump formed in her throat and tears welled in her eyes. She knew that Yew and Sun would be out of sight for a while. She could hold Ling and feel her warmth against her. Kim's knees quivered and her palms moistened. She reached in her purse for the key, but it wasn't there. She reached in her own pocket and found only her key. She had given Yew the only key. She reached for the door.

"Ling," she pleaded at the door, "Ling, are you there?"

The stainless steel handle felt cool in her hand as if it hadn't been opened in a while. She twisted the handle, but it jammed. It was locked. She leaned against the door.

"Ling, baby. Ling?" she said, tears running over her cheeks.

There was no reply. Kim turned from the door, trying to control her sobs. She marched back to her room, disrobed, and crawled into her bed.

# -35-

## CREEPING OVER THE DECKS

Chance tried to sleep as much as possible during the day to conserve his energy for the evening, but he couldn't. Sweat rolled off him, as if he was a WWII prisoner in a Japanese prisoner of war camp, locked in a wooden sweatbox, doing solitary. He listened intently for the sounds of crewmembers coming down the long ladders into the dark holds. They were like steel boxes, silent as tombs, when the ship was still and the engine stopped. When underway, the noise was deafening combined with the vibration and crates flexing under powerful sea currents.

Judging by the time, 1730, the crew would be off work and at chow. Chance dug through his box of tools. The pry bar was his predominant weapon for escape. He pulled at the most slack corner of the lid and the 1/2-inch plywood screamed at his efforts as the fresh nails pulled against the pressurized plywood. He slowly worked his way around the box, prying at one spot or nail after another with limited success.

Chance worked the material but couldn't budge the roof. The lashing chain held the hinged door to his wooden coffin firmly in place. He lifted the edge by 1 inch, that's all. If anything, the more he worked the edge, the more the lid seemed to crush in on him. After an hour of painful efforts in the tiny box, he sat against the crushed cardboard garment boxes packed with multi-hued sarongs and turned on his mag light. He looked at his watch. It was 1845. He flashed it in the bag of tools and dug through his bedroll.

Chance had a habit of always assuming he would win a game of cards or anything he rolled the dice at. In this case, he had to win or lose Ling, or worse. He didn't know, but the tension drove him hard. It was a given in his mind. No matter how deep his well of fear, he needed to break out, but he was burning daylight.

Time was critical. He didn't think about the box crushing in on him as it creaked and whined. He took a batch of cable ties and shoved them in his back pocket. He put a 6-inch long, single-edged dagger under the leather belt around his waist and pulled a Phillips screwdriver from his tool selection. He pointed the light at the thick 4-by-4 containing the sheet metal screws holding the hinges in place and began to unscrew them. He knew he couldn't get out through the side. He wished they built another escape hatch in the other coffin end, but no time for what-ifs. As he started to back out the screws, the whole box screeched and the box began to fold.

Chance dropped his mag light and scrambled to retrieve it. The hinged side of the plywood box creaked and the roof started to cave in on him. As he picked up the light and aimed it at the hinge, the stud split and the hinge pulled free overhead; under the tension of the chain it began to collapse inward. Chance pushed his torso against the far wooden wall, pulled his knees to his chest and pushed with his feet to avoid being crushed.

The lid pulled at the nails against the chain. With the box end disconnected from the framed structure, the box lost considerable structural strength and the chain was free to crush the contents, especially when they rolled in the open ocean and cargo shifted, drawing the chains even more taut. His crew didn't anticipate this deadly scenario during the construction process. How could they? He dug in his bag of tools for another alternative and came up with a short single-handed saw. For another hour, he cut at the corner nails to release the door of the box.

He sweated profusely, and the sawing noise was fortunately muffled by the roar of the diesel engines. Crew members, who finished their chow of curried rice in the galley, strolled toward the main deck to smoke cigarettes and jaw.

Yew took the tray of food up to Ling's room and stepped in gingerly. The room smelled of dirty body odor and sweat. Again he attempted to roll her over and feed her, but was only able to force a couple of swallows of water down her throat. She looked more parched everyday, more lethargic and distant. She never spoke and neither did he. He went to the head and snatched a dry unused wash-cloth off the stainless towel rail and moistened it in the sink with cool water, and then returned to her side. She already sipped at the hot tea with fumbling digits, spilling most of the tea, then dropping the cup. Her strength was gone.

When he returned and tried to wash her face, she attempted to roll away from him, but when she couldn't, she simply shut her eyes. She moved like a woman in her nineties, slow and deliberately as if it would be her last. Her hair was filthy and matted. All the color was gone from her features.

Chance grabbed the pry bar and pried at the sawed edge of the wood corner until it was free. Then he heard crew members jumping onto the hold doors. He froze. The chain fell away and was slack. He couldn't replace the corner of the box. He didn't want to leave evidence of someone in a crate, but that was going to be impossible to avoid.

He pushed enough nails out of his way to crawl out of the box. He packed his pockets with everything he would have left behind and grabbed his bottles of piss and protein bar wrappers. He set the stuff and his bedroll on the adjoining crate and pulled himself out of the box onto the top of the next one and stretched out. It was painful and everything ached but he was unbelievably pleased to be free of his wooden cell. He looked around the dark hold but could only see slivers of light in the distance. It was difficult to differentiate between the myriad of ship sounds. They were all abrupt, mechanical, and sounded too close. He put the crate back together, as best he could. Terrified, he moved quickly.

Chance straightened as many nails as he could to indicate that the crate had just crushed under the powerful chain, but he knew the sawed-off fasteners wouldn't work, or would they? Time was running out. He wanted to get out of sight as quickly as possible. Crawling from crate to crate, he scrambled to the edge of the cargo boxes and jumped down to the second-tiered deck. He scurried along the pas-sageway toward the superstructure. He didn't want to open a hatch and find himself exposed in a manned engine compartment.

He had some notion of the cargo holds, so he stayed within familiar turf. With his bedroll slung over his shoulder, he crawled up a long narrow ladder until he reached a hatch adjacent to one of the steel housings for a dual 20-ton crane, just forward of the Mac Gregor folding hold hatches. He opened the small square hatch slowly and peered outside. It was still somewhat light as the ship neared the equator. He looked around and didn't see anything or anyone, and crawled out of the hatch onto the grimy deck and hid behind the base of the crane out of visibility of the bridge.

Carefully, he moved toward the edge of the deck and tossed his used water bottles overboard with his debris. He moved back toward one of the lashing hatches and climbed inside. He had to wait for darkness and for the crew to crash after a tough day of harried loading and unloading, coupled with departure duties, handling the lines and all the preparations for being underway. He squatted in the corner of the narrow storage area and considered where Ling might be and how to reach her. He was so fucking excited that his skin crawled with determination. He was close, but fearful. If he had a gun, he would have just walked in the main passage and taken the ship. At least that's how he felt. Nothing or no one was going to prevent him from reaching his girl.

After 2300, Chance came out of his hiding place and moved carefully towards the superstructure. It was dark, and with the captain and crew trying to navigate in a dark ocean, no lights were allowed on the deck, so Chance could slither from one hatch to the next without being seen. He changed in the crate to a black sweatshirt and some black sweatpants and running shoes. As he moved along the greasy passageway, he heard the clank of hatches opening and dove to the filthy deck. Lying perfectly still, he looked at the thick dark grimy, rust filled grease on his gloved hand, and smeared it on his face. Listening for footsteps against the iron deck, he froze. He glanced over the top of the hold and saw one of the Chinese guards searching the main deck. He crept toward the stern and away from the Chinese security.

The warm night smelled of moisture and diesel fumes. He was as black as he could be as he reached the hatch to the inside passageways. This was the sister ship to the Leon and basically the same configuration as his ship. He stepped inside and heard voices. He immediately stepped to the left into the crew's laundry and plastered himself to the bulkhead behind lockers used to store dirty overalls. The voices passed and he moved carefully into the passageway.

Chance could take the stairs or the elevator to E deck where he suspected Ling was being kept. All the other floors would be packed with crewmen. The only deck with extra cabins was E and that was going to be his first shot. He heard more voices and Karaoke music filter down from the deck above. He stepped out of the laundry and into the passageway and outside. It was too risky to go inside. He moved around the superstructure, stumbling over wire cables, latches and gear on the dark deck. Everything was covered with a coat of oily slime.

He reached the stern portion of the superstructure and started up the steel, pulled-metal, outside stairs. The railing was filthy, but he moved up the grimy steps quietly and huddled on each deck landing to inspect his progress and look for someone who might spot him. He was exposed in the moonlit night. Too big to be considered a Filipino, he would immediately be reported to the captain or shot by the Chinese guards. He crept up another flight of stairs and crouched down again on the landing and looked around.

A steward came out from the door on the lower deck leading into the galley with a large bag full of trash and headed to the stern trash containers. He put the bag in the appropriate container and returned, stepping over the various mooring lines, as he returned to the galley. As he opened the rear door, the interior light threw a beam out across the deck, and startled Chance. It disappeared again as he closed the door.

Chance started up another flight of steps when a door opened again. He froze on the rungs as the Filipino kid started across the stern once more. Chance was too driven, and while the kid walked away from him, he continued up another level until he reached E deck. He checked below and the kid returned to the galley, whistling. Chance leaned to the side of the dented aluminum door, and then peered into the porthole.

Lights were on in the stark passageway constructed in a horseshoe configuration. If he went in the door and followed the passage, it would head forward and then to the left across the bow portion of the superstructure and back out on the port side. He remembered a guests' head on the starboard side and perhaps he could slip his bedroll behind the door for the moment. It was still warm outside and the humidity was high as the ship rocked slightly in the tepid Karimata Strait.

He opened the door and made his way slowly towards the head leaving greasy footprints in his wake. The first door on the right just inside the creaking aluminum door was a cabin, Ling's cell, but he didn't know. On the left was a radio room. Past it on the left was the guest restroom and dead ahead was the captain's cabin. It was closed.

Chance crept slowly to the guest bathroom and tried the door. He opened it with a noisy click. He stepped inside the dark steel box and felt along the steel bulkhead adjacent to the door for the light switch. It was a massive cast unit with a dial that snapped in place every 90 degrees for the light to be turned on and off. He twisted it, and again the sound was startling and unnerving. The two 4-foot fluorescent tubes blinked then came on, showering him with light. He looked around the room, high and low for a place to stash his bedroll. He had a couple of tools on him and two knives, his long straight-blade, single-edge knife around his waist and an easy to snap open 4-inch locking blade Elishewitz folding knife. He looked at the toilet and desperately needed to use it. It was a very plain empty restroom with no shelves or cupboards. He had to take the bedroll with him.

The next door on the left led to the stairwell up to the bridge and down to the main deck five floors below. He crouched and crept along the passageway when he heard footsteps on the stairway beneath him. He ducked back into the guest bathroom and closed the door as quietly as possible.

The footsteps continued up the interior stairwell to E deck and Yew stepped into the passage way. He noticed that the captain's door was shut. Yew walked in the direction of the captain's cabin, turned left and headed toward the port side of the ship and his cabin at the stern. If he had turned in the other direction, he would have spotted the greasy footprints on the deck to the guest head.

Chance could barely make out the cabin door closing and the footsteps in the halls were distant quickly. He opened the door again and peered around it carefully. Moving stealthily, he crept toward the captain's cabin. On his right were three circular bell alarms. One was a general fire alarm, then a smoke detector and the larger general alarm. He passed the captain's cabin and discovered another door on the left.

It was marked Elect. Wireway Space. There was a small wad of paper shoved in the jam that indicated to Chance that someone had opened it recently. Often the doors on the vibrating steel ship are padded with foam or anything to restrain the vibration and rattling noise.

He gingerly placed his hand on the door handle and twisted it. Again it clicked like the hammer on a revolver snapping against an empty chamber. He pulled the door and it opened quietly. Inside was a boxed electrical panel a foot deep against the back wall only two feet from the door. The whole area was the same size of a small broom closet cut in half. Chance thought he heard a noise, dropped to his knees and shoved his bedroll in under the panel against the looms of wiring disappearing below the deck. He shut the door quickly.

He took only a large black towel he stole from the Fullerton Hotel, folded it and stuck it under his arm. He looked down the port passageway and noticed two open cabins on the outside past the elevator. The elevator wasn't moving. The first open cabin was noted to be the conference room by a plaque above the door. It had a chalkboard, a narrow table with several odd shaped chairs and a small desk used to hold a copy machine.

Chance stuck his head inside and determined that it was unoccupied. If it was anything like the Leon, it was rarely used. The next room down was another communications room and it was packed with radio equipment, telex units and satellite phones. Directly across from it was another cabin. Chance wondered if Ling was inside and wanted to reach for the door. He heard someone shuffling around, and then he heard the footsteps again.

The door, less than five feet from another stern exterior entrance and an aluminum hatch led to the outside. It was the other end of the horseshoe. He stepped to it quickly and turned the handle. It was locked. He fumbled with the deadbolt, unsnapping it as he heard the door handle turn on the cabin door. He stepped outside and closed the door as quickly as possible, panting like his chest would explode. He tossed the towel at his feet and held the handle of the long knife. He peaked around the edge of the porthole when the door opened and the small Chinese guard stepped into the passageway, holding a ceramic coffee cup.

Chance was tempted to take him right then and there. Chance thought about stabbing the short man and dragging him back into his cabin, but he still wasn't sure where Ling was. By morning the others would know about the attack and they could move Ling before he even got a chance to see her.

He needed to check two more doors on the port side of the ship marked Lockers #2 and Electric Equipment Room. Chance watched the small Asian walk up the hallway and disappear around the corner heading toward the stairwell. Chance waited and listened intently. He moved across the outside level to the other stern door and watched the small man enter the door to the stairs. Chance moved immediately back to the port door, and as quietly as possible entered the linoleum passageway and moved to the two doors in question. Both were locked. He stopped for a second and thought about the floor layout. Perhaps that left Ling unconfirmed in the cabin at the other end of the corridor.

Chance heard climbing steps in the internal stairwell again and moved quickly to the outside door. He stepped through it and closed it hurriedly and quietly. He watched as the small Chinese man strode down the passageway and opened his door. He didn't seem to be an angry, hateful man, but Chance knew he might be forced to kill him.

As the man opened the door to his cabin, he turned and looked at the porthole as Chance moved away. He went inside and closed his cabin door. Chance climbed up the stairs to the bridge deck, then up again to the small deck above the bridge. It was basically the communications floor scattered with various whip and fixed mast antennas. At the stern was a hearty mast containing the radar antenna spinning around at the top and flags flying from the halyards on the booms. He moved along the deck in total silence. He knew there were perhaps two or three men on the bridge navigating the ship below him.

He unfolded the towel and laid it carefully on the steel deck. He pulled his running shoes off and set them to the side. He laid down on the towel and tried to sleep. The next morning would be crucial. He sensed how close he was to her and felt nervous. He prayed she was physically all right, but concerned about her mental condition. Had she been able to cope? He was so damn close, but unsure of his next move. How the hell could he find her? He knew in his heart, if she had been mistreated or neglected, he would find that broad and tear her hair out and make her eat it.

# -36-

## Cᴏᴜʟᴅ Cʜᴀɴᴄᴇ Rᴇꜱᴄᴜᴇ Lɪɴɢ Wᴜ?

Chance awoke in a flash of brilliant sunlight and sat up on the hard steel antenna deck in the summer-like warmth and humidity. There was something wrong with his plan. He looked at his ticking watch. It was 0630. He had no notion of how he was going to get into Ling's room, or even which room she was in, without being detected. He knew the approximate deck, since he had scoured most of the ship last night. He had to find her before a crewmember spotted him. He was lost in a mind packed with singular determination.

"Fuck it," he said aloud and got to his feet. As usual, his mouth was pasty. He hadn't brushed his teeth in days. His stomach crawled with hunger pangs and his clothes were stuck to his sweat-soaked frame. He was downright uncomfortable as he looked out at the sea and wondered where the ship was headed. The Leon was scheduled to hit Jakarta after Singapore and Vietnam before Hong Kong.

He wondered how much time he had before they arrived in the next port. He scrambled down the rusting set of corrugated steel stairs, crouched low and dashed across the stern portion of the bridge deck to the rusting exterior stairs leading to the main deck below. Some of the railing, so corroded sharp-edged and jagged, it could snag, tear, and break fingers. He scrambled down the stairs to the E deck platform and tried to look in the dirty porthole in the door. He watched passenger level doors hoping for a clue, while glancing to the stern of the ship. He was outside and visible.

He could hear movement in the passageways. Most of the crew headed toward the two mess halls for chow and he banked on the fleeting notion that someone might provide a clue to her whereabouts.

Crewmembers stepped out onto the stern deck for their first smoke of the morning. The sea remained calm as the shipped motored comfortably. Chance slammed himself against the bulkhead. If just one crewmember looked up, he would be busted. More Filipino crew hustled out onto the main deck. Most of them smoked or had pre-breakfast duties.

Terrified, Chance waited. Then a stubby member turned while chatting with a fellow sailor. Chance watched his features change, then he pointed, spoke in a harried manner, and other crewmembers turned. It was just before 0730 breakfast call, and a Chinese guard appeared in the passageway with a tray of meager food and a pot of tea. He noticed the greasy footprints on the deck. He strode to the stern, outside cabin and propped the brushed stainless steel tray on the safety railing in the hallway with his left hand, while reaching for the key in his right pocket. As he pulled the key out of his pocket and inserted it in the lock, Chance burst through the aluminum door to the outside stairwell.

Yew was taken aback by someone erupting in the stern door, but not alarmed. The doors were generally left unlocked as crewmembers made repairs all over the ship. It wasn't completely uncustomary to find someone on any deck, but then he thought about the unfamiliar greasy footprints. He turned and saw the big Anglo man, recognizing immediately it wasn't one of the Polish officers or a grubby Filipino crewmember. There was something obviously American about the man, but before he could react, Chance had a knife at his throat.

"Unlock the door," Chance demanded, "or they'll be mopping your blood off this deck for a week."

Yew felt the blade cutting at his throat and didn't budge except to turn the key and the door swung open.

"Don't say a word," Chance said. "Just take the tray and step in slowly."

Chance saw Ling in the bed, turned away from the door and he lowered his voice. "Set the tray on the desk along with the key," he muttered low, "and lean with both hands on the desk."

Chance kicked the door shut and locked it from the inside. He searched Yew and pulled his pistol from his shoulder holster. Other than the semi- automatic, he was unarmed. He yanked two-foot long cable ties out of his back pocket and wrapped Yew's wrists tight, cutting his wrists and hindering his circulation. Then Chance shoved him to the floor. He pointed the gun at the little man and the hatred boiled in his sparkling green eyes. He cable-tied Yew's ankles and set the gun on the table without a word and crawled on the bed.

He put his hand on Ling's shoulder for the first time in almost three months and rolled her toward his arms.

"Baby," Chance said full of trepidation as a man making love with a woman for the first time. "It's Chance, honey. I've come to get you."

Her skin was clammy and cold. Her eyes opened just slightly, as a druggie would who hadn't had anything to eat for a week. Her eyes were red and dry, but they brightened and a skinny hand reached for his arm. Her lips cracked as she attempted to speak and her body smelled of death. Chance looked at the woman he fell in love with and adored and hardly recognized her. She was a concentration camp refugee in his arms. Outrage churned in his stomach and he turned to the tray of food and reached for the tea.

"There's opium in the tea," Yew said.

Chance snatched the gun off the counter and turned to Yew. He aimed it at the man's forehead and pulled the trigger. Yew's face went completely white with fear, but the weapon didn't fire. He looked at the gun and unsnapped the safety. He cocked it and checked the chamber to ensure that a round was securely in place.

Yew was never so terrified in his life. He knew that his part in this matter was unquestionably wrong. He had certain death coming. He deserved nothing less. Chance looked at him again, but didn't utter a word. He stood and grabbed the key to the room; he unlocked the door, and stuck the weapon in his waistband above the belt holding the knife. His mind whirled with abject anger. He asked himself why he shouldn't kill this sonuvabitch for blinking. He dragged Yew into the passageway and along it to the guest restroom. He pulled him inside and slammed the back of his head against the toilet bowel. Yew was knocked unconscious.

Chance knew that if he didn't confront these bastards immediately, they would come to Ling's room to find out what the hell was going on. Chance heard other activity around the ship as he backed out of the head into the passageway, but he didn't care. He stepped into the hallway, took one step toward the bow and opened the inner stairway down the center of the superstructure. He bounded down one flight of stairs after another. As he reached the C deck, a Filipino kid stepped into the stairwell and looked at Chance with question in his eyes. At first he noticed Chance's unfamiliar features and bright angry eyes, then the gun in his waistband and the long knife hanging at his hip.

"Good morning, goddamnit," Chance said and walked passed. The kid tried to step back onto C deck where most of the crew slept, and get the hell out of the way.

Chance stormed down two more decks and out into the A deck passageway. Following the Leon's format, he turned to the right towards the officer's mess and followed the narrow hallway around to the right. The ship rolled slightly in the Java Sea south of the equator as Chance burst into the mess hall. He faced the passengers sitting for breakfast with the officers.

At the left end of the long table sat the Captain the Chief Engineer and the Chief Officer. The steward stood with his back against the long wooden silverware cupboard behind the Captain, and grimaced as the big, unshaven biker stepped into the dining room armed.

The rotund Chinese guard at the other end of the table, directly in front of Chance, spun from his chair, reaching for his shoulder holster. Chance yanked the pistol out of his waistband, raised and aimed it at the Chinese guard's head and pulled the trigger. The man died instantly and brains blew all over the officer's end of the table. Chance kept coming and stepped up onto the table as Kim pushed back and tried to jump to her feet. Chance kicked her in the face with his running shoe and drove her against the bulkhead under the large brass framed portholes.

"Captain," Chance shouted, "did you know that this woman has my fiancée kidnapped on your ship and she's using your vessel to smuggle opium?"

The officers were in a state of shock.

"Do you have a doctor on board?" Chance demanded as he jumped down off the table, crushing one of Kim's hands under one foot and pistol-whipping her. He pulled a cable tie out of his back pocket and put it around her neck as she screamed in agony from her busted fingers. He pulled it tight around her throat and as she lifted her hands to her neck he slipped one cable tie around her wrists and pulled it furiously tight. Then he stepped away from her as she gagged, scratching at her throat with both hands strapped together, unable to breathe. He walked around the table and pulled Sun's weapon and shoved it into his waistband along with the other one.

"Captain," Chance spoke directly, his voice on the verge of being loud, "can you speak English?"

"Yes," the Captain said, getting to his feet.

"Do you have a doctor on board?" Chance asked again.

He looked at the Captain as if he might shoot him if he didn't receive the correct answer. Chance stood at the end of the dinner table with his back against the wall. He was still dressed in all black, but now he had a long knife on his hip and two pistols stuck in his waistband.

He was anxious; the Captain could read everything in his dire features. The dinning room table was splattered with blood. A dead man lay against the cloth. Two officers still sat in their seats, wondering if they were next.

"No," the Polish Captain admitted, "We don't have doctor."

"I want you to explain to your men what I'm about to tell you," Chance said angrily, "then I want you to follow me to a cabin where I will prove my statements. Is that clear?"

The Captain nodded, visibly shaken. Kim still lay on the linoleum grasping at the cable tie around her neck desperately. She couldn't breath.

"This woman is running an opium cartel," Chance said. "She kidnapped my Chinese girlfriend and is holding her hostage on this ship. She made a sizable delivery of opium, probably in Genoa or she wouldn't be here. I will introduce you to my fiancée, who is in the pilot's cabin and has been drugged and maybe dying. Now, tell them what I have told you. I'm not here to harm anyone. All I want is my girl and to get off the ship in Hong Kong. Is that clear?"

The Captain nodded and quickly explained Chance's story to his men.

"They want to know what to do," the Captain said.

"Tell them to perform their duties as usual. I wish we had some medical help, but everything will be back to normal, shortly. The other guard is tied up in the guest head on E deck. I will allow you to hold them for the authorities."

The Captain began to explain, then a series of questions began to badger him from the officers and Chance interrupted.

"Captain, please," he said urgently. "The sooner I can show you and we can deal with this, the sooner the ship will return to order."

"But what about this girl?" the Captain questioned apprehensively. Kim was turning blue.

Chance pulled his pocket knife out and knelt beside Kim. The officers gasped as he slipped the razor-sharp point of the knife under the hard plastic tie around Kim's neck and cut it. A small trickle of blood ran down the side of her alabaster neck.

Chance stood and pulled on her wrist restraint. Pain shot down her arms and she struggled, stumbling and gasping, to her feet. He wanted to shoot her. He could give a shit, whether she lived for two seconds or not, but needed her when he spoke to Chang. He shoved her forward and indicated for the Captain to lead the way. He glanced back at the assortment of officers. He nodded deliberately, as if to assure them of something. He wasn't sure.

They walked up the stairs as Chance pulled and yanked on Kim's restraints as she attempted to gather her breath and thoughts. Chance pointed out Yew in the guest head and led them down to the Pilot's cabin and opened it.

Ling was sitting on the edge of the bed trying to keep her eyes open. The Captain went to her side to exam her while Kim stood back and looked at the woman she fell in love with. She couldn't believe the stark figure who drooped before her, drawn and gaunt.

"I need medicine and help," Chance said. "I also need to have this woman under arrest in some quarters, separate from her other man."

Kim dropped to her knees and began to cry. The fight was gone from her as two Filipino crew members came into the room and took her away. They moved Yew onto another deck in a locked cabin. Chance went to Ling's side and held her.

"Captain, I haven't eaten a meal in a couple of days. I could use some chow, and I would like to have a couple of jugs of water sent up. Could you have someone bring me a bunch of scrambled eggs and lots of fruit?"

"Let's get you out of this cabin," the Captain said and indicated for the steward to prepare the cabin Kim had been using and to deliver food and provisions.

"I'll want to stay with her for a couple of days straight," Chance said. "They had drugged her with opium in her tea. We need to find the drugs, because if she goes cold turkey now, it could kill her."

"I understand," the Captain said. "I will have one of the stewards look after you. About the guns…"

"I will not give them up until that woman is off this ship or I am." Chance said and picked up Ling, who couldn't weigh over 90 pounds. They made their way down the passageway to the owner's cabin and went inside.

"Put all of that woman's stuff here on the couch," Chance said. "I want to go through it."

He laid Ling in the freshly made bed and asked the curious crew to leave. The stewards delivered food, fruit, and water, and then backed out the door and left. It was the first time Chance had been alone safely with Ling since the night before she was kidnapped. He held her close.

"Baby, I want to give you a shower if you can stand long enough."

She nodded weakly and tried to get up, but couldn't. Chance peeled her out of her soiled clothes and then undressed himself. He turned on the shower in the head and returned to help Ling to her feet. She stumbled and Chance had to carry her into the shower where he pressed her body to his.

"We'll pull you together, baby. Just hang on," he said.

Tears ran down the sides of her cheeks and mixed with the warm water from the shower as Chance ran his soapy hands over her body and shampooed her hair. Still wet, he helped her out of the shower, dried her off carefully and carried her to the bed. He turned on the reading light above the bed and poured her a glass of water.

"Please, try to drink this. I know you're going to have a very tough go of it, but I'll do whatever I can to make you feel more comfortable."

Chance returned to the bath and dried off. He dug through his bedroll and slipped on a pair of shorts and a t-shirt. When he returned to Ling, her eyes were weary. He fed her some eggs and cut up some banana and peeled an orange; she ate a few pieces of each, and then laid down. Chance crammed down a few mouthfuls of food and swallowed it quickly with some water before snuggling up beside her. He wrapped his arms around her as she fell asleep.

At noon, she awoke in a cold sweat as the ship rolled in the Gaspar Straits heading into Jakarta. She was drenched in sweat but holding onto Chance with all her might. She licked her lips.

"I love you, Chance. I'm sorry."

"Don't say a word, baby," he said. "You're going to go through hell week and I need you to work with me."

He picked up the phone and called the Captain.

"Did you find out anything?"

"Yes," the Captain said. "I have the drugs. I spoke to the remaining guard. He will help us."

"I need a half dose of the drugs this afternoon," Chance said. "See if he'll do it."

"I don't think that will be a problem," the Captain said. "We'll be arriving in Jakarta tomorrow morning. I need to keep all of you out of sight of the immigration people. I will send a steward, Clemet, to your room with lunch. Do you want anything in particular?"

"No, just lots of fruit, green tea, and water," Chance said. "Oh, and I need to make a call this afternoon. We may need to put that woman on the phone."

"That won't be possible until we leave Jakarta," the Captain said.

"Okay," Chance said, "but I'll still need to call Ling's family."

"No problem," the Captain said.

Chance hung up and rolled over to Ling and kissed her on the neck. She moved into his arms and her sweat-soaked body formed into his.

"Baby, I'm going to have food and some of your tea brought up, but it will be a lesser dose," Chance whispered near her ear. "You'll have to eat food and fruit. You may get sick, but you need nourishment badly and water while we pull you off this shit."

"I'll try," Ling said, her stomach turning in knots. "I want to go home."

She held on tight, but her grip was as weak as a newborn's. Chance's heart cried out for her to hang on. She felt like a bag of bones from a Nazi concentration camp. The other side of him wanted to find the other woman's cabin and snuff her out deliberately and slowly.

Chance scrambled out of bed. Dressed in shorts and a T-shirt. He opened the door for Clement to come in with a tray of food and a pot of tea.

"Can I get you anything else?" he asked, looking concerned.

# -37-

## JAKARTA BROWN WATERS

Chance woke Ling before dinner. "Baby," he said, "wake up for a little while. I need to get some more food in you."

She turned slowly in the bed, her eyes full of tears. Her skin felt strange to Chance, like she was coming down with the flu. Chilled and covered with goose bumps, he didn't understand her condition. The drug's imbalance in her brain interacted with the nervous system, producing standard opiate withdrawal symptoms. She looked at him longingly, but he knew that it wasn't for him; it was for the drug.

Clemet brought a fresh tray of food and no tea. He fed her some food, including meat, vegetables and salad, and encouraged her to drink a glass of water.

The next morning, he gave her a small cup of the drugged tea, hoping it would help him get more food into her before she fell completely to the whim of the withdrawal symptoms. She ate an egg and some toast. He began to massage her body between meals and helped her into the shower again, and this time she stood for a few moments on her own. She was so frail and fragile. Scared to roll over at night, Chance thought he might smother her.

They pulled into the port of Jakarta in the early afternoon, and while Ling slept, Chance locked her door and climbed the steel stairs to the bridge.

"How's it going, Captain?" Chance asked, standing back from the older gentleman as he stared at the radar screen. The water around the ship was muddy brown, and everywhere Chance looked were rusting hulks of ships at anchor. It was foggy and overcast and the scene was eerie.

"They told me the pilot would be on board at 1330. It's 1415 and I haven't seen him yet."

The Captain stood straight and watched an old tanker motor out of the harbor.

"Maybe he's on that ship? Who knows?"

The Captain straightened.

"Dead slow," he said to the Filipino second office and turned toward Chance. "How is she?"

"She's trying," Chance said, "I won't know for a couple of days."

"Can I help you with something?" the Captain asked.

His eyes were dark with weariness. His face was drawn and the dark bags under his eyes were heavy. His hair grayed rapidly. He didn't comb it or have it trimmed. He didn't seem to care. His breath smelled of liquor.

"I believe the people behind this will try to get their woman back," Chance said, concern written all over his face. "I will need security at the gangplank constantly. I'm not even sure that will be enough. Can we set up walkie-talkies to the gangplank so I can monitor the situation there?"

"Yes, of course," the Captain said.

"I don't want any of your crew hurt," Chance said. "This is none of their business. I would like to speak to the guard we captured."

"I will see that you have access to him," the Captain said, "but why?"

"I may be able to encourage him to work with me," Chance said. "It's worth a shot."

The Captain looked at Chance long and desperately. With only a rough knowledge of English from an American's standpoint, he missed messages related in slang words. He nodded and picked up the internal phone of the bridge and dialed a number.

The 3rd officer, a stout Filipino kid named Jesse, came directly to the bridge. He indicated for Chance to follow him down to the Cdeck to a cabin on the port side of the ship. He opened the door to the sparse room containing only a small narrow bunk, one chair, a restroom, and one porthole. The cabin hadn't been cleaned in months.

Yew was chained to a large steel sewage pipe that ran from deck to deck, from head to head. The chain ran out of the bathroom and gave him enough slack to reach his bed, and that was all. The rusty chain strapped around his leg was supported by irons locked to his wrists. Yew sat on the bunk when they entered.

Chance stared at him as he pulled up the chair and sat down.

"I'll wait outside," Jesse said and backed toward the door. Concern for his life filled Yew's facial features.

"Thank you," Chance said, nodding in Jesse's direction and turning back to Yew.

"I have a proposition for you," Chance said to Yew, "but first, what's your goddamn name?"

"Yew," he said, looking earnestly at Chance.

"Okay ,Yew," Chance said, staring the young man straight in the eyes. If he noted the slightest indication the man would betray him, he would just beat him to death and leave him chained in the room.

"I'm here to get my girl and take her home. That's it, understand?"

Yew nodded fervently.

"I'm not in the drug business. I'm not your competitor, and I don't like killing people," Chance said. He spilled his guts, and he knew it was a long-shot. "I just want my girl back and to go home. I hope to get off the ship in Hong Kong and fly out, but your people have caused problems with her family and they won't be happy to find out we have Kim and I now have Ling back. They will attempt to grab her and prevent me from going home. I need you to help me. I don't want you to shoot anyone; just let me know if the wrong person is on the ship or something is happening that will harm my girl or me. I don't know why I came to you, but something told me that you didn't want any part of this."

"You are right about many things, but this won't end. The Wong family wants the Wu family's land," Yew said concern filled his face. "What can I do?"

"I need someone who can watch the gangplank for me in Jakarta," Chance said. "Like I said, I don't want anyone hurt. I just want to get to Hong Kong and go home with my girl. If you see anyone approaching from the Wong family or industry, I don't want you to do anything except let me know and then step out of the way."

"What about me?" Yew asked. "What will happen to me? They will kill us all to get Kim back."

"If you work with me," Chance said, keeping his eyes on how Yew reacted to each statement, "I'll see if I can get you off the hook and maybe a job with the Wu family."

"Thank you," Yew said, but didn't mean it. He knew that he could never go to work for the Wu family. He had no skills. He wasn't even a good bodyguard and would be considered a traitor. He looked at the grimy carpeting at his feet then back up at Chance's intent gaze.

"I will do whatever you need, but this will not end easily."

Chance sat back in the chair concerned.

"I'm know. I just want to get her home safely."

He stepped out of the door and indicated for Jesse to unshackle Yew and give him a walkie-talkie. Jesse was leery of the action, but he didn't want to have anything to do with fighting the Hong Kong mafia as the rumors spread through the crew.

Yew went down to the gangplank area on the main deck, as the ship motored slowly into the harbor. It began to rain in this dark place. The floods floods had taken a massive toll on the already impoverished area racked with terrorism and poverty.

As the gangplank lowered next to the dilapidated dock, several men waited on the pier under umbrellas to come aboard. The aluminum gangplank, with scooped convex steps, and ribs for use at any angle was awkward at all angles. It banged against the dock and the last hinged step bent to fit any dock surface, clanged and bounced against the concrete unevenly. It was lowered with the same system used by the heavy cranes on the ship. A series of grease-soaked steel cables looped around pulleys on the stairway, lifted or dropped it into position. The grease from the cables coated the railing and guests who mistakenly bumped into the cables or handrails, ruined their clothes.

As soon as the plank landed securely on the concrete, agents, immigration, and customs officials began to board. In addition, two prostitutes jogged up the steps along with a tattoo artist and his apprentice. Two more women with bundles of shirts and souvenirs tried to scurry on board but were turned away.

For two days it rained. None of the crew or officers left the ship. Jakarta held a nasty, dirty reputation and they had their own problems aboard. Chance used the Captain's computer to study opiate addiction. He learned how much drug users consume in a day, as many as seven to ten shots a day. He slowed Ling's use of the drug. She drank water, ate fruit and protein, more each day, but she began to get anxious and agitated. He knew the worst was yet to come with abdominal cramping, nausea, vomiting and diarrhea. The first week would be the worst.

Several little folks set up shop at the base of the gangplank and hung out 24/7 hoping for customers. As shipping duties took place, crewmembers never departed the ship except to the dock to take part in the makeshift shops at the bottom of the gangplanks selling trinkets, street food, and drugs.

On the third day, a professional looking man approached the ship. He had a brutal scar on his left cheek and another one splitting his opposite eyebrow. He watched the ship from afar for several hours before he boarded. He used his umbrella to hide himself from onlookers until he saw Yew standing in the corner of the deck under an overhang, holding a walkie-talkie.

Yew stood watch daily. At first he was very concerned about his future. His boss, Kim, busted, he was left with few options in China, but the big white American gave him hope. Maybe he could escape to the States and start a new life. As the days passed in Jakarta he became more relaxed. Maybe no one would come from the Wong family anymore and they could arrive safely and somehow fly to America? But a lingering sense said he was wrong. Kim wasn't checking in and hadn't for several days.

As Yuro slowly lifted the edge of the sopping umbrella he recognized Yew and pulled it back. Yew froze in his shoes. Yuro was a nasty, violent man who relished the use of a knife as a tool for maiming someone over assassinating cleanly and quickly with a bullet. Yuro walked directly to Yew while reaching inside his black sport coat.

"What has become of Kim?" he said. "No daily reports to the family."

"She's up stairs," Yew stammered. He just wanted to avoid more trouble and find a way to escape. His hopes backfired as Yuro shoved him through the hatch to the stern in the rain. It was dark and overcast with heavy clouds and the dense humidity combined with the rain. As he stepped through the hatch, he felt something move across his neck quickly. He immediately began to gurgle as his small throat filled with his own blood. He dropped the walkie-talkie and tried to stop the bleeding. He took two more steps before he stumbled and fell. The hatch clanged shut behind him and he had no voice to call for help.

Jesse straightened the bridge and docking paperwork after they started preparing and planning for departure. Every night he locked the bridge area from onlookers and petty thieves who snuck aboard to steal whatever they could get their hands on. As he left the bridge and locked the door, he was reminded of Yew and suspicious.

He grew up in the remnants of Subic Bay where the US set up an active port and operations for U.S Naval ships traveling to and from Vietnam in the '60s and '70s. The prostitutes who tried to survive after the Navy returned to the States, raised him. They had a tough time of it and some turned to drugs. He loved his mom and some of the girls, but didn't get along with many of the men who tried to take advantage of them once the American servicemen were no longer around to watch over them. He recognized some of the slipperiness in Yew's features and didn't trust the man. He locked the door as he heard agents and an official stepping out of the creaking elevator and speaking in the island tongue. He wondered how Yew was doing. He would check.

He knew officials would be using the elevator, so he took the steps down the inside of the steel structure to the main deck, but Yew wasn't there. It rained densely hard, similar to the monsoon season in the Philippines. The sky was gray and foreboding and the stevedores ducked the downpour into one of the adjacent corrugated steel warehouses. Work stopped, but women still huddled against the walls with their stores to sell. More men approached the gangplank as Jesse pulled his walkie-talkie out of his overalls and called to Chance.

"Sir Chance," he said, "Jesse here."

"Yeah," Chance said.

"I'm at gangplank," Jesse said in his bumbling English. "No Chinese here."

"Did you look around?" Chance asked. "He's either escaped or he's still on board."

"I'll have a look, sir," Jesse said. "I will stand by here until you tell me."

"Look around," Chance said urgently, "then call me. I know you have other duties and you won't know the people I'm looking for, but thank you. And watch your back and for strangers."

"Yes, sir," Jesse said and put the walkie-talkie deep in a pocket protected from the rain.

He walked around the superstructure, but there were only crewmen in greasy overalls trying to avoid the deluge of rain. He moved to the back corner where he could stand out from under the rain, and then he noticed that the hatch to the stern was partially open.

He turned one of the dogs and pulled on the handle. The door was rarely opened and heavy to pull against corroded hinges. He pulled it open just enough to stick his head passed the opening. He saw nothing until he looked down at the vast pool of blood and rainwater mixed with the oily grime of the deck. Yew was a few feet away laying face down in the rain.

"Sir," Jesse stammered in the walkie-talkie.

"Yeah?" Chance said.

"I found him," Jesse said stumbling. "He's dead behind the hatch on the main deck."

"Close the hatch," Chance said, "and get away from that area. I don't want anyone to be suspicious of you. Just go back to your duties. Where are they keeping the woman?"

"She is on the upper level in the hospital compartment," Jesse said.

"Is she chained?" Chance asked.

"Yes, I believe so," Jesse answered.

"Thanks," Chance said and clicked off the mike.

He clamored to the bedroom and pulled on his long sweats, a black t-shirt then Yew's shoulder holster and one pistol. Then he threw on a jacket and put on socks and running shoes. As always, he grabbed the key to the room and his locking-blade knife. He recently fed Ling and massaged her legs, which were already beginning to cramp. He figured by the next day, she might have enough nourishment in her to sustain the withdrawals, but he monitored her every move. She reached out to him. Her lips began to soften and show some color.

"Where are you going?" Ling asked.

"I'll be back in a minute," Chance said. "You stay in bed and don't open the door for anyone!" He kissed her lightly on the lips.

She grabbed at him and he held her tight for a few long moments.

"Don't be long," she whispered, her voice still feeble.

Chance went out and down the passageway to the guest bath and opened the door wide and stepped in. He waited until the elevator door opened and two officials got out and proceeded to the Captain's quarters. The elevator made considerable noise, so Chance stepped into the interior passageway and began working his way down the stairs.

Yuro followed two officials into the superstructure of the vessel and to the elevator, where he faked that he had forgotten something and headed back to the exit. When the men stepped into the elevator and it started to climb to the Captain's office on E deck, Yuro stepped back into the passageway and began to check cabins and knock on doors. One was the electrician's office and the big Polish man opened the door.

"Can I help you?" he said abruptly to the stout Chinese man. "You are not in the right place."

He closed the door in the man's face and went back to his repairs.

Yuro moved to the next cabin, which was the residence of the Russian sand blaster. As he was about to knock on the door, he heard the sounds of a woman squealing with delight as she was being fucked. He lowered his hand and moved on. The hospital cabin was like most others, except a white piece of cardboard was taped to the metal door with a Red Cross insignia printed on it. It was smudged with dirt and taped on the door at an odd angle. Yuro tried the door. It was locked. He knocked. No one answered.

"Ms. Kim," he said.

"Yes," she returned.

He was startled, surprised, and then interrupted as crewmen came down the passageway. He knelt quickly with his briefcase and umbrella and acted as if he had dropped it. One of the Filipino men stopped to help him pick it up.

"I've got it," Yuro said, "thank you."

The Filipino kid pointed the opposite direction down the passageway.

"That's the way to the Captain's office."

Yuro looked at his smiling brown face and nodded. Filipinos were consistently helpful and friendly. Yuro focused on his briefcase and acted as if he was pulling himself and his belongings together. When the crewmember disappeared up the stairs to the galley, Yuro stood and pressed his back against the bulkhead for all the support he could muster as he kicked the hospital door with all his might. He was due to be paid big if he brought Kim home safely. The door jarred and jiggled, metal against metal. He kicked again and it sprung open and the components that made up the dead bolt scattered around the deck.

He burst into the room with his gun pulled and slammed the door behind him. Kim was a mess, secured to a long chain leading into the head and wrapped around a sewer line pipe. Yuro didn't pay much attention to Kim. She was just a tall paycheck for him. He jumped into the bathroom and kicked at the pipe. It did nothing but creaked against the deck and the overhead. He kicked again, but he couldn't get the support he needed and the steel tube damaged the arch of his foot in the soft leather shoes he wore.

He slammed the briefcase against the lid of the toilet and opened it. Inside was a variety of tools from a miniature hacksaw to a foot long set of bolt cutters and wire side cutters. He yanked the bolt cutter out of the leather case and snapped through the chain. Then went to Kim and cut through the chains around her ankle. She stood, her right hand bandaged and her wrists still held firmly with cable ties.

He darted back into the head and grabbed the side cutters. He put them to the taught plastic bindings and clipped them. For the first time, he looked at her face and saw the scar from the pistol whipping she took. It was partially bandaged, but he instantly knew that her face was struck with similar bad luck to his. She would never be beautiful again. He flinched but grabbed her good hand and headed toward the door.

Mad as hell, Chance descended the stairs, while grinding his teeth. He yanked the pistol from the holster, cocked it and checked the safety. Then he slammed it back in the holster and took the downward steps three at a time, grabbed the overhead railing for rough seas and swung down the remaining six steps to the next level.

He flew down the stairs in leaps and burst onto A deck across the passageway, and then down the double stairs to the main deck. The stairs were designed to drop crew or passengers toward the bow of the ship so they could turn to whatever side of the ship was against the dock and proceed to the exit.

Chance spun to the port side, then pulled the weapon and peeked around the corned just as Yuro and Kim initiated the turn toward the exit. Yuro pulled Kim's wrist behind him and didn't see Chance, but Kim did.

Kim had one concern and that was to get off the ship and away from Chance. She didn't care about the little hit man in front of her anymore than he gave a shit about her. She was startled to see Chance glance around the corner holding the weapon. She knew that if it was up to him, he would kill at the drop of a hat.

Kim dashed toward Yuro's back. She knew she had less than 15 feet to spring out of the hatch, across the narrow deck and onto the gangplank to freedom. When she got back to the mainland and had the power of the Triad gangs behind her, she could have Chance and Ling both killed anywhere on the planet. They would have nowhere to run or hide.

Yuro was startled by her rapid advance and tried to keep his footing but slipped on the oily mat and fell toward the oval hatch.

"Out of my way," Kim screamed and stepped on Yuro, while trying to scramble through the hatch to escape. Yuro was confused until he rolled to get on his feet and saw Chance round the corner. The white man looked ominous as he charged into the passageway after Kim.

Yuro spun and kicked Chance in the solar plexus as he tried to get to his feet. The kick stopped Chance as he held the semi-auto in both hands. Chance stopped short but didn't go down. Yuro jumped to his feet, pulled his knife, and lashed out at Chance, who backed up while trying to reorient himself. He remembered what Mark had drilled into him over and over. If a man has a weapon, and is foolishly swinging it, charge him and catch the arm.

Yuro, also well trained at similar self-defense schools, leaped at Chance before he could raise his weapon to a firing position.

Chance spun, blocked the arm wielding the razor sharp knife, while dropping the pistol to the man's abdomen and pulled the trigger.

The bullet tore through the man's stomach and shattered his spine. His eyes widened as his torso was nearly lifted from the deck and then he crumbled into a ball as he fell, still alive, but in terrible agony as he lost all control of the bottom half of his body.

Chance dashed past him through the hatch onto the main deck. Kim had already run across the oily deck, slipping and grabbing at the corroded railing before jumping onto the gangplank. She made the abrupt right off the ship onto the first step and stumbled, catching one leg between two rungs of the grease-coated gangplank. She stumbled and fell screaming as the fall twisted and fractured her ankle. She pulled herself up by the grease-soaked tubular railing and started to hobble down the steps as Chance burst onto the deck.

She was halfway down the gangplank and close to freedom. Chance dashed to the lever controlling the pulleys raising and lowering the gangplank and pulled on the greasy switch. It sputtered and began to draw the cables. The gangplank started to rise off the concrete dock.

Kim didn't notice the whirring noise above her as the aluminum gangplank vibrated. She stumbled for the diamond plate base. As she reached the end, she discovered what was happening. She got down on her knees and squatted into a position to drop from the edge while holding the aluminum corner with her fingers, but she struggled for a solid grip.

Chance realized what was happening. He wanted the bitch dead in the worst way, and if she jumped, she would break her leg on the concrete dock, lose her balance and fall between the hull of the ship and the jagged wooden pillars covered with mussels and barnacles holding the dock in place.

She was trying to crawl over the ledge of the diamond plate platform at the bottom of the gangplank as Chance let go of the switch and the gangplank jerked and stopped.

Some eight feet off the dock, just as she was going to attempt the jump, Chance grabbed a hemp line and jumped over the side, swinging to the concrete dock.

Kim paid little attention to him. She tried to escape. It was her last shot to slip away to safety far from port officials before Chance arrived in Hong Kong. She slid over the side of the platform and tried to hold onto the grimy edge. She wasn't strong enough. She fell directly into Chance's arms. He swept her away from additional injuries on the dirty concrete in front of various Muslim stevedores.

Initially, she was relieved not to strike the cement deck, but when she turned and discovered Chance with his big arms around her, she tried to fight, taking a swing at him with her good hand. Chance saw it coming and dropped her like a hot potato on the hard oily surface of the pavement, spinning her so she landed face down. He jumped on her back and grabbed both of her wrists. Screaming at the top of her lungs, Chance pulled her wrists together and strapped them into submission with a cable tie, pulling it so tight that she cried out with pain. By her wrists, he pulled her to her feet and she stumbled, consumed with the pain of the fractured ankle. Kim hobbled, barely able to walk as Chance pushed her aboard the ship once more.

Jesse came to his aid and returned her to the interior of the ship.

"You'll have to find another cabin," Chance said.

"I will," Jesse said.

Chance sat down on a chair on the rough deck next to the gangplank and stood watch. He didn't budge until 1730, when it was time to get dinner for Ling.

Jesse told him that he would watch the gangplank and radio him if he saw anything strange. Chance took the food up, helped her eat, massaged her and tried to get her up to walk around, unsuccessfully. She started to vomit and he helped her to the bathroom. Then she returned to bed and fell asleep again. Chance returned to the main deck in the driving rain and stood watch over the gangplank.

The two whores on the deck tried to solicit Chance and they chatted with him regularly. Constantine, the short Romanian sand-blaster, sat on the line chalk while the tattoo artist inked him with a couple of classic tattoos for a measly 30 bucks while the rain came down around the ship.

When it poured, the stevedores stopped work and stood in the doorways to the warehouse and waited for the torrent to let up. The harbor was full of brown dirty water from the Java island runoff and cluttered with debris from the city. Little skiffs buzzed around the harbor in the driving rain with scoop nets on their bows picking up trash from the water and sorting it into various containers.

Chance looked out at the sheets of rain, listening to it pelt the steel decks and splash in puddles on the dock. Everything was dark and humid. The people didn't smile, but looked angry and grim. Chance sensed negativity hovering over the town and hoped they could finish off-loading and be on their way.

# -38-

## Opium Voyage

Chance checked on Ling from time to time, during the approaching evening, but returned to the main deck and maintained surveillance over anyone coming aboard or even hovering around the ship. The rain came and went as the sun dipped deeper in the grayness of the dense depressing clouds as darkness enveloped the ship. Chance wrapped himself in an old blanket and stayed as deep in the corner of the grease-soaked bulkheads as possible.

As the rain stopped and started in waves of warm wetness, the crews followed the same pattern, working off and on throughout the long night. Chance caught the shift change, as light penetrated the dull gray of the clouds. His watch indicated 0630 and another group of men began to clamor up the gangplank. He could see and hear the squeaking of the hatches being shut and saw signs that the ship was preparing to depart the port. The cargo superintendent came aboard and headed to the interior ladder to the Captain's cabin.

"Aren't you the same agent for the Leon?" Chance said to Dierk.

"Yes of course," Dierk said, extending his hand, "the Leon is not far behind."

"I hope to pick it up in Hong Kong," Chance said.

"That shouldn't be a problem," Captain Dierk said in his usual dour demeanor. "The Leon is due to deposit cargo in Vietnam. You won't be stopping there but going directly to Hong Kong."

"That's good news," Chance said as Dierk turned and entered the passageway. His short gray hair was covered with a dripping wet ball cap.

Jesse stumbled out of the interior hatch onto the main deck, rubbing his eyes from a long night's sleep.

"I'll take over if you want to get some chow and sleep," he said.

"I'll take some food up to Ling," Chance said, "but then I'll come back. I want to make sure that no one comes on board before we sail, and I don't want you in any danger."

Chance climbed through the hatch and walked briskly to the galley. The chef prepared a plate as Chance entered his small space. He reduced the amount of the drugs added to her tea each day in a powdery form. He didn't have any way of telling how much she had been using except what Yew told him before he was killed. He knew what was going into the tea but not the strength. Each teapot carried a fraction of the opium strength she consumed previously. She faced the throws of withdrawal.

Chance entered their cabin on a cold, wet and dismal morning. Death and fear still blanketed his thoughts. He was unsure about everything except that he wanted the ship to pull away from the filthy port without another threat.

He thought he would be relieved once he had reached Ling, but he wasn't. He still felt threatened. She wasn't well and he feared something to do with the drug would harm her permanently. He wished Kim had fallen to her death and he didn't need to deal with this treacherous aspect of the war between the families. He prayed Chang hatched a bullet-proof plan and he could whisk Ling off the ship and to safety far away from the Triad gangs who roamed the streets of Hong Kong and controlled the drug trade.

Chance became terribly aware of a dismal fact. His long battle to find his girl wasn't over and wasn't as it should be. He sought a personal nirvana for himself and Ling, but it was evasive.

"Chance!" Ling cried out as he opened the door to the cabin.

"Yeah, babe?" Chance said and set the tray down on the long couch in the day room.

"I was worried," Ling said through sobs. "Where have you been?"

"I was down below," Chance said, rushing to her side. "I checked on you last night several times, but you seemed to be sleeping soundly. I need to make sure no one tries to sneak on board, again."

He purposely did not mention the two deaths. She was so delicate looking.

"I can't sleep without you," Ling whispered. "I need you."

Chance looked at her and saw age and deterioration. He was still afraid he might lose her. Every fiber of her being seemed wracked with anxiety. She still shook, unable to hold a glass of water. He faced seven more long days until they reached Honk Kong and medical assistance. She could be healed or dead before he reached a place where he could seek help.

In a quivering state, she tried to hold onto Chance for all she was worth, while he carried her to the head where she vomited violently. She shook like a fragile, dry-as-dust leaf as he held her and cleaned her with a warm washcloth.

Then he noticed a familiar vibration as the diesel engines came to life six decks below. Soon they would be pulling out of the port.

Chang made several calls to the Wong family without a reply. He sat in his office in the Bank of China tower on Hong Kong Island and waited. His cell phone began to ring and he looked at the printout of the incoming number on the digital pad. It was Wing.

"Yes," Chang said, his heart heavy. He knew she had betrayed him, but he loved her still, and he couldn't deny his feelings. He didn't understand her actions and wished in his heart she would somehow make it right. In his head, he knew she was detached and he lost her.

"I am leaving you," Wing said.

Chang knew for weeks those words were near.

"I know," Change said. "I have made arrangements. You must leave. You have betrayed my family. Try to be honorable in your future actions."

He hung up quickly. As much as he knew she was gone, he prayed she would change and hang on. He loved her. He couldn't deny it, but she succumbed to the will of the Wong family. He would have waited until she killed him herself. His love was too strong and as destructive as she had become, he couldn't turn on her, and labored over decisions to protect himself. Now, he knew a time might come and he might be forced to kill her.

He didn't know what to do. He never felt such emotional pain and loss. If he used drugs, he would have run to them, but he wasn't even much of a drinker. He tried to remember back when he was so strong and confident. No one could tell him anything, including his father. He thought of himself as a strong, death-defying knight who could not be brought down. He sensed now, it was the exact time Wing turned on him. She had to be submissive to his every whim. He would never listen to her pleadings for more reasonable actions on his part. He was tough and unrelenting and she couldn't sway him from his bitter line of thinking, so she turned to his enemies.

Everything changed when Ling was taken. There was nothing he could do, no one he could fight or kill face to face.

He knew his father blamed him for his harsh approach, and he wished now he could see him and seek guidance. The phone rang again. It was Chance.

"Hello?" he said apprehensively.

"Are you all right?" Chance asked.

"Wing has left me," Chang replied.

"I know why," Chance said. "You know she was disloyal, don't you."

"Yes, I know," Chang replied, "but I could not let her go."

"Believe me," Chance said, "I've been in your shoes. When did it happen?"

"Minutes ago," Chang said and his voice was swept with sadness.

"Listen." Chance sat up straight in his armchair. He knew Chang faced a distracting time, yet Chance needed him to focus. "I know why she left now. Is someone watching her?"

"Yes," Chang said, "I've had a man on her ever since she betrayed you. I was hoping…" His voice trailed off.

"You're going to have to let her go from your mind and your heart," Chance said. "You're going to need to see only what she has done to you and your family. She left because she knows the Wong plan is unraveling and she can be of little help to them and will be exposed soon. They sent someone to the ship to find Kim. He failed and is dead, and I could have killed Kim and wish I had."

"It's best that you didn't," Chang said, "I've tried to make contact with them since you reached Ling, but can't. They lost their edge with me."

"You might hear from them now, but you have the upper hand," Chance said sternly. "They may even try to use Wing against you. Beware. Stay in touch with me. In a few days, I will know if Ling will survive the shit that they gave her. Call me when you're feeling down and we can talk. This is an important time to stay strong for your family. You need to stay focused."

"I understand," Chang said. "Thank you." He hung up.

Chance remembered when Ling was taken, how desperate he felt, how much he needed her. He was completely in Chang's corner, knowing the emotional loss he encountered. His mind whirled with advice to give him, knowing none would help without Chang's desire for a cure. He needed to wait. He ran back to Ling and curled up in bed beside her and held her close. He could feel her move against him, her cold body quivering like some mechanical toy terribly out of tune and about to break under the strain.

He didn't sleep much, and neither did she. As the dose of opium was reduced, the inhibited neurons started to pump neurotransmitters. The chemical imbalance in the brain melded with the nervous system to fabricate the typical opiate withdrawal symptoms as nausea, muscle spasms, cramps, anxiety, fever consumed her.

Chance was unaware how reducing the drug had similar effects as withdrawing it altogether. Most addicts must continually increase their intake to assume the same level of high. Sometimes receiving the same amount of the drug can cause withdrawal symptoms. Her body set up oppositional processes to restore itself, so more of the drug was needed to correct these highly efficient procedures. As her withdrawal progressed, elevations in blood pressure, pulse, respiratory rate and temperature occurred. Symptoms of overdose, which included shallow breathing, clammy skin, convulsions and coma, could end in Ling's death.

For five days, the ship motored north in relative calm seas as they passed Borneo and entered the South China Sea along the coast of Vietnam and neared the Tonkin Gulf where the Leon would enter and deposit cargo in Haiphong. Chance stayed at Ling's side, although occasionally he clamored up the steel stairway to the bridge and checked the ship's progress. Each day, he bathed Ling and fed her carefully, constantly reducing the daily drug intake until he removed it all together.

It the afternoon on a calm day she slipped into convulsions and he was tempted to allow her a modicum of opium-spiced tea, as she shook violently. His heart cried out as her skin turned hot and her eyes rolled back. He couldn't stand what this monster did to his woman. He bathed her with cold small white ship towels. They smelled of diesel fuel and bleach.

Just as he prayed for color to return to her features, these spasms occurred in a more terrible fashion than ever before. He wished he could call someone, anyone, to help, but there was no one on the ship trained to treat heroin addiction. He held her through another night, trying to massage her cramped legs and fight the fever engulfing her. At 4:00 in the morning he finally collapsed and slept.

His satellite phone awoke him at 6:30 and he jumped out of the still damp bed to answer it.

"Yeah," Chance said.

"Chance," Chang said, "They contacted me. How far are you from Hong Kong?"

"Two days," Chance said and waited.

"I don't know what to say," Chang stumbled. "There's going to be a struggle. They have contacts and so do I, but it may be a fight to see who reaches the ship first."

"No," Chance said angrily. "Call them back. I will kill Kim in the next 24 hours, if they don't allow you to send a boat for Ling and me. I am told we won't dock but will anchor in Victoria Bay. Does anything mean anything to these people?"

"What do you mean?" Chang said.

"Tell them about Kim," Chance said, "as a guarantee that they will not harm Ling when she leaves the ship. You need to ride out on the skiff, or I will not get on it and risk your sister's life again."

"It's such a risky plan," Chang said.

"Think about it," Chance said. "I must check on your sister now. She was near a coma last night. I'm not sure…" His voice trailed off, he shut off the phone and ran back to the bedroom.

Ling was sitting up in the bed drinking a glass of water. She had deep dark circles under her eyes, but her face brightened with a smile of stained teeth. She set her glass down and outstretched her arms.

"I love you," she said. "Thank you."

Chance ran to her arms and for the first time he sensed muscle strength. She broke the opiate spell. He helped her to the shower and again for the first time she relished the warm water. After the cleansing, she dressed in a red silk robe owned by Kim and sat in the day room and ate a full breakfast of eggs, Canadian bacon, toast and coffee. She refused the tea.

"Don't think I will ever drink tea again," she said.

Chance was in awe of the transition. He called the steward and had the bed changed. He could see the rich color and beauty returning to Ling's cheeks and kissed her several times while staring at her.

"What's next?" Ling asked, finishing her breakfast.

"We have to get off this fuckin' ship in Hong Kong and get the hell out of China," Chance said. "I'm not sure if it will be easy or how much danger Chang is in. I'm a little lost as to what to do. I still have Kim on board."

"She's here?" Ling questioned.

"Yes," Chance said, "her guards are dead."

# -39-

# Hong Kong

It was a miracle, but Ling overcame her opium addiction, and the following day, her appetite returned. Together for two days straight, as the ship entered Chinese waters, the couple ate and worked out twice a day. Ling's color returned and although she was thin, she quickly regained some strength. As they neared the Victoria region of Hong Kong, Ling's ability to move around the ship increased immensely. The withdrawal process wasn't over. She could encounter effects for months.

At 17.3 knots, the Bibi motored into the East Lamma Channel and was scheduled to drop anchor three miles from Hong Kong Island and the Kowloon Peninsula. Located dead in the center of the channel, Chance called Chang as soon as the pilot boarded the ship.

"Chance," Chang said, "how's my sister?"

"She beat it," Chance said. "It was like playing with a marked deck toward the end, but she pulled through. We need to get off this ship safely. Has that been arranged?"

"Yes, I'm sending a boat to pick you up," Chang said. "I will be aboard a 40-foot, high-powered service boat. Call my cell phone the minute you drop anchor. Our deal is that you leave Kim on the ship and they will pick her up."

"I'll call," Chance said, "This time, I will look forward to seeing you."

"Me, too," Chang said. "Thank you for all you have done."

It took the Bibi two hours to motor into Victoria Bay. Chance sat with Ling in her room as she collected a few things and stuffed them into his bedroll. Chance watched as her lithe form moved around the cabin. He looked out the forward portholes at the colorful array of high-rise buildings clustered along the coast of Hong Kong Island. A similar array of neon and Chinese New Year decorations adorned the tall buildings on the Kowloon Peninsula. It looked foreboding and sprawling from the bow of the ship. He was concerned about so many things. He couldn't focus on the fact that he was getting off this ship for good and Ling was healthy.

"What's wrong, baby?" Ling asked.

"I don't like it," Chance said. "Something is too easy. These people have tried everything under the goddamn sun. Now suddenly a boat will come out to pick us up and it's all over. I'm not going for it."

She came to him and kissed him deeply.

"It will work out. I have faith in my brother."

"It's not your brother I'm worried about," Chance said and picked up the phone and dialed Chang again.

"Chang," Chance said, "Listen to me. Do you have Wing with you?"

"Yes, she is here," Chang said.

"Is she coming with you?" Change questioned.

"No," Chang said, "she stays here until we are home."

"Change the plan," Chance said. "Take her with you. And put her on the boat coming out here. I want to meet her, but stay off the boat yourself. Make up some excuse."

He could sense the ship rattling beneath him in a furious attempt to back down and stop.

"Okay," Chang said, "I'll do as you say."

"If everything goes as planned," Chance said, "no problem. If something goes wrong, you'll be cool. They are about to drop anchor. Get moving and be careful."

Chance rang Jesse.

"Meet me at my cabin in five minutes."

"Yes, sir," Jesse said.

"Baby," Chance said, "I don't have a good feeling about this first boat, but we need to get off this ship as soon as possible, so be ready. I'll be right back."

Chance looked out the portholes one more time and could see a cluster of barges and service vessels moving around the harbor and some motoring in the direction of the Bibi. Chance stepped out of the cabin into the passageway and walked briskly to the Captain's cabin.

He wanted to be there before customs and immigration agents arrived, not to mention the ship's agent, the cargo superintendent and representatives of the stevedores.

"Captain," Chance asked, barging into his cabin, "may I speak to you for a second?"

The Captain stepped out of his office, drink in hand. His eyes were tired and indicated his lack of desire for what was about to engulf him from another port.

"Yes, yes," the Captain said and took a slug of his drink. In his day/conference room, he already had a case of whiskey and a carton of Marlboros prepared for the authorities, to make swift work of their papers.

"I'm leaving with my girl and the prisoner just as soon as humanly possible," Chance said. "I just wanted to say thank you for your help, and I wish you all the best in the future. Get the fuck out of this business and take a break."

The Captain brightened and nodded, and then shook Chance's hand briskly.

Chance stepped over the threshold of the Captain's cabin and headed up the stairs to the bridge. He walked out onto the bridge wing, grabbing a pair of binoculars and looked around the ship. There were vessels everywhere. Barges motored along under their own steam and each barge had a 20-ton crane mounted securely on the stern. Already they were pulling up beside the Bibi and throwing lines to the crew. Off to starboard, more powerboats were headed from the island. The harbor was crowded with ships. Chance lifted the binoculars to his eyes and watched as the boats came closer.

As he turned to run back downstairs to meet with Jesse, one of the harbor vessels exploded in the bay. At first, Chance thought it was just the popping of more Chinese New Year celebrations, which constantly filled the night air, and then as he picked up the glasses, he realized that the boat was aflame in the harbor. As Chance put the binoculars back on the bridge, his phone began to ring.

"Yeah," Chance said.

"Chance," Chang sobbed into the phone, "The boat blew up with Wing on it. She didn't want to go. I could tell."

"Never mind that," Chance said. "Get away from there and protect yourself. I'm coming. I can see a Sheraton Hotel on the Kowloon side. I'll meet you there."

Chance hung up and jogged down the corridor to meet Jesse, who was standing at the foot of the owner's cabin.

"Take me to the girl," Chance said, and then heard the elevator just a few feet away stopping on E deck.

"Wait," Chance said, as a young Chinese man stepped out of the small steel box.

"Are you the agent?" Chance said.

"Yes," he said, caught off guard.

"We need a lift into Kowloon," Chance said, "Do you have a boat below?"

"Yes," the young man with a heavy jacket and a backpack said, stammering. "I will be a few minutes."

"That's fine," Chance said. "Can you call the boat and tell them to expect three passengers?"

"Sure," he said, reaching for the cell phone strapped in a neat phone holster on his waist.

As he dialed, Chance returned to Ling and grabbed his gear. They followed Jesse down the stairs to the C deck and to a cabin marked for Cook's assistant. Jesse opened it and Kim was strapped securely to a chair. Chance cut the bindings off the chair as Jesse unlocked the chain around her ankle, then with wire cutters snipped the cable ties from around her ankles and wrists. She was scarred in both places and Ling eyed her face, perplexed. She had been so beautiful and now she looked worn and wounded.

Chance was wearing his vest with one of the semi-automatics in a shoulder holster under the flap. He pulled her to her feet and she limped awkwardly without saying a word.

"You're going with us on a boat right now," Chance said. "If you so much as blink, I'll blow your head off and throw you in the bay. As far as I'm concerned, I can handle this and get home safe with Ling. I don't need to be bothered with you. Am I clear?"

Kim nodded and looked at Ling longingly.

"I'm sorry," she said to Ling.

Ling didn't know what to say or how to react; she just stepped back as Chance led Kim out the door and through the corridor to the stairs. Kim's legs were weak and her ankle hurt like hell as she struggled to get down the steps to A deck and across the corridor to the main deck stairs, down the steps, then along the corridor to the exit and the gangplank.

Jesse ran to the controls and lowered it as a large 40-foot service boat pulled up alongside the ship in the tossing bay. Chance helped Ling into the boat first. He took only a moment to look out at the bay to see other boats heading his way. He went back to the top of the gangplank to assist Kim down the awkward steps. She stumbled and fell onto the bow of the rocking vessel, but one of the crewmen helped her to her feet.

They grabbed the stainless handrails and worked their way down the side of the powerboat to the doorway to the interior. The boat was strong looking and powerful, but the interior was plain with several rows of benches for passengers. It was designed to haul people from ship to shore quickly and efficiently. No frills. The exterior had a black deck with a white cabin and hull. The edge of the ship was lined with chunks of tires to prevent damage during alongside missions.

The Captain sat on a barstool affair with a padded back on it, on the starboard side of the bridge. The powerboat jerked and jumped in the choppy waters of Victoria Bay as Chance looked out the windows. He was hoping that the Triad families would be pleased with the killing of Chang and leave them be, but that was too easy. They still wanted Kim back, and if they could get their hands on Ling, they would have twice the influence over the Wu family.

He wanted to kick this cargo ship poker game in the ass and get the hell away. He tried to sit still but couldn't and paced the interior deck waiting for the agent. Less than five minutes passed when the agent jumped on board and the boat pulled away.

"You are in a hurry," Wang Duo said to Chance, handing him a card.

"My girlfriend lives here and her brother is waiting for us," Chance said, beginning to relax as the powerboat picked up speed in the rough water.

Aside from the Captain, there was one scrawny Chinese crewman and the agent on board with them. The crewman held the bow of the boat near the gangplank for them to depart the ship then returned to the interior.

In the center of the dash was a doorway leading to the bow of the ship. The crewman disappeared down the hatch to the bow and the agent went to the dash on the port side and stood looking out the large square windows at the glistening lights of the city and the high-rise buildings adorned with New Year's neon. Chance looked out at the windblown seas that seemed extremely rough for a bay surrounded by over 200 islands.

The powerboat lurched in the waves as he motored along at 10 knots. Chance decided that he didn't care where the boat was going. As soon as they were on shore, they could grab a cab for the hotel, even if they had to take an underground tunnel from the island to the mainland. Chance, sitting in the first row of bench seats, couldn't see above the tall control area in front of him and was looking at the back of the pilot and the agent on the other side when the agent pointed to his right and spoke in a loud fast Chinese tone to the Captain.

Unconcerned, Chance followed his index finger to the Captain and then out the windows. Suddenly, the Captain was shouting at what Chance discovered was another powerboat bearing down on this fiberglass graft at high speed. The Chinese pilot started screaming and reaching for his radio to alert the craft while trying to steer clear of the careening vessel.

Chance's first reaction was to reach for Ling, who sat directly behind him on the next upholstered bench. Kim suddenly lunged over the seat and grabbed Ling by the arm, yanking her to her feet.

Chance reached under his vest and snatched the 9mm, but as he spun he saw Ling's eyes widen and her gaze went beyond him to the cabin door in the bow. The crewman ran topside, armed with a machine gun.

"She's coming with me," Kim said, lifting Ling as the oncoming vessel plowed alongside the rocking service craft holding them. Bullets followed and the Captain was immediately hit and spun out of his chair, falling to the deck. Chance, knocked off his feet in the collision, tried desperately to figure out all the violent elements surrounding him. He focused on the crewman with the machine gun. Between the roar of the engines and the violent pop of guns, Chance moved to protect Ling and before the Chinaman could re-aim his weapon, Chance shot him twice, while Ling struggled with Kim.

Chance turned to discover another armed agent clamoring from the other boat. He shot the first soldier off the other craft from the floor through a Plexiglas window, and the man fell into the bay. Another armed man jumped onto the deck and hurried to the door at the stern. Chance followed him with bullets through the shattering glass but ran out of ammunition. He crawled to the dead guard with the Uzi and took the weapon, then rolled to the edge of the hull and stuck the gun out the doorway before opening up. He sent a swath of bullets up the side of the powerboat to the captain through the windshield. He shattered the protective windshield with bullets and drove the captain away from his post.

The pursuing boat's engine drifted and died and the boat fell away from the hull of the service craft. Chance dove out the door as the soldier entered the cockpit at the stern. They struggled. Chance lost the automatic weapon over the side of the boat and almost went over into the rough waters himself. Desperately, he pulled himself up onto the narrow runner. He crawled to his knees and dove upwards onto the roof of the cabin. The guard charged to the controls and tried to maneuver the heavy-seas powerboat while the guards on the other craft tried to get control of the adjacent vessel. Chance scrambled in his direction, as the guard turned his Uzi on Chance.

Chance rolled his dice once more, dropping into the stern cockpit next to the boxed motor housing, as a single weapon was heard at close range. Ling grabbed the other pistol from her bag and put a round in Kim's foot. Kim screamed, but the struggle continued and Ling's pistol fell to the deck. Ling knelt to recover the revolver, when Kim hit her in the face.

Chance prepared to tear the distributor cap off the powerful engine, when the guard fired the machine gun.

The other craft bore down on them once more, and Ling screamed as it lurched just off the starboard side. Chance discovered a crescent wrench and threw it at the guard at the controls just a few feet away. It smacked him hard enough to distract him. Chance yanked the man away from the wheel and hit him as hard as he could, pulled him away from the wheel station and threw him overboard. Chance ran into the cabin, grabbed Kim, who was screaming in pain, but still fighting to control Ling. He shoved her to the rear door and into the exterior cockpit visible to the other powerboat.

Spotlights from the other craft blurred Chance's vision as he shoved Kim forward, so that they could see her. Bullets stopped and the man at the wheel attempted to curb the swaying steaming vessel, as Chance pushed Kim into its path off the side of the powerboat. She fell into the rough oil-laced brine between the two 40-foot powerboats churning the waters around them.

Chance jumped back into the cockpit, grabbed the controls, threw the powerful boat into gear and yanked the throttle lever. They spun away from the other craft, which tried to stop. Men rushed to the edge of the deck to see if Kim had floated to the surface.

Kim sank in the murky brine and disappeared. Guards dove in after her.

Chance pulled away and disappeared behind the Bibi and headed off in the distance toward Kowloon. Ling came to his side, took the empty 9mm out of his shoulder holster and put it in her purse and then stuck the still-loaded revolver back in the shoulder holster. "I'll reload them both when we get to the hotel," Ling said.

"Hopefully, we won't need more bullets," Chance said.

"I just need you," Ling said.

Chance spun and embraced her. "You're right!" He said and kissed her deeply. "But wait."

Ling looked startled and looked out the shattered windshield, anticipating another surging vessel, but there were only choppy waves in the bay.

"What?" she asked.

"I need my chopper," Chance said and smiled.

Ling punched him playfully in his shoulder and wrapped her arms around him once more.

K. Randall Ball is an old grubby biker and a so-so writer, who's hung around with many of the greats in the custom motorcycle world. He's built a handful of bikes, set Bonneville records and traveled around the world. He spends most of his time working in his Wilmington, California shop, writing for his web site, Bikernet.com, and wondering why he's so attracted to redheads.

Other works by K. Randall Ball

*Prize Possession*
*Outlaw Justice*
*Sam "Chopper" Orwell*
*Harbor Town Seduction (A WIld Chance Hogan Ride)*


Other books and connections to K. Randall Ball can be found at:

Bikernet.com.

\* 9 7 8 0 9 6 5 1 6 0 5 5 1 \*